Collateral Damage

TITLES BY THE SAME AUTHOR
  A Good Liar
  Forgiven
  Fallout
  Cruel Tide
  Fatal Reckoning
  Burning Secrets
  Out of the Deep
  Corruption

COLLATERAL DAMAGE

RUTH SUTTON

First published in UK by Hoad Press in 2021.
2 Lowther Street, Waberthwaite, Millom, Cumbria LA19 5YN

ISBN: 97809929314-7-6

Copyright ©Ruth Sutton 2021

This is a work of fiction. Any resemblance to actual persons, living or dead, is entirely coincidental.

All rights reserved. No part of this publication may be used or reproduced in any manner whatsoever without the prior written permission of the copyright holder, except in the case of brief quotations embodied in critical articles or reviews. The right of Ruth Sutton to be identified as the author of this work has been asserted in accordance with the Copyright, Designs and Patents Act 1988.

A CIP catalogue record of this book is available from the British Library.

Editorial: Sharon Keeley-Holden
Typesetting and Page Layout: Chris Moore
Cover Design: Kevin Ancient
Proofreading: Sharon Keeley-Holden
Typeset in Adobe Garamond Pro 11.5/14.5pt

Printed and bound in Great Britain by TJ Books Limited, Padstow, Cornwall

Acknowledgements

Thanks to Sharon Keeley-Holden for both her insightful critique of several drafts, and her meticulous proofreading. Chris Moore and Kevin Ancient have both done another great job with typesetting of the book and design of the cover respectively.

As ever, special thanks are to Mick Shaw for his unfailing encouragement as the book developed.

Author's Note

Many of the places mentioned in this novel are real, and specific locations have been carefully researched in the 1999 setting.

All of the characters however are entirely fictional, and any resemblance to real characters, living or dead, is purely coincidental.

RS, Waberthwaite, July 2021.

Chapter 1

December 1999

The house near the beach in Parton was quiet. It was a Saturday morning in December and most people in the small village were at home. The long kitchen was full of light, although the room was cool. The wind had swung round during the night, bringing frigid air from the east, and the offshore breeze flattened the sea that lay just beyond the garden wall.

Sam Tognarelli sat at the kitchen table with his second mug of tea and the newspaper, reading yet another article about possible impending disaster when the clocks ticked into the new millennium in about two weeks' time. Must be a slow news week, he thought, if this is all there is to talk about. Y2K, the 'Millennium Bug', he was sick of it, but re-booting his life as well as the computer sounded an attractive idea.

He felt stalled, blocked at work by the same cohort of senior officers that he'd been accountable to ever since he joined the police force. Sam had reached the rank of Detective Inspector in 1984, fifteen years ago, and had stuck there. His seniors seemed to fall into two camps: one group were the old boys who'd trained before all the new legislation in the 1980s and hankered after the way things used to be. The other group were the modern bean counters, happy to add up everything that was countable, regardless of its real value. Quantification had gone mad.

Below Sam in the great hierarchy of policing were another tribe, this time of younger officers who seemed to have mysterious technology skills and an arcane language of their own, leaving Sam and his generation marooned in the middle. Even the police station where he worked felt frozen in time. The old Nook Street building in Workington was clearly outdated, and a new one was planned, but not for another year or two. In the meantime, they just plodded on, with buckets catching the drips whenever it rained.

Judith's voice from upstairs broke through his mood. 'Sam,' she called. 'Can you come up?'

At least she's awake, he thought. The painkillers she was taking seemed to knock her out and the effect lingered long into the morning. Too much wine wasn't helping. Judith was sitting on the edge of the bed, her broken leg in its plaster cast sticking out awkwardly. 'It's hurting,' she said, 'and my crutches are too far away. Can you pass them over?'

They struggled for a while until the hated crutches were in place and she managed to get to the bathroom.

'Only another week or two,' he said, 'then you'll have a new cast that you can walk on.'

Judith was not prepared to be cheered up. 'I hate this,' she said. 'And don't tell me again that I brought it on myself. It was an accident. Anyone can trip at the top of the stairs.'

'OK, I know that,' Sam said. To himself he added, 'But it doesn't help if that person has had too much to drink.' He kept that thought to himself.

Judith looked at him. 'You think I was drunk, don't you? Well, I wasn't, I was half asleep.' She shook her head, and long curls fell over her face. 'I feel bad enough about this, please don't make me feel any worse.'

'Sorry,' he said. 'Do you want me to go down the stairs ahead of you, just in case?'

They came down the stairs slowly, one step at a time and went through into the kitchen where Judith lowered herself onto a chair.

'Has Ted been in touch?' Sam asked. He wondered if thinking about her work at the newspaper office would make his wife feel better, or only increase the frustration.

'Out of sight, out of mind with him,' Judith said. 'I know he's busy, but he's editor of the Workington Star, not the Observer or the New York Times.'

Sam tried again. 'Now you're using email, it should make things easier, shouldn't it? Can you send things to him that way, rather than by fax or post?'

'Yes, if he would give me things to do. Heaven knows, I've got time.' She hesitated. 'You'll be out all day on Monday, will you?'

He nodded. 'I have to be, sorry. With Bell away we're short-handed, and there's a new DC starting, so Skaife says.' Sam smiled. 'The new bloke's name is Sergeant, DC Sergeant. That'll confuse things.'

She laughed, and Sam was relieved. He hadn't seen his wife laugh for a while.

'What about Maureen Pritchard?' Judith asked. 'She's been around for years as a DC. Why don't they just promote her to sergeant, and push the ghastly DS Bell off somewhere else?'

'Good question,' said Sam. 'Work's been easier without Dinger winding people up all the time.'

Bill the Lakeland terrier responded to company in the kitchen by getting up and standing expectantly by the door that led towards the path down to the beach. 'I'll take him out,' said Sam. 'You be all right for an hour or so?'

'Go,' she said. 'I can use the outside loo if I need it. And turn the heating up, it's cold down here.'

It was even colder on the beach, and Sam pulled his coat tight around him. The dog was ahead of him, following the usual route down the path towards the top of the shingle. Sam's mood was as grey as the sky overhead. Even before her fall down the stairs he'd been worried about Judith and the rut they seemed to be in. They both worked hard, too hard probably, and spent less and less time together. Now that she was at home all the time, he realised how anxious she was. It wasn't just the pain that was bothering her. She was drinking more, but was that a cause of her anxiety or its effect? He wasn't sure about that, but he was sure that something had to change.

The dog was snuffling around the high tide line, nosing into seaweed looking for sticks. Sam walked along watching his feet on the pebbles, thinking about the meeting he'd had with DCI Skaife the previous afternoon. The DCI had asked about two relative newcomers to the Workington team, DS Findale and DC Sharp, as if they had nothing to do with him: he had no sense of responsibility for them, just a mild avuncular interest. Sam had watched Skaife's bland face across the DCI's desk, which was completely empty apart from a redundant blotter and a telephone. Skaife's computer, a more up-to-date version than the rest of the squad's, sat in a corner gathering dust. 'Tidy desk, tidy mind' was one of the DCI's little sayings. More like empty desk, empty mind.

DS Rob Findale was a bit of a puzzle. He'd been with them only three months on a voluntary transfer from the Met, and Sam still couldn't work out why he'd wanted to leave the London action and move up to Cumbria, even if it was only for a year or so. It felt as if he was doing missionary work in the benighted provinces. Maybe there's a woman in the picture, Sam wondered, but there was no sign of a local attachment. The man lived like a hermit, work, takeaways, swotting for his next promotion. How old was he, not yet thirty? He seemed like a good copper, but inexperienced and lacking any real interest in the area. He'd have to stay a very long time to lose the 'offcomer' tag. Sam was Lancashire born and therefore qualified as a 'northerner', but he still felt like an outsider in West Cumbria after nearly thirty years.

The memory of his first conversation with Rob Findale came back to him, unheralded and unwelcome. 'I've heard good things about you, sir,' Rob had said. Sam was puzzled. He couldn't think of any previous connection with this brash young man from the Met.

Rob went on. 'I met an old friend of yours who asked to be remembered to you.' He paused. 'Marianne Gordon.'

Thinking about it now, Sam felt sick, again. The last time he'd seen Marianne Gordon her warm body had been next to his in bed, her dark hair spread on the pillow. That was fifteen years before, and still the memory burned. 'Don't tell your wife,' Marianne had said, and he never had. Sam hoped the shock of hearing her name hadn't shown on his face. 'Well, well,' he'd managed to say. 'Not seen Marianne in a long time. What's she doing now?'

'Something big in the Home Office,' Rob had said. 'I met her at a conference.'

So did I, Sam thought.

He was jerked out of the memory by the sight of Bill sprinting away across the gleaming sands, having spotted another dog far out where the tide was inching towards the shore. No amount of calling and whistling would bring Bill back: there was nothing for it but to go after him. By the time the over-excited dog was safely on the lead, Sam was out of breath from the exertion, aware of feeling older and less fit with every year that passed.

In the quiet kitchen, Judith glanced at the newspaper but quickly pushed it to one side. Keeping the truth from Sam was wearing her down. Right from the start, when the accident happened, she'd said that she'd tripped at the top of the stairs. Maintaining that half-truth was getting harder. She knew that if she admitted to him that she'd had another dizzy spell he would assume that she'd been drinking. She was sure that the blood pressure pills had made her dizzy. She'd flushed them down the toilet and felt better. The only drugs she really needed were painkillers for her aching leg. Once that was healed, she would go back to work and Sam would stop nagging her. They might even start having sex again. It was weeks since they'd last made love, but she didn't want to talk about it. Sam hadn't mentioned it either and the silence lay between them like a bolster in the bed.

The phone rang. It was Helen, Judith's sister-in-law. 'Do you mind if we bring Dad with us tomorrow? We can't persuade Mum to leave her chair at Rosedale, and Dad needs a reason for not going there to sit with her. He's very patient, but he hates the place.'

'Is Maggie getting worse?'

'The doc says as she gets worse, it might get better.'

'How come?'

'Well, every now and then she realises that her mind is failing, and it upsets her. That's when she gets so angry. Soon she won't understand how limited she is, and she'll calm down. That's what happens apparently.'

Judith closed her eyes at the thought of it. 'That's so sad.'

'Well, anyway, can we bring Dad? We won't stay long, promise. We've got some more pictures of the grandkids. I'll bring them.'

'OK,' said Judith. 'About eleven, as usual?'

'See you then,' said Helen.

It was strange, Judith thought, how much closer she felt to John Pharoah, her stepfather, than to her mother Maggie who'd given birth to her in the middle of the war that had killed her real father. Judith had heard the phrase 'high maintenance' used to describe some celebrity or other and it fitted Maggie to a tee. It was John who'd always supported Judith, encouraged her to follow her own dreams not the social ambitions of her mother. Seeing him on Sunday without Maggie's dominating presence would be a pleasure. Of course, John missed Maggie after they'd been together over fifty years, but Vince and Helen loved him dearly and were happy to have him living with them now that their own children had grown up and gone.

When Sam came back, Judith was thinking about their future together. 'How long will it be before you can take your pension?' she asked even before Sam had taken off his coat.

'Pension? I'm not old.'

'Your police pension. You can get it after thirty years, can't you? I could retire too, and we could have some fun before we end up like my mother.'

Sam looked at her. 'I joined up late, remember. My pension doesn't come due until 2001.' He hesitated. 'Making it to DCI before that would help.'

'What's the chance of that?' Judith asked.

'If Skaife sticks around, slim to none. I wouldn't mind if he was pulling his weight, but he's not. Since his wife died, he comes to work just to avoid the empty house. He doesn't earn his pay, and nobody makes any demands on him.'

'So, you just have to wait?'

'That's how it feels.'

Judith shrugged. 'Anyway, it doesn't really matter about not getting to DCI. We don't really need the money.'

'Maybe not, but I want to feel that I've made it that far. I'm good at my job.'

She leaned over and took his hand. 'I know you are, really good at it. But it's grinding you down at the moment. I hate to see you so low.'

Sam raised her hand to his mouth and kissed it. 'I worry about you, too' he said, 'and about us. We seem to have got stuck.'

'You need a proper case to work on,' she said. 'Something complicated, to take your mind off things.'

Neither of them could know that, not far away, a young man whose death would occupy Sam's mind, skill and experience for weeks to come was beginning the last day of his life.

Chapter 2

Monday morning started early as Sam had to make sure that Judith was washed, dressed and downstairs before he could leave her to fend for herself during the day. She didn't complain, but he knew that her day would be long, tedious and lonely, and Bill would fret about being in the house. If only Ted, her Editor at the newspaper, hadn't cut her off from work so abruptly. Sam wondered about having a word with him but decided against it. Judith wouldn't want him to interfere.

Sam's office adjoined the large CID room where desks, cupboards and shelving seemed to be randomly scattered about. No wonder DCI Skaife hardly ever came in: his sensibilities would be disturbed by the normal clutter of a busy workspace. The room was empty when Sam arrived. Findale was usually in early, but not today. Sam picked up the training manual for his long-promised new computer and leafed through it. No doubt Rob Findale would understand it all, and Marion Sharp too. Bob Carruthers, another DC under thirty, had adopted the role of the team's computer expert as soon as the chance had arisen some years ago. He seemed to do little else but tap away at the big machine in the corner of the room, but it was useful to have someone who could navigate the police HOLMES system where the details of major crimes were stored. And now the internet was more accessible, Bob was finding his way round that too.

Someone knocked on his office door. 'Yes Geoff?,' said Sam, as the bulky form of Geoff Simpson, the Duty Sergeant, filled the doorway. 'Call came in just before you got here, boss. Looks like a hit and run near Axelby. DS Findale picked it up, and DC Sharp's gone with him.'

'Details?' Sam asked.

'A woman called it in, dog walker, a Miss Taylor. She gave us the location, but she was a bit vague about the rest. It's near the main gate to Axelby Hall. Man's body at the side of the road.' Simpson glanced at his watch. 'Ambulance should be there by now, and Findale in about ten minutes or so. Sharp's driving so they should get there pretty fast.'

Sam smiled. DC Sharp had certainly established her reputation in the few weeks she'd been on the team.

'I reckon those two can handle it for now at least.' Sam said.

'Aye,' said Simpson. 'Sergeant Findale needs to see more of the locals. He still thinks we're all country bumpkins and a bit thick.'

Sam smiled. 'Well, he's got that wrong, hasn't he?'

'Aye, 'appen,' said Simpson.

'Anyone else around out there?' Sam asked.

Simpson looked behind him. 'Not that I can see.'

Sam gestured the man into his office and closed the door. 'What do you reckon to those two, just between us?' he asked. Geoff had been around for years and Sam knew he didn't miss anything.

'Mm,' said Geoff. 'I reckon Findale's a good copper, bit hasty maybe, but he's very London, isn't he? Maybe it's the voice, sounds like 'Eastenders' not 'Coronation Street'. And he's very smart, too smart. Must spend a fortune on those suits.'

'Does that matter?' Sam asked.

'It does if it stops him really talking to people, or them talking to 'im. People round 'ere, well you know what they're like. They think anyone from south of Manchester is a southerner or a tourist, not to be trusted.'

'And what about DC Sharp?' Sam asked.

Geoff raised his eyebrows. 'Well, she's a piece of work, no mistake. Karate black belt or something, isn't she? Calls herself black, too, but she's more brown than black, I reckon.'

'Scottish mother, Kenyan father apparently,' said Sam.

'And she's another one with a foreign accent. Glasgow isn't it?' Simpson added. 'Can't wait to see what Dinger makes of her. You could sell tickets for the first time those two meet. When's he coming back, by the way?'

'Soon, probably. He's part of our squad officially, and with the budget like it is he'll have to stop swanning around in Carlisle and get back here.'

Sam thought for a moment about what Geoff had said. 'Dinger might surprise us about getting on with Sharp,' he said. 'There was a woman we worked with on another case, years ago. A bit fierce, like Sharp, ran the women's refuge in Carlisle, big woman, pink hair, piercings everywhere. She was older, and he treated her more like a man, maybe that was the difference.'

'Yes, but Sharp's young isn't she, more of a threat? I still reckon he'll rub her up the wrong way,' said Simpson. 'Bet you a pint they're shouting at each other on Day One.'

'Thanks Geoff. Just what I need,' said Sam.

Sam had been looking at the new budget figures for only a few minutes before his radio crackled and Findale's voice said, 'You there, boss?'

'Here. What have you got, Sergeant?'

'Young male, in the ditch, looks like an RTA. No sign of a vehicle braking or swerving. Could be deliberate. Forensics are on the way.' A pause. 'I think we might need you, sir.'

'What's the problem?'

'Well, the witness here thinks the man is James Bramall, from the Hall. His dad's some big shot apparently who'll expect a DI to turn up, not a lowly sergeant.'

Sam knew the name. 'Axelby Hall is Edward Bramall's place. Yes, he is a big shot, and he'll know all the top brass. His son, eh? OK, I'll be there in half an hour, Sergeant. Tell Forensics to get a move on. What about Dr Patel?'

'On her way, sir.'

'Right,' said Sam. 'Don't go to the Hall until I get there, OK? This one might take a bit of handling.'

It wasn't difficult to spot the location on the quiet empty road outside Axelby Hall. Sam pulled his car over and got out. 'No ambulance?' he said to Rob Findale, who was standing looking down into the ditch over the yellow police tape, his hands in the pockets of a very expensive coat.

'Nothing for the paramedics to do,' Findale said. 'They've gone back to base. Can't move the body till the doc gets here and anyway the man is definitely dead.'

'You decided to use the radio this time, Sergeant,' said Sam. 'What happened to that tiny phone of yours?'

'No signal, again. Technology's no use if the basics aren't here, like a decent signal.' He tapped the radio that was clipped to his jacket. 'I'm sure there are people listening in on this thing,'

'You flatter us, Sergeant. Most people round here aren't that interested in what we're doing.'

Sam stepped carefully down into the ditch and leaned over to look at the body more closely. The dead man was lying with only the right side of his face visible, one arm over his head, the other underneath his body. One of his legs was at an awkward angle. Sam leaned in closer. 'Facial injuries,' he said, 'and the left leg looks broken.' He peered closely at the man's leather jacket. 'Tyre marks on the back of the jacket. Looking at how the body's lying, it might have been dragged into the ditch by someone after impact. Hard to tell until we see all the injuries.'

'Drunk maybe?' Findale asked.

Sam looked up at him. 'Give us a hand up, will you? I can't see enough really, have to wait for Patel.'

Findale said, 'Looks like he was going out somewhere, or coming back. That leather jacket cost a bob or two. Shoes too. Not the kind of clobber for hanging around at home, or at work.'

'Where's this witness?' Sam asked.

Rob pointed to the car. 'In the car with DC Sharp. She was fretting about getting home so I thought Sharp might keep her calm until you got here.'

'Name?' asked Sam.

'Taylor, Miss Taylor.'

'First name?'

'Yvonne.'

'OK.'

Sam walked along to the car. Marion Sharp got out of the front seat as he approached. She unfolded her long legs and stood up straight, taller than Sam. 'Morning, sir,' she said. 'Miss Taylor would like to go home as soon as possible. She says her elderly mother will be worried.'

'We won't keep her long, thanks, Constable. Can you and Sergeant Findale close this road, make sure no traffic comes down before Forensics have finished?'

Marion walked away and Sam opened the rear door of the car, leaned down and introduced himself to the pale-faced woman sitting there.

'Sorry you've been kept waiting,' he said. 'Shall I get in with you, or we could talk outside?'

Miss Taylor answered by getting out of the car on the other side and looking across at him. A paisley headscarf was knotted under her chin. Light rain was beginning to drift down the road.

'I've been here over an hour,' she said, 'and my mother will be worried.'

'This won't take long,' Sam said. 'You've given your name and details to the officer, haven't you? So I just need to confirm when and how you discovered this unfortunate young man.'

'It's James Bramall,' said Miss Taylor. 'I've known him since he was a boy. What a terrible thing. His poor mother..'

'When exactly did you find him?'

'Well I left home as usual at eight o'clock and it takes me about ten minutes to reach here with Meg. I had her on the long lead, and she must have smelled something. She pulled me along the road and then off towards the ditch. That was when I saw him lying there.'

'How did you know it was Mr Bramall? His face is almost hidden.'

'Well, it's just outside their gate isn't it, and I know his profile, the look of him, you know. I'm sure it's him.' She looked towards the gate. 'Has someone told them, the Bramalls?'

'Not yet.'

The woman sniffed and shook her head. 'How awful for them.'

'What did you do when you found him?' Sam asked.

'Well, I was just standing here when a van went by and I flagged it down. The man driving had one of those mobile phone things and he let me use it to dial 999.'

'Do you have this man's name?'

She shook her head. 'It was a BT van. He asked if I'd be alright, but he didn't want to wait. Already late for something he said. I hoped he would stay with me, but he just drove off. I had to wait a long time before your man turned up. It was nearly quarter to nine by then. I looked at my watch. And then it started to rain.'

She pointed towards the dog, who was tied to a tree on the other side of the road, lying still and watching them with one eye. 'She wants her Bonio,' said Miss Taylor. 'Can we go now?'

Sam called to DC Sharp, 'Can you take Miss Taylor home, Constable? Thanks for your patience, Miss Taylor. DC Sharp will take your statement at home, not to delay you any further.'

As Sam watched the car drive away, a man appeared in the gateway to Axelby Hall, a tall figure wearing a dark green padded coat and a cap pulled down against the rain. Sam walked towards him quickly, to prevent the man from seeing the object of their attention in the ditch.

'What's going on?' the man asked. 'Our driver told us there was something happening out here.'

Sam held his ID card out. 'DI Sam Tognarelli, Workington CID,' he said. 'Mr Bramall?'

Edward Bramall held out his hand and Sam steered him back towards the gateway. 'Sir,' he said. 'There's been an accident here, early this morning by the look of it, and we have found the victim in the ditch, down the road there.'

'Who is it, do you know?'

Sam turned to face the man, looking into his tanned confident face. 'I'm sorry to say, sir, that we believe it may be your son, James.'

Bramall jerked back, and then dodged round Sam and began to run in shocked disbelief towards Rob Findale who walked towards him with outstretched arms, catching him before he could reach the body. Sam caught up with them. 'Sergeant,' he said. 'Take Mr Bramall so that he can see more clearly.'

Edward Bramall stood on the side of the road, looking down, his hand over his mouth. 'It's him, James,' he said, looking round at Sam. 'What happened, for God's sake? What was he doing out here? Is a doctor coming?' He stepped down into the ditch, crying out, 'James, James.'

Findale pulled him back. 'The ambulance has been, sir, and the paramedics confirmed that there's no hope. We're very sorry for your loss. The doctor is on her way to examine the body before it's taken to the mortuary. Everything must be undisturbed until then, sir. Please step back.'

Edward Bramall stood mute, staring down, his face contorted. He turned to Sam, but no words came.

'We'll go back to the Hall,' said Sam. 'Can you walk, or do you want me to drive you there?'

Still silent, Edward set off towards the gate, shuffling as if he'd aged ten years in as many minutes. Sam gestured to Findale to stay where he was and walked along the road until he and the bereaved father turned into the driveway.

Sam had many questions, but he didn't speak as they walked towards the colonnaded porch at the front of Axelby Hall. He noticed the Georgian façade and the circular gravelled driveway where carriages would have turned in times past. Edward Bramall opened the front door and walked in, still silent. He took off his coat and cap and threw them onto a chair. Sam kept his coat on and followed Bramall across the entrance hall, past the foot of an elegant staircase and into a high-ceilinged room to the right. Bramall walked across to a small table, picked up a decanter, poured some golden liquid into a glass and drained it in one gulp. He gestured to Sam, but Sam shook his head.

Finally, Bramall spoke. 'You say James was in an accident of some kind? Hit by a car or something?'

'That's all we can see at present, sir. We'll know more when the forensics team and the doctor have done their work.' Sam hesitated. 'You've no doubt that it is your son, sir?'

'I know my own boy, Inspector.' Bramall's voice was recovering some of its usual authority.

'I know there will be questions, but first I have to talk to my wife, and that means you will have to wait.' He pointed to one of the large chairs, steadied himself with a hand on the small table and then walked slowly across the room, closing the door behind him. Sam tiptoed across to listen behind the heavy door, and heard a woman's voice cry out, harsh in the silence of the house.

Sam walked away from the door and sat down, taking out his notebook to make a few notes while he had the chance. Presently the door opened, and Edward Bramall came back into the room. 'My wife, Angela,' he said. 'She,' he hesitated. 'She's, well, fragile. The housekeeper is with her. We've telephoned our daughter who lives in Penrith. You can't speak to Angela yet, Inspector, but I'll answer your questions if I can.'

'Do you need anything, sir?' Sam asked. 'Coffee?'

Edward shook his head. 'Just get on with it, man. And don't take long, right?'

'Can you tell me a little about your son James,' Sam asked. He closed his notebook to focus his full attention on everything Edward Bramall said and did.

Bramall senior looked towards the window. 'Twenty-four, our younger child. Usual things, Sedbergh School, Cambridge, then back to the family firm.'

'That's your engineering firm, based at Sellafield, I believe?'

Edward looked at him. 'That's right. You know our business, Inspector?'

'Only by reputation, sir' said Sam. 'Your son was working there for you, since he left university?'

Edward nodded and looked at his knees. 'James was no great scholar. I wanted him to do something useful like Physics, but no, it had to be History of Art.' He shook his head. 'So, he was working on the management side of the business, not the sharp end.'

'And this past weekend, sir,' said Sam. 'Can you tell me about James's movements?'

'From Friday?'

'Yes, please.'

Edward Bramall took a deep breath. 'Well, we were both at work on Friday, in different parts of the plant, but I saw him at his desk after lunch, and when I got home around six, he was already here.'

'You saw him?'

Yes, he was in the kitchen, and then in the utility room doing some laundry'. He hesitated. 'We have a housekeeper, but recently James has insisted on doing his own.' The man's eyes filled with tears and he tried to blink them away. 'Sorry,' he said. 'It's just a shock. I can't believe…'

'I'm sorry to be asking you questions at such a time, sir, but you realise I'm sure..'

'Yes, yes,' said Bramall. He took out a large handkerchief and blew his nose. 'Anything I can do to help. And I'd rather be answering questions myself than putting Angela through it.'

'We will need to talk to your wife, sir,' Sam said.

'All right, but not now, Inspector.'

Sam thought about insisting that he speak to Angela Bramall before he left the house. He wanted to get both stories before they had any chance to confer about it, but he also knew that Bramall would have friends in high places and Sam didn't need any more spats with senior officers. He opened his notebook. Sometimes he decided to make notes during an interview, just to put a bit of pressure on the person he was questioning, and to slow things down, give himself more time to think. He always used a small pencil and wrote very neatly. When Sam looked up, Bramall was peering at the tiny marks on the page.

Sam continued. 'What about later on Friday evening?'

'James was here. I was surprised, he usually doesn't hang around here on a Friday night, but he seemed pretty low and stayed in his room watching TV. I could hear it. Football, I think.'

'Any idea why he might have been 'low'?'

Edward shook his head. 'Best not to ask. I guessed it had something to do with the girl he's been seeing, but that was just an assumption.'

'Any problems at work?'

'No, not as far as I know. People are careful about what they tell me, boss's son and all that, but nothing was reported to me. And James didn't say anything, but then he wouldn't. Home and work were kept well apart.'

'So,' said Sam. 'Saturday?'

Edward Bramall sniffed, blew his nose again. 'James is, was, not an early riser at the weekend. You'd have to ask my wife about Saturday, I was out most of the day at the golf club. I got back about four I should think, and he was still at home. At least I think he was. It's a big house, you know. Sometimes he went out early on a Saturday, sometimes later, and then he'd be out for the night.'

'You mean. He stayed out overnight?'

'Yes, regularly on Saturday nights. He's an adult, Inspector. Living at home has its conveniences but we can't keep questioning where he is.'

'Any idea where he would be on Saturday night?'

'As I said, we never asked. I assumed he was with his girlfriend. Angela will know more about her than I do.'

'So, James had a girlfriend?'

'Oh yes. James usually had someone on the go, so to speak. We never asked for any details, at least I didn't. Ask Angela. Mothers and sons, I think they talk more about things like that.'

'Were you and your wife at home on Saturday night, sir?'

'No, we were out, at the golf club, actually. Dennis took us in the big car.'

'Dennis?'

'Dennis Pickthall, our driver. Well, he does all sorts of things around the place. He drives if we want to have a drink while we're out. James has the Mini.' He looked up, puzzled. Sam guessed he was wondering about James's car, but that question could wait.

'What time did you get home?'

'Late. About one, I think.'

'And was there any sign of James in the house at that time?'

'No. As I said, he often stayed out Saturday night, came home Sunday.'

'Did he usually take his car when he went out?'

Bramall looked irritated. 'Of course he took his bloody car. How else would he get to see anyone?'

'They might have picked him up here, sir.'

Bramall looked at him. 'Yes, I suppose they might.'

'Is James's car here?'

Bramall didn't respond but stretched for the phone that sat on the sideboard behind him. 'Can you find Dennis? Ask him to come to the sitting room.' He turned back to Sam.

'Dennis will know whether James's car is here,' he said.

There was a light tap on the door and a man came in. He was quite short, wearing overalls that looked too big on his slight frame. He stared at Bramall and Sam, unsure what to say.

'Sir,' he said, 'I just heard.'

Edward Bramall ignored the man's obvious distress. 'James's car,' he said, 'is it in the garage?'

Dennis nodded. 'Saw it this morning, sir. In its usual place.'

'Do you know if James took it out yesterday?'

The man thought for a moment. 'It was there when I had my lunch. I was thinking I needed to check the tyres.'

'Check for what?' Sam asked.

Dennis shrugged. 'You know, for wear and that. I check both the cars regular.'

Bramall asked, 'Did you see the Mini after that?'

'It was still there on Saturday night when I brought the big car round for you and Mrs Bramall at seven, sir.'

'And you saw it this morning?' Sam said.

'I told you that,' said Dennis, and he seemed about to say more, but Bramall waved him away again and the man left the room, closing the door behind him.

Edward Bramall looked close to tears. 'What time,' he began, stopped and tried again. 'What time do you think James was hit? You do think he was hit, don't you?'

Sam nodded. 'Yes, but we'll know more when the doctor has finished her work and made her report. Until then…'

'Yes, OK. How long will that be?'

'Later today, I should think. We need to be very thorough.'

Bramall shook his head. 'Will there have to be a post-mortem?'

'Oh, yes, sir,' Sam said. 'That's vital to our understanding of what happened.'

Bramall nodded. Sam wondered if he was thinking about his son's body lying on a slab, cut open.

'Before we check James's car, sir,' said Sam, 'what can you tell me about yesterday, Sunday?'

Edward looked out of the window. 'I'm afraid I don't know where my son was yesterday, Inspector. He was living under my roof, but I never thought to check whether he was in the house. As I told you, he lived his own life.' He blew his nose again. 'You'll be asking my wife, I'm sure. As far as I know, she was here yesterday.'

'You were not here yourself?'

'Until about noon, but then I went shooting with some pals. Got back for dinner around six. James didn't appear, but that wasn't unusual. My wife didn't say anything about it, as far as I recall.'

'You mentioned a housekeeper?'

'Mrs Harvey, yes of course. Sunday's her day off, but she has a flat in the grounds. She might know something.'

Sam got to his feet. 'About James' car,' he said. 'Can you show me where it's kept?'

Edward led Sam through the house to the back and then out to the side door of a large garage. The air was fresh and cold. A robin perched on the garage roof, singing. The garage door was unlocked and the Bramalls' black BMW was the first thing they could see. Edward pointed. 'There it is, James's Mini, next to my car, where it usually is'.

'We'll need to examine it, sir,' said Sam. 'Can you ensure that it's not touched before we do?'

Edward nodded. 'We bought it when he came back from America, a sort of welcome home present.'

'When was that?' Sam asked.

'Early in September.' Bramall blew his nose again.

'A holiday, was it?' Sam asked.

'Some business for the firm,' Bramall said, 'but mostly holiday, yes.'

Sam wondered what kind of business James might have been entrusted with, but that question could wait. 'If James didn't take his car out this weekend,' he said, 'we need to ask what he was doing out on the road. Perhaps someone was picking him up, or dropping him off?'

'That's for you to find out, isn't it?' Edward said.

'Does James's girlfriend have a car, perhaps?'

'I've already told you, Inspector, I don't know her or anything about her.' He paused. 'Not even her name.'

'Right,' said Sam. Edward Bramall had already turned away and was walking back to the house.

When they reached the main hall, Sam extended his hand to Bramall. 'Thank you for your help, sir,' he said. 'I'll keep you informed as our investigation proceeds.'

'No stone unturned and all that?'

'Of course. When would it be suitable for us to talk to your wife?'

Bramall took a deep breath and let it out slowly, thinking. 'This evening? She should be more herself by then.'

'One of our officers will come back. About six? And could you ask Dennis to make a few minutes for us?'

'Dennis? Now?' Bramall queried. 'Right, if you must.'

'I'll let you know of any further developments when I get reports from Forensics and Dr Patel. I could telephone you, no need to disturb you in person again, if you wish.'

'We're not going anywhere, Inspector. You do whatever you need to do.'

Bramall led Sam towards the front door. 'And who do you report to, Inspector?'

'DCI Skaife is my immediate superior officer,' said Sam. He was surprised it had taken Edward Bramall this long to assert his standing.

Bramall nodded. 'Of course,' he said. 'Pass on my regards to him, will you?'

Sam didn't respond. There was no need.

Chapter 3

Sam walked back down the drive to the road. It was nearly eleven. He needed to talk to Brian Fothergill, the Scene of Crime Officer, about his late arrival at the scene, again. In fact, he needed to talk to Fothergill about a number of things. The man was a dinosaur. Forensic science was moving rapidly and he just wasn't keeping up, and now this failing was verging on incompetence. Everyone knew, but of course no one was prepared to do anything about it in case it upset their old mate Brian.

Fothergill's van was pulling up when Sam reached the yellow tape surrounding the ditch where James Bramall's body lay. Fothergill eased his bulky body out of the van, followed by a young man carrying a camera who saw the expression on the DI's face and stood well back.

'It's about time, Brian,' Sam said, tapping his watch. 'This young man's father lives right here, at Axelby Hall, and he's probably already on the phone to his old mate the DCI. So now you're finally here, make a proper job of it. We need to know whether the deceased was put in the ditch or fell there. We've already marked some shoe or boot marks on the verge, so have a good look at those.'

Fothergill stood listening but didn't react. 'We're pretty sure about the ID,' Sam went on, 'but check his pockets now, will you, so we've got something to go on straight away? And look for a mobile phone.'

'OK, OK,' Fothergill said. 'One thing at a time. Let's have a look at him.' He climbed carefully down into the ditch, gesturing to the photographer to take the shots he needed before the body was moved. Once that was done, Fothergill peered closely at the jacket and felt in the pockets of both the jacket and the trousers before he looked up at Sam and shook his head. 'No wallet, no phone. Who is he?'

'James Bramall, son of Edward Bramall.'

Fothergill pursed his lips. 'Bramall Engineering? Oh God. That man's a force of nature. He'll be all over us like a rash.'

'You know Edward Bramall?'

'Oh yes. Known him for years. Rotary and such. Have you seen him yet?'

'Just now,' said Sam. 'He's more upset than he's letting on.'

'Well, it's the son and heir, isn't it? Bit of a waste of space though, I heard.'

'What have you heard?' Sam asked.

'Playboy type,' said Fothergill. 'I'll get the lab to check for drug traces.'

Another car arrived. It was Dr Patel, who'd driven from Carlisle. At least Sam had confidence in her and knew that the PM report would be prompt and thorough. 'Morning, Doctor,' Sam said, shaking the young woman's hand. 'I know you hate being rushed about time of death, but it would be really useful.'

'I'll do my best, Inspector,' said Patel, 'but don't take anything as definite until I have a proper look back at base.' She looked down at the body. 'Hit by a car?'

'Looks like it. We're not sure whether he ended up in the ditch through the impact, or someone put him there out of sight. That would be useful to know.'

He left Fothergill and Patel to their respective tasks and walked down to Findale and Sharp who were standing by the barrier they'd erected across the road.

'We've got a couple of woolly suits coming up from the local nick to control the road for now, sir,' Findale said.

' "Woolly suits" sounds like Met-speak to me, Sergeant. Round here we call them "uniformed officers".'

'Right, sir,' said Findale.

'I'll take you both down to the house,' Sam said, 'and introduce you to Mr Bramall senior. I want to brief the DCI and alert the press boys, so they don't crawl over the place as soon as word gets out, which it will.' He looked at both the officers standing in front of him. 'Mr Bramall appears to be personally acquainted with our DCI, and probably with half the senior officers in the county. So, watch your manners. I want you to talk to the driver, Dennis Pickthall, and to the housekeeper, Mrs Harvey. We need to know everything there is to know about James's movements on Saturday and Sunday. Bramall senior hasn't been terribly helpful on that score, too busy golfing, dining and shooting. Mrs Bramall, Angela, is too upset to talk yet, but one of us will have to do that before the end of the day. I just hope she's not full of tranquilisers by then. Edward Bramall says she's 'fragile', but men often say that about their wives when they have no idea how strong they are. Ask all of them about James's friends, and the girlfriend, who apparently the father knew nothing about.' He paused. 'Got all that?'

'Do you think the family are covering something up, sir?' Sharp asked.

Sam shook his head. 'No, not necessarily, but reputation obviously matters for them. They might want to massage things a bit, protect the memory of their son, you know how these families circle the wagons when something goes wrong'.

They both nodded.

'I know we're stretched without DS Bell,' Sam went on, 'but he should be back soon. This is a chance for both of you to shine. High profile case, do the best job you can. Call me any time, and I'll expect detailed reports from you at tomorrow's morning briefing, eight-thirty sharp. OK?'

'Yes, sir,' they replied in unison.

'Right, we'll take both cars down to the house to get them off this road. I'll introduce you both and get back to Nook Street.'

Sam did exactly that: he formally introduced DS Findale and DC Sharp to Edward Bramall, explained that they needed to take statements from the driver and the housekeeper, reassured Bramall that one of them would return to speak to Mrs Bramall later, shook the bereaved man's hand and left. Dr Patel was waiting for him on the road. The initial report was vague, as Sam guessed it might be. Time of death, between midnight and four in the morning, probably. Everything else would have to wait.

At Axelby Hall, Edward Bramall was none too pleased to be left to deal with two underlings. 'I'll speak to the driver,' Rob said, taking charge as the ranking officer present, 'while my colleague speaks to the housekeeper. That should mean we can be out of your way a little more quickly.'

Bramall didn't respond, except to indicate where the two people they wanted might be found. 'Which one of you will be speaking to my wife?' he asked.

Rob said, 'DI Tognarelli will assign that task, sir.'

'Whoever it is, not before six. She needs to rest,' said Bramall before he turned away to trudge slowly up the long, curved staircase.

Rob Findale found Dennis in the garage. They stood outside to talk, in the low morning sun and away from any listening ears in the house.

'Tell me what you know about James Bramall,' said Rob.

Dennis looked around. 'Honestly?' he asked.

'Definitely,' said Rob. 'This is between us.'

'Well,' said Dennis, rubbing at the oil on his hands, 'between us, he was a waste of space. Typical bloody public school, flash, posh, plummy voice, spoiled. He's my employer's son, but if he'd been a son of mine, well…'

'Well what?' Rob said, pleased that the manly chat was paying off.

'Well, I'd have got him away from the drugs for a start.'

'How do you know James was on drugs?'

'He was on something, for certain. Half the time when he was round the house, he couldn't see straight. His mam covered up for him, said he just needed to grow up a bit, but he's twenty-four, for God's sake.'

'Anything specific about the drugs, that you saw yourself?'

Dennis shrugged. 'I only know about drugs from the telly. It's cocaine, isn't it, that these yuppie types do? Makes them sniff a lot.'

Rob tried another tack. 'OK. Over the weekend, when did you see James yourself?'

Dennis screwed up his face thinking. 'Friday night I was out, with the missus.'

'Do you live in, here?'

'Good God, no. Lose the job, lose the house. Too risky. We live in the village,' he jerked his thumb in the direction of Axelby, just down the road.

'Saturday?'

'I came up to the house around six in the evening, had a cuppa with Audrey – the housekeeper – before I went to fetch the big car, to take them out to the golf club. James came in to see if Audrey could get a stain off his leather jacket.'

'How did he seem?'

'Same as normal. He was always a bit smarmy with Audrey, but she liked it. She asked if he was going out and he said he wasn't sure.'

'Did he say anything about where he might be going, or who with?'

'No, just out. He looked excited I thought, but it wasn't my place to ask why. That was the last I saw of him. Ever. Weird, to think I'll never see him again.'

'What about Sunday, yesterday?'

Dennis shook his head. 'I wasn't here. No, wait, I popped in around lunchtime. My Susan was at her mother's and I thought there might be some lunch stuff here in the pantry. And while I was here, I thought about checking the tyres on the Mini, but didn't bother in the end.'

'But you saw the car in the garage yesterday?'

Yes, it was there, with the BMW. Mr Edward took the old Landrover to his shoot. That's kept in a shed, not in the main garage.'

'And did you see James at any time after that?'

'No. I went home about two yesterday afternoon and came back here as usual half eight'ish this morning. I could see there was something going on. Van was stopped in the middle of the road and a woman was standing there, but I was a bit late, so I kept going. Can I go now?'

Rob Findale found DC Sharp coming out of the back door of the house with a middle-aged woman who was wiping her hands on her apron. 'Sir,' said Marion, 'this is Mrs Harvey, the housekeeper.' Audrey Harvey nodded a greeting. 'She's told me she knows James was in the house on Saturday morning. He came to ask her something at around six the same day, and then she saw him walking down the drive that night, about nine.'

Rob frowned. 'It would be properly dark by then.' He looked at Mrs Harvey. 'Are you sure?'

Mrs Harvey rubbed her hands together. 'Yes, the drive is well lit, and I know Mr James's walk. It was definitely him, and I know the time because a programme I'd been watching had just finished. It was pretty cold and wet by then and I could see his long coat flapping, as if he hadn't done it up properly.'

'He was definitely wearing a coat?'

'Well, he would be when it was raining. Wouldn't want to spoil that leather jacket.'

Marion added. 'I've asked Mrs Harvey if anyone rang the house for James, but she says not as far as she knows.'

Audrey chipped in, 'But he had one of those little mobile phones, so he might have had a call on that. Or one of those messages you get on the phone, texts they call them. He was always clicking away, using his thumbs on that little tiny keyboard. Like a whole new way of writing, isn't it?'

'If someone was picking him up, why didn't they come down to the house, I wonder?' Marion asked.

Audrey shrugged. 'Maybe Mr James asked them not to. Some young people don't want their parents to know about their friends, do they? Anyway, do you want to see where I saw him from, or not? It's cold out here.'

'Lead on,' said Marion, and Rob followed the two women across the yard. Audrey opened a bright blue door and led them upstairs. The flat above the old stables was warm and tidy. 'In there,' Audrey said, pushing open a door. 'Go in, it's OK. Look out of that window, you'd be able to see someone walking up the drive. But the drive goes round a corner, so you can't see the road from here. Just after nine, Saturday night. That was the last I saw of him.'

'Nothing yesterday?'

She shook her head. 'It was my day off, but I don't miss much that goes on in the house.' She remembered something. 'I popped over there about noon yesterday, just to check on the lunch arrangement. I'm pretty sure Mr James wasn't there then. I took some laundry up for him, no noise from his room, and it was locked, so I left the things outside on a chair.'

'Was it unusual for him not to come home after Saturday night out?'

'It's my day off, as I said, but he's a young man, you know. Had money to spend, friends, so he could stay away all weekend if he wanted to. He could have been anywhere. James had a friend in the village, Ian Dawes. He might know. They used to be close, but I'm not sure whether they still are.'

'Well, thank you, Mrs Harvey,' said Marion, turning back towards the stairs. 'Someone will be coming back later to see Mrs Bramall. How is she now?'

'Much better, thank you. It was a terrible shock, but she knows you'll need to talk to her.'

'Who's this Ian Dawes?' Findale asked Sharp as they walked back to the front where the car was parked.

'A friend of James that Audrey mentioned, and he lives just down the road so I thought we might call while we're out here. He might be there, worth a try.'

They drove into Axelby, looking for the address Mrs Harvey had provided. It turned out to be a post-war semi on a small estate in the village.

'This looks like a normal house to me,' said Marion as she drew up outside. 'More like the house I used to live in, not that great echoing place we've just been to.' Rob didn't comment, but she went on. 'I went to a posh school, on a scholarship. First week in school, in Art we had to draw our own house. The other girls drew enormous houses and I asked how many families lived in them. They thought that was very funny.'

There was a car in the paved front yard and when they knocked on the front door a grey-haired woman opened it a fraction, peering round at the pair of strangers standing on her doorstep. They both held out their ID cards for her to see.

'What's happened?' she asked anxiously

Rob introduced them both. 'Is it Mrs Dawes?'

A nod.

'Nothing to worry about, Mrs Dawes. We'd like to ask your son Ian a few questions, if he's at home. He's done nothing wrong, just a routine enquiry.'

The woman hesitated, and then opened the door, ushering them into the narrow hall. 'Ian', she called up the stairs. 'It's the police, they want to talk to you.'

A young man clattered down the stairs, hair flopping over his eyes. He stopped at the bottom of the stairs. There were too many people in the hall for him to go any further.

'Well get them in the front room, Mam,' he said. 'We can't all fit in here, and it's too cold outside.'

Mrs Dawes went into the front room, which was almost as cold as outside, but at least they could sit down. Ian took his mother's arm and ushered her out. 'Make us a pot of tea, Mam. Don't know what this is about but we might as well have a drink, it's freezing in here.'

'It'll be about what happened on the road by the Hall, early on,' said his mother. 'Mrs Andrews next door said there was summat up.'

Ian waved her away and she left the room.

'Monday's my day off, only just got up,' Ian said. 'What did happen this morning?'

Rob leaned forward. 'Do you know James Bramall, from the Hall?'

'Yeh,' said Ian. 'Why? What's he done?'

'I'm sorry to tell you he's dead, sir. Accident on the road this morning. We're checking Mr Bramall's movements over the weekend and the housekeeper, Mrs Harvey, said you were a friend of his.'

Ian's head dropped and he put his hands over his face. 'Oh, my God. Jimmy? What happened?'

'That's what we're trying to discover, sir. Do you have any idea where James might have been over the weekend, or who he might have been with? Apparently, he went out about nine on Saturday night and wasn't seen again until someone found his body by the side of the road near the Hall gate early this morning.'

'What about his car?' Ian asked.

'Still in the garage at the Hall. He may have walked out to meet someone. Do you know who?'

The door opened. 'Do you both take milk?' Mrs Dawes said. She saw Ian's face. 'What's happened?'

'It's Jimmy Bramall,' said Ian. 'He's dead.'

Mrs Dawes was as shocked as her son and sat down beside him on the low sofa. He put his arm round her, and they sat for a moment while Findale and Sharp watched and waited, before the young man stood and pulled his mother up and steered her once again out of the door.

Ian lowered his voice. 'Was he, you know, on something? Not booze, something stronger?'

'Did Mr Bramall have a drug habit, Mr Dawes?' It was Marion Sharp who asked. Time was ticking on and she wanted Ian to tell them what he knew about Bramall before the old lady faffed around any further.

Ian nodded. 'He was OK while he was at school, but when he went off to uni it all started. He could have been bragging to me, the poor local lad left behind, but he showed all the signs of being on stuff. God knows how his parents didn't notice. He was never short of money of course, and you can get anything you want in Carlisle or Manchester or wherever he went on those weekend binges, if you've got the cash.'

Findale took out a notebook and began to scribble. 'Friends?' Sharp asked. Ian shrugged. 'We'd been mates from primary school, but I don't see much of him now. I'd see him in the pub every now and then, or in the shop, and sometimes we went shooting.'

'Any mention of other friends?'

'Well, there was the new girlfriend. Newish, I think they got together after he got back from a holiday in the States. Sandy, he called her. I met her with Jimmy actually, just once when I took Mam Christmas shopping to Carlisle one Saturday.'

'Recently, then?' said Findale.

'It was October, for Christmas shopping, would you believe?'

'Description?' Sharp asked.

'Blonde, quite pretty, a bit standoffish, I thought. Sort of 'cool but doesn't give a shit'. She looked a bit older than him, but it's hard to tell with girls. Jimmy said she was different, not like the girls round here. 'Cosmopolitan,' he said. But she worked in Workington, I think. Not exactly Monte Carlo, is it, Workington?'

'Second name?'

Ian thought for a moment. 'What was it? Something Welsh sounding. Evans, that's it. Sandy Evans.'

Ian got up and closed the door. 'Thing is, Jimmy was a bit of a show-off, a fantasist,' he said. 'That personalised number plate he bought for his car, I ask you! And he was always making up stories about the glamorous life he led, meeting models, coke parties, that kind of stuff. I didn't believe most of it.' He looked up. 'He was pretty thick, you know. He used to ask me for help with schoolwork – me! And God knows how he got into Cambridge. Same college as his dad, well, that says a lot. The family's loaded, Dad probably paid for a new library or something.'

Rob asked, 'Any particular fantasies that you remember, apart from the parties?', but before Ian could respond the door opened again and Mrs Dawes shuffled in with a tray, complete with large teapot in a red cosy, mugs, milk jug, sugar bowl and a plate of biscuits.

For several minutes the conversation was interrupted by the rituals of tea making and by the time these were complete, and Mrs Dawes had disappeared again, Ian had to ask what the question had been.

'Fantasies? Well, here's a typical one. Just after the American trip, we were out shooting crows one Sunday and Jimmy said that he had joined Greenpeace – I think it was Greenpeace, something hippy – and was off to the South Pacific on one of their boats. I said it was strange that he was still shooting defenceless creatures, but he didn't get it. Thick as a brick. The new woman, Miss Wales, was going with him, of course, sailing off into the sunset. I knew there was no point in arguing with him.'

'And that was?'

'End of September. I thought of asking her about it when we met them in Carlisle, but I didn't want to show him up.'

Findale looked at his notes. 'So, you're telling us that either James had a fairly exotic private life or else he made most of it up.'

'That's about right. I'd known him since we were five, starting school, before he went to some posh prep school and then off to

Sedbergh. He never really grew up. I reckon his dad bullied him and his mam spoiled him.' He closed his eyes. 'Oh God, they'll be in bits. I ought to go and see them or something.'

'Just one last thing about the drugs,' Findale was scribbling as he spoke. 'Did James ever mention any names, dealers, suppliers, or anyone he might have owed money to?'

'I doubt he owed money. He had loads, not just from his parents but from some family trust. Came into it when he was twenty-one, three years ago. And he never mentioned names of people he got drugs from, but I'm sure he was on cocaine. All the signs were there. I had a mate who had the same problem, and I recognised it. Jimmy often stayed out all weekend and must have got home looking pretty wasted, but 'Mommy Dearest' would patch him up. They should have confronted him about it, but that wouldn't be the Bramall way of doing things.'

'Did you ever confront him yourself?'

He shook his head. 'Should have done, but he would have just fobbed me off. And it's too late now, isn't it?'

Sharp said, 'We've heard that James would be away from home all weekend sometimes. Do you have any idea where he might stay?'

Ian shrugged, 'With a friend, or the girlfriend. For all I know, he might have had a flat in Carlisle, or stayed in a hotel. He wasn't short of money.'

Findale closed his notebook and got up to leave, and Ian looked up at him. 'Wait a minute. What happened to Jimmy? Was he killed by a car? Why was he on the road, right outside the house? Have you found who did it?'

Sharp stood up, looking even taller in the low ceilinged room. 'We can't discuss an on-going investigation, sir.' She handed Ian a card. 'Please thank your mother for the tea, and if you remember anything else that might help us, call anytime. And where would we find you, during working hours?'

'Taylor Building Supplies in Workington, not far from your place actually.' He paused. 'If you do come, make sure my boss knows it's not me in trouble, right?'

'No problem,' said Rob. 'One more thing, sir. Please don't tell all your mates that we might have a drug connection in this case. We don't want to scare off the people we need to find.'

Ian nodded.

They made their way to the door and Ian ushered the two detectives out into the cold. 'You don't think someone ran the poor bugger over deliberately, do you? He was an idiot, but harmless, really.'

'Too early to speculate, sir,' said Findale. 'Thanks for your help.'

Sharp looked at her watch before she got back into the car. 'It's nearly two o'clock, no wonder I'm hungry. One of us will have to come back here before we can get home tonight.'

'That's the boss's call,' said Rob. 'Not like him to leave us to it like this. He's usually all over a new case.'

'His wife had an accident, didn't she?' Marion said. 'Maybe he has to get home for her.'

Rob smiled. 'Have you met his wife?'

'No, what's she like?'

'Fierce,' said Findale. 'Red hair, doesn't take any prisoners. And she's a journalist. Can't imagine her playing the little woman who needs looking after.'

'I hope Sam doesn't ask me to go back to the Hall again,' said Marion. 'What did Ian Dawes say about the Bramalls? The dad bullied James and the mother spoiled him. Sounds about right.'

They'd just got back to Nook Street when Duty Sergeant Simpson walked through, holding a paper in his hand. 'Sam around?'

Sam's office was empty. 'I'll pass it on, Sergeant,' said Findale. The paper was handed over.

'Call from Whitehaven nick,' Simpson explained. 'Drug OD reported, and they think CID need to check it out. Young woman, taken to Whitehaven hospital. Name of Sandra Evans.'

Chapter 4

Findale stared at the paper in his hand, then handed it to Sharp. Geoff Simpson was watching the reaction his announcement had produced. 'Someone we know?' he asked.

Sharp summarised the note. 'Landlady hadn't seen the tenant for a while, went to check, found the flat ransacked and the tenant unconscious, possibly already dead.'

Findale looked around. 'We need to find the boss,' he announced to the room. 'Anyone know where he is?'

Sam walked into the room. 'Here I am,' he said. 'What's the fuss?'

'OK, boss,' said Sharp. 'Here's the short version: a friend of James Bramall mentioned James's girlfriend, and thinks her name is Sandra Evans and that she works in Workington. We just got back, and this has come in from Whitehaven – a woman of that name has been found, apparent OD.'

'Why did they call us?' Sam asked.

'Place had been ransacked. Same name? No way that's a coincidence.'

'Where's Evans now?'

'Whitehaven hospital.'

Sam said, 'OK, Sharp, get up there, check all the details, speak to the woman if you can. Sergeant, fill me in on all the rest.

We'll need more information from the landlady and the officers first on scene.'

Sharp asked, 'What about Mrs Bramall? Mr Bramall said we could see her at six o'clock.'

'I'll sort that out,' Sam said. 'You go. If this Evans woman has anything to say, I want to know what it is.'

The heavy Sellafield traffic on the main road was mostly going the other way but it still took Sharp nearly an hour to get to West Cumberland Hospital, which sat on a hill on the south side of Whitehaven. The A&E area was crowded, and it was a few minutes before Sharp got the attention of the nurse who was calmly checking patients on arrival, while the mayhem of an obvious emergency swirled around them. As she waited, Marion looked around, wondering if anyone had come in with Sandra Evans, and whether the young woman was alive or dead. To one side she noticed a middle-aged woman with grey hair trying to use a public phone, straining to speak with one hand over her ear.

Finally, the nurse was able to tell her that Miss Evans was in one of the cubicles reserved for emergency patients, and that a lady called Mrs Allan had come in with her. 'There she is, on the phone,' she said. Marion picked her way across the crowded space just as the grey-haired woman was heading towards the main entrance. 'Mrs Allan?' she said. The woman turned and Marion held out her police ID. 'Can we talk outside, where it's quieter,' she said, keen to get the basic facts before she checked on Sandra.

It was damp and windy outside, and they huddled behind a pillar. 'What do you want?' said Mrs Allan. 'My husband's coming to pick me up, he'll be here in a minute.'

'Can you tell me when you found Miss Evans? She's your lodger, isn't she?'

'Tenant,' Mrs Allan insisted. 'She's my tenant, the only one, she has the flat upstairs.'

'Address?' Marion asked.

'19 Sebastopol Terrace, Whitehaven.'

'And your full name please?'

'Philippa Susan Allan. I don't use Philippa, people call me Susan.'

'OK Susan, when did you find her?'

Mrs Allen took a deep breath. 'About four this afternoon. I was taking some fresh bedding up to the flat. I knocked of course, but when there was no response, I let myself in.' She shuddered at the memory. 'What a sight, never seen anything like it, not in my house. Drawers open, papers everywhere, all the cushions off the sofa.'

'Was Sandra there?'

'No, that's her living room. She has a bedroom and a bathroom at the back. I went through into the bedroom and that's where I found her, lying on the bed, straight, like one of those things you see in old churches. Looked as if she was asleep, and I shook her, but she just lay there.'

'She was fully clothed?' Sharp interrupted.

Mrs Allan looked shocked. 'You mean?... Yes, she was wearing a skirt and a blue blouse, no shoes. One sleeve was rolled up, but I don't think…, you know.' She grimaced at Marion. 'Anyway,' she went on, 'I didn't know what to do. I tried her pulse, and I could feel something but it was very faint. I just went downstairs and called 999. A policeman arrived after about five minutes and the ambulance a bit later. I kept out of the way, but I thought I ought to come in the ambulance with her. I don't know why, this is an awful place, all those sick people.'

A car drew up at the kerb and Mrs Allan pulled open the door. 'I'm not staying here,' she said with a rush of energy verging on panic. 'You'll have to come to the house if you want to ask me any more.'

Marion didn't try to stop her. She went back to the reception desk. 'I need to find Miss Evans, brought in about an hour ago, possible overdose.'

This time the nurse said, 'Number three'.

Marion opened the curtains of the cubicle and a white-coated figure turned towards her, taking the proffered police ID and casting a careful eye over it before handing it back. 'I know most of the Whitehaven police,' said the doctor, 'but you're new, aren't you?'

'Workington CID,' said Marion. She checked the doctor's name badge, 'Dr Kimani.' She looked up into his face. 'That's a Kikuyu name isn't it?'

He smiled. 'Are you Kenyan?' he asked.

'Half,' she said. 'My father was from Nairobi. Came here as a student.'

'Well, Officer, here we both are. Small world.'

'Will she live?' Marion asked.

He shook his head. 'Too far gone, we couldn't save her.'

'Accident or deliberate, do you think?'

He shrugged. 'Hard to tell that too. I'll know more when the blood tests come back. Sometimes it's a combination of drink and drugs that does it. Careless more than deliberate. Any indication of her state of mind?'

'Not that we know of,' said Marion. 'The landlady didn't mention anything, but I'll ask her about it.'

'Right, Officer, we'll let you know if there's more information.'

Outside, under the canopy of the main entrance Marion unclipped her radio and checked in.

'Go ahead DC Sharp,' said Sam's familiar voice.

'Miss Evans died without coming round,' Marion said. 'We think she was James Bramall's girlfriend, is that right?'

'I'll be asking Mrs Bramall about that. I'm just off to see her now.'

'I spoke briefly to the landlady who came in with Sandra,' said Marion. 'But she rushed off home, Sebastopol Terrace in Whitehaven. Shall I follow her there?'

'Not now. It can wait till tomorrow. Check with Whitehaven police that Evans' flat is secure. We'll get Forensics there in the morning and get more details out of the landlady.'

'Mrs Allan,' said Marion. 'Susan Allan.'

'Right. Briefing at 8.30 tomorrow. This case is getting messy.'

'You go home if you want to, Rob,' Sam said to DS Findale. 'I'll go to Axelby Hall to talk to Mrs Bramall before I head home, and we'll pick up on the Evans break-in in the morning.'

'What about Evans?' Rob asked. 'Accident? Suicide?'

'Nothing much to go on as yet,' Sam said. 'Forensics from the flat might help, and whatever the landlady can tell us when she's calmed down, but for now it's wide open.'

'The two events are linked, aren't they? Too much of a coincidence.'

'Oh, yes, they're linked all right, but heaven knows how. If you're here in the morning before me, get Bob Carruthers checking anything he can find on the Bramalls and Sandra or Sandy Evans, and Ian Dawes too, come to that. He and Bramall were mates, could be some other connections.'

The porch light was on at Axelby Hall when Sam parked the car and crunched across the gravel to the front door. Curtains were drawn in the room to the right but a sliver of light shone out and Sam could hear voices inside. It was Edward Bramall himself who opened the front door and stood back as Sam walked into the hall.

'A little later than planned, my apologies, sir,' said Sam. 'I would very much like to speak to Mrs Bramall, if she's sufficiently recovered?'

'She's upstairs, resting,' said Bramall, 'but I'm sure she'll be able to talk to you, Inspector. I have guests in the living room. Can you wait in the dining room while I ask her to come down?'

The dining room was cold and formal, with a long polished table and a high sideboard laden with porcelain and silver. The door creaked open and a small figure entered. Angela Bramall was short and thin, simply dressed, with grey hair pulled away from her face. As she walked towards him Sam could see both grief and incomprehension in her face. She stretched her hand to him, and he shook it gently. The hand was dry and cool.

'I'm so sorry for the loss of your son, Mrs Bramall,' he said.

She gestured to a large chair on one side of the fireplace and sat down on the edge of the chair opposite, her small feet planted side by side on the rug. 'Do you have children, Inspector?' she asked.

'No,' said Sam.

'James is our younger child,' she hesitated. 'He was our younger child. Edward says I spoiled him. He's always been firm with James, much more than me.' She dabbed at her eyes with a handkerchief. 'You have questions for me?'

Sam left his notebook in his pocket. He asked how long James had been living there.

Angela hesitated again, pulling scattered thoughts together. 'He'd had a place of his own when he started with Edward at the firm, but that didn't work out very well, so when he came back from America he came to live here with us. Edward suggested it.' She dabbed at her eyes with a hankie. 'I'm not sure it was really what James wanted, but it certainly saved him some money and it's comfortable here. We try not to intrude…' Her voice trailed away and she looked down at her hands, twisting the handkerchief between her fingers. 'I'm sorry, Inspector,' she whispered. 'It's…this is such a shock, I'm sure you understand.' She unfolded the hankie and blew her nose. 'Do go on.'

Sam said, 'I do appreciate your time, Mrs Bramall. I'll try to keep it short. Maybe you'd prefer me to come back?'

'No, no, let's get this over. I know you have your job to do.'

'You said earlier that James living on his own didn't work out. What did you mean?'

'Oh, you know, the usual young man things. Washing piling up, the place was a mess, no proper food. He didn't seem able to look after himself.' She shook her head. 'Edward said it was because we'd done too much for him, that he hadn't grown up properly. I had a word with James, and it did get a bit better, but it was easier for him here with us.'

Sam waited while she sat quietly for a few moments. 'What can you tell me about James's friends?' he asked.

She shook her head. 'Not a lot. There was Ian Dawes in the village of course, they went back to primary school although I wouldn't say they've been very close recently. Used to go shooting together, to the pub, that kind of thing. And there were boys from school, but James didn't seem to bother with them much. One of them came to stay, just the once. His parents were abroad.'

'What was his name?'

'Marcus Fenton, nice boy.'

'What about friends at work?' Sam asked.

She shook her head again. 'It was hard for him, you know, being the boss's son. I had the feeling that people at work steered clear of him. There must have been people he was close to at university, but no one ever visited here. Before that trip to America James just seemed to muddle along. Never short of a girlfriend but none of them were serious enough to introduce properly to his father and me.' She shrugged. 'I was disappointed, he seemed a bit adrift. Edward and I married quite young. I wanted James to have that security, you know, a family of his own.'

'You mentioned the trip to America,' said Sam. 'Mr Bramall said that James was on business?'

'Partly, yes,' she said. 'Edward arranged some meetings for him in New York and Washington. Some of the firm's work involves links with the Pentagon. Edward wanted James to meet some of the key people out there, part of his induction into the firm, I suppose. But that was only a few days at the start of the trip. After that James was away another four weeks, and he would have stayed longer if Edward hadn't insisted that he come back to work.'

'Do you think the trip changed him at all?'

'Did I say that?' she asked.

'You said that before the trip he was muddling along.'

'And that sounds as if things were different when he got back? Well, yes, they were different, in some ways. James was never very political, not interested in the big issues, but he started talking, ranting even, about the state of the planet, plastic waste, global warming, all that kind of thing. Edward got tired of it very quickly, I'm afraid. When you work at Sellafield you have to be careful about those kinds of opinions, Inspector. There's been so much trouble with Greenpeace and the like over the years.'

'Did you ask James about it?'

'I tried, but he got annoyed. I think he forgot sometimes where his allowance comes from, and his salary, and all the comforts of this house.'

'Do you know if James was in any kind of group, with like-minded people?'

47

'How would I know that?' she asked. 'He lived in this house, but he had his own life.'

'What about his girlfriend? Your husband said you would know more about her than he does.'

'Fathers and sons,' said Angela. ' "Don't ask, don't tell," is that what they say? Those two could talk about rugby, but not much else. Anything to do with James's private life and Edward didn't want to know.'

'And you, did you know?'

'He told me about a girlfriend called Sandra Evans. But then he said, "Don't bother asking around, no one you know will know her." I took that to mean that we wouldn't know her family.' She looked across at Sam and then looked away. 'I even wondered if he'd taken up with someone common just to spite us.'

'Common,' thought Sam. 'That's a word you don't hear much these days.' He kept the observation to himself.

'Do you know where this woman lives, or works?'

'No, I'm afraid not. James did mention that he'd spent time with her in New York. I don't know whether he met her there for the first time, or travelled with her, or met her by accident. I should have asked, I know, but he clearly didn't want to talk to me about her. Maybe they had friends in common, I don't know.'

'Have you ever met her?'

She shook her head. 'It was never suggested that she should come here, and I didn't ask. To be honest, Inspector, I hoped it would blow over, like all the others.'

'What about these new ideas James appeared to have? Do you think they were coming from her?'

'Well, it felt like they were coming from somewhere, or someone, and quite recently. James wasn't a reader, Inspector, not even the front pages of the newspaper, so where was he getting all this anger from?' She closed her eyes for a second. 'Will we be much longer? I'm very tired.'

'Just one last thing, Mrs Bramall. When James was in the house, on Friday night and Saturday before you and your husband went out, did anyone call the house to speak to him?'

She shook her head. 'He had his own phone, you know,' she said. 'Since he got it, he never used the house phone. Haven't you found it?'

'I'm afraid not,' said Sam. 'And James didn't mention any reason why he would go out without his car?'

Angela Bramall shook her head. Tears came to her eyes. 'We went out. When we got back, he was not in the house, and now I'll never see him again.' She bowed her head. 'I can't tell you any more. I'm sorry.' She flapped her hands, willing him to leave.

The drive back to Parton wasn't long enough to process properly all the odd fragments of information that the day had produced. In his mind Sam was putting together the wall display he would create in the morning. That meant another early start. He wondered what kind of day Judith would have had, and what mood she would be in when he got home.

In the house in Parton Judith looked at her watch. It was past seven, and Sam had promised earlier in the day that he'd be home by six. Bill was sitting by the back door, fretting to go out. He needed a proper walk but a run round the back garden would have to do for now. When she was first confined to the house, two weeks before, she'd hoped that Bill would keep her company, but he just lay moodily round the house, his frustrated energy reminding her of her own incapacity.

Judith's irritation with the Parton house had been growing with every passing tedious day. It was too small, too exposed to the westerly wind, and even before she broke her leg it felt too far to walk into town for a coffee or an occasional meal out.

Parton was useful for taking the dog out, straight down to the beach, but who chooses a place to live just to suit the dog-walking? Both of them worked long hours and they hadn't really connected with the small community that lay around them. The neighbours nodded and passed the occasional 'You all'reet?' but that was all.

No word from the newspaper. It felt as if they'd forgotten her, but Ted said he just didn't want to bother her for a few weeks while she recovered. 'It's not just the broken leg,' he'd said, 'it's a shock to the system.' He was right about that. Like someone had hit the emergency brake on her life. She knew it was temporary, but maybe this was a chance to change direction. The community newspaper in Egremont was looking for someone to take over. Might be fun, but not real journalism, not like the days when she was tracking down corruption in local government, making the headlines. It had taken her a while to get over all that, but the big corruption case in 1984 was a long time ago and she seemed to be going backwards. Not having children had meant she could devote all her energy to work, but even if she'd had a kid or two earlier, they would be off her hands by now. 'Listen to yourself,' she said. 'What's the point of having children and then just waiting for them to leave home?'

Past seven-thirty now. Where the hell was Sam? She'd waited to eat with him and now she was hungry and dying for a drink. 'Sam doesn't like me drinking on my own,' she said to herself, 'but it's too bloody bad.' As she hobbled across the room towards the tempting bottle of Cab Sav on the sideboard she caught sight of herself in the big mirror over the fireplace. The red hair had faded as she aged and was unbrushed, framing a face that looked strangely unfamiliar. There were grey bags under her eyes and wrinkles round her mouth that she hadn't noticed before. The stains on her dressing gown weren't visible in the image that stared back at her, but she knew they were there. And she needed a wash too. 'No wonder Sam doesn't seem to fancy me these days,' she thought. 'Does he fancy other women? No, he's never been that kind of man. Do I fancy other men? Oh yes, but they're always younger, funny and cheerful.' Looks mattered less to Judith than whether a man made her laugh.

In the quiet of the house, the phone rang and made her jump. As she picked it up, she was expecting to hear Sam's latest apology for being late, but it wasn't Sam. A man's voice, unfamiliar, not local. 'Is Sam Tognarelli there, please?'

'He's not home yet,' said Judith, 'but I'm expecting him soon.'

There was a short pause, before the voice said. 'Righto, I'll call again, in about an hour?'

'That should work,' she said. 'Can I…?'

The question was unfinished as the line went dead. The man had asked for Sam by name, not as 'Detective Inspector Tognarelli'.

She heard the car pull up outside and the key in the front door. Sam was full of apologies, but apparently more concerned about Bill than about her. Without taking off his coat he walked through the house into the yard and she heard the backgate creak as he whistled the dog away to the beach. Judith opened the bottle of red wine. Making food for them both was what she'd planned to do when he came in but that would have to wait, or he could do it himself. She'd finished her second glass when Sam finally returned.

For a while Sam busied himself with finding food and putting it together for them both while Judith sat, glass in hand, watching.

'Busy day?' she asked.

He shook his head. 'Ridiculous. One young man dead in a ditch, his alleged girlfriend in hospital, dead from an overdose by the look of it, and no clear information what happened in either case.'

'They're connected though, aren't they?'

'Must be, but I can't see exactly how. Just lots of questions.'

They ate. Judith drank. She forgot the earlier phone call until the phone rang again while Sam was washing up and she answered it.

'Is Sam Tognarelli there?' said the voice she remembered.

'Yes, he is. Can I tell him who's calling?'

'My name's Tom Phelps,' said the man. 'My mother is his sister Elspeth. Sam's my uncle.'

'Tommy!' Judith cried out. 'It's been twenty years. Where have you been?'

Chapter 5

It was still dark as Sam set off for work the following day. His mind was too full and sleep had been fitful as memories and problems tumbled round. The phone call with Tommy had lasted a long time, but all they could glean was that Elspeth's marriage to Andy Phelps had failed and for some reason she'd never been able or willing to get back in touch with her brother Sam.

'I was never really part of that family,' Tom had said. 'I left home as soon as I could.'

Sam could imagine how that might have happened. Tommy was born when Elspeth was very young, after a one-night stand with a fellow student whose wealthy family had basically bought Elspeth off, leaving her with a son that any future husband would have to take on. But why no contact from her over all these years?

'We need to talk properly, Tommy,' Sam had said. 'I can't get to London right now to visit you, and Judith can't travel because of her broken leg, but could you come here to us for a day or two? It would be so great to see you.' Judith had been standing close, listening to the conversation, and she smiled and nodded at the suggestion.

'That's what I was wondering,' Tommy had said. 'I've got a meeting in Carlisle next week, and it's not far on the train from there, is it?'

The date was agreed, and Sam was delighted to see how much Judith had perked up at the prospect of a visitor, even though he could only stay for one night. What puzzled Sam as he drove to work the next day was why Tommy had waited so long before tracking him down, making contact only after he'd been in London more than a year. That question had to be pushed to the back of Sam's mind for the time being.

The CID room in Nook Street was still in darkness when he arrived. Sam cleared space on the big whiteboard on one wall above the messy desks and stood back to bring the picture together in his mind. He'd done this with every case he'd ever worked on. The first time he'd used a big wall display flashed into his mind. He'd been working as a postman in 1971 after resigning from the police force in Barrow but had helped Judith's family to find their missing son, Frank. They'd found him dead on a beach, and it was that investigation that had drawn Sam to rejoin the force. Not for the first time, Sam wondered whether he'd done the right thing.

He put two names in the centre of the whiteboard, with a clear space between them. Pictures would follow when they had good images, to add life to the facts. Round James Bramall's name he wrote the key names – the parents Edward and Angela Bramall, friend Ian Dawes, Dennis Hayward and Audrey Harvey, the driver and housekeeper. 'Change of mood?' Sam wrote. 'America?' The word 'girlfriend' linked the left-hand section of the board to the right-hand section, where Sandra Evans' name was bereft of further information so far, apart from the name of her landlady Susan Allan and the address in Whitehaven. 'Drugs?' Sam wrote, and also included an arrow linking Sandra to 'America'.

It was pitifully thin, but they should know more when James Bramall's PM report arrived, and the Forensics information from the apparent break-in at Sandra's flat. The PM on Sandra would help, and Mrs Allan needed to be properly interviewed. Sam began to allocate strands of enquiry to the various officers and realised as he did so that he really needed DS Bell to provide the local knowledge that Findale and Sharp lacked. And there was a new DC on his way too, according to DCI Skaife. DC Sergeant, another novice on probation with CID, who would need his hand holding by someone.

By eight-thirty Sam had added as much as he could to the display, and members of the team were filtering in for the morning briefing. By the time he called them together his mind was the sharpest in the room and he'd had the chance to read Fothergill's preliminary report on the Axelby site that had come in by fax. Grainy photos of tyre tracks, footprints and fragments of glass were added to the whiteboard.

'Lines of enquiry?' Sam asked, looking round the room. He'd already made his list but wanted to get them thinking.

'Trace the car involved, make and model from the glass from the headlights and the tyre tracks?' said Carruthers from his corner.

'Chorley forensics lab say they'll have those results by tomorrow, sir,' Findale chipped in. 'Fothergill says there's no sign of braking on the road, so it looks as if the vehicle could have been aiming to hit Bramall, not an accident. Also looks as if Bramall was already down on the road before the vehicle hit him, but we'll know more when the PM report comes in.'

'What about the girlfriend?' said Sam, pointing at Sandra's name behind him. 'Carruthers, anything you can find on her, any drugs connections, here or in Wales. And what about the girl's flat? Pretty well trashed apparently.'

'She could have done that herself,' said Sharp.

'What about James's frequent weekends away from home?' Sam asked.

Findale checked his notes. 'Ian Dawes said James might have his own place to stay in Carlisle or stay in a hotel. He had enough money, by all accounts.'

A phone rang in Sam's office and Marion Sharp got up to answer it. When she came back into the room a moment later, she raised her hand to attract Sam's attention.

'Sir,' she said. 'That was the hospital. Initial blood tests on Sandra Evans showed evidence of cocaine, alcohol and large amounts of heroin.'

Sam pointed to the whiteboard. 'Two young people dead, both in highly suspicious circumstances, but we still need to avoid assumptions until we have more. In the meantime, Maureen I want you to follow up with the landlady, Mrs Allan, and Sandra's workplace too when you've pinned that down. Findale, get back to Dr Patel and ask her for as much as she has already and the full report on both bodies as soon as possible. I'm due to brief DCI Skaife later this morning and I need more than this by then.'

As if summoned, DCI Skaife came into the room. Behind him was a young man who looked as if he were truanting from school. Sam guessed this was the novice DC that Skaife had mentioned, and the uncharitable thought came to him that strings must have been pulled somewhere to get this youth attached to CID while other more promising candidates were still in uniform.

Skaife stood next to the young man. 'This is DC Sergeant,' he announced. 'He's starting a probationary term with us, and I expect you all to support him any way you can.' He smiled benignly, tapped Sergeant on the shoulder, nodded to Sam and left the room. The young man looked round and the team looked back at him. Carruthers – it would be him, Sam thought – made the obvious remark. 'DC Sergeant, eh? In a few years it could be Sergeant Sergeant.' There were a few snickers.

'Well, for now,' said Sam, 'it's either 'Constable' or, what's your first name?'

'Bill, sir,' said the young man.

Sam shook his head. 'Won't do, my dog's called Bill. How about William?'

'That's what my mam calls me,' said Sergeant.

'Me and your mam,' said Sam. 'It'll feel just like home. Ok, work to do. Let's get on with it.'

He looked across at Maureen who was putting her jacket on ready for the off.

'DC Pritchard,' Sam said. 'Take William with you, give him a chance to see the patch.'

Maureen didn't speak but Sam could see reluctance and annoyance in her face.

'Can I have a word, Maureen?' Sam asked. He led her into his office and closed the door.

'You look thrilled,' he said. 'Sorry I've dumped the new boy on you. No good attaching him to the other 'offcomers' if I want him to get a feel for the place.'

'He's local, isn't he?' said Maureen.

'Another émigré from Barrow,' Sam said, 'it's closer than London or Glasgow, but it's still a bit different up here, and anyway, there's no one better for him to learn from.'

'Is that a compliment?'

'Of course, it is,' he said. 'You know how I highly I rate you, Maureen.'

'Not highly enough to get me promoted.'

He rolled his eyes. 'I've tried, believe me.'

'Paddy says I should just give up the idea, stop fretting about it. And he wants me at home a bit more. Now our Jack's away, he misses the company.'

'Well, that's between you two,' said Sam. 'In the meantime, you can do an important job training the next generation. He's probably about the same age as your Jack.'

'God help us,' said Maureen. 'Not much to go on so far, have we? Forensics should have finished at Evans's flat by the time we get up there. I'll see what I can winkle out of them.' She opened the office door, then turned back. 'It could have been a suicide attempt after the boyfriend's sad demise, but it sounds a bit melodramatic to me. They'd not known each other long, had they?'

'According to Mrs Bramall, only a few months.'

'Maybe she's tried it before, depressive.'

'She might have some mates at work you can ask about that. We're still tracking down the next of kin, a sister according to the hospital records. Carruthers is on to it.'

'OK, I'll take the Boy Wonder off your hands for a few hours and we'll see what we can turn up. See you later.'

'Come on then, William,' said Maureen to the young man hovering outside. 'Whitehaven first, then we'll see where this Evans woman worked and check that too.'

'Right, Sarge,' said William.

Maureen turned to him. 'OK, let's get this straight, shall we? You're not a sergeant even though you're called Sergeant, and I'm not a sergeant, even though I'm old enough to be your mam. It's DC Pritchard. The only difference between you and me, sonny, is twenty years' experience. The boss says you have to learn, so that starts now, OK?'

'Yes,' he hesitated. 'What do I call you?'

'Maureen, like everyone else does.'

It took a while to find the entrance to the house in Sebastopol Terrace. The row of tall Victorian houses looked out over the town, with front gardens dropping down a steep slope to the main road, but they were built before the onset of motor cars and there was nowhere to park. In the end Maureen parked the car in the supermarket carpark further down the road and they walked up the hill and steep steps to the front door.

'Did anyone mention Sandra Evans having a car?' William asked.

'Good question. If she had one, it's probably parked round the back somewhere. The landlady should know. Make sure you ask her.'

It took a while before the door was opened. Maureen introduced them both to the grey-haired woman who stood in front of them.

'What happened to the other officer, the dark-skinned one?' Mrs Allan asked.

'Other duties this morning, Mrs Allan. May we come in?'

'There's a pile of you lot already upstairs in the flat,' said Mrs Allan. 'It was a mess to start with up there, it'll be worse when they've finished.' She pointed to a door off the hall. 'In there,' she said. 'I hope this won't take long. I've got errands to run.'

Maureen could hear people moving around upstairs. 'Is that the flat?' she asked, pointing upwards. 'Two rooms and the bathroom,' said Mrs Allan. 'Will Miss Evans be coming back?'

'I'm sorry to tell you that Miss Evans died without regaining consciousness.'

'Oh, my God!' said the landlady. 'She died! I thought it was just one of those, what do they call it, 'cry for help', just to get attention.'

'That's a possibility,' said Maureen. 'We cannot rule anything out. That's why it is so important to find out exactly what happened before you found her yesterday.'

DC Sergeant spoke suddenly. Maureen had almost forgotten he was there. 'Did she have a car?' he asked, notebook in hand.

Mrs Allan looked at him, and then back at Maureen. 'What's that got to do with anything? As a matter of fact, she didn't.'

'OK, Constable,' said Maureen. 'Why don't you go upstairs and check with the Forensics blokes, see what they've got so far?'

When Sergeant left the room Maureen said, 'Just started today, bless him. Now, can you and I sit down and have a proper chat? My colleague who saw you last night said she wasn't able to have much of a talk with you.'

Mrs Allan sat down. 'I couldn't get out of there fast enough, to tell the truth. I hate those places, full of sick people and drunks. There was nothing I could do anyway. I'd no idea…,' she pulled a handkerchief from her sleeve and dabbed at her eyes. 'She was so young.'

'Do you know how old?'

'I've got the form she filled in when she took the flat,' said Mrs Allan. 'Hang on, I'll fetch it.'

She handed the single sheet over to Maureen who scanned down the items. 'OK, this is very useful, thanks. So, she's been with you only a few months, from September this year. Contact address is in Llanelli?'

'Her sister, I think. Do I have to talk to her?'

'No, we'll handle all that. I need to know everything you can tell me about Sandra's movements over the weekend, up to when you found her, OK? Timings will be really important, so think as hard as you can. When was the last time you saw Sandra?'

The woman stared at the ceiling, recalling the details. 'Well, it must have been Friday morning when she went out to work, but Bob says he heard her come back in the middle of the day on Friday while I was out, and then she went out again. Bob's not here now, but that's what he told me.'

'What about after that?'

Mrs Allan shrugged. 'We were out and about over the weekend, as normal, and I thought it was odd that she didn't seem to be around at all, but I can't keep tabs on her.' She sniffed. 'I'm not one to pry.'

'So why did you go up to the flat on Monday, when you found her?'

'Well, I'd been thinking we hadn't seen her for a few days and I had some clean sheets for her bed, so I took them up. Knocked on the door, but no response, so in the end I used my key. Well, it was a shock I can tell you. The living room, the one above here, was all over the place. Papers everywhere, drawers pulled out, cushions off the sofa. Looked like someone was looking for something. No sign of Sandra though. I called out to her, thought maybe she was asleep or something, so I went through to the bedroom, and there she was.'

'Where?' Maureen asked.

'Like I told that other officer last night, she was lying on the bed, on her back, like one of those things in old churches, an effigy. Looked as if she was asleep, so I went over and shook her, but she didn't stir. I felt her pulse and her cheek. She was warm, but I knew there was something badly wrong. She had one sleeve rolled up, and there was a syringe on the table. There were empty bottles on the table as well, those little ones they put pills in. And a bottle of vodka, that was empty too. It looked like something off the telly.' She put her hand to her mouth. 'Then suddenly I had the feeling there was someone else in the flat. Maybe I heard something.'

'What did you do?'

'I got out of there as fast as I could. I shouted for Bob. He wanted to go up, but I told him not too. I was scared, what with the mess and everything. So we dialled 999 and waited.'

'Did you hear anything upstairs?'

'No, thank God. The ambulance came pretty quick and just after that a policewoman came.

I was in such a state. The policewoman said she had to stay here, to make sure no one disturbed the mess until someone had been to check. I went with Sandra to the hospital. Just didn't want her to be all alone.'

'It must have been a real shock for you,' said Maureen.

'Didn't sleep a wink,' said Susan Allan. 'And now she's died.' She sat back in the chair for a moment. 'What about the room?' she asked.

'They'll be finished soon,' said Maureen.

'I mean, after that. I'll need to find another tenant.'

Maureen was tempted to suggest that she might wait until the last one was buried.

'While I'm here, Mrs Allan, what can you tell me about Sandra, as a person. What was she like?'

'Well, we weren't close or anything, you know. She was quiet, tidy.'

'Friends? Boyfriend?'

'There were a couple of people who came here. One came a few times, I assumed he was her boyfriend, Sandra never said. What was his name? Jimmy. Nice boy, well-spoken, better than most round here. He had a car, a red sporty Mini, used to leave it parked right in the middle of the road at the back when he came to pick her up. Cheeky.'

'Second name?' Maureen asked, although she had already guessed who this might be.

Susan shrugged. 'No idea.'

'And when did you see him last?'

'Saturday before last it must have been. They always went out on Saturdays.'

Mrs Allan leaned forward. 'Sometimes I don't think she came back till Sunday morning, but I never asked. None of my business.'

'So where would she be, any idea?'

'I assumed they were at his place. These young people, it's not like it was in our day.'

'Did Sandra have people to stay here, over the weekends?'

Mrs Allan shook her head. 'Oh, no. We wouldn't have been happy about that. Family maybe, if she asked me beforehand, but no one else.'

'Of course,' Maureen said. 'You mentioned that Sandra had a couple of people who called. One was this Jimmy, what about the other one?'

'A woman came, a couple of weeks ago. She asked if Sandy Evans lived here. I said that she did but she wasn't in, and she went away.'

'What can you remember about her?'

'I asked her name, but she just said she would come back.'

'Tall, short?'

'Quite tall, in her thirties maybe. Hard to tell these days isn't it. Striking looking, you know, unusual. Funny voice, couldn't place the accent, but she wasn't from round here.'

'Did you mention it to Sandra?'

'Yes. She seemed surprised, pleased actually, but she didn't say any more about her.'

'Right, Mrs Allan,' Maureen said, 'I'm just going to pop upstairs and see how they're doing, make sure they don't make too much extra mess.' She pointed up the stairs. 'Is this the only way into the flat?'

'There's a fire escape door at the back, between the bedroom and the bathroom. It's one of those you have to push open, can't be opened from the outside. And there's some stairs down to the back garden.'

'OK, thanks. Now you'll need to wait downstairs, Susan. Can't have too many people in there. And I have to put on these plastic covers over my shoes, and gloves too, so off you go. I'll let you know when we're done.'

Inside the flat two officers in plastic coveralls were still at work, one of them dusting for fingerprints, the other checking among the papers and belongings scattered around the room. DC Sergeant was wearing shoes covers and gloves too, but he was standing to one side, where he'd been told to stand.

'We've finished in the bedroom, Maureen,' said Brian Fothergill.

'Bagged up all those bottles and drug works by the bed?'

'All done, quite a lot of stuff to look at. And we found something else too, come and look.' He stepped towards the firedoor and pointed at the floor. There was something with a label next to it.

'What is it?' said Maureen, peering into the shadow.

'Just a folded-up scrap of paper. There are marks on the floor where it's been wedged under the door to stop it closing properly.'

'So, someone could enter and leave the flat without going through the front door?'

'Right. We'll check the door inside and out for prints. Might even find something on this wedge, but I doubt it. And we'll check the handrail down the outside stairs, but what with the weather and people wearing gloves that's only a faint chance too.'

'OK,' Maureen said. 'I'll ask the landlady if there's anything obviously missing. Can I bring her up, to jog her memory, just to the door?'

Susan Allan seemed pleased to be involved. She stared round the messy room. Maureen spoke to her. 'Have a look around, Susan. Do you notice anything portable that might be missing in here?'

'The telly's there,' said Susan, 'but that's too big to take away. I can see her little radio over there still, and the couple of lamps I got to make it look more homely, you know. What about her phone? She had one of those little phones, very proud of it she was.'

Fothergill shook his head.

'Anything else?'

Mrs Allan shook her head. 'Not that I can see.'

'Handbag?'

'We've bagged that,' said another plastic-suited man who was standing in the doorway that led to the back landing and the bedroom. 'No phone in it though.'

'Any questions, Constable?' Maureen said. 'DC Sergeant,' she said to Fothergill. 'He's with us on probation.' She saw his smile. 'Yes, I know, the name could be confusing.'

'Well, my girlfriend has more than one handbag,' Sergeant ventured.

'There's another couple of bags in the wardrobe,' said the other man. 'We're taking those to check for traces.'

'We need anything you can tell us, Brian, ASAP,' said Maureen. "The young woman's dead, so the case goes up the urgency list, OK?'

'OK,' said Brian, turning back to the job. 'I'll get the preliminary report to Sam, but some of the stuff might take a few days.'

Maureen, DC Sergeant and Mrs Allan went back down the stairs. 'Nearly done, Mrs Allan,' Maureen said. 'Now we need to go to Sandra's work to pester them with questions as well. Where is that?'

'Oh, did I not say? Sandersons in Workington, in Accounts. I think she was quite a clever girl you know. Just the way she spoke, something about her, serious. I wondered how they got together, her and that Jimmy? Chalk and cheese, it seemed to me. But he had money, I reckon, so that helps.'

'So,' Maureen said, flicking back through the notes she'd been making as they talked. 'Just to make sure we've covered everything here…Your husband heard somebody in Sandra's rooms in the middle of Friday, but neither of you saw her after that until you found her on Monday evening. Is that right?'

'Right. It must have been about five o'clock.'

'When were you out on Saturday, Sunday and Monday? Sandra might have come back at some point, maybe while you and your husband were out.'

'Right, so on Saturday we went to Bob's mother in Silloth for lunch and stayed out till after dark.'

'Were there any lights on in the flat when you got back?'

'No, I don't think so. We stayed in Saturday evening.'

'And Sunday?'

'I went to church, about ten like I always do, and Bob went to the club. He picked me up afterwards and we got back here around one. All quiet. I never really thought about where she was.'

'So that takes us to Monday, when Sandra would normally be at work, wouldn't she? What time would she usually set off for work?'

'I think she usually got the train from Corcickle just before eight. She usually went out just before that, the station's just across the street.'

'And you didn't see or hear her go out on Monday morning?'

'No, but I was probably in our kitchen at the back.'

'So, the last time either of you definitely saw or heard Sandra was on the Friday,' Maureen said.

Mrs Allan looked up at Maureen and put her hand to her mouth. 'Oh Lord,' she said, 'when I went up to the flat on Monday, she could have been there for hours, or days even, and I never knew.'

Back in the car, Maureen radioed in. 'Another missing mobile phone,' she said to Sam. 'Still no idea who trashed the flat, but Mrs Allan said she thought there was someone in the place when she found Sandra, about five on Monday afternoon. Just a feeling, nothing more. I think she likes a bit of drama. And there's a fire escape at the back of the house that looks as if it's been wedged open so it could have been used for entry as well as exit. Forensics are checking it.'

Sam asked, 'Do we know how long Sandra had been in the flat before she was found?'

'No, the last time Mrs Allan saw her was Friday morning, so there's three days unaccounted for. It's possible Sandra came back to the flat later on Friday, but that's less certain. I'm going to see if there are CCTV cameras in the supermarket carpark that might pick up movement on Sebastopol Terrace, and we'll need a house to house at the back as well. The fire escape goes from the flat to the back garden and there's a gate from there out into the street. I'll check with Sandra's work first and then sort that out.'

'I'm due to report to Skaife, so have we got anything else?'

'Mention of Sandra having another caller, apart from Jimmy Bramall. A tallish woman, thirties. I'm on my way up to

Sandersons to find Sandra's workmates, see if they can tell me more about her personal life.'

'How's the new boy doing?'

'Not saying much, but he's taking everything in.'

'OK, see you later,' Sam ended the call.

'That's you we're talking about,' said Maureen to Sergeant. 'You're lucky to be working under DI Tognarelli. He's a bloody good detective, so learn as much as you can. Oh, and by the way, there's someone else you'll meet soon, another sergeant. He'll probably try winding you up right from the start, so don't let it get to you. That's DS Bell, quite a character.'

Chapter 6

Sanderson's engineering works sprawled unattractively across part of the industrial estate outside the town. The reception area was spruce and gleaming, belying the external appearance of the plant. Maureen and her sidekick made themselves known, asked to see the head of Miss Sandra Evans's department and waited.

'Ever thought of working somewhere like this?' Maureen asked, eyeing the photos of machinery on the walls. DC Sergeant shuddered. 'My idea of hell, spending all day inside. Noise and fumes and people shouting. No thanks. I wanted to be out and about, that's one reason I joined the force.'

'Noise and fumes and people shouting,' Maureen said, smiling. 'Sounds like a Friday afternoon at Nook Street.'

'DC Pritchard?' said a voice behind them. Maureen turned to face the man who was standing with his head inclined to one side, looking oddly obsequious.

'Peter Coleshaw,' the man said, 'Accounts office manager. I believe you have some questions about one of our employees?'

'Sandra Evans, sir,' said Maureen.

'Ah yes, Miss Evans,' said Coleshaw. 'She left us, quite suddenly and without notice, on Friday. I thought that was very strange. Has something happened?'

'I'm afraid so, sir. Is there somewhere we could talk?'

He led them through to an empty meeting room and the three of them sat down. Maureen said, 'I'm sorry to tell you sir that Miss Evans was found unconscious in her flat on Monday afternoon and subsequently died.'

Coleshaw looked genuinely shocked and upset. 'Oh, how dreadful. How did it happen?'

'That's what we're investigating, sir. We need to know when she was last seen at work, which you've just told us, and I need to speak to any friends Sandra has here, to help us piece together where she might have been since Friday.' He nodded. 'You say she left without notice. Any idea why that might have been?'

'No, none,' said Coleshaw. 'Her work here was quite satisfactory. She'd only been with us since the summer but I had high hopes for her actually, a good candidate for further training, I thought. No, she just came to me late morning on Friday and said she was leaving, right away. I explained that if she left without notice she'd forfeit a week's pay, but she practically laughed in my face. It was most uncharacteristic, Constable. I wondered if she was drunk.'

'Drunk, or on drugs perhaps, to make her react that way?'

'Not in the morning, surely. She seemed, what's the word, euphoric, that's it.'

'High as a kite?' Sergeant contributed.

'Exactly,' said Coleshaw. 'And now… how dreadful,' he repeated. 'What a waste.'

'We'd like to talk to any close friends or workmates, sir.'

'Yes, of course.'

Coleshaw went out to the reception desk and picked up the phone. He spoke very quietly, but Maureen saw that the receptionist heard the gist of what he was saying. It would be all round the works within minutes.

'Follow me, please,' said Coleshaw and he led the way down various corridors. He opened the door to a small windowless office and ushered them inside. 'Wait here, please.'

He left and they waited. A few minutes later there was a light knock on the open door and a young woman stood in the doorway. She had very short blonde hair and bright red lipstick. 'Are you the police?' she said.

Maureen introduced them both.

'And you're asking about Sandra?'

'Sandra Evans, yes. Is she a friend of yours, Miss…?'

'Anne-Marie Corbett,' said the young woman, looking intently at Maureen. What's happened to her? She just downed tools on Friday, and not a word since.'

Maureen gestured for the young woman to sit down. She didn't look at DC Sergeant but hoped he'd assumed the role of note-taker.

Anne-Marie said, 'Me and Sandra work in Accounts, at least she did until Friday.'

'What happened on Friday?'

'Well, she got a phone call mid-morning. Our supervisor was pretty mad about that. We're not supposed to get personal phone calls. I couldn't help listening, Sandra's desk is right next to me. Anyway, she didn't talk for long. Just said OK, a few times. Then she leaned back with this big smile and marched straight into old Coleshaw's office. Two minutes later she was back saying she'd resigned and started packing up her stuff. She was really excited, never seen her like that before. I asked her what she was going to do, but she just shrugged and said she'd be fine.' She looked at Maureen curiously. 'Anyway, why are you here? Has she done something wrong?'

'I'm afraid she'd dead,' Maureen said. 'She was found unconscious at her flat on Monday and died without coming round.'

Anne-Marie cried out and stood up, hands over her mouth. 'She's dead?' She looked around, and then ran out of the room. Sergeant jumped up and ran after her, with Maureen struggling to follow. The young woman was leaning against the wall outside the room, breathing heavily, obviously very shocked. 'I need a cig,' she said and began to walk down the corridor. Sergeant made to pull her back, but Maureen gestured for him to leave her and they followed as Anne-Marie went through a door into the open air and walked towards a wooden seat.

Maureen sat down beside her, gesturing to Sergeant to stand close enough to hear. Anne-Marie lit a cigarette with a shaking hand.

'Sorry that was such a shock,' said Maureen. 'Were you two very close?'

The young woman shook her head, 'No, not really. But she was young like me, there was nothing wrong with her, and now she's dead. I can't take it in.' She looked up. 'Was it drugs?'

'What makes you say that?'

'Well, I wondered. That boyfriend of hers, he looked like a druggie to me, you know. Not shambling around and drooling, but sort of hyped up. And he had money, and they went clubbing in Carlisle every weekend. Monday mornings sometimes, she looked wasted. I just assumed they were getting high on something.'

Someone else approached the seat, looked at the two women and the young man hovering to one side and walked away again. Maureen wondered how long it would take for rumours about the police visit, Sandra's disappearance and Anne-Marie's tears to spread round the employees.

'I'll come back to that,' Maureen said. 'Tell me what you know about Sandra.'

Anne-Marie drew on the cigarette. 'What's to tell? She'd knocked around a bit, more than the rest of us. When she started here, she talked a lot about New York. Said she went early in the year because it was cheaper, but it still costs, doesn't it? I think there was a man or an old friend involved, but she never said directly, or mentioned anyone. Could have been someone she'd known for a while. And she'd lived in Brighton you know, in a commune or something.'

'Recently?'

'Don't think so, quite a while ago. She must have been just a kid.'

'And where did she live before moving here?'

'No idea. Can't you ask her parents?'

Maureen tried another angle. 'Did you like her?'

Anne-Marie hesitated. 'She was complicated, you know? I get on easy with most people, but I always thought she was holding back, very private. And she got on her high horse every now and then about politics and stuff, lecturing me about the planet like I was a public meeting. I had to tell her to lay off, I wasn't interested.'

'You mentioned the boyfriend. Did you meet him?'

'Yeh, sometimes he'd pick her up after work. Jimmy. Posh. I asked her where she met him and she said in New York. I thought that was funny. Fancy going all that way and meeting someone from here.'

'When did they start seeing each other?'

'Just after she started here, end of September.'

'You said they went clubbing in Carlisle at the weekends. Do you know if they stayed anywhere, to get some sleep?'

Anne-Marie shook her head. 'She did say something about how good it was that James could afford whatever they wanted. That could have meant a hotel, I suppose.'

'And did Sandra ever mention any other friends?'

Anne-Marie looked up. 'I think there was someone that Sandra kept quiet about, a woman. I saw them in Carlisle one Saturday afternoon, couple of weeks ago.'

'What did this woman look like?'

'Tall, short black hair. She was wearing a long coat, and boots, looked like Doc Martins. They were further down the street and I tried to catch up, but then they sat down and I felt a bit awkward and hung back.'

'Did you speak to them?'

'No, they hadn't seen me, and they seemed really wrapped up in each other.'

'What do you mean?' Maureen asked.

Anne-Marie shrugged. 'Don't know. They just seemed so, you know, close.'

Maureen smiled. 'Maybe you were jealous.'

'Jealous? You think we're lesbians or something? I'm certainly not, but I did wonder about Sandra after I saw them together. There was something about that woman, she walked like a man, long stride.'

'Did you ask Sandra about it?'

'No, but I wish I had done. It might have made us talk properly, like real friends.' She paused, sniffed. 'I don't think Sandra wanted to die, but then you realise how little you know about someone.' She wiped her eyes, took a last drag on the cigarette and ground the stub under her shoe. 'What's going to happen now?'

'Well, we think she has relatives who'll presumably look after the funeral. Anyway, I'll contact Mr Coleshaw if I hear anything about that. We'll keep on checking until we're clear exactly what happened.'

'Will they have to do a post-mortem, cut her open and that?'

'I'm afraid so, yes. It's an unexplained death.' She paused. 'Anne-Marie, you said you don't think Sandra would have taken her own life.'

'No.' Anne-Marie shook her head. 'No way.'

'Not even if something drastic happened?'

'Well, on Friday she was pretty chuffed with life I reckon, packing in the job and swanning off somewhere, happy as Larry. Have you found her journal? There might be something in there.'

Maureen's eyes widened. 'Sandra kept a journal?'

'That's what she told me. Said she'd done it for years, every day or two. She waved it at me once, it was bright red I remember.'

Sergeant asked, 'Any idea where she might have kept it?'

'Well, it was in her handbag when she showed it to me. It wasn't something she'd leave lying around.'

Anne-Marie took the pack of cigarettes out of her pocket, but then put it away again. She bit her lip. 'I can't believe she's dead. And she can't have wanted to die, she can't.'

'It could have been an accident,' said Maureen. 'Once drugs are involved, accidents can happen.' She paused. 'You mentioned that the boyfriend, Jimmy, might have been on drugs. Why did you think that?'

She shrugged. 'Dunno really. Just the look of him, like I said, hyped up, fidgety. Sandra never said anything about it.' She sniffed. 'Look, she's dead anyway, what does it matter? You'll make sure we know about the funeral? Promise?'

'I'll do my best,' said Maureen. 'And thanks for your help, Miss Corbett.'

They left Anne-Marie and went back inside. 'Where now?' said Sergeant.

'We have one more question to ask here, don't we?' Maureen said.

'The phone call that Sandra got?'

'Right. So, back to reception. You can deal with this.'

Sergeant went to the desk while Maureen stood off to one side.

'Last Friday morning,' he said, 'a call came for Sandra Evans. Can you tell where it was from?'

'The number will be in the system, and I log all the calls,' said the woman. She leafed back through the large book on her desk. 'Here we are, Friday morning, 10.53am, put through to Miss Evans in the Accounts department. I reported it to Mr Coleshaw, employees aren't supposed to take personal calls.'

'So why did you put the call through?'

'The caller said it was an urgent family matter. It only lasted a minute or two.'

'Do you remember the caller's voice at all?' Sergeant asked.

'It was woman, I think,' said the receptionist, 'and she had an accent but I couldn't place it.'

'American?' Maureen interjected.

'Possible. Hard to tell from just a few words.'

Sergeant leaned towards her and lowered his voice. 'You didn't listen in on the call, did you?' The woman smiled. 'Like in some old film, you mean? Too busy, love. I only know the call's finished when the light goes off.' She pointed to the console in front of her.

'And can you give us the number of the caller, please?'

The woman looked at him. 'Certainly, hang on.'

A few moments later she handed Sergeant a scrap of paper with a long number written on it. 'It's one of those mobile phones,' she said. 'Could have been from anywhere.'

'Is it always like this?' William Sergeant asked Maureen as they walked back to the car.

'Like what? Driving around and talking to people, you mean? Yes, that's the job. Forensics people look for traces, pathologists look at bodies, and we look at what they tell us and use it to decide who to talk to and what about. And sometimes it's the other way around. We talk to people and use what they tell us to decide what evidence we need to look for.'

'And sometimes people get upset, or forget things, or can't be bothered to remember,' he said. 'Then you have to be really patient, like you are when you're talking to people. You just let them talk.'

'Of course,' said Maureen. 'I know all the science stuff helps, especially now with DNA and all that, but it's people who matter most. I let Anne-Marie talk and now we know that Sandra had a friend who could have been American, that she kept a journal which appears to be missing, and that she probably didn't kill herself because of what happened to James Bramall.'

'Yes, OK,' said Sergeant, 'but until we get the post-mortem results we won't know when Sandra died. And the Forensics blokes might be able to say if anyone else had been in that flat. That's where the science comes in.'

'You're learning,' she said. 'We'll stop off at Nook Street to check in with the boss, and then go back to Sebastopol Terrace to start on the house-to-house. I think Sandra went back to that house after leaving work on Friday lunchtime. Then she went out again. Between Friday afternoon and Monday afternoon she could have been in and out a few times, but the Allans missed her. If there was someone else in the flat during that time, we need to know who and when. Every little piece of information helps.'

The CID room was quiet when they got back, apart from Bob Carruthers in his usual spot. 'You found anything, Bob?' Maureen asked.

'Plenty,' he said. 'Looks like our Sandra had a past, and another name. Arrested in 1990, poll tax riot. Sometimes she called herself Sandra Dryden. And she's 28, older than young Bramall. Sam says there's a sister coming up from Llanelli, Thursday probably.'

'Anything from the post-mortems?'

'Nothing yet but it shouldn't be long. Sam wants a briefing later on, five-thirty, just to catch up with everything before the end of the day.'

'Anything from Chorley about the hit and run car?'

He laughed. 'Oh, that'll be ages. I could hassle them I suppose.'

'Hassle away,' said Maureen. 'I've been telling our new boy how every little detail helps.' She pointed at the whiteboard. 'Everything goes up there,' she said to Sergeant. 'The DI's really good at bringing it all together. That's why we need to do the house-to-house before people forget the details.'

Together, the two of them knocked on doors up and down the road behind Sebastopol Terrace and the houses that overlooked the back of Sandra's flat, asking about lights and any movement in the first floor flat at number 19 over the weekend. They were drawing blank looks and shaking heads until a man in a wheelchair rolled down the dark hallway of a house just behind number 19. 'You want to know if there was anyone in that upstairs flat across the road, Bob Allans' place?' he said. 'Well, someone was there last Saturday afternoon, it was before the footie started, so before three. I was in our downstairs back room. It was still light but I saw someone draw the curtains in that flat, the big window at the back.'

'Did you see who it was?'

'I don't think it was her, the girl who lives there. She's quite short. This person was taller and I thought it might have been a man. I thought, aye, aye, bit of nookie on a Saturday afternoon. All right for some.' He hesitated. 'Mind you, I'm not sure about it being a man, not 100% like.'

'Did you see anything else, later on?'

The man shook his head. 'It was dark at four, wasn't it? I didn't see a light on over there, but if the curtains were still drawn, I wouldn't have seen light anyway, would I? They were still shut all day Sunday. Monday I was at the Day Centre and didn't notice.'

Sergeant said, 'There's a fire door and stairs coming down from the flat. Did you see anyone on those, at any time?'

The man shook his head. 'Never noticed anyone on those stairs, actually, although the way the wheelchair fits in that room I don't see out at the right angle. I have a carer who comes in a few hours a week. You could ask her. I've got her number.'

Sergeant proffered his notebook and a pen, and the man wrote the number down on an empty page.

'Right, thanks' said Maureen. 'Can you deal with that, Constable?'

Sergeant nodded.

'OK,' she said as they drove back to Workington. 'We still need any CCTV coverage that picks up the front of the house, but it was worth knocking on doors. We know there was someone in the flat on Saturday afternoon who for whatever reason wanted to close the curtains, but we're not sure whether that person was male or female.'

'A tall person. Anne-Marie saw Sandra with someone tall in Carlisle, didn't she? It's in my notes. She thought it was a woman, but walked like a man.'

'Tall and possibly a woman isn't much to go on, but every little helps,' said Maureen. 'Do you want to do the report at the briefing?'

'OK. What's the boss been doing today?' Sergeant wondered.

'Something important I expect,' said Maureen.

Chapter 7

Sam's plans for the afternoon had changed, and not in a direction he welcomed. When he'd mentioned to DCI Skaife that he had asked Forensics to examine James Bramall's room and car, Skaife began to fidget. 'What do you expect to find?' he'd asked.

'Evidence of drug-taking,' Sam said. 'We already suspect that James had a drug habit, and involvement with dealers might have caused trouble. Someone ran over James that night and drove away.'

'When do you propose to make these searches?' Skaife asked.

'This afternoon, I'm heading up there now myself with Findale.'

DCI Skaife pushed back his chair and stood up. 'Give DS Findale another assignment. You and I will go to Axelby Hall, Findale won't be needed.'

The surprise must have registered on Sam's face.

'Of course, you're very competent, Inspector,' said Skaife, 'but Findale is relatively green and I've done many years in CID. Sometimes a case needs a very experienced team. The Superintendent said as much when I saw him yesterday, and he wants to put this case to bed as rapidly as possible.'

Sam had already suggested to Findale and Sharp that this high-profile case might be good for their careers, but obviously

Skaife had other ideas. Strings were being pulled that were causing Skaife to take the unusual step of doing some real police work.

'Yes, sir,' was all Sam could say. 'Shall we take my car?'

'Tell the Forensics boys to wait until we call them, OK?' Skaife said. 'I'd like the Bramalls to have a few minutes' notice before they are invaded by men in plastic coveralls.'

Sam stopped. 'Is that wise, sir? The whole point of a search is that it finds what's there, not what people want us to find.'

Skaife shook his head. 'I'm sure you're not suggesting that Edward Bramall and his wife would interfere with our investigation of their son's death. Make the call, Inspector. Tell them to hold off for an hour, and I'll make sure the Bramalls are ready to see us.'

There was nothing Sam could do, and he knew it. When they arrived at Axelby Hall Edward Bramall greeted his old mate Arthur Skaife. Murmured condolences were offered, and enquiries made about Angela, who didn't appear. 'Mrs Bramall is still very distressed, obviously,' Skaife said to Sam, 'but Mr Bramall has no problem with us searching James's room and car, so let's get the team in.'

Skaife played very little part in the activity that followed. The first search was of James's rooms, a large comfortably furnished bedroom, a smaller office which had probably been a dressing room in earlier times, and the modern bathroom, all on the first floor at the side of the house, overlooking large trees where noisy rooks were settling down to roost. Sam followed Fothergill and his assistant as they worked round the room, picking up and bagging various items, while Skaife and Edward Bramall watched from the doorway. There was no sign of a mobile phone, address book or a palm pilot where contacts could be stored digitally. In a desk drawer were various pamphlets and papers. Sam picked one of them out of the pile before they went into a bag. It was a polemic about global warming complete with charts and statistics. Sam peered at the address printed at the bottom. '*Earth Liberation Front, 47 East Street, Stepney,*' There was a phone number and email address too and Sam made a note of them.

In the bathroom Sam whispered to Fothergill, 'Don't bring anything to my attention while we're here, OK, Brian. I don't want Bramall senior poking his nose in.'

'What's Skaife doing here?' Fothergill whispered back. 'Not seen him at a crime scene for weeks. His appraisal interview must be due.'

'He's a busy man, isn't he?' said Sam. 'All those targets to check.'

Fothergill's assistant picked up a tiny polythene sachet from the bathroom cabinet and held it up for them both to see. Sam put a finger to his lips. 'Bag it,' said Fothergill, 'and everything else you find in there.' He nodded to Sam. 'No problem, if anything's here, we'll find it.'

When they were finished in the house, Edward Bramall led the way to the garage, where James's red Mini sat gathering dust. He handed over the keys and looked as if he would stay and watch, but Sam asked if they could all go back to the house as he had some more questions. He wanted to give Fothergill the chance to do a proper search without Bramall hovering around. Skaife looked uncertain but he followed Sam and Bramall back into the house. In the comfortable drawing room, Sam reached for his notebook as Angela Bramall pushed open the door. Skaife stood up to greet her, obliging Sam to follow suit. Edward Bramall guided his wife solicitously to a chair.

'What have you found, Inspector?' she asked.

'Too early to tell,' said Sam. 'But there were some interesting pamphlets in James's room, about the environment and such like.

Big headline, "Liberate the Earth". Can you or your husband shed any light on that?'

He handed one of the pamphlets to Edward Bramall who scowled at it before handing it back. 'James knew better than to talk about that kind of stuff,' he said. 'I honestly don't know if or why he had anything to do with people like that.'

Angela spoke up quietly. 'He never mentioned it before he went to America,' she said.

'And that was when he started knocking about with that girl,' said Edward.

'Do you mean Sandra Evans?' Sam asked.

'Is that her name?' Edward looked at his wife. 'Did James tell you anything about her?'

She shook her head. 'I asked him, but he just said we wouldn't know her family, and I left it at that. I didn't think he was very serious about her.'

'Have you talked to her, Inspector?' Edward asked. Skaife looked at his hands.

Sam said, 'I'm afraid we only became aware of Miss Evans whereabouts when she was unable to talk to us.'

'You mean she refused?' Edward asked.

'No, sir,' said Sam, 'she was found unconscious, and has since died.'

Angela gave a small shriek and stared at her husband, who reached a comforting hand towards her. 'Is there some connection with James's death, Arthur?' Edward asked.

Skaife said, 'It's too early to draw any firm conclusions. It's possible that the young woman accidentally overdosed. She had a drug habit, apparently.'

Angela had tears in her eyes, 'Might she have, you know, taken her own life?'

'That's possible too,' said Sam. 'We're waiting for the results of the post-mortem.'

'And what about James's post-mortem?' Edward asked. 'Do you have that report yet?'

'It's due to reach us by the end of the day,' Skaife said. 'I'm afraid these procedures do take time.'

'And in the meantime,' said Edward, who was now holding his wife's hand, 'you feel the need to rake over James's life and possessions. You must understand how distressing this is.'

Skaife began to respond, but Sam interrupted him. 'It's standard procedure, sir, when a death is unexplained. We all need to be clear exactly what happened to your son, and the Coroner will expect us to be thorough.'

'Of course, of course,' said Bramall. He stood up, clearly agitated. 'Will they be finished in the garage yet? I need the keys back.'

'I'll go and check in a moment,' said Sam, 'but could you help us with any names from James's college that we could talk to? And any other of James's friends? We've already spoken to Ian Dawes.'

Angela said. 'James's tutor at St Catherine's was Professor Auerbach. What about his friends? Edward?'

'You would know better than me,' said Edward. 'What about that Sedbergh boy who came to us one holiday, just before James went away?'

'Marcus, Marcus Fenton,' said Angela. 'Yes, I told the inspector about him. I have his phone number somewhere. He went to Cambridge too, but a different college. James did mention him once or twice.'

While Angela searched for the number, Sam went to check on Fothergill's progress in the garage. He was holding several plastic bags in his hand. 'Our boy was either careless or naïve, or both,'

Fothergill said. 'All sorts in here. Not sure his parents are going to be thrilled.'

'Too bad,' said Sam. 'I'll be interested to see if any of this ever hits the news, which would definitely upset them. Let us have the report as soon as you can, Brian. Skaife's under pressure by the look of it, so questions will be asked I've no doubt.'

'Will do,' said Fothergill. 'By the way, do I hear Dinger's coming back to Nook Street?'

'Apparently so,' Sam said. 'I'm thrilled, as you can imagine. I don't think the Bramalls will be seeing much of DS Bell, unless six months in Carlisle has improved his interpersonal skills.'

Brian Fothergill laughed. 'I doubt that,' he said. 'Good luck.'

As they drove back to Workington Sam tried to clarify the tasks that faced them and who they should be assigned to, but Skaife was only interested in the progress of the PM report on James Bramall, and what the Forensics team had found at Axelby Hall. 'Do these reports always take so long?' he asked Sam.

'Generally, yes, sir. We're also still waiting to hear from the lab at Chorley about the headlight glass found at the scene. That would give us some idea of the car that hit James.'

'Leave all that to me, Inspector,' said Skaife. 'It's time these people felt a bit of pressure. Things are getting slack around here.'

Yet again, Sam mused silently on Skaife's unwillingness to acknowledge his responsibility for what happened "around here". Out loud, he asked, 'What would you like me to focus on, sir?'

'Follow up with the Cambridge tutor, and that name the Bramalls gave us.'

'Marcus Fenton?'

'Yes, quick as you can.'

When they got back to Nook Street one item of business was quickly crossed off the list. The post-mortem report on James

Bramall was in. Skaife led Sam through to the DCI's office to read it. He began to read while Sam waited.

'Time of death's a bit vague.' Skaife commented almost immediately. 'Between midnight Sunday and three on Monday morning.' He read on, turned the page to read further and then looked up, closing his eyes. 'Oh God, here we go. The Bramalls aren't going to like this.'

He handed the page over to Sam.

Sam skimmed the information. 'Cocaine and heroin as well as alcohol, he must have been well-nigh incapable.' He read on, 'Signs of long-term drug use.'

'There's more,' said Skaife, 'Read the rest of it.'

Sam summarised what he was reading. 'From the position of the injuries from both the impact and the wheels of the car, it looks as if James was already lying on the road when the vehicle hit him.' He looked again. 'Injury to the head may have happened before the final impact… looks as if he was dragged into the ditch.' He read on, 'Bruising to the torso and hands from about two weeks earlier.'

Sam looked up from the report. Skaife was gazing out of the window.

'Not straightforward at all,' Sam said.

Skaife shook his head. 'Edward doesn't want to hear any of this. He thinks his precious son was "immature", not a hardened druggie. And Angela, well…' Skaife shook his head.

Sam was thinking not of the Bramalls but the evidence that would need to be followed up.

'My list of questions is getting longer all the time,' said Sam. Skaife might not be interested but Sam was determined that he should realise how much work they had to do. 'We have to find out why James was on the road,' Sam said. 'Had he just walked up from the house, or was he being dropped off? Who was driving the car? How did James get those previous injuries? Who was supplying James with drugs? Where did James go on his weekends away from home? What's the connection with this 'Earth Liberation' group?'

Skaife shook his head. 'And this is all compounded by the link to the young woman, Miss Evans. What do we know about her?'

'DC Pritchard and DC Sergeant have been checking all that, sir,' said Sam. 'Knowing Pritchard, they'll have done a good job.'

'Pull it all together, Inspector,' said Skaife. 'Let's get everything on that whiteboard and set some priorities.' He checked his watch. 'Tell everyone, briefing at five-thirty. We've been on this case for nearly three full days and going round in circles.'

'Are we thinking of Bramall and Evans as one case now, sir?' Sam asked. He suspected that Skaife really wasn't interested in Sandra Evans. 'No alternative,' said the DCI, 'but I think we're missing something or someone that connects these two.'

Sam thought for a moment. 'There is one thing,' he said. 'They'd both been in New York recently.'

'Were they there together?'

'Not as far as we know, but we need to check dates and where they were staying. I can get Findale on to that, he might have some contacts over there from his time in the Met.'

Later in the afternoon the team assembled in the CID room. The strip lighting was harsh and the windows black against the dark December sky. Wind moaned through the ill-fitting windows of the old building and in one corner a persistent drip from the ceiling tapped into a bucket. Skaife took up his place on one side of the whiteboard. Sam noticed an exchange of looks between Findale and Sharp as they noticed Skaife standing at the front of the room rather than hovering at the side. He wondered what the two offcomers from big cities talked about when no one else was around. He also wondered how on earth Dinger would fit into the new team when he returned.

Skaife asked for a report from the Evans' side of the investigation, which DC Sergeant read from his notes in a monotone while Sam wrote up the salient details on the whiteboard.

'This journal,' Sam said, 'was anything found in the flat?'

'Some old ones, sir,' Pritchard said, 'but not this year's. The old ones show that she recorded all sorts of personal information. It could have been what someone was looking for when they ransacked the place.'

'Red cover, you said? Shouldn't be hard to spot.' Sam added 'Red journal?' to the whiteboard near Sandra's name.

Maureen added, 'The phone call that Evans received on Friday morning is clearly significant,' she said. 'It was from a mobile phone. Do we have a number for James Bramall's mobile?'

Sam pulled his notebook from his pocket. 'The number was among the papers found in his room,' he said, 'but no sign of the phone itself.' He read out the number, and Maureen shook her head. 'Not him,' she said. 'So, there's clearly someone else in Sandra's life important enough to cause her to leave her job.'

'Family?' asked Skaife.

'The sister, Mrs Lewis, is coming up from South Wales tomorrow,' Sam said. 'She might help with that.' Pritchard raised her hand. 'We think Sandra returned to the flat on Friday and then went out again and wasn't seen there again until the landlady found her on Monday afternoon. A witness says that someone closed the curtains in the bedroom of the flat around three on Saturday afternoon, but that person was probably not Sandra herself. The witness could be mistaken but seems sure that this person was taller than Sandra, and could have been male or female. The landlady told us that a tall woman called to see Sandra at the flat, and there's a mention from another witness of an unidentified person, female, linked to Miss Evans, but no further details as yet.'

Sam had more questions, but Skaife interrupted. 'As for James Bramall,' he said, pulling the report from his pocket and holding it up like a rabbit out of a hat. 'We have the PM report, which raises more questions than answers.' He read out the salient parts of the report that he and Sam had found earlier. 'This raises the following questions,' he went on, and proceeded to list the questions, word for word, that Sam had outlined in their previous conversation. He glanced at a list of assignments that sat on the desk just in front of him. 'Sergeant Findale, DC Sharp, house-to-house in Axelby close to the Hall about anything seen or heard on the road in question overnight, from midnight onwards. DC Sergeant will work with DC Carruthers on any CCTV in the village and vehicle checks where necessary.' He looked across at Bob Carruthers who was peeking as usual over the top of his large computer. 'Chorley should have the results on the glass fragments found at the scene by tomorrow morning. Tracking down the vehicle involved is a high priority, OK? Report your progress directly to me.'

'Sir,' said Bob.

Skaife went on, pointing vaguely at Sandra Evans's image on the whiteboard. 'DI Tognarelli and DC Pritchard will focus on the Evans enquiry. I will work with the Bramall family and their staff. Any approaches to the Bramalls come through me, understood?'

Sam looked around. Everyone understood: the Bramalls would be given personal attention by the DCI. Everyone else, hands off.

'One last thing,' Skaife added. 'DS Bell will be returning to duty with us here from tomorrow morning. He will join this investigation once he's up to speed with developments. That's all. Thank you everyone. Next briefing this time tomorrow.'

The meeting broke up, but not before Sam saw some whispering, and guessed it was in anticipation of Dinger's imminent arrival. DS Bell would be reclaiming his desk which had been freely used by others in his absence, and Carruthers would get his best buddy back. He hoped they could keep young DC Sergeant out of Bell's clutches but assigning him to work with Bob Carruthers could be a mistake. Bell thrived on the witless admiration of younger male officers who giggled at his sexist jokes and the rudeness that masqueraded as 'honesty'. He seemed to believe that every true Cumbrian bloke was scornful of women and suspicious of 'foreigners' and that he was the only one brave enough to say out loud what all of them were thinking. The man was a menace.

When Sam got home, Judith had managed to have a shower by wrapping a plastic bag round her plaster cast. She'd washed her hair and got dressed, putting on a long skirt that hid the hated cast.

'I've tidied up a bit,' she said. 'Can you do the vacuuming and wash the back windows before Tommy comes? All that wind has streaked them with salt and sand.' She pointed to the cooker. 'I found some spaghetti sauce in the freezer,' she said, smiling. 'And we've even got parmesan.' She looked so pleased with herself that Sam gave her a big hug.

They were just sitting down to eat when the phone rang. Judith looked at him, but Sam knew he had to answer it. It was DC Sharp. 'Fax just came in, sir. I thought you'd want to know that the initial examination of Sandra Evans showed that she was pregnant. Twelve weeks gone. If it wasn't showing already, it soon would be. Should I tell the DCI, sir?'

'Leave that with me,' Sam said. 'It'll keep till the morning.'

Sam thanked her, put down the phone and turned back to the table and his dinner. Judith had made an effort and he mustn't spoil her evening, but his mind was turning.

Chapter 8

There was no sign of Skaife when Sam arrived at work. He had got the clear message that the Evans enquiry was far less important to the DCI than the James Bramall case, so it wasn't worth trying to find him. If Sandra Evans' pregnancy could be linked back to James Bramall, that would be a different story. He rang Dr Patel to check how long it would take to extract DNA from the foetus and check that against DNA from James's body. A week? That long? They could probably get it done faster, she told him, but that might mean spending more. He wrote a note and left it on the DCI's desk. 'Sandra Evans twelve weeks pregnant. Checking DNA for paternity. Could take a week.' He wondered how Skaife might approach the Bramalls if it turned out that Sandra's death might have deprived them of a grandchild. Now he had to make the most of the morning, before meeting Mrs Lewis, Sandra's sister, off the train in the early afternoon.

No sign of DS Bell, despite the promises of the DCI the previous evening. Sam wasn't unduly surprised, and certainly not disappointed. Bell often used lateness as a way of emphasising how important he was, and he had probably found plenty to delay his departure from Carlisle. He'll probably turn up for this afternoon's briefing, Sam thought, to make a good entrance. In the meantime, Sam had some tasks to tick off the list in his head.

James Bramall's tutor from St Catherine's, Cambridge, Dr Auerbach told a familiar story when Sam managed to track him down. There was shock at James's untimely demise, but the same estimation of James's capabilities as Sam had already gathered. 'A nice enough young man, Inspector, but I did wonder how he managed to squeeze through the academic qualifications we expect here.'

'He wasn't up to it, intellectually?'

'Well, a third-class degree speaks for itself really, doesn't it? I wish we could manage to fail someone, at least every now and then, but we'd probably have a lawsuit on our hands if we did. Something about 'silk purses and sow's ears' comes to mind, if you understand me.'

Sam caught the drift and marvelled at the drawl in Auerbach's voice, like something out of 'Brideshead Revisited'.

Sam asked a question he had already guessed the answer to. 'James's father Edward read Physics at St Catherine's, I understand. Do you think that might have helped James find his place with you?'

Auerbach gave a short laugh. 'Well, that plus a hint of generosity might have done the trick.'

'A bribe?' Sam asked.

'Bribe?' Auerbach laughed again. 'Good heavens, Inspector, nothing so crude. A contribution to the new Library wing, perhaps. But that's all history now, isn't it? The poor young man is dead, run over, you said. Ghastly.'

'One last thing, sir,' said Sam. 'Do you recall any difficulties James might have had with drugs?'

The response was categoric. 'I doubt it. The odd whiff of cannabis possibly, but nothing more than that. We may not succeed academically with some of our weaker students, Inspector, but we do take their supervision very seriously. Any sign of serious drug issues would have been followed up assiduously.'

'And what about James's political views?'

'He was a child of the Thatcher years, Inspector. He and his peers seemed tediously conventional to me. And more than that, James was still very young for his age. I doubt whether he'd developed any firm views about anything significant.' There was a short silence. 'Is that all, Inspector? I have students due in a few minutes. Please convey my condolences to the poor boy's parents.'

It took a while to track down Marcus Fenton from the home phone number that Mrs Bramall had given Sam. When Marcus finally answered Sam could hear quite a racket going on in the background. 'Can you speak up?' Marcus said. 'We're running a simulation of a Y2K catastrophe scenario and things have got a bit noisy.'

'Are you expecting a crisis on New Year's Eve?' Sam asked.

'Well, you never know, do you? Big banks like ours have had to plan ahead. If there is a glitch we'll have to respond fast. What can I do for you?'

'I'm enquiring about someone you know, Mr Fenton, James Bramall.'

'Jimmy? Not seen him for a while. What's he done?'

'I'm afraid he was involved in an incident a few days ago. He received injuries from which he died.'

'He's dead? Christ. What kind of an incident?'

'He was run over.'

'He wasn't driving then.' Fenton paused. 'Was he drunk?'

'We believe so, sir, and there were drugs in his system also. Do you know anything about James's habits in that regard?'

Marcus Fenton paused again. Sam heard a door close and the noise lessened. 'I saw him last just after he got back from America.

I was up for the weekend and we got together. I admit we got pretty wasted. James said he had some hard stuff, but I declined.'

'What kind of stuff?' Sam asked.

'Cocaine, I think. He said they were all into it when he was in New York.'

'What else did he tell you about that trip?'

'Just what a blast it was. He said it had changed his life, but I'm not sure what that meant really. He said stuff like that, you know, over-dramatised things. Always did.'

'Did you hear anything about his political ideas or affiliations?'

'Well, he had a real go at Thatcher and her legacy, which surprised me as she was the big hero when we were younger. There he was, spouting on about saving the planet. Tried to force some pamphlets on me, said they needed people with influence. I told him I've no influence at all.'

'Did he mention anything about "Liberate the Earth"?'

'That's it. Sounds like a kids' game. I told him to grow up, he didn't like that. I haven't seen him since then,' he hesitated. 'And now I never will. Christ. What about the funeral?'

'You'll need to ask the family about that, Mr Fenton. I'm sure Mrs Bramall would appreciate hearing from you. She gave me your home number.'

'Yes, sure. Well, thanks for letting me know,' said Marcus and he went back to his noisy colleagues.

Sam went to the whiteboard and wrote up 'Marcus Fenton' and 'Liberate the Earth' close to Bramall's name. Rob Findale was out with Sharp chasing up information in Axelby about the night James died, and Sam scribbled a note, pinned it to the Earth Liberation Front leaflet and left it on his desk. The note asked if Findale would check the address and contact details on the leaflet, and did he know someone in the Met with links to the New York police department or even the FBI? Something had happened there during the summer that had an impact on young Bramall. It sounded like the environmental equivalent of a religious conversion.

Next stop was Bob Carruthers, still ensconced in his corner with DC Sergeant sitting alongside him. They both looked very pleased with themselves. Carruthers picked up a piece of paper and waved it. 'Report from Chorley, sir. They've analysed the glass from the damaged headlight at the Bramall hit and run. Toyota, 1998.'

'When did that arrive?'

'Just an hour ago. We're making a list of all the garages that could have done a repair. And we're looking for reports of abandoned vehicles over the past three days.'

'Anything more on Sandra Evans?' Sam asked. He wondered whether Skaife had prioritised Bob's online activities.

'We know she was arrested in 1990, but there's nothing more after that, unless she used another name, apart from the two we know about. Did I mention she's twenty-eight, older than Bramall?'

Sam nodded. 'What about CCTV from last weekend? She didn't have a car, went to work by train. We think she went from Sandersons in Workington to the flat in Whitehaven last Friday afternoon and then out again shortly afterwards. Check for CCTV around Corkickle Station for that Friday. See if you can find out where she was going when she left around mid-afternoon and then check with the destination.'

Carruthers rubbed his hands together and smiled. He loves this, Sam thought, and he's good at it even though he rarely gets off his backside. 'OK, gentlemen,' Sam said, 'here's another little job. It's a long shot, but worth trying. See if you can find where

James Bramall stayed in Carlisle most weekends. Could be a flat, or a hotel, but city centre probably, near the nightlife. We need to know where he was, when and who with. OK?'

Now both the young men were smiling, and Sam left them to it.

Sam's phone was ringing when he reached his office. It was Maureen. 'Was it your idea to give the Boy Wonder to Bob for a while?'

'Skaife's decision. I hope we don't regret it. He and Bob look very pally, side by side peering at the big computer. Where are you Maureen?'

'I'm at Ian Dawes' workplace. Sergeant Findale asked me to get more information from him about James. Dawes has been talking about James's trip to New York and it sounds interesting. I'm taking him for a coffee if you want to join us.'

Ten minutes later Sam found Maureen talking to a young man in the Pelican café. It was quiet after the lunchtime rush and they sat well away from the two other customers.

'This is DI Tognarelli, Ian,' said Maureen, 'one of the investigating officers on this case.'

Ian checked his watch. 'I haven't got long. Thanks for making sure they know it's not me in trouble, but they'll moan if I'm away for too long. Anyway, I thought you'd finished with the questions.'

'You've been very helpful with our understanding of James Bramall,' said Sam, 'but since you spoke to us last, something else has come up.'

'And I want the DI to hear what you told me about the people James was with in New York,' said Maureen.

'What's come up?' asked Ian. He was clearly anxious to get back to work.

'It was from James's post-mortem,' Sam said.

Ian winced.

'Apart from the injuries caused by the car hitting him,' said Sam, omitting the details of that collision, 'there were old injuries, bruising to the body and hands, that were from around two weeks ago, according to the medic who examined him.'

'Well,' said Ian. 'There is something else that I've remembered. I saw James in the Axelby shop, middle of last week. He was moving awkwardly, grimacing as if something was hurting. I asked him what was up and he said he'd got into a fight. Some guy in a pub just went for him. He showed me his hands to prove how he'd defended himself.'

'Did he say who this guy was?'

'No, just some drunk. I guessed he had Sandra with him and wanted to impress her. Not like James to look for trouble.'

Sam got out his notebook and made a note of the date. 'Did he say where this happened?'

'No, but he and Sandra mostly went to pubs and clubs in Carlisle. Could have been there, maybe the previous weekend.'

'Do you know where they stayed, or which places they went to?'

Ian shook his head.

'Did he report it to the police?'

'Doubt it. He would have told me if he had, and he certainly wouldn't have wanted his dad to know. I told those other coppers that James was a bit of a fantasist, so he could have made it all up, or just exaggerated. And I was so shocked about James being dead that I didn't really think of it at the time.'

Sam said, 'And what do you know about his time in New York?'

'OK, well, James said he met some people there. Very impressed by them, so he said. Said they were 'activists' whatever that means.' He stopped, looked at Maureen and then at Sam.

'Look I don't want to speak ill of the dead and all that, but I did wonder about James sometimes, about whether he was a closet homo, you know, gay.'

'My son is gay,' said Maureen. 'What makes you think that about James?'

Sam looked across at Maureen, but she was still looking at Ian Dawes.

'No offence,' said Ian.

'None taken,' said Maureen. 'Did you ever see James flirting with men?'

'God, no,' said Ian. 'Nothing like that. He just seemed to admire some blokes, for their looks and style and that. He had this mate Marcus that I met once, I wondered about him too.'

'No advances to you?' Maureen asked.

Ian shook his head. He pushed back his chair, 'I should be getting back,' he said.

'Hang on, Ian,' said Sam. 'This is important to us only because we need to know who might have been involved with James, and there might be a link to his girlfriend too.'

'Sandra, what about her?'

Maureen stepped in. 'She's dead too,' she said. 'They were both in New York over the summer and what happened to them might have some connection with that. I think that's what the DI is interested in.'

Ian sat down again. He rubbed a hand over his face. 'This is awful.'

'Yes,' said Sam, 'So can you remember anything else James told you about these people?'

Ian shook his head. 'I wish I could now, but it was just about how cool they were.'

'Any mention of them coming over here?'

'No, but people do move around, don't they? Other people I mean. I don't move anywhere.'

He got up. 'And now I have to get back. Don't come to work again, right? If you want me, call me at home.'

'What do you reckon, boss?' Maureen asked as they finished their coffee.

'One more piece of the puzzle,' said Sam, 'but I still can't see the picture. Did you know Sandra was pregnant? Twelve weeks or so apparently.'

Maureen was counting. 'So, she must have conceived around mid-September, before she started at Sandersons. Is it James's?'

'They're checking DNA. It could take a while to get the results.'

'Does the DCI know?'

'He might by now. He's not around. I assume he's gone to see the Bramalls about James's PM report.'

'Yes, you said James had old injuries, and Ian confirmed that.'

'The other thing in the report was that it looks as if the car ran over him as he was lying in the road.'

'Nasty,' said Maureen.

The walk back to Nook Street took only a few minutes, long enough for Maureen to explain to Sam that she'd known her son Jack was gay for some time before the lad shared it with them himself. 'Couldn't miss it,' she said, 'and it's no big deal. Paddy was a bit surprised, but only a bit. Jack's happy, doing well in London. So long as he's careful.'

'They've got AIDS under control now, haven't they?'

'It's treatable, yes, but he still has to be careful. His boyfriend is lovely. I think they'll be fine.'

'Don't let Dinger get to you,' Sam said. 'I don't expect he's changed much.'

'It's been good not to hear him queer-bashing all the time,' she said. 'But frankly, Bell is pretty pathetic, and I just ignore people like him. Dinosaurs. And he's a good copper some of the time. How's Judith by the way?' she added.

'Fretting,' said Sam. 'She hates being immobile.'

'I bet,' said Maureen. 'I could drop in on my way home, if she wants a chat.'

Sam nodded. 'She does love company. And next week we're going to have a visitor, a real blast from the past. My nephew Tommy.'

'Elspeth's boy? I thought they were in New Zealand.'

'He's working in London. Called out of the blue the other night and he's coming up to see us. That cheered Judith up no end.'

Still no sign of Skaife. Sam poked his head round the duty sergeant's door. 'Do you know where the DCI is, Geoff?'

'Said he was going out to Axelby,' said Geoff, 'but that was early on. Not seen him since. Findale's back, by the way. He said you were looking for him.'

Rob was at his desk.

'Anything from the house to house?' Sam asked.

Rob shook his head. 'Total waste of time.' He checked around the office and lowered his voice. 'Is the DCI just trying to keep us away from the Bramalls by giving us shit jobs to do?'

'Shit jobs?' Sam said. 'Surely, DS Findale, that's no way to describe routine police enquiries.'

'But that's what they are, right? Routine police enquiries, good for the uniformed lot, links with the community and all that. You'd never get a DS in the Met to do a job like that.'

'So, you're saying we're no nearer knowing exactly when the accident happened that killed James Bramall?'

'Any chance he was already dead before the car hit him?' Findale asked. 'Skaife gave us the PM report before he went out.'

Sam shook his head. 'Not sure Patel would have enough to go on for that conclusion. James could have just fallen down, drunk or drugged or both. Anyway, have you seen the note I left you?'

Sam spotted it among the litter on the desk and gave it to him. Rob read and raised his eyebrows. 'Yep, I'll check that address, and see if I can find some contacts in New York.' He looked at Sam and smiled. 'That's more like proper police work. I know someone who did a few months over there. Why?'

Sam pointed to the whiteboard. 'Bramall and Evans were both in New York and both came back shouting about saving the planet. I'm looking for things that connect them.'

'Apart from sex, you mean,' Rob said, making a gesture with his arms which Sam chose to ignore.

'We're not sure whether they went to New York together, but they were together when they came back, around the end of September.'

'Any names mentioned over there?' Rob asked.

'James said they were 'activists'. We're not sure what that means, but James was very impressed with them.'

Rob was scribbling in his notebook. 'What sort of activists? Covers a multitude of sins.'

'Something environmental, save the planet sort of stuff. That leaflet I've given you was among James's things. Is that enough to go on?'

'It's a start. You want me to ask this mate of mine to ask around? He's back in London now, but he'd probably be able to contact a few people. Have you asked Bob to check on the internet?'

'Not yet. He's got some more concrete stuff to work on right now. See what you can find.' He leaned down, closer to Findale's ear. 'And let me know first if anything turns up, right?'

Chapter 9

Only two people got off the northbound train at Workington and Sam knew straight away which one of them was Valerie Lewis, Sandra Evans's sister. He had only seen photos of Sandra, both alive and dead, but he could still see a family resemblance as Mrs Lewis put her bag down and looked around. He walked up to her with his hand outstretched and introduced himself.

'You could be from Swansea with a name like that,' said Valerie Lewis. 'Lots of Italians there.'

'Quite a few here too,' said Sam. 'But my dad lived in Preston. That's where I was raised. Call me Sam, by the way,' he said, 'it's easier.'

'Well, thanks for meeting me, Sam. It's a long trip and the last hour or two seemed very slow.'

Sam picked up the bag and steered her towards the back entrance of the station where he'd parked the car. 'We're all very sorry about the loss of your sister,' he said. 'It must have been a great shock.'

He opened the car door for her, put the bag in the boot and got in beside her. 'I asked your local police to come and visit you, rather than you just getting a phone call. I hope that was OK.'

'Still a shock when you open the door to the police,' she said, 'but the policewoman they sent was very good. Women are better at those kinds of things, aren't they?' She found a handkerchief and blew her nose.

'There are some official visits we'll need to make, Mrs Lewis, and I'd like the chance to sit down with you for a proper chat about Sandra.'

'Call me Valerie, Sam. Yes, I'll need to arrange about Sandra's remains, but can we have a cup of tea somewhere before that? It's been a long day so far.'

'Of course. There's a café close to the police station and we can have a chat there, then I'll take you wherever you need to go. We booked you into a B&B too.'

The owner of the Pelican café raised her eyebrows when Sam came in for the second time that day. This time it was busier. 'Can we have a table upstairs?' Sam asked. 'We need some quiet.'

'No problem,' she said. 'You sit where you please up there and I'll come up in a minute.'

'We'll need tea for two for a start,' said Sam, looking at Valerie, who nodded.

'This is nice,' Valerie Evans said, looking around at the old photos on the walls of the upstairs space where they were sitting alone. 'Just like the cafés back home.'

'Workington's an industrial town, built around the pits, much like your towns in South Wales I should think,' said Sam. 'This is much nicer for a chat than the police station.' He was thinking of the drab interior at Nook Street and the bucket in the corner catching the drips.

Once the tea had been brought, and a plate of sandwiches ordered, Sam said, 'Is there anything you want to ask me, Valerie, before we talk about Sandra? I'm not sure what you've been told already.'

She sipped her tea and put down the cup carefully on its saucer. 'They just said that she'd been found unconscious at her flat on Monday afternoon and taken to hospital, but they couldn't save her, and she died.'

'The doctor said she had a heart attack, brought on by the drugs in her system.'

Valerie's eyes filled with tears. 'I knew it would be something to do with drugs. I've worried about her for years, but there was nothing I could do. She went her own way, always did, right from being a teenager. After Dad died, Mam tried to rein her in, and I tried too, but off she went to London. After that she was on her own.'

Sam said, 'We know she had some trouble in 1990, from our own records.'

Valerie shook her head. 'The people she was living with then, they were all, you know, rebel types. Living in a squat, she said, my poor mam didn't even know what that meant. That's when it all started, the drugs, moving around all the time. We never knew where she was.'

'How long did that last?'

'About five years. Then one day she rang up and said she'd got a job and was going to college. And she got a proper address in Brighton. We could write to her, send things. Mam sent Welsh cakes and scarves and things. She seemed to think Sandra would be cold in Brighton.'

'Can you let me have that address?' Sam asked.

'Do you want the other ones too?' Valerie said, rummaging in her handbag. 'She was moving a lot, getting better places, she said, when the money started coming in.'

'What was she doing?'

'Accounts jobs. She was always good at maths at school, got that from her dad, and the people she worked for sent her to college, paid for her. Mam was thrilled.'

Sam skimmed down the addresses, all in the south-east.

'We know Sandra went to New York earlier this year,' he said. 'And then she came to live up here, working at a local firm and living in a flat in Whitehaven. Do you know why she went to New York?'

The sandwiches had arrived, and Valerie was obviously hungry. She picked one up and took a small bite out of it before she spoke. 'No idea,' she said. 'We just got a letter in February saying that she was taking a break to do some travelling. She'd always wanted to travel, so I wasn't surprised really. It showed she had the confidence and the money to follow a dream, you know. I was pleased for her.'

'Do you think she was taking drugs at this point?'

'No, I thought she must have stopped all that, how else could she have saved the money to go to America? But people don't get off things forever, do they? When the policewoman said she'd been found unconscious it was still the first thing I thought of. Thank heaven Mam passed away last year, she'd have been heartbroken with all this.'

'Have you seen Sandra since she came back from America?'

'No, the last time was at Mam's funeral, about a year ago. Just before Christmas it was. Sandra came up from London, just for the day. I wanted her to stay but she wouldn't. She looked thin, but much the same. Very smart, black suit. She wasn't rude to people, just distant, like she'd grown apart from us all.'

Sam asked the question that had been forming in his mind. 'Valerie, did Sandra ever mention joining a group, something to do with saving the planet?'

'Well,' she said, 'that's what I wanted to tell you about. It was at Mam's funeral, she might have had a glass or two afterwards, like we all did, and she started a long speech about how the earth was being destroyed by humans and we all needed to wake up. It wasn't just what she was saying but how, you know, that got people's backs up. It was a funeral, not a public meeting. You could tell folk didn't like it. Poor Mam would have been mortified. In the end I just pushed her out of the room and told her to calm down. Then she went really off on one, said I was as bad as all the others, she didn't know why she'd bothered coming back, and she just stormed out. It was really embarrassing.'

'Did she go back to London?'

'Yes, next train back. She couldn't wait to get away from us. That's why I was surprised when she telephoned me about a month ago.'

'She did? To say what?'

'It was like a different person talking. She said she'd met someone in America and had some news for us, but she couldn't say over the phone and she promised she'd come and see us.' She counted back. 'Yes, it must have been around the middle of November. I asked her to come to Llanelli for Christmas, and she said she would.'

'What did you think the news might be?' Sam asked.

Valerie smiled. 'I guessed she was going to get married to this person she'd met, whoever he was.'

Sam looked down, avoiding her eyes. 'Valerie, after Sandra died, it was found that she was pregnant. That might have been what she wanted to tell you.'

Valerie's face clouded. 'Oh God. So the baby died too.' Her eyes filled with tears. 'Why did she do it? I don't understand.'

'And you have no idea who the father might be?'

'She never mentioned a name, just that she'd met someone in America. Do you know who it is?'

'We know she had a boyfriend in the past few months, and that this man was in New York at the same time as she was. But at present we can't say if he was the father of the child.'

'Who is he? Where is he?' Valerie asked.

Sam said, 'I'm afraid I can't tell you about that, not yet.'

Valerie was crying now and took a moment before she said, 'We didn't really know her, did we? I should have spent more time with her, but she was never around, and I was busy, married, kids.'

'Don't blame yourself,' Sam said, recognising the guilt. He should have tried harder to find his own sister.

Sam spent another hour or so with Valerie Lewis, taking her to the mortuary to make arrangements for Sandra's body, and then to the B&B. It was around four o'clock when he got back to the station. Carruthers and Sergeant were bursting to tell him that they'd found Sandra on CCTV, first at Corcickle station taking a northbound train on Friday afternoon, and then they'd got access to the CCTV at Carlisle Station and seen her there too. 'There she was,' DC Sergeant said, barely containing his excitement, 'bold as brass, walking out of the station carrying a suitcase.'

Carruthers added, 'But she turned a corner and we lost her. Now we'll have to check all the other CCTV footage in Carlisle city centre to see where she went. But we're on it, boss.'

Sergeant jiggled in his chair. 'And that's not all, boss.' This time Carruthers interrupted. 'We've found a Toyota car that might be the one that did for James Bramall,' Bob said, while Sergeant nodded and smiled alongside him. 'We checked all the car rental places in Carlisle to see if any of them had rented out a Toyota that had been returned with damage or was overdue. Bingo! And guess who signed the rental papers on Saturday morning?' Sergeant was still nodding. Bob carried on, 'A woman called Sandra Dryden!' He paused for effect. 'Remember, that was the name that Evans had used when she was arrested. She had a proper driver's licence, everything in order. Rented for three days, so it's overdue for return.'

'Where's the car now?' Sam said, his mind working to process the implications.

'Not been found,' said Sergeant. 'That's our next job.'

'And we're checking round the places in Carlisle where James might have stayed. There's lots of cheap places, but I think someone like James Bramall would have wanted something posh.'

'I think you're right, William,' said Sam. 'Good thinking, so start with the expensive places first.'

Sam pulled up a chair and sat down. 'Two DCs and a computer,' he said. 'Give them a couple of hours and they'll close the case.' They beamed, first at each other, and then at him. 'Seriously,' Sam said. 'This is good work. When we get to the briefing in an hour or so you can share what you've found, so forget the repair places and start checking any reports of Toyota cars abandoned or burned out. If Sandra rented it, then it might be somewhere near her place in Whitehaven, or at one of the stations. Did she pay cash at the rental place?'

'Yes, cash,' said Sergeant.

'So,' said Sam, 'the next thing will be to check her financials. I'll get DC Sharp to help with that. You've got an hour to see what else you can find and to work out who says what at the briefing. DCI Skaife will be leading it, so this is your chance to impress him as well as me.'

As Sam stood up, he heard a familiar voice from the other side of the room. 'Nelly!' boomed the voice. 'I'm back. Have you missed me?'

Before Sam could reply, Bob Carruthers had sprung to his feet. DS Bell had returned to Nook Street and at least one person in Workington CID was pleased to see him. Sam was still deciding about any words of welcome when DCI Skaife appeared. He shook Bell's hand, said a few words to him and then turned his attention to Sam. 'A word, Inspector,' he said, 'in my office.'

Sam followed the DCI down the corridor towards Skaife's sterile office and stood as he always did, in front of the desk, his hands behind his back. Skaife did not invite him to sit down.

'I went to see the Bramalls this morning,' he said. 'That'll come up in the briefing. For now, I need to tell you that you and I are to report to Penrith HQ tomorrow morning at nine sharp.'

Sam's mind raced. 'May I ask what it's about, sir?' he asked.

'The Chief Constable said only that it was a matter of great importance. Be ready to leave here at eight. We can't afford to be late.'

Sam hesitated. 'Should I be worried, sir?'

'I don't know, Inspector. Have you something to be worried about?'

'Not as far as I know,' said Sam.

'Good,' said Skaife. He checked his watch. 'Let's get this briefing underway. I hope to God we've made some progress.'

If we have, it's no thanks to you, Sam thought, but he turned and left without a word.

Sam checked his desk to make sure he had everything he needed for the briefing. There was a note about a phone call that he'd missed during the afternoon. He didn't recognise the name Tracey Tyson, but the number was local. He picked up the phone and a woman answered.

'Miss Tyson, this is DI Sam Tognarelli, Workington CID.'

'Oh, I wanted to speak to a woman. Pritchard, I think.'

'That's one of my officers, you can talk to me.'

'Well, it's about that girl, what's her name? Sandra.'

Sam checked his watch. In the big room outside his office he could see people gathering for the briefing. He leaned over and pushed the door closed with his foot. 'Sandra Evans, yes. DC Pritchard has been checking on activity at Miss Evans' flat in Sebastopol Terrace over the weekend.'

'Yeah, and she spoke to one of my clients, Alf, he's in a wheelchair. Lives just behind that place on Sebastopol Terrace. I was away this week, see, and he only told me today about what he'd seen and that.'

'Yes,' said Sam. 'Are you telling me you saw something yourself?'

'Yeah, only I didn't think anything of it till today, and Alf said I'd better ring up, so I did.'

Sam reached for his notebook. 'What did you see, and when?'

'Well, it was Monday morning, early. It was just getting light and I was in the back room getting something out of a cupboard in there and I saw someone on those steps, the ones from the upstairs flat.'

'What time?'

'Just getting light, so around eight.'

'Man or woman?'

'Well, I'd say it was a woman, although I couldn't be sure. I couldn't see the face but the person was quite tall, whoever it was. Big coat, collar turned up, and boots. I thought someone had let them out the back, easier to get to a car if it's parked back here, instead of walking all the way round.'

'Did you notice if the curtains were closed in that big window at the back?'

'Yes, I think they were.'

Sam sat down to scribble the details. 'So, this person came out of the door and down the stairs. Was he or she carrying anything?'

A moment's silence. 'Yes, I think so, slung over one shoulder, quite a big bag it was.'

'Where did the person go? Could you see?'

'No, I can't see into the back garden, not from that window.'

'So you don't know which way the person went?'

'No, I told you, I couldn't see, and then I was busy with Alf and thought no more about it until he said that woman had been round.'

'Right, OK, Mrs Tyson. I've got your number. Someone will call you to arrange to take a proper statement from you. That's really helpful, thank you.'

'What happened up there?' the woman asked.

'We're still investigating,' said Sam. 'Thanks very much, Miss Tyson.'

A timeline, he thought to himself as he rang off. We need a detailed timeline of all these movements.

Skaife opened the briefing with a comment about Bell being back to bolster the capacity of the team, and Sam saw Findale's eyes move from Skaife to Bell and back again. Findale's wondering whether Bell will push him out, Sam thought. Bell was standing at the back of the room, expressionless, but clearly paying close attention and, to Sam's surprise, seemed to be taking notes.

One by one, different parts of the two investigations were reported on. Bob Carruthers played his cards well, working up to the final flourish as he revealed that Sandra Dryden aka Evans had rented a Toyota car which in terms of both make and year could be the car involved in the death of James Bramall. Skaife didn't seem to be surprised, so Sam guessed that Bob had made sure that the DCI knew about their success as soon as possible.

The forensic evidence from Evans's flat was disappointing. 'Forensically aware,' Fothergill had said in his report, to describe whoever had been in the flat apart from Sandra herself. Most fingerprints were Sandra and Mrs Allan. There were some others too, but probably not enough for a positive ID. Bedding had been closely examined and sent to the lab, but Fothergill wasn't optimistic about the outcome. Sam waited until he had the chance to reiterate the growing evidence of the links between the two halves of the investigation. 'We know that Evans and Bramall were in a relationship, and that both had been in New York during the summer months of this year. Both of them at some point appear to have signed up with an environmental group who want to "liberate the Earth" and there's been mention of people in New York who could be connected with that too. DS Findale is following up.'

Sam looked across at Rob Findale. 'Any joy?' he asked. Rob shook his head and Sam continued. 'The Toyota car is still missing and therefore cannot be confirmed as the vehicle involved in the Axelby hit and run. Bramall had told a friend that the previous injuries noticed by Dr Patel were caused in a pub fight. Evans' overdose could have been self-inflicted, but the question remains of how and when she could have found out about James's death, if that would have prompted her to suicide.'

Maureen interrupted. 'The picture we're getting of Sandra doesn't fit with someone who would take her own life over the end of a relationship.'

'And she was pregnant,' DC Sharp added.

Skaife interrupted, 'We could speculate about the psychology of a pregnant woman, DC Sharp, but it's still speculation and not what we need.' Sharp looked away and Sam could sense her annoyance.

'The other possible link,' said Sam, 'is the person who has been seen in various places, with Evans in Carlisle and then – by the sound of it – by three witnesses in Whitehaven. Let's assume it was a woman.'

'Three?' Maureen queried. 'Mrs Allan saw her, and then the man in the wheelchair saw a tall person draw the curtains on Saturday afternoon. Who's the other one in Whitehaven?'

Sam said, 'The neighbour in the wheelchair has a carer, Tracey Tyson. I spoke to her a few minutes ago. She says she saw someone leaving Evans' flat by the fire door exit around eight on Monday morning. The person was dressed like a man, but she thinks it was a woman.'

A phone rang and as DC Sergeant answered it there was a rattle of conversation in the room. 'Settle down, everyone,' said Skaife.

Sam went on, 'What's needed urgently is a detailed timeline covering both parts of this investigation. DC Sharp, could you do that please, as quickly as possible?'

Sharp nodded but said nothing.

'Right,' said Skaife. 'DS Bell, liaise with Carlisle about the CCTV, follow up Evans' financials and the whereabouts of the missing Toyota. DS Findale, follow up the evidence taken from Bramall's rooms and car, and James's financials, and tell your New York contacts to hurry it up.' Rob nodded. 'And,' Skaife added, 'Mr Bramall tells me that James wouldn't go anywhere without his mobile phone, so we need to find it. I know we searched the area before but go out there and search again. But tread lightly, OK? Bramall Engineering has sensitive commercial links with the US which need to be respected, understood?'

Sam realised yet again that Skaife was obviously talking to Bramall privately and responding to his influential friend's demands.

DC Sergeant suddenly put his hand up. 'Sir, sir,' he cried, like a keen pupil in a schoolroom. 'What is it?' Skaife said. 'We've found where James Bramall stayed in Carlisle last weekend. It was the Royal. He stayed there quite a lot at weekends.'

'Right, good work,' said Skaife.

'He didn't use his own name, sir, that's why it took us a while to find it.' He pointed at the whiteboard. 'The room was booked for a Mr and Mrs Fenton.'

Skaife looked confused, but Sam laughed. 'What a cheek! Are you sure it's Bramall? We'll need to double check.'

Skaife raised his hand. 'DI Tognarelli and I will be at County HQ tomorrow morning. In our absence, DS Bell is temporarily in overall charge of this investigation.' He ignored the silence that greeted this announcement. 'DS Bell, with me. The rest of you, dismiss.'

Chapter 10

'You should have seen Bell's face when Skaife put him in charge,' said Sam to Judith when he got home. 'A smirk, pure and simple, and directed right at Findale. I thought Rob was going to rush over and deck him.'

'What's Skaife up to?' Judith said. 'You and he are going to Penrith for a meeting, aren't you, not being spirited away somewhere, so why does Bell have to be put in charge for just a few hours?'

They were sitting at the kitchen table, a bottle of wine between them, waiting for the potatoes to cook. Judith had washed her hair and it gleamed in the light that hung over the table. 'That's what's worrying me,' said Sam. 'Skaife wasn't letting on, and he was out most of yesterday. Even Geoff Simpson didn't know where he was.'

'Have you had a row with him recently?'

'No,' said Sam, 'by a supreme effort of will I've managed to avoid telling him what a waste of space he is.'

'Could he be about to retire and you're in line for his job?'

'No sign of that, but there's definitely something going on. I wish I knew what it was.'

Halfway through dinner the phone rang. 'Tommy!' said Sam. 'Good to hear from you. When are you coming up?' He listened for a few moments. 'OK,' he said, 'I can move things around to meet you off the train next Wednesday, or you could get a taxi from Whitehaven. Judith's stuck at home, so she'll be here even if I'm not... Busy? Oh yes. But evenings are usually OK. How long can you stay? Well, one night's better than nothing. We'll just have to talk fast. Do you like Chinese food? That's about the best you can get round here.... OK, great. See you, bye.'

'Bye, Tommy,' Judith called before Sam put down the phone. 'Thanks for saying we'll go out to eat,' she said. 'I don't want to be hopping around trying to cook when he won't be here for long.'

'He's got a meeting in Carlisle on Wednesday that should be over by four, so we'll have the whole evening, and I'll get him back to the train on Thursday.'

'What does he do?' Judith asked.

Sam shrugged. 'Don't know, one more thing to ask him. Funny to hear that accent, he was talking broad Barrow last time we saw him.'

Judith poured them both another glass of wine. 'What time do you have to leave tomorrow?'

'Skaife wants to be on the road by eight,' he said. 'That means we'll be there long before nine, but you know what he's like.'

'So, you'll need to get up early, won't you?' She pulled herself up and reached for the crutches. 'Pick up those glasses and bring them upstairs,' she said.

Sam looked at his wife. 'I was going to wash up,' he said.

'No, you're not going to wash up, you're coming to bed with me.'

It had been a long time since they'd made love. The leg in plaster was a challenge, and caused some giggling, but Sam was happy to stroke her pale skin and feel the warmth of her. When it was over he lay beside her, his mind at rest for the first time in weeks.

He woke to the sound of rain on the window. It was not long after six in the morning, but he knew that his night was over, and the prospect of the day ahead rushed into his mind. Judith was still asleep, snoring gently, as he got out of bed, covered his nakedness with his dressing gown, picked up the empty glasses and went downstairs. Bill stirred in his basket but didn't get up. Sam would take the dog out before he left the house, but not yet. With any luck the rain would ease off.

Wondering again about the summons to Penrith, the only reason he could think of was some serious string-pulling by Edward Bramall that had reached as far as the Chief Superintendent. Sam went over in his head the possible reasons Bramall might have for complaint, which could have prompted the summons to HQ. They were still waiting for the results of the DNA tests on Sandra's unborn child, but Sam couldn't be held personally responsible for delays at the lab. The Bramall family might be embarrassed by revelations about James's drug-taking, but that too was out of Sam's hands. It was a mystery, but in a few hours he should know what was going on.

By seven-thirty Bill had been walked, cups of tea had been drunk, cereal and toast eaten, Judith was up and prepared for the day and Sam was out of the door and in the car. He was wearing his second best suit, an almost new tie, polished shoes and the coat he usually wore for funerals. Whatever the day had in store, he felt ready.

'Good luck,' said Judith and gave him a kiss that was more than the usual peck on the cheek.

Skaife insisted that Sam drove them to Penrith while he sat silently looking at various budgets and spreadsheets. Sam wondered if the DCI's job had to be so desk-based. He'd known other

DCIs during his career that did more real policing, but times were changing, and CID work was changing too. The science seemed to be taking over, and now there were computers and mobile phones to contend with. Men like Rob Findale would keep up, but Sam felt himself being left behind.

Beside him in the car Skaife shut the folder he'd been leafing through and looked across at Sam, 'How's your wife?' he asked. 'Judith, isn't it?'

'Yes, sir, Judith. She's recovering from her accident, but not back at work yet. She can't drive either, feeling a bit stuck.'

'How does she manage during the day with you at work? Does somebody come in to help?'

'Oh, no,' said Sam. 'No need for that. We'll manage, and it's only for a few more weeks. Come the new year she should be able to get around.'

'What do you make of all this 'Millennium Bug' business?' Skaife said.

'Scaremongering, I reckon,' said Sam. 'There may be a few computer glitches, but I can't see everything grinding to a halt.'

'My daughter's hoarding things as if we're heading for a siege,' said Skaife. 'Their house is stuffed with toilet rolls and bottled water, and she says I might have to go and stay.'

'That's very thoughtful of her, sir,' said Sam. It was hard to think of DCI Skaife having a family.

'Too noisy for me, Inspector. You've no grandchildren, have you?'

'No, sir. It's just me and Judith, and her brother's family in St Bees.'

'What about you, any siblings?'

'A sister, but she's been living in New Zealand for twenty years or so. My nephew's in London at the moment, actually.'

Skaife lapsed once more into silence, and when they parked the car and headed into County Police HQ he marched towards the building.

It was one of those times when Sam wished he hadn't given up smoking. What he wanted was to slow everything down, slope off to the bins at the back with the other misfits and have a quiet ciggie. As it was, he felt as if he was being pulled into something by forces he couldn't control, and seeing Skaife striding purposefully ahead of him wasn't helping at all.

Skaife pulled open the door and turned, waiting for Sam. 'Come on, Inspector, we haven't got all day. Not sure who's going to meet us.'

They signed in and got their visitor's passes. Skaife went to sit down and Sam joined him.

'Why are we here, sir?' he asked. 'What's going on?'

'All in good time, Inspector. Glad to see you're wearing a decent suit.' He lowered his voice. 'Officers from the west aren't always given due respect in this place, and first impressions matter.'

Sam had no time to make sense of the mystery before a young policewoman appeared. 'DCI Skaife?' she enquired. Skaife and Sam stood up. 'Follow me, please,' she said, and led them down gleaming corridors and upstairs to a far corner of the building.

She tapped on a door. 'Come,' someone called. She opened the door and ushered them through.

The room was an outer office, and a large man stood in the doorway into a further room beyond. 'Ah, Skaife,' said the man, extending his hand to the DCI. 'And DI Tognarelli? Chief Superintendent Williams, pleased to meet you.' Sam mumbled something appropriate and took the man's hand as confidently as he could muster before following him into the inner room. There were long windows and bright light, carpets and gleaming wood. Photographs adorned the walls, alongside various certificates and coats of arms. There were people too, who stood up as the visitors entered. Sam registered two men and a woman, but their features were unclear against the white morning light through the windows.

Williams turned and smiled. 'Prompt as ever, DCI Skaife. Thank you for coming and bringing your DI along.' He gestured towards one of the men, who was too short and round to be a serving policeman. The man had a smooth pink face and grey hair combed over a balding crown. 'Arnold Truelove, Home Office,' said the man. The other man, who was not much taller but thinner and younger, introduced himself. 'Smith,' he said, 'from the Met.'

Sam looked at the third face, the woman, and caught his breath. She was fifteen years older than the last time he'd seen her, but he knew her at once. 'We have met, Inspector,' she said, smiling. 'Morecambe, I think, 1984, one of those conferences about the new policing legislation. Marianne Gordon, Home Office.' She held out her hand and Sam took it, hoping against hope that his face didn't betray what he was feeling. Skaife shook hands with her too. Chief Superintendent Williams retreated behind his desk. Sam, Skaife, Truelove and Gordon sat in easy chairs facing him, while Smith sat apart, at the back of the room. Sam could feel his heart thumping. The shock of encountering Marianne was still affecting him.

Williams took charge. He smiled at Sam. 'You probably have no idea what this is about, DI Tognarelli. I had to ask DCI Skaife not to divulge the purpose of your visit, and I'm sure he's told you nothing at all.'

Sam shook his head, hoping he didn't look too ridiculous. He was already speculating that the Home Office presence denoted something to do with security and guessed that Mr Smith from the Met was probably Special Branch, but Marianne's presence still bothered him.

'Long story short,' said Williams, 'the Home Secretary has some concerns about possible disruption around the Millennium, and various teams are being deployed round the country to check potential risks.'

'May I ask a question, sir?' Sam asked.

'Of course, Inspector.'

'What kind of risk might that be?'

'Shall I answer that, David?' said Truelove. 'You're no doubt aware, Inspector, that the Millennium seems to be occupying people's attention as it gets closer. All sorts of speculation about what might happen at midnight on New Year's Eve, some of it frankly ludicrous.'

Sam nodded.

Truelove went on, 'There's to be a special event at the Millennium Dome in Greenwich. Hundreds of the great and the good all gathered together in one place, and a nightmare for the security services.'

'Not much fun for the guests, either,' Marianne said.

'I can't comment on that,' said Truelove. 'But that business threatens to divert all our attention from anything else that might be planned by people who want to use the Millennium to score some political points.' He looked around. Sam was no nearer understanding what he was getting at.

'You ask what kind of risks we are talking about, Inspector, and the answer is, we're not sure. It could be as inconsequential as demonstrations of the type that we've seen in recent years, mostly harmless, or it could be something much more serious.'

'Like the IRA bombings in London?' Sam asked.

'Exactly,' said Truelove. 'Mercifully those have reduced in recent years as the peace process has continued, but we're all aware what havoc can be caused by a small group of determined and well-organised people who want to disrupt our society for whatever reason. Does that answer your question? The risks we're considering around the Millennium could be anywhere on that spectrum of possibilities.'

Marianne Gordon leaned forward. 'Anyone working in this part of the country knows from long experience that London and the south-east exert far more pressure on policy than they should.' She looked at the others. Williams and Truelove didn't flicker, although both of them knew she was right. Sam nodded. Marianne went on, 'We're very late coming here only two weeks away from the event, because we've been over-focussed on London and that ghastly event at the Dome. Those of us who hail from north of Watford have worked hard to get our political masters to acknowledge that whatever threat they envisage may actually happen somewhere other than London.'

Sam marvelled at her confidence, and her capacity to string words together so effortlessly. Her message was clear to him. 'Sellafield,' he said, 'are you worried about Sellafield?'

She nodded. 'And places like it, iconic places that would make headlines right round the world if anything untoward were to happen. We're not necessarily talking about someone charging in to steal nuclear material. It's pictures that make headlines these days. HM Government certainly doesn't want the international embarrassment of something dramatic happening, quite apart from the encouragement that it might give to future terrorist action.'

'Ms Gordon makes the situation quite clear, as ever,' said Truelove. 'Better late than never, we should say. The Minister finally agreed to send small teams to various parts of the country to investigate possible security issues, to ensure that we are not caught napping, as it were.'

'And our job,' said Williams, 'is to assist this effort in any way we can.' He pressed a button on his desk. 'And now,' he said, 'we'll have some coffee, and resume our meeting in twenty minutes or so.' He pushed back his chair and stood up as the door opened and a trolley nudged through the gap and into the room.

Sam stayed where he was, trying to think through the implications of what he'd heard so far, and why he and Skaife had been summoned. 'Coffee, Sam?' said a voice. He looked up and Marianne was smiling, very close to him. He stood up and stepped away from her, fearful of what she might say. Then he stood watching while she poured a coffee and handed it to him. The others were exchanging manly small talk, although Sam noticed that Mr Smith – was that his real name? – still hung back, standing by the window talking into his mobile phone.

'How are you?' she enquired.

'Fine, thanks.' said Sam.

'Surprised to see me?'

'Yes, I thought you were with the CPS.'

'I was until early this year. New opportunity, you know.' She looked at him. 'You're still at Workington, then. You've been a DI for a while.'

Sam shrugged. 'Things move a bit more slowly up here.'

'So it seems. You could always move away, pastures new and all that.'

'Maybe, but there are other things to consider.'

'Family?' she asked.

'Yes, family.'

She nodded.

He turned away from the other people and lowered his voice. 'Why am I here, Marianne?'

She smiled. 'All in good time, Sam,' she said. 'Have a biscuit.'

Sam took a biscuit and walked over towards the window. Smith came to stand beside him. He brandished his mobile phone before putting it back in his pocket. 'This thing could take over your life,' he said. 'One of my colleagues sleeps with his under the pillow. You're never off-duty.'

'Special Branch?' Sam asked.

'Well spotted,' said Smith. 'I'm keeping my head down for a while, but you and I might be having a proper talk soon, once the niceties are out of the way.'

'And what will this proper talk be about?' Sam asked. He was getting tired of the dancing around.

'Patience, Inspector,' said Smith. 'Let the old boys do their thing. It should get clearer before lunch.'

'I hope so,' said Sam. He noticed that Skaife was watching them and he gave the DCI a smile which was not reciprocated. Does he know what's going on? Sam wondered.

Someone came in to take the trolley away and Williams resumed his seat, beckoning to the others to do the same. 'Gentlemen,' he began, 'and Ms Gordon, I'm sure DI Tognarelli is asking how all this might concern him, assuming that DCI Skaife has not enlightened him already?' He glanced at Skaife, who shook his head.

'Right,' said the Chief Superintendent. 'Our colleagues from the Home Office approached me earlier this week to ask me to assign a local officer to them for the duration of this – what can we call it? – this investigation into potential threats. This officer would obviously have to be very efficient, with expert local knowledge and also absolutely trustworthy. There's far too much rumour and speculation about the Millennium to risk adding to it.'

Williams opened a file that lay on his desk. Sam realised that the file might refer to him and began to feel uneasy.

'DI Tognarelli,' said Williams, not looking at Sam, 'has been with the Cumbria force since 1971.' He hesitated. 'Well, actually, he was stationed in Barrow as a DC before that, but resigned, before rejoining in 1971 based first in Whitehaven and then in Workington.'

Truelove said, 'May I ask what prompted DI Tognarelli to resign, and for how many years?'

Sam turned to him. 'Two years, sir. After a difficult case in 1969 I was told that there was no chance of making a career in CID and felt I had no option but to leave.'

Williams turned pages in the file. 'Ah, yes,' he said, 'There were some particular difficulties in the Barrow team at the time. The senior officers involved all moved on quite quickly.' Sam remembered the business all too well, and he knew why Williams wasn't giving much away.

'What did you do for those two years, Inspector?' Marianne Gordon asked.

'I worked overseas in construction for a while, and then as a postman in Whitehaven.'

'Really?' she said, smiling. 'How interesting.'

Patronising, Sam thought, but he replied, 'Yes, it was. Very instructive. I learned a lot.'

Williams continued, still without looking up. 'You joined the Workington CID team in 1971 and have been with them ever since, promoted to DI in 1984, is that right?'

'Yes, sir,' said Sam. He hesitated. 'Am I being vetted?'

It was Arnold Truelove who answered the question. 'Oh no, Inspector,' he said, with a thin smile, 'you've already been vetted, or you wouldn't be here.'

'Let's just say,' Williams said, 'that our colleagues here need to have a sense of your career with us, Inspector. Now, looking back a few years, there has been some trouble with protestors from Greenpeace at various times. All to do with Sellafield?'

'Yes, various issues,' said Sam. 'We've had a Greenpeace boat out at sea, and they tried to blockade the plant in 1995 which resulted in a number of arrests. I was involved in all that, obviously.'

'Any views on Greenpeace or other political issue that we should know about?'

Sam shook his head.

'And your wife? Does she have any political affiliations?'

'You'd have to ask her about that,' said Sam. He noticed Marianne smile and nod her head.

Truelove coughed and interrupted. 'Can we move on, Chief Superintendent? I believe we need to ask Inspector Tognarelli about the case he's currently working on.'

'Ah, yes,' said Williams. 'You're currently investigating two fatalities, one involving James Bramall and the other a woman thought to be his girlfriend,' he checked his notes, 'Sandra Evans, also known as Sandra Dryden.'

'That's correct, sir,' said Sam. 'Mr Bramall was run over on the road just outside his home last Sunday night, and it looks as if it was deliberate. Miss Evans was found unconscious by her landlady on Monday afternoon, and died shortly afterwards, but we don't yet know whether her death was an accidental overdose, suicide or possibly murder.' He hesitated – how much to tell? 'More lab results are due today,' he added, deciding that if they wanted to know more, they would have to ask.

'Inspector,' Marianne asked, 'what do you know about Sandra Evans?'

'So far we've spoken to her landlady, employer, friends and her sister. She seems to have been out of touch with family for ten years or so, in Brighton and London we understand. We have an arrest on record at the poll tax riots in 1990. Nothing much more until she went to the USA earlier this year and returned early in September, took the flat in Whitehaven and started work at Sandersons in Workington. She sounds like a bright woman with strong views about environmental issues.'

'Anything odd about her relationship with Bramall?'

Sam thought for a moment. 'Well, she was older than him, and more intellectually serious, as far as we can tell. But they both enjoyed the night life, and possibly drug use. And we know they were both in New York during the summer.'

'Do you know what they were doing there?'

'No, sir. I have an officer making enquiries about the New York link.' He paused, making a connection in his mind. 'One of Bramall's friends told us that Bramall had met some people in New York who he seemed to be impressed with, and that since his return he'd been handing out leaflets about "Liberating the Earth".'

'You think the people in New York might be the origin of Bramall's interest in this cause?'

'It's circumstantial, but yes.'

Truelove and Gordon looked at each other. 'Any names mentioned?'

'No,' Sam hesitated. 'But we also know that Miss Evans has been visited by a woman since her return who has a non-English accent and might be from the USA, although that's a guess. She called at the flat in Whitehaven and was also possibly seen by another witness in Carlisle with Miss Evans.'

Truelove said, 'Can you give us a minute, Chief Superintendent? I need to check something with my colleagues.'

'Certainly,' said Williams, and Sam watched as Truelove, Gordon and Smith walked a few paces away and talked in low whispers.

'If I may,' said Truelove as the three of them sat down again, 'I think we need to clarify some things with Inspector Tognarelli before we continue.'

'Carry on,' said Williams, and Truelove turned to Sam. 'Inspector, we've come here today to ask for your help with a matter relating to the Government's anxieties about the Millennium. To be more specific, it's possible that the momentous date might be hi-jacked by a group looking for publicity. One of the groups under scrutiny is called the 'Earth Liberation Front'. They've been around since 1992 and were based in Brighton for a while. They have an environmental agenda much like Greenpeace but advocate much more radical direct action. They're organised in cells, like the Provisional IRA, and hard to monitor because they have no formal structure. We know that some of their key people are based in New York.' He smiled. 'Quite a rum bunch apparently. They call themselves 'Elves', after the initials of the title.'

Marianne leaned forward. 'Some of what we know about them is pretty bizarre. Apparently, a few of them use a special language among themselves, based on Tolkein's 'Lord of the Rings', although one of our informants said it's actually Welsh.'

'You have informants in this group?'

'Naturally,' said Marianne. 'Well under cover, but they can be useful. That's one of the sources for this worry about the Millennium, but it's hard to separate real information from the eccentric ideas these people cling to. They could be sending us on a wild goose chase and laughing about wasting our time.'

'Well, well,' said Truelove. 'What more do we know about these 'Elves', Smith?'

Smith spoke up from the back. He had a notebook open and read from it, 'Earth Liberation Front, linked with an American outfit called Crimethinc, leaderless like the Animal Liberation Front. They stand for economic sabotage and guerrilla warfare to stop the exploitation and destruction of the environment.' He paused, before addressing a question to Sam. 'Inspector, does this person who's been seen with Evans know that you're interested in them?'

'I doubt it,' said Sam.

'What about your colleague who's making enquiries about the New York connection? Is the FBI involved?'

Sam shook his head. 'No word from there yet. I don't know about the FBI.'

Smith pressed on. 'Could you stop that enquiry?'

Stop it? Why? Sam thought, but he said, 'Yes, I expect so. It would take a phone call.'

Chief Superintendent Williams leaned forward. 'If you're suggesting an interruption to an on-going investigation, we need to know why. What are your worries about the American connection?'

The question was addressed to Smith but it was Truelove who answered. 'If those enquiries involve information from the US, that would inevitably involve the FBI,' he began.

Marianne interrupted, 'And possibly the CIA too.'

'Indeed,' Truelove went on. He hesitated. 'For reasons I won't trouble you with, we want to keep our American cousins out of this, at least for the present, time being of the essence, you understand.'

Williams nodded sagely, and Sam wondered if he really understood what Truelove was hinting at. The only thing that made sense was that involving other agencies would inevitably slow things down and add yet another layer of complication.

Truelove smiled. 'So we need to keep this business "in house" for the time being,' he said, 'and close down any enquiries in New York before the American agencies get too curious.' Smith nodded. 'If we may take a short break, Chief Superintendent,' Truelove said to Williams, 'while the Inspector makes that call?'

'Certainly, if you think it's so important?'

'We do,' Truelove said.

Williams pressed a button on his desk and a middle-aged woman came in. 'Mrs Keenan, can you place an outside call for Inspector Tognarelli, from your office?'

He gestured to Sam, who followed the woman out of the room. He was being strong-armed, but he knew he had no choice.

Fortunately, Rob Findale was at his desk when Sam called him. 'But I only set this in motion yesterday,' he said when Sam told him to drop the New York enquiry.

'Well, unset it,' said Sam. 'Don't ask me why, orders from on high, OK?'

'OK, boss,' said Findale. 'What's going on over there?'

'Can't talk now,' said Sam. 'Bye.' He handed the phone back to Mrs Keenan and went back into Williams's room. He had no idea what was going on, or what would happen next.

Chapter 11

When Sam walked back into the room another low-voiced huddle was in progress, with Williams still seated behind his big desk watching. They all resumed their seats.

'I've asked the officer to halt the enquiry in New York,' Sam said. 'I didn't give a reason, because I don't have one.'

'No need to explain, surely, Inspector?' said Williams.

'No, sir, but as I said, it would be useful for me to know what the purpose is.'

Truelove coughed again. 'Perhaps we need to be more explicit about why we've asked you and DCI Skaife to meet with us.' He paused. 'To be frank, we have little to go on apart from some shreds of intelligence regarding a possible security threat timed around the Millennium. Other teams are working on the same track in other parts of the country. We need some rapid checking to be done before New Year's Eve, but there's a little more to it than that. The group calling itself the 'Earth Liberation Front' is of particular interest to the security services and has been for some time. It has no formal leadership but one of the key organisers, who goes under a variety of names, is a tall woman in her thirties who may be American.'

In Sam's mind, light began to dawn.

Truelove went on. 'The fact that this person may be involved in your current case presents some problems for us. If you follow your enquiries too rapidly, it might push her into slipping away, as she's apparently done on previous occasions. Having her here in the UK, if this is indeed the woman we want, would make life considerably easier and could allow us to discover more about the ELF than we have managed to date.' He paused, looking at Sam. 'Am I making myself clear, Inspector?'

Sam said, 'You're asking us to leave this person at large, to assist you in building a larger case against this group?'

'That's about the size of it,' said Truelove.

Williams intervened. 'You don't have anything specific against this mystery woman, do you, Inspector?'

'No, sir, not yet, but I'm very curious about a possible link between the two fatalities.'

'Explain, please,' said Marianne.

Sam cleared his throat, thinking about putting the case as succinctly as he could. 'Clearly, both Bramall and Evans were interested in environmental issues, and the two were closely connected. Evans was pregnant and it's possible that Bramall was the father. We're waiting for DNA results. We're sure Bramall's death was not accidental. Evans' death very soon afterwards could have been an accidental overdose, or even suicide, although that appears to be unlikely. There is a great deal yet to learn, and the investigation is in its early stages.'

Truelove asked, 'Would it undermine your current case to pull back on your search?'

Sam thought about this. 'It goes against the grain, sir, to hold back if we suspect someone to be involved in a capital crime.'

Williams and Skaife looked at each other, before Williams spoke. 'My officers will need to be very clear about this,' he said. 'You're not asking them to sabotage the enquiry in any way?'

'Not at all,' said Truelove. 'But if your officers do find the American woman we're all interested in, we would need them to check with you, Chief Superintendent, and through you with us, before moving in on her. That's just until the New Year, of course. It's her possible plan to create mayhem for the Millennium that we're worried about. If she's working with others, they may not reveal themselves until much nearer the time. Hence the need to let her remain at large, but under surveillance.'

'May I, sir?' said Smith from his seat behind them.

'Carry on, Mr Smith,' said Williams. 'We all need to be very clear about the implications.'

'Finding this woman and keeping her under surveillance will not be easy,' he said. 'We suspect that she may be able to disguise herself very successfully, including passing as a man. Your officers will be doing well just to keep track of her.'

'How would the investigation proceed if DI Tognarelli were no longer in charge of the case?' Marianne asked.

'Another officer would be assigned to the case,' Skaife said, as if it had all been pre-arranged.

Sam felt suddenly angry, as if they were all ganging up on him. 'But why should I be removed from this case?' he asked, his voice louder than he'd intended.

Williams began to respond, but Truelove held up his hand to intervene. 'Inspector,' he said benignly, 'you would drop your involvement in this case because you would be working for us. To be precise, between now and the New Year you would be working intensively with Mr Smith to check any weak links in national security in this area. He will bring the security expertise to this task and you provide the local knowledge and experience.'

'And who would manage our investigation in my absence?' Sam asked.

DCI Skaife said, 'I would take command, Inspector, assisted by DS Bell.'

Sam took this in. So that was why Dinger had been called back from Carlisle. The thought of Bell and Skaife leading Sam's team made Sam rub his chin to disguise his expression. 'With all due respect to you, sir,' Sam said to Skaife, 'I'm not sure DS Bell is a wise choice. He's not been involved in the investigation so far and,' he hesitated, 'two of the team are new and DS Bell sometimes has problems relating to people he doesn't know.'

Marianne smiled. 'So, if we want to slow your investigation down, we've got the right man for the job, haven't we?'

Sam saw the expression on Skaife's face as he opened his mouth to respond but Truelove cut across him. 'That sounds worse than it is, I'm sure, Chief Inspector. As we've already heard, the case is still under investigation, in mid-stream we might say. What we want you to do at this point is keep this case under close watch, but not move in prematurely. As we explained earlier, we believe the Millennium threat, if it's real, will be concerned with a dramatic gesture. We don't anticipate a serious threat to innocent lives. That's not been part of this group's goals in the past.'

'Are you saying that no-one might be harmed by this 'dramatic gesture' if it happens?' Williams asked.

'Of course, we could never guarantee...' Truelove left the sentence unfinished, before turning again to Sam. 'Do you have any further questions, Inspector?'

Sam tried to think about practicalities as his world shifted around him. 'If you want me to step away from the case to work with Mr Smith, for how long?' he asked.

'Most likely, from now until the new year, a few weeks, no more.'

'And what would we tell my team?'

Marianne said, 'Well that could be tricky. If we tell the truth, that could spark speculation that could frighten our target off. So, we need a coherent reason why you might be away from your post for a few weeks.' Sam looked at Skaife. What had he agreed to?

'A disciplinary?' Sam asked.

'No, no, nothing that might damage your prospects,' said Skaife. 'It could be a personal reason.' He hesitated, 'Your wife has recently had an accident, I understand?'

'Yes, sir, she fell and broke her leg.'

'Is it plausible that you need to take some time off to care for her?'

'Well,' said Sam, wondering how Judith would react to being used as a reason to keep him off work. 'I wouldn't want to agree to that without checking with her.'

'You couldn't tell her much of what you've heard this morning,' said Marianne. 'You will be required to sign the Official Secrets Act before you leave today, and none of the details could be divulged by you elsewhere without breaking the law.'

'Severe penalties involved,' added Williams, looking gravely at Sam, who was beginning to get a headache.

'Are you feeling trapped, Inspector?' asked Marianne.

Sam nodded.

'Would you like a little time to consider?'

'Yes, I would,' he said.

Williams stood up. 'I've asked for some lunch to be brought in. Would this be a good time to break for that?'

'Good idea,' said Truelove, standing up and stretching his short back. 'Breakfast seems like a distant memory.'

Sam didn't want lunch. He just wanted to think. He went to the outer office and asked Mrs Keenan to direct him to the gents'.

Luckily there was no one in the gents' toilet as Sam needed privacy and time to think. He went into one of the cubicles and locked the door. Too much was happening too quickly. He felt manipulated and under pressure, and still hadn't recovered from seeing Marianne after spending so many years trying to forget about her. The whole business of fanatical elves and dramatic gestures sounded fanciful, like something out of a Hollywood film. And he was in the middle of it, unless he could find a way to wriggle out.

But something else was nagging at his mind too, something that made the adrenalin pump a little faster. Suddenly, unexpectedly, the potential for change existed, and without some change the future looked tedious. DS Bell was back, whether or not he was put in charge of the case. That meant a return to the point-scoring, the challenges, the frustration of dealing with him day after day. And another thing. If Skaife was now "in command" as he put it, that would make him Bell's closest supervisor, which might push the DCI over the edge into retirement and open up Sam's chance to take his post. You're being given a choice, Sam thought to himself in the quiet of the cubicle, a chance to change the future. Take the risk.

People were standing juggling small plates and drinks when Sam returned to the room. He'd splashed his face with cold water, taken some deep breaths and combed his hair, and could feel his confidence returning. He helped himself to a sandwich and walked over towards the long windows, looking out at the bare trees that flanked the building. A figure was at his side. It was Marianne. 'How are you feeling?' she said quietly without looking at him.

'Better than I was,' said Sam. 'I needed time to think.'

'And what have you thought?' she asked.

'That this is a chance I don't want to miss,' he said.

'Excellent,' she said, and drifted away.

Arnold Truelove now emerged next to him. 'All this must seem a bit sudden, Inspector,' he said. 'Your superior officers were informed, of course, but it was thought better to brief you properly this morning, not before. I hope you understand.'

'Yes, sir,' said Sam. 'I can see why you wanted to keep these plans under wraps.' He turned to face him. 'I have to say though that it all seems a bit far-fetched.'

Truelove smiled. 'We spend our days dealing with people who want to upset the order of things, Inspector. We need to try and think like they do. Does that make sense?'

Sam shook his head. 'Not really.'

'But you're a rational being, Inspector. Many people are not.'

Skaife was approaching Sam, obviously keen to say something, when Chief Superintendent Williams tapped a spoon on his coffee cup to draw their attention and Skaife turned away. 'With an eye on the time,' Williams said, 'and the train to London that will not wait, shall we resume?'

Plates and glasses were returned to the trolley and someone came in to roll it away. They all sat down in the same places they had occupied before.

'Arnold,' said Williams, 'would you like to suggest our next steps?'

'Well,' said Truelove, 'much depends on DI Tognarelli's response to the question. Is he willing to step back from his normal duties for a short period to assist Mr Smith in the task to protect security in this area over the Millennium period?'

All eyes turned to Sam. 'Yes,' he said. 'If a plausible reason can be found why I should leave the investigation that does not affect my career here in Cumbria, I would be willing to do so.'

'Admirably clear,' said Truelove, smiling. He patted Sam's shoulder. 'I think our best plan is to offer the Inspector a few weeks' personal leave while his wife is temporarily incapacitated by her injury. DCI Skaife and DS Bell would take over the investigation of the deaths of Bramall and Evans but try to avoid apprehending the person who may be connected with the ELF, at least for the time being. When we feel it's the right time, we shall ask some questions of our American counterparts, but leave that to us.' He looked at Marianne, who nodded.

To Sam, Truelove said, 'Conall Smith from Special Branch will be your co-worker, Inspector, and report directly to us. It's quite possible that nothing will come of the rumours about this particular 'Millennium Bug', at least in this area, but we cannot afford that uncertainty.' He pushed back his chair and checked his watch. 'Right,' he said, 'Ms Gordon and I will be in good time for our train, Chief Superintendent. Mr Smith will be staying in the area. May we leave the details about the Inspector's proposed leave of absence to you?'

Williams stood up. 'You may indeed, Arnold.' He pressed the button on his desk. 'Mrs Keenan, can you ask the driver to be at the main entrance in ten minutes, please?'

For a few minutes there was movement, hand shaking, platitudes and all the various signs of a meeting coming to an end. Marianne took Sam's elbow and turned him away from the others as she said, 'Good to see you, Sam.'

He wanted to tell her that he remembered everything, and that he longed to see her again, but he said nothing. The moment passed, Marianne and Arnold Truelove departed, and Smith walked them down to the main entrance, leaving Williams, Skaife and Sam looking at each other.

'Well,' said Williams. 'That was interesting. Ms Gordon is doing well for herself. She's with MI5 now, of course, but tells people she's at the Home Office. Nobody likes a spook, do they?' He turned to Sam. 'You've met her before, have you?'

'Long time ago,' Sam said. 'When the PACE legislation was going through. She's very articulate.'

Williams went on, 'I suppose we'll have to do something about women in senior CID posts before the Home Office make any more barbed remarks about our, what do they call it, 'gender balance'. The old boys won't like it, but they'll just have to lump it.' He turned to Skaife, 'And we both know who else won't like it, don't we, Arthur?' Skaife didn't respond.

'Right,' said Williams, 'I'll do the paperwork awarding DI Tognarelli personal leave for three weeks. If they're right about the timescale, that should be plenty. If it's not, your wife may need to take a turn for the worse, Inspector.' He fingered some papers on the desk in front of him. 'You'll need to sign the OSA, as Ms Gordon explained, so what you can tell your wife or anyone else is strictly limited. And that lasts all your life, remember. When Smith comes back, you and he can make any necessary arrangements before you go back to Workington. Just clear your desk of anything essential, Inspector, and you'll be based at home for a while. OK?' He checked his watch and turned to Skaife. 'Smith said he would need an hour or so with the DI, Arthur, no more, so you find yourself something to do and I'll find a room for the two of them for whatever they need to do.'

Sam was sitting in a much smaller room wondering about what he'd let himself in for when the door opened and Conall Smith came in. He sat down heavily in one of the plastic chairs and loosened his tie. 'Thank God that's over,' he said. 'We could have got through the whole business in less than an hour, but your boss wanted to do the full hospitality thing, and Truelove beats around the bush sometimes. Marianne Gordon would have sorted everything out in half the time.'

Sam agreed, but just smiled.

'Right,' said Conall. 'I didn't bring the whole file as we couldn't be sure that you'd be willing to step up. My suggestion is that you do what you need to do at your end, think through all the specifics, and you and I meet tomorrow to do some detailed planning. I don't want to be seen with you on your patch, so we'll find somewhere else, more discreet. Anything you want to know right now?'

Yet again, Sam wanted to slow things down. He was about to start a working relationship with this man and had no idea who he was or what made him tick.

'Who are you?' he asked.

Smith leaned back in his chair and laughed. 'Fair enough,' he said. 'Where do you want me to start?'

'At the beginning,' Sam said. 'I assume you already know a fair amount about me.'

'True. OK, here goes. Conall Smith, named after one of the old kings of Ireland, born Ballycastle 1968.'

'Interesting year,' said Sam.

'So it was. I wasn't much good at school and scared stiff most of the time growing up. Parents panicked every time us kids were out. Protestant Dad, Catholic Mam. That made life a bit complicated. I joined the RUC in 1987. Mam was convinced the job would kill me and I escaped to London as soon as I could. Home was stifling, you know? So, I joined the Met. What I really wanted was MI5 but I didn't fit the profile they wanted, Oxbridge graduate, all that English snobby stuff. So Special Branch was the next best thing, I joined in 1994, five years ago. I'm useful to them because of the Irish connections. That brought me up to this area in 1995 when we thought the Provos were linked to the Sellafield protests in '95.'

Sam was surprised, 'You were here then?'

'Well under the radar, of course,' Smith said. 'Remember that day in April when all those people were arrested?'

Sam laughed. 'I do indeed,' he said. 'Whitehaven and Workington police stations were both swamped. It was chaos for a while.'

'Well,' said Smith, 'there was I, sitting at the back in some of those interviews, just like today, saying nothing but taking everything in.'

'Have we met before, then?' Sam asked. Nothing about the man seemed familiar.

Smith shook his head. 'I don't think our paths crossed. As you said, there was a lot going on. Press all over the place. I kept a low profile.'

Sam smiled and shook his head. 'Well, well. Small world.'

'To be sure,' said Smith, his Ulster intonation very clear.

'You don't think there's an Irish connection with this bloke in our case, do you?'

Smith shrugged. 'The FBI call these ELF people 'eco terrorists'. Terrorism makes for strange bedfellows.'

'Talking of bedfellows,' said Sam, 'we already know that Sandra Evans was about twelve weeks pregnant when she died.'

Smith winced. 'That's unfortunate,' he said. 'Do you know who the father was?'

'We're waiting for DNA results,' said Sam. 'The parentage might be important, but I'm not sure how.'

'Me neither,' said Smith, 'but there's a bigger issue here. We need a way to keep tabs on your investigation when you're not part of it. Can we rely on Skaife for information? That Bell bloke you mentioned sounds dodgy.'

Sam laughed. 'Bell "dodgy"? That's about right. DCI Skaife? Well, he's not dodgy but he's not very bright either, between you and me. And he's too close to the father of the Bramall boy who died and may well miss things.' He shook his head. 'Marianne Gordon was right about those two not helping the investigation along. Less Starsky and Hutch, more Laurel and Hardy.'

Smith laughed again. 'Good one,' he said. 'Is there anyone on your team that you could trust to keep us up to date, discreetly?'

Sam looked at the phone that hung on the wall of the room. 'Give me the number of that phone in your pocket,' he said. Smith wrote down the number on his notebook. Sam picked up the wall phone. A minute later he had the outside line he needed and dialled a familiar number. 'Geoff, Sam here, can you find Maureen for me, or get her on the radio? Tell her to get somewhere quiet and call me back on this number.' He spelled out the long number. 'Tell her it's important, OK, and keep this to yourself. I'll be in later, about four.'

They waited, watching Smith's phone that lay on the table between them. When it rang, Smith picked it up. Sam heard a voice saying, 'Sam? Are you there?' He took the phone. 'Maureen, it's Sam. There's something I want you to do for me, 'off the record'. I can't explain right now, but can you call me tonight at home? Thanks. Bye.'

He handed the phone back to Smith.

'Well, well,' said Smith. 'The plot thickens, as they say. Who's this Maureen?'

'DC Pritchard. One of the best. She'd knock spots off DS Bell but won't get the chance. She's been around too long, doesn't suffer fools, and she's female. They've been blocking her for years.'

'Can you trust her to keep you in the picture without really knowing why?'

'I'll tell her I won't be away for long, and that I'd rather be updated by her than by Bell or Skaife. She'll understand that.'

'What will you tell your wife?' Smith asked.

'What can I tell her?'

'That you're working on a special assignment at the request of the Chief Superintendent. That's about it. It won't be for long. When did Judith's accident happen?'

'Judith? You know her name?'

Smith smiled and tapped the side of his nose. 'Special Branch, we know everything,' he said.

'She fell down the stairs about two weeks ago.'

'Is she still immobilised?'

'She's on crutches,' Sam said, 'but she should have a weight-bearing cast sometime soon. Until then she has trouble getting around in quite a small house with stairs.' He thought about the next few weeks. 'It'll be odd seeing more of her during the day.'

For a while on the way back to Workington Arthur Skaife said nothing at all, staring straight out at the road ahead. Sam could feel that something was brewing. When it came Sam was surprised by Skaife's vehemence.

'Never do that again, Inspector, do you understand?'

Sam didn't respond. Skaife went on. 'In front of the Chief and those Home Office wallahs, you start criticising a fellow officer, and me too by implication.' He was looking at Sam, who kept his eyes on the road. 'You're an arrogant bugger, Tognarelli,' said Skaife. 'How dare you?'

'I didn't,' Sam began, but Skaife cut him off. 'Typical,' he said. 'You've never really been one of us, have you? I've read the file about that business in Barrow. You were an arrogant bugger then and you still are. Think you're better than all of us. DS Bell is a good officer. He understands how things work around here, better than you ever will.'

Sam was almost tempted to pull over and talk this out properly but thought better of it. There wasn't much he could do anyway. Skaife had obviously been harbouring this grudge for years.

He kept quiet, and for a while Skaife said no more. As they drove the last stretch into Workington Skaife spoke again. 'You're off the case as of now, Inspector. In fact, you're no longer part of Workington CID until this nonsense is over. I'll be promoting DS Bell to Acting DI in your absence. At least I'm sure of his loyalty,' he said.

'What will you tell the team?' Sam asked.

'What they need to know,' said Skaife. 'Those are my orders and that's what I'll do. It's my business, so keep your nose out, understood?'

When they reached the Nook Street carpark Sam waited, not bothering to find a parking spot. Skaife got out without another word, slammed the door and marched into the police station. Sam wanted to say, 'Thank you for clearing the air,' or something equally loaded, but he kept his mouth shut.

Chapter 12

'He called you an arrogant bugger?' said Judith when Sam got home. She laughed. 'He must have been chewing on that for years.'

'That's what I thought,' Sam said. He could see the funny side of it now, and at least he knew where he stood. He'd always wondered why Skaife was so wary of him. 'The cardinal sin was criticising Bell in front of strangers,' Sam said. 'All that Skaife and the old boys care about is how people respect rank, and Bell can lick arses with the best of them.'

'Maybe you need to learn that lesson,' said Judith, 'More touching of the forelock required, Inspector,' she said, making the gesture.

'Fat chance,' said Sam. 'Oh, and the main outcome of all this is that I'm on leave for a few weeks.'

'On leave?' said Judith. 'Why? Are you suspended?'

'No, I'm not in trouble.' Sam had been thinking about how much he was able to tell her. 'I've been asked to work on a special project, but it's secret. As far as anyone else is concerned I've been offered three weeks' personal leave to look after you while you're incapacitated.'

'What?' Judith said. 'Wait a minute. What's this special project?'

'I'm not allowed to tell you, Official Secrets Act.'

Her journalist's eyes lit up. 'OSA stuff. Wow. And you have to pretend to be looking after me. Is that what I have to say if anyone asks why you're not at work?'

'Yes. So, you can recover as slowly as you want. I'll have to push you around in a wheelchair if we go out.'

She frowned. 'A wheelchair. We'd have to get one from somewhere.' She looked at him. 'This is crazy. What's really going on?'

'Honestly Judith, I can't tell you. The man I'm working with is from Special Branch, he's called Smith.'

She laughed. 'Smith! Better and better. I need a drink. Want one?'

He didn't really want anything but a cup of tea, but he didn't want to mention her drinking yet again, not now. He watched as she hobbled over to the sideboard and poured herself a glass of red. The bottle was almost empty, but it had been full the night before.

'I have a meeting with Smith tomorrow morning,' he said, 'but I'm not sure what other things we'll need to do. I should find out more details. I think there might be work to do from home, but we'll be doing various visits as well.'

'And you can't tell me anything about it?'

'Apparently not.'

'How long is this for?' she asked, holding the glass close to her mouth.

'About three weeks, until the New Year.'

'Tommy's coming next week. What will you tell him?'

'That I'm on leave to look after you. It's perfectly feasible. God knows, they owe me leave, and it's not easy for you with that leg. You can't get up and down the stairs safely, can't go out. Why shouldn't I take time off to help out?'

'OK,' she said. 'Who's looking after your work?'

'Skaife and Bell.'

She threw up her hands. 'God help Workington CID! Skaife hasn't done any proper police work in ages.'

'I know that, and you know that, but he couldn't admit that to the Chief Superintendent, could he?'

'It might tip him over the edge into retirement.'

'That thought struck me too, which was one of the reasons for saying yes to this other assignment.'

Judith took a sip of the wine, her mind working on the new information. 'How will you find out what's going on?'

'That could be tricky. Skaife is the official link of course, but I'm the last person he'll want to confide in. The only person I can really trust is Maureen, and I can't ring her at work. I asked her to ring me here tonight.'

'Let's hope she leaves it for a while,' Judith said. 'It's Friday night, can you go and get us fish and chips?'

An hour later, the phone rang. Sam guessed it would be Maureen and picked it up.

'Sorry about earlier on,' he said. 'I wanted to make sure that we could talk tonight.'

'Whose phone was that?' she asked, 'I didn't recognise the number.'

'That's just it, Maureen.' He paused. 'I can't say. Look, what I'm going to tell you is strictly between us? I know I can trust you Maureen, and it's really important, OK?'

'OK,' she said. 'My lips are sealed.'

'They're giving me a special assignment, but it can't be made public, so officially I'm on leave for a few weeks, looking after Judith while she can't get around.'

'You're not in trouble, are you?'

'No, nothing like that. It's not for long, but it could be interesting, and I want to do it. The downside is that I have to leave the current cases with Skaife and Bell.'

'Bell? God help us. Why not Findale?'

'Not enough local experience apparently. Anyway, I want to keep an eye on what's happening, not what Skaife wants to tell me, so I'll need you to let me know. Can you do that?'

'With those two in charge, there may not be anything happening at all,' Maureen said.

'What about today, while I was out?' he asked.

'We got the DNA results that ruled out Bramall as the father of Evans's baby.'

'Well, that'll be one less thing for the Bramalls to think about I suppose, but doesn't help us much. No match with DNA on our databases, I suppose?'

'No, not so far.'

'What about forensics on Sandra's flat?'

'Oh, yes. There were prints in various places that don't match either Sandra or Mrs Allan. Bob couldn't find them on the police computer. Nothing about the New York connection. We keep drawing blanks. The briefing tomorrow morning should be interesting. There are bound to be questions about what's going on with you.'

'Do me a favour, Maureen. Tell anyone who asks you that Judith has been really struggling and I decided to ask for a week or two off, now that Bell is back.'

'OK, boss. And you'll call me at home if you want to know about the case?'

'If that's OK?'

'Fine by me. First thing to find out will be what Bell makes of our various newcomers, and vice versa?'

'There's definitely a briefing tomorrow morning?' Sam asked. 'Skaife didn't mention anything about it.'

'Findale said there is. Will you be there?'

'No, I have to be somewhere else. I think my leave starts immediately. It all seems a bit hasty, I know.'

'And you can't tell anyone what it's about?'

'No, sorry. There'll be all sorts of speculation, no doubt.'

'Naturally,' she said. 'Let's see how we get on without you. It'll be different, that's for sure.'

'Not for long,' he said. 'Good luck, and thanks Maureen. I knew I could trust you.'

'Always, sir,' she said.

Judith had been listening in. 'Maureen's a good woman,' she said to Sam as he rang off. 'You lot don't deserve her.'

'That's harsh, love,' Sam responded. 'We're no worse than any other bunch of coppers.'

Judith shook her head. 'Just way behind the times. Really Sam, I think you are.'

Sam was still thinking about that as he drove east along the A66 towards Bassenthwaite the following morning. He and Smith had agreed the day before that they would meet in a layby by the lake on the A66, close to Smith's digs and an easy drive for Sam. The miserable winter weather had given way to high pressure and northerly wind, and overnight snow sparkled on the fell tops in the clear air. Were they really as behind the times as Judith claimed? He wanted to distance himself from the narrow-mindedness he heard around him, but it affected him too. He might be more open to change in some respects, but all the new technology was baffling and part of him just couldn't be bothered trying to come to terms with it. He had a choice: make some changes or stay as he was, which meant falling further behind as the rest of the world overtook him. As he pulled into the layby where he and Smith were to meet, Sam felt optimistic about the risk he had taken in agreeing to this assignment, and more alive than he'd felt in years.

He was early. There was no one around and Sam got out of the car and walked across to the edge of the lake. Bassenthwaite sparkled in the morning light, ruffled by the breeze. On the far side were the whitened western slopes of Skiddaw, and the wooded cone of Dodd. There was talk of ospreys being sighted over the lake, but not at this time of year. He was walking back to the car to find the binoculars that were in the glove compartment when a car pulled in and Conall Smith got out.

'What a great spot,' Conall said. 'I thought the Lake District was full of tourists and chintzy teashops and steamers on the lakes.'

'It is in some places,' said Sam. 'The further you get from the motorway, the quieter it is, thank heaven. On the coast where we live it's like another world. You'll see that when we start checking out the places you'll want to visit.'

'It's bloody cold, I know that,' said Smith. 'We can talk in my car, and then find somewhere for a coffee.'

'Any second thoughts?' Smith asked as they sat side by side in his car, looking out over the water.

'No,' said Sam. 'I think it'll do me good. The idea still sounds pretty far-fetched, but you presumably have reasons for concern. The whole Millennium thing seems to be winding people up.'

'Possibly,' said Smith. 'But sometimes you have to think outside the box, as they say. Think like a terrorist. This is the soft underbelly of England, far from normal surveillance, rich pickings to be had.'

'If I was a terrorist looking for publicity I wouldn't be looking here,' said Sam. 'When Sellafield was on fire in '57 the media coverage was pretty pathetic.'

Smith shook his head. 'That was forty years ago, things were different, easier to hush up. The internet changes everything.'

'It does?' said Sam.

'How old are you?' Smith asked.

'Fifty-nine,' said Sam. 'Born in 1940. You?'

'Thirty-three. Different generation. Kids at university are comfortable with technology that I struggle with and you wouldn't have a clue about. No offence.'

'None taken,' said Sam. 'I've seen the same with the young officers coming through. All this emailing and playing around on the computer. It's mostly Greek to me.'

'You need a crash course,' said Smith. 'That's why I've arranged for someone to come and see you, tomorrow as it happens. She's going to bring you some kit and show you what to do with it.'

Sam smiled, 'Who's that bloke in the Bond films, Q isn't it? The man with all the gadgets.'

Smith laughed. 'Don't raise your hopes. No ejector seats and Aston Martins. Do you have a laptop at home?'

'You mean a little computer?' Sam shook his head. 'My wife has, for her work. She thinks I'm a dinosaur.'

'She may be right, but Chris will sort you out. Tomorrow at six, she'll come to you.'

'Does she know where I live?'

'We're Special Branch, remember? We know everything.'

'But you don't know as much as you need to about possible security targets in this area, or I wouldn't be here.'

'True. The only place on my list so far is Sellafield.'

Sam remembered something he needed to mention. 'When you were talking yesterday about these ELF people you're interested in I realised that the two victims in our investigation are both linked to Sellafield. James Bramall's father owns Bramall Engineering, which is based at the Sellafield site. And Sandra

151

Evans worked at Sandersons in Workington and they have Sellafield links too.' He paused, 'Mind you, that could be said for most of the engineering businesses in this area. Sellafield employs thousands of people directly but the various supply chains involve thousands more. And then there's Barrow, further south. Nuclear subs built in the shipyard, and the nuclear material brought in and out by sea.'

Smith frowned. 'Don't people up here care about the risks?'

'Of course some do, but it's about jobs. Real jobs, not tourism and hospitality stuff. It used to be mining and shipbuilding on the Cumbrian coast, and those are the kinds of jobs people respect.'

'Interesting,' said Conall Smith. He rubbed his hands together. 'But too cold to talk here. Is there anywhere we could get a coffee? You don't know loads of people round here do you, not going to be spotted talking to a strange man?'

'This is well off my stamping ground,' said Sam. 'There's the Pheasant, just down the road. They might even do us a bacon butty.'

The bar of the pub was quiet and mercifully warm after the chill wind off the lake. The two men shed their coats, enjoyed their late breakfast and looked at a map that Conall Smith spread on the table between them. Sam pointed with his finger, leaving a spot of melted butter behind on the paper. 'Here's Sellafield,' he said, 'and here's the railway line that runs right along the edge of the plant, north through Parton where I live, on to Workington where Sandra Evans worked and up the coast to Carlisle. South from Sellafield the train runs down the coast to Barrow. Nuclear material is shipped in and out of the Ramsden Dock, just outside the town centre.' He sat back and thought for a moment. 'If you're looking for places with some iconic importance, to make a big splash, then Sellafield has to be top of the list.'

'I thought that,' said Smith. 'So, you and I will visit there on Monday. I've told them we're interested in security, but they don't know the specifics. Their head of security is meeting us at the Visitors' Centre.' He shook his head. 'A Visitors' Centre, for heaven's sake! It's like hanging a 'welcome' sign over a potentially lethal place.'

Sam smiled. 'Most people are surprised that it's there,' he said. 'West Cumbria's always been ambivalent about having a nuclear plant on the doorstep. At first it was a big deal when it was going to generate cheap electricity, then we had the fire in 1957 which was a PR nightmare. Before your time, but I remember it. The grass was so contaminated they had to pour all the milk down the drains for miles around. Thirty years later they built the Visitors' Centre. It cost a lot, so they must think it's worth having. And now BNFL, that's British Nuclear Fuels, are trying to butter up the community. 'Stakeholder Dialogue' they call it. Maybe something will happen soon, and they'll have to tighten up again, but the welcome sign's still there for now.'

Conall Smith peered at the map. 'You're saying that they carry nuclear material on this railway line, from Barrow to Sellafield, past all these villages?'

'Yep, in special containers. Have done for years. Greenpeace were interested in it for a while, but nobody seems bothered about it these days. And it's not just Sellafield.' Sam pointed to another spot on the map. 'There's the site at Drigg where they dump the low-level waste. That's on the railway line too.'

'Why don't they bring it by sea?'

'Too shallow. They'd have to build miles out to find water deep enough for ships to dock. Barrow's the closest they can get by ship.'

Conall stared at the map. 'All these places would be interesting to the ELF agenda, but it's such a long way off the track. They must be able to find somewhere to shout about closer to home.'

Before they ventured back out into the cold, Sam and Smith had agreed a time to meet at the Visitors' Centre at Sellafield on Monday morning. 'By that time, I should be loaded down with all the kit I need, right?' said Sam. 'Invisibility cloak, the lot.'

'You'll need to pay attention when Chris is showing you how to make things work,' said Smith. 'She's one of the new generation, and it shows. I've told her to go through it slowly and make sure you take it all in.' Smith rubbed his gloved hands together. 'I might have a look round this stunning landscape while I've got the chance,' he said. 'Any suggestions?'

Sam thought for a minute. 'Have a look at Derwentwater if you can,' he said. 'Crummock Water might be quieter. Depends how much you want cafés and shops.'

'I'll be in touch about Monday,' said Smith. 'I'll use the new phone that Chris will be giving you.'

'OK,' said Sam, wondering what technological complications he would have to adapt to. Heading home, he was glad that Judith would be there to help him if he needed her. Maybe this change would be good for both of them.

While Sam and his new best friend were sitting in a warm pub enjoying bacon butties, the investigation team at Nook Street in Workington had been enduring, rather than enjoying, their Saturday morning briefing. Overtime was in the air, but all of them knew it probably wouldn't amount to much with budget cuts also in the offing. Rob Findale led the briefing. There was no sign of DCI Skaife and Bell was lounging at the back of the room, listening as Findale and the rest of the team shared the information they had gathered. DC Sharp had completed the timeline that Sam had asked for, which helped to focus attention on how the two lines of enquiry overlapped with each other.

'Let's go over this one more time,' said Findale. 'Sandra leaves work suddenly on Friday, following a phone call that didn't come from Bramall's number, and we don't know who made that call. She seemed excited about whatever she was going to do next. She went back to her flat, picked up a suitcase and headed back to the train, going to Carlisle. After that we don't know where she was, but someone was seen closing the curtains of her bedroom in the flat on Saturday afternoon. We know she rented a car in Carlisle on Saturday morning, so presumably that's how she got back to Whitehaven.'

Findale looked for Bob Carruthers sitting in his corner. 'Bob, was anyone with her when she rented the car?'

'No,' said Bob. 'The rental people said she was on her own.'

'And no sightings of the car?'

'Not yet. Word's out to all patrols and the traffic police, so if it's in Cumbria it should turn up sometime soon. Then we can check for prints.'

Bob looked across at Bell after this contribution, looking for approbation, but Dinger was too busy taking notes to respond.

'Going back to the timeline,' said Findale, 'James Bramall appears to have been at home Friday night and most of Saturday, although we can't be absolutely sure about him being in the house. He was seen leaving the house around nine on Saturday night, on foot, not in his car. We assume he was meeting someone or being picked up. That's the last we see of him until his body is found early on Monday morning. We had another look for his phone on the roadside near where he was found but no joy.'

'Hang on,' Bell said from the back of the room. Heads turned. 'First, if Carruthers is right about the hotel in Carlisle, we might get some more information about Bramall's movements last weekend. And, there's another thing.' He paused for effect, waiting for everyone to turn towards him. 'The PM report on Bramall said he was full of drugs and booze before he was struck by the car. He could have been staggering around all over the place. And the doc reckoned he was probably dragged from where he was hit into the ditch, to be out of sight,' said Dinger. 'We need to widen the search for that phone. It could be a long way from where the body was found.'

Heads turned back to Findale. 'OK, right,' he said. 'Let me know about the hotel as soon as you've been there. I'll organise the wider search for the phone.'

'Good,' said Bell. 'Do it.'

The two men glared at each other until Maureen broke the tension. 'What about the person seen leaving Evans's flat on Monday morning?' she asked. 'Sam mentioned it last night. We need a statement from the woman who called it in, Tracey Tyson.'

'And a fuller description would help too,' said Findale. 'Can you chase that up, Maureen?'

'There's still a big hole in that timeline,' said Dinger. 'How long had Evans been in the flat before she was knocked out by the drugs and vodka, and how long did she lie there before the landlady found her around four on Monday afternoon? Can't somebody pin the medics down on that? Who went to see Evans at the hospital?'

'That would be me, Sergeant,' said Marion Sharp, turning towards Bell, who looked at her.

'You're new here, aren't you?' he said. 'What's a darky like you doing with a Scottish accent?'

Silence. Bob looked at Dinger, Maureen looked at Findale, Findale looked at Sharp, Sharp looked at the ceiling. Then DC Sergeant giggled. Maureen had had enough. 'Sir,' she said to

Findale, wanting him to say something, but all he said was, 'Can you check back with the doctor who treated Evans in A&E, DC Sharp, and see if he can tell us when the overdose might have happened?'

Sharp said nothing more, but Maureen could see in her face that she was struggling to restrain herself.

Findale finished the briefing and there was muttering as people reacted to what Dinger had said. Maureen found Sharp at her desk. 'You don't have to put up with him, Marion,' she whispered. 'The man's a moron. Tell Skaife what he said, "Darky"? For God's sake.'

'I've heard worse,' said Marion. 'But not at work. Is it worth making a fuss?'

'If you do, I'll back you up,' said Maureen. 'If Sam was here, Dinger wouldn't dare. Maybe he's testing how far he can push Rob as well as you. Do you know the Police Federation rep? He might advise you what to do.'

'I'll think about it,' said Marion. 'Thanks for the support anyway.'

'Anytime,' said Maureen.

The group dispersed quickly to salvage what was left of the weekend. Dinger was edging his car out of its parking place when Maureen spotted him and walked over. Dinger rolled down his window. 'Don't think much of our friend from the Met,' he said.

'And our friend from Glasgow doesn't think much of you,' Maureen said. ' "Darky?" for pity's sake Dinger, it's 1999 not 1899. What kind of language is that?'

'It's a joke, right? Black face, Scottish accent, it's funny.'

'And who was the only one who laughed? New boy Sergeant who's barely out of school. You're just stupid kids, the pair of you.'

Dinger rolled his eyes. 'Oh, you fucking feminists, can't take a joke. Humour bypass, that's your problem.'

'No, our problem is men like you. If Sam was here you wouldn't bloody dare, and you know it.'

'Well, he's not here, is he, and don't go running to him telling tales. Go home and henpeck Paddy. I'm off.' And with that DS Bell rolled up the window and drove out of the carpark.

Chapter 13

The Royal Hotel in Carlisle had seen better days, but it was still the most expensive hotel in town. It stood proud in Cumbrian sandstone opposite the station, close to the bars and clubs that James Bramall had used to escape from his family.

Dinger was glad to have something to do on this cold Saturday afternoon. After the nagging from Pritchard he couldn't face another weekend of being nagged by his wife and ignored by his kids. He relished time he got to himself and enjoyed the power that the ID card in his pocket gave him. Even off-duty, he was somebody.

The hotel was quiet. He guessed they would have been pleased to have guests that came for the weekend, when the business types weren't around. He pushed the bell on the reception desk and waited. A young man emerged from the back office. He was sharply dressed and his hair was full, black and glossy. He smiled. 'Good afternoon, sir, how can I help?'

Another foreign accent. Dinger glanced at the young man's name badge. 'Well, Pavel,' he said, 'I need some information.' He pulled out his ID and opened it up. 'DS Bell, Workington CID,' he said. 'That's just down the coast,' he added.

'Yes, sir,' said the young man. 'I know where Workington is.'

'Splendid,' said Dinger. 'And where are you from?'

'Krakow,' said Pavel. 'Have you been there? It's very beautiful, very old. What can I do for you, sir?' He was six inches taller than Bell and looked down at him. Dinger stepped back and pulled out a photo of James Bramall. 'Do you recognise this man?'

Pavel took the photo and looked at it carefully. 'It looks like one of our regular guests, Mr Fenton.'

Dinger smiled. 'I'm afraid Mr Fenton is having you on, sir. This man is known to us as James Bramall. We believe he's been staying with you during weekends for a couple of months. Can you check your records please?'

'You're saying Mr Fenton is actually called Mr Bramall? What about Mrs Fenton?'

'Probably Mr Bramall's girlfriend, sonny.'

'Mrs Fenton is called Sonny?'

'Just check the records,' said Dinger. 'I haven't got all day.'

Pavel lifted a large book onto the desk and opened it.

'No computer?' Bell said. 'Bit behind the times, aren't you?'

'Personally, I prefer a computer, but the hotel's owners like the big book. They think it's more classy,' said Pavel. He began to leaf back through the pages. Finding the entry he was looking for, he turned the book around and pointed. 'See here, Mr and Mrs Fenton. Last Saturday night, and Sunday too. The previous weekend, just Saturday, and the previous weekend. So it goes.'

He stood back, watching while Bell turned back through the pages, looking for when the Fenton visits started. 'First time seems to have been early in October, then almost every weekend since.'

'Yes, sir, the gentleman obviously enjoys his stays with us.'

'Here's one reason why,' said Dinger, proffering a photo of Sandra Evans. 'Is this the wife?'

'Yes,' said Pavel, 'that's her. A charming couple.'

'What's the pattern?' Dinger asked.

'Pattern?'

'When do they get here? Where do they go?'

'I couldn't say where they go, sir, but they usually check in on Saturday, maybe the afternoon or early in the evening. Sometimes they stay until Monday morning, mostly they leave on Sunday.'

'Spend any time in the bar or the restaurant, do they?'

'The bar, certainly. They don't usually eat with us.' The young man hesitated. 'You're sure about this?'

'About them not being Mr and Mrs Fenton? Oh aye,' said Dinger.

'What should I say to them when they come in again?' Pavel asked.

Dinger laughed. 'Not much chance of that,' he said. 'The bar is through here, right?'

A couple were in the far corner of the bar, hunched over their drinks, and a young woman in black was perched on a stool behind the bar tapping on her phone. She had long dark hair tied back and very pale skin. She looked up as Dinger walked in, put the phone away and smiled. He noticed her blue eyes. 'Good afternoon, sir,' she said, 'what can I get you?'

Dinger peered at the name on her badge, sensing the smell of something flowery on her skin. 'Mary,' he said, 'thank God for a British name. Local, are you?'

'Born in Dublin, sir,' said the girl.

Dinger smiled. Another bloody foreigner. 'So what brought you over here, Mary?' he asked.

She shrugged. 'Work. Things haven't been great in Ireland the past year or two.'

'And how are you finding it here?'

'It's a job, but Carlisle, well, it's not very exciting.'

He leaned forward. 'Maybe you don't know where to look.'

'Maybe, sir,' she said. 'So, what can I get you?'

Dinger reached for his ID. 'I'm a police officer, Mary, Acting Detective Inspector Bell. If anyone knows how to find excitement in Carlisle, it's me. Remember that.'

She looked nervous now, much to his satisfaction. He took the photo of James Bramall out of his inside pocket and held it out for her.

'Have a look at this face. Recognise him?'

'That's Mr Fenton. He and his wife are in here a lot at the weekends. Always a pleasure to serve them.' She frowned. 'Why are you asking?'

'I'll tell you all about it, Mary, but I could do with a drink. It's thirsty work, asking pretty girls questions.' He tapped one of the beer taps on the bar. 'A pint, please.'

Mary pulled a pint with care and handed it to him. He took a sip, smacked his lips and smiled.

'Better. Now, about this Mr Fenton. I have some news for you, Mary. First, the man's name is James Bramall, second, the woman is not his wife, and third, they're both dead.'

Mary dropped the photo on the bar and stepped back, her hand over her mouth, while Dinger raised the glass to his mouth.

'Jesus,' she said. 'What happened?'

Dinger shook his head. 'I get to ask the questions, pet. What's your full name?'

'Mary Brady,' she whispered.

'Well, Mary Brady, these two were here in the hotel last weekend. Did you see them?'

Mary recovered herself. 'Yes, they were here. Not Saturday, but Sunday. They came in around seven, and then another woman joined them.'

'Another woman? Young, old, what?'

'Maybe a bit older than Mr Fenton...Mr Bramall.'

'Anything you remember about her?'

'Tall, very short hair, American accent, but sort of soft.' She hesitated. 'She's not..

'Dead?' Bell asked. 'Not as far as we know. Have you seen her here before?'

Mary hesitated.

'Don't waste my time, pet,' he said. 'It's a simple enough question. Yes or no?'

'No,' she said.

Bell reached for his notebook. 'So, did they all come in together?'

'Mr Bramall and his… and the woman were here first. When the other woman arrived, they seemed pleased to see each other.'

'Could you hear what they were saying?'

'No, they were sitting over there, in the corner by the window.'

'How long did they stay?'

'Too long,' Mary said. 'Usually the man and his wife leave here about nine, to a club I guess, or to eat. It got to well past eleven and I wanted to go home, but they always tip really well, so I hung on. They were pretty far gone by then. Not the tall woman, she was drinking Coke, the other two.'

'When did they finally leave?'

'About eleven-thirty. They gave me a tenner, so it was worth it.'

'The tall woman paid, did she? Cash or card?'

'Cash.' She hesitated. 'What happened to them?'

'Can't tell you that, love,' said Dinger. He took another sip of his pint. 'What time do you finish?'

'I'm on the early shift today,' she said. 'My boyfriend's picking me up at six.'

Dinger laughed. 'All right, pet. Hint taken,' he said, taking a card from his pocket. 'This woman, if you see her again, give me a call,'

'What do want her for?'

'Well, the two people she was drinking with both died pretty soon afterwards. That should be a good start to a conversation, shouldn't it?' He drained the rest of his pint. 'Don't forget now, Mary. If you remember anything, ring DS Bell – that should be easy to remember, eh?'

Dinger didn't pay for his drink or leave a tip. And he didn't see the gesture that Mary made behind his back as he walked back to the reception desk. Pavel looked up. 'Is there anything else, Officer?'

'Sergeant,' said Bell. 'Last weekend, there was a woman with the Fentons, as you call them, in the bar, Sunday evening. Any idea who she is?'

Pavel shook his head. 'We do get business people from time to time but not many ladies on their own.'

'Not that kind of lady, I'm sure, in a posh place like this,' said Dinger. 'Right,' he handed over a card. 'If you have any more information about any of those three, ring me, OK?'

Bell pushed through the revolving door and out into the busy street. Carlisle United were playing at home and the town would be full of rowdy fans in an hour or two. Thank God I'm not still in uniform, he said to himself as he headed home. Sunday in the Bell household unfolded in its usual way. While his wife made her weekly visit to see her mother, Bell leafed through the Bramall/Evans case file he had brought home and thought about the people he had to work with. Skaife was still just going through the motions. Pritchard was a pain, but she was good at her job. Bob and the new lad would do as they were told and loved fiddling about on the computer, which could be useful. Findale and the Sharp woman, now they could be a problem. Findale might bugger off back to London if he was given enough shit jobs to do. Sharp was another issue. She was the tallest woman Dinger had ever seen, built like a brick shithouse. He could wind her up, no problem, but if she ever played the race card and claimed that she was being discriminated against, that could be tricky. Good thing Sam was out of the frame for a while. With any luck and a bit of pushing, by the time Sam came back, Skaife could have decided to pack it in, Findale and Sharp might have had enough and Acting DI Bell could climb another rung up the career ladder, where he belonged.

❖ ❖ ❖

Saturday afternoon in Parton: Sam wanted to find out how the morning briefing had gone. He knew Skaife was under orders to slow down the hunt for anyone connected with New York, but he wasn't sure what those instructions really amounted to. And what if the tall woman or man was clearly involved in two murders? Sam was very uneasy about trading a murder suspect for some short-term security advantage, but it was a clear choice. He must either step back from the investigation or else back out of the assignment with Smith.

The doorbell interrupted this dilemma, and Sam was surprised to find Maureen standing on the step.

'Come in,' he said. 'I was just wondering how things went this morning.' He ushered Maureen through to the kitchen where Judith was sitting. 'Look who's here!' Judith said, smiling. 'Not seen you in ages, how are you?'

'Never mind me, how are you?' Maureen said, pointing at the damaged leg. 'Is it still painful?'

'Not bad, really. Itchy, under the plaster'. Judith brandished a knitting needle. 'High tech solutions!'

Sam had put the kettle on and was gathering mugs on the worktop. 'Coffee?'

'Please, and make it strong,' said Maureen. 'I went shopping after the briefing just to calm down, but coffee might help too.'

Sam looked round. 'What happened? Not Dinger, not already?'

Maureen nodded. 'Didn't take him long.'

Sam said, 'Geoff bet me a pint that there'd be a shouting match on his first day back.'

'Well, you owe him.'

'Who did the shouting, DC Sharp?'

'No, me,' said Maureen. 'She's young, so I did the shouting for her. Not in the briefing, afterwards.'

Judith leaned forward. 'What did he do?'

Maureen winced, remembering. 'He said to Marion, and I quote, "What's a darky like you doing with a Scottish accent?"'

Sam and Judith groaned in unison. Sam had lifted the kettle and put it down again. 'The man's a liability. What did anyone say?'

'Nothing,' said Maureen. 'That was the worst part. New boy Sergeant just giggled. Sharp said nothing, what could she say? She's never met the man before. She looked more shocked than upset.'

'So, when did you shout at him?' Judith asked, enjoying the drama.

'In the carpark afterwards. He proceeded to call me a 'fucking feminist with no sense of humour'. That's why I need that coffee.'

Judith looked at Sam. 'When is someone going to do something about him?' she said. 'It's 1999, for heaven's sake.'

'That's what I said. The man's a throwback.'

'He needs throwing back,' Judith retorted. 'Preferably into very deep water.'

Sam carried on making the coffee. 'I have tried. Skaife won't take him on, and it's hard to get past him to the higher ranks.'

'Is Dinger in the Masons?' Judith asked.

'Probably. I've given up asking about that.'

'What about Marion, is she OK?'

'She says she's used to racial stuff, but not at work. I've suggested she talk to the Fed. rep. Not much the rest of us can do if she doesn't say something herself.'

Sam put large mugs of coffee in front of his wife and his guest. Maureen sipped and smiled. 'Great, thanks. Anyway, I've got that off my chest now. Do you want the rest of the news?'

She recounted the rest of the information from the briefing. 'The two computer lads get through a fair amount pretty quickly. Young Sergeant seems to have found his niche, right by Bob's side.'

'You said he giggled at Dinger?'

'That's the downside,' said Maureen. 'Bob sucks up to Bell and maybe Sergeant's copying him. I should have a word.'

'Well, Sam won't be around for a bit,' said Judith, 'while he's looking after me. By New Year I should have my new cast and be able to walk properly. All I can do now is hobble on the hateful crutches.'

Maureen finished her coffee and stood up. 'I'll leave you to it,' she said. 'Thanks for this. If anything important happens, Sam, I'll let you know.'

'Fine, thanks,' he said. He thought briefly about sharing his anxiety about the new assignment but decided not to do so. 'It's only a few weeks,' he said, 'You'll all cope without me, no problem.'

'What are you going to do about Bell, Sam?' Judith asked.

'For the moment, nothing. Once this other project is out of the way, but not now.'

When Maureen had gone, Judith could see that Sam had something on his mind.

'Tell you what,' she said. 'Why don't we go and sort out a wheelchair for me at that hire place? Then you can push me round the shops and people will talk down to me like an invalid. That'll be fun.' There was frustration in her voice but Sam didn't respond.

Sunday dawned drear and cold and Sam felt as grey as the day. He worried that he'd made a mistake, risking his career for a few weeks away from the routine of work. He worried too about Judith. Spending more time with her had meant he'd noticed things that he hadn't registered before, that she was sleeping less and drinking more. With that and the lack of exercise, she was looking fatter, her face more puffy than before. The only thing she seemed to care about was getting back to work as soon as she could, even though the newspaper didn't seem to be missing her.

On Sunday morning he made two cups of tea and brought them upstairs. Judith lay with her back to him. 'Is it work that's bothering you?' he asked. 'Do you want me to have a word with Ted?' She turned towards him, angry. 'I'm not a child, Sam. You don't need to plead with him on my behalf. If he hasn't got anything for me to do, I'll have to talk to him, but that's my worry not yours. Just leave it, OK?'

He offered to help her get up and dress, but she shook her head and lay down again after she'd drunk the tea. 'There's someone coming to see me this afternoon,' he said. 'She's bringing some kit for me to use while I'm doing this work with the Special Branch guy.'

'Lucky you,' she said.

It was almost lunchtime before Judith agreed to accept his help. By the time Sam's visitor had arrived Judith was in her chair at the kitchen table, glad to have something new and different to interrupt the tedium of the day. Chris, the young woman sent by Conall Smith, looked very young indeed, early twenties at most. Her fair hair was cropped short and a small stud glinted at one side of her nose. Judith envied her energy.

Chris's obvious technical expertise was intimidating, and Sam had to concentrate as she explained details of the equipment she'd brought. The new laptop computer was the latest model, with security software loaded up. Chris took Sam through it, slowly, while Judith added explanations and suggestions. Chris seemed impressed with Judith's easy grasp of the processes and Sam felt old and slow in comparison.

Next came the new phone, again top of the range and Judith's eyes lit up. 'That's a beauty,' she said.

'This is just for use with this project,' said Chris. 'Use your own phone for everything else.'

'He hasn't got one,' said Judith.

Sam defended himself. 'We use radios for work, and I can't be bothered keeping a phone charged up. And there's no signal half the time. One of my sergeants is from London, and he complains all the time that Cumbria seems like one big black hole.'

Chris nodded. 'I know how he feels,' she said. 'We are a wee bit behind in that respect. This one uses whichever network has the best local signal, but, even so, there will places where the signal is pretty poor, although by the coast here there seems to be a strong signal from the Isle of Man. Weird isn't it? London is much better, obviously.'

'Have you ever worked in London?' Judith asked.

Chris nodded. 'Did most of my training there. It's great in some ways, but I couldn't wait to get back here. Too many people down there, too much traffic, too much noise. I found it exhausting.'

'You're lucky to have the choice,' said Judith. 'I don't think we'll ever leave this place. It's beautiful, but sometimes I feel so hemmed in.'

Sam looked at his wife, wondering why she'd never said that to him. He realised that Judith's accident and now this new assignment for him might give them a chance to rethink. He hoped they didn't let the chance slip by.

'There are a few different things about this phone,' Chris was saying. 'Some special features, quite exciting actually.'

Judith leaned in, fascinated.

'We've put in some of the numbers you'll need on speed dial. Mr Smith's direct line is in there already, and my number. Are there any others that should be there?'

'How about 999?' said Judith.

'Yes, we can do that, if you're expecting trouble. Are you?'

Sam shook his head. 'I'm not sure,' he said. 'You know about this work I'm doing with your boss?'

She nodded. 'It could get tricky,' she said. 'We'll put 999 into the phone, just in case. As I said, the phone's programmed to find the best available signal for emergency calls. I'm sure Mr Smith would want you to call him first if there was any trouble, but you'll be working together most of the time, I expect.'

She lifted the little phone up so they could see it clearly. 'This is a feature you need to be aware of. If you press this key and hold it down, the phone will record what's being said, not just by you but within a few feet of where you are. Look.' She pressed the key and held it and a tiny red light began to pulse on the phone. 'There, see? When the light's blinking like that, it's recording. And if you do that and press the speed-dial number, the person you call will also hear what's being recorded.'

She gave the phone to Sam. 'Here, try it.'

It worked. 'Now,' she said, 'you need to practice that just by feel, without looking at the phone. The whole point is that you might need to record something or let someone else listen without the person you're talking to knowing what's happening.'

Sam looked puzzled. 'Now it sounds like you're expecting trouble.'

'But we can't discuss those details, can we?' Chris said, smiling. She was warning Sam off.

Judith looked at the phone. 'Can't some of the new phones do that?'

'Not yet. This one's ahead of its time. It's got an extra powerful microphone, and a longer lasting battery too.'

Judith laughed. 'There you are Sam, a special phone for a special agent.' She handed it back to him. 'Don't worry Chris,' she said. 'I'll make him practice. It could be a life-saver.'

Before Chris drove back to Carlisle, Sam took her and Bill for a walk on the beach. The cold sea fret was beginning to lift. On the horizon to the west the setting sun blazed for a few minutes before disappearing into the sea. They stood and watched. 'This business with Smith must feel a bit strange,' Chris said.

'It does, you're right,' said Sam. 'I had a choice of course, but I felt I was getting a bit stale, needing a bit of a challenge.'

They turned and walked back towards the house as the darkness intensified. Chris said, 'Your wife's impressively up with all this stuff, isn't she?'

'I'm impressed, that's for sure,' he said. 'She's frustrated at not being able to work until her leg is better. We've no kids, and work's always been important to us.' He looked across at her. 'What about you?' he said. 'Do you enjoy what you do?'

'Love it,' she said, 'but it's only a job. Life's more important than work, isn't it?'

Half an hour later, as Chris drove away from the house, a dark blue van that had been parked by the beach pulled out and followed her, but Sam was too preoccupied to notice.

Chapter 14

DS Bell was ready for the new week at work, more ready than he'd been for quite a while. He'd taken the temporary transfer to Carlisle just for the sake of a change, but it was good to be back, especially with Nelly out of the picture. Bell didn't really understand why Nelly wanted personal leave to look after his harridan of a wife, but it didn't matter. DCI Skaife was pretty much a waste of space, but at least he'd had the sense to realise that the new bloke Findale was just passing through and couldn't give a toss about the patch or the people in it. Dinger would have his day, and he was determined to make the most of it.

Unusually, the office was almost empty when he arrived. A head popped up in the corner. 'Morning, sir,' said the boyish voice. 'DC Sergeant, sir,' the voice went on. 'I just started last week. Me and DC Carruthers have been working together.'

'Good stuff,' said Bell. 'Who realised that Bramall had used someone else's name at the hotel?'

'That was me, sir,' said Sergeant, standing up. 'The name was on the whiteboard. It was just a guess really, and it worked.'

'That's what we're doing most of the time, son,' said Bell, 'guessing. Sometimes you have to think like the criminals we're tracking down.'

'Yes, sir,' said Sergeant, enjoying the attention.

Bell walked through for a word with the Duty Sergeant. 'Anything interesting overnight?'

'Good timing,' said Geoff. 'I was just coming to find you. A call came in just after eight, someone looking for the senior officer in charge of the Bramall case. That would be DCI Skaife, wouldn't it, now that Sam's on leave?'

Bell looked at the sergeant, who'd been around as long as he had, and smiled. 'OK Geoff, Skaife or me, take your pick.'

Geoff nodded and handed over the paper. Bell scanned it, 'Information about the night of Bramall's death? That was a week ago.'

'Bloke said he's been away, just got back last night and heard about Bramall. He rang us straight away.'

'OK, thanks. Is the DCI in, by the way?'

Geoff checked his watch. 'Not nine o'clock yet, have a guess.'

Back in the office, Bell followed through on a decision he'd made over the weekend. He picked up a few items from the desk where he usually sat and walked into Sam's office. He cleared to one side the sundry pieces of paper that lay on Sam's desk and put his own items down, arranging the assortment of pens and paperclips and the plastic trays he'd brought with him. He wanted to change the name on the door, but that might be a step too far and for once discretion prevailed over ego. If the rest of the team didn't like it, they could stuff it. He was Acting Inspector Bell now. Skaife had put him in charge in Sam's absence, and that's what he would be, in charge.

Out in the main office, Rob Findale had arrived. Bell could see him through the open door and waited. He wanted to see what Findale would do about this obvious assertion of control. To his disappointment, Findale did not react immediately, but a moment later he walked across and stood in the doorway.

'OK,' he said. 'You've made your point. People told me you like pushing everyone around, and they weren't wrong.' He stepped into the office and closed the door. 'Just so you know,' he said quietly. 'In the Met, if you spoke publicly to a fellow officer like you spoke to DC Sharp on Saturday morning, you'd be in trouble. Things are obviously different here, but my advice to her would be to make an official complaint.'

Bell leaned back in his chair. 'Well, things are different here, thank God. Maybe it's time you buggered off back to the smoke.'

'When I'm good and ready,' said Findale. 'In the meantime, watch yourself.'

'Or what?'

Findale raised a finger at Bell, who raised two in reply.

'Off you go,' Bell said. 'The DCI and I have some proper work to do while you're wiping that lass's tears. Got something going with her, have you?'

The office door opened and they both turned. DCI Skaife was standing there. 'Ah, Bell,' he said. 'You've moved into DI Tognarelli's office, I see.'

'My usual desk seems to have been taken over in my absence, sir,' Bell said, getting to his feet. 'DS Findale and I were just discussing the new plan.'

'Splendid,' said Skaife.

Findale said nothing, turned on his heel and left.

'Everything OK, Sergeant?' Skaife asked.

'Couldn't be better, sir,' said Bell. 'I took all the paperwork on the two cases home over the weekend, and I also made some enquiries myself. Fully up to speed.'

'Splendid,' said Skaife, again. 'I'm sure they've all got plenty to be getting on with. I'm going to suggest a briefing at five this evening, just for an update. That OK?'

'Shall I tell them?' said Bell, making for the door.

Skaife held out his hand to bar Bell's way. 'No, Sergeant,' he said. 'That's for me to do. And then come down to my office, will you? Geoff tells me we may have another witness.'

An hour later, DS Bell was ringing the doorbell at a house in Axelby. A man in his sixties muffled in a heavy sweater opened it. 'Mr Johnson?' said Bell, holding up his ID. Skaife introduced himself and the man registered surprise when Skaife mentioned his rank. Bell said, 'You rang Nook Street police station this morning with some information for us.'

'Yes, that's right,' said Walter Johnson. 'I thought you might call us back, didn't think you'd bother driving out here. Hang on a minute.' He opened a door at the end of the hall. 'Winnie, we've got company. The police, two of them.'

A woman appeared, taking off her apron. 'Winnie Johnson,' she said. 'How do you do?' The two visitors shook the outstretched hand. 'I'll bring some tea,' she said. 'And put the fire on in the front room, Walter. The house is cold, we've been away.'

In the frigid front room Walter fiddled with the gas fire and it popped into life. Skaife and Bell kept their coats on as they sat down. Bell reached for his notebook. Skaife was the ranking officer present and would expect to take the lead, leaving Bell to take the notes.

'My sergeant tells me you may have some information pertaining to the sad death of young James Bramall last week,' said Skaife.

'Aye,' said Walter. 'We've been away like, didn't know owt about it till we got back yesterday. I said to Winnie…'

As if on cue, Winnie pushed open the door and came in bearing a tray. She fussed with the tea rituals until her husband ushered her out again.

'Like I said,' Walter began again, 'we've been away.'

'Yes,' said Skaife. 'Let's start at the beginning, shall we?'

'Right,' said Johnson, looking at Bell who was poised to write whenever something worth writing emerged. 'Well, it was last Sunday night, not last night, the Sunday before. Well, it was probably Monday morning actually. We were driving out of Axelby, like…'

'Why so late?' asked Bell.

'Well, we booked this flight to Alicante because it was the cheapest, that is, Winnie booked it, not me. The flight left Newcastle at six-thirty in the morning and Winnie didn't realise that meant we'd have to be there by four. All that check-in malarky, it's not like catching a train is it? So anyway, not worth going to bed was it? Winnie said we could sleep on the plane, but it's only a couple of hours to Spain…'

This time Skaife interrupted. 'What time were you driving through Axelby, Mr Johnson?'

'Must have been about half past midnight. We were going slow because Winnie wasn't sure we'd got everything and she said we might have to turn round. I was trying to talk to her, you know, and we were just passing Axelby Hall, t'other side of the main gate, when this car was stopped in the middle of the road. Headlights were still on, and I could see two people standing in the road in front of the car.'

'Two people?' said Skaife. 'What were they doing?'

'Looked like they were having an argument. I rolled the window down. One of them could have been local, but the other one sounded American, you know, like off the telly.'

Bell said, 'Can you describe them, sir?'

'Well it was dark, like, but they both looked young, younger than us, maybe twenties? One was wearing a long coat, that was the one with the accent.'

'Man, woman?' Bell asked.

Johnson hesitated. 'It could have been a woman. Hard to tell in the dark. The other one, looked like he was wearing a shiny jacket, the light sort of bounced off it.'

'Leather, perhaps?' said Bell.

'Aye, I thought that. I noticed cos it was raining and rain's not good on leather, is it?'

'You say you slowed down?' said Skaife. 'Did you stop?'

'I wanted to,' said Walter, 'but Winnie said we had to get on. It might have been something we had to help with, you know, and we had a plane to catch. I felt bad, but when they both looked at us and never said anything I just drove on. Good thing I did too 'cos there was roadworks…'

'Yes, yes,' said Skaife. 'Have you got all this, Sergeant?'

Bell nodded. 'May I?' he asked. Skaife sat back. 'You say both of them were young,' said Bell. 'Anything else you noticed about them, in the light from the car?'

'Well, now you ask,' said Walter, 'as I said, the one in the long coat could have been a woman. It was the bloke in the jacket who was waving his arms. Tell the truth, he looked completely blotto. When the other one poked him in the chest he staggered back. I thought he was going to fall down. That's why Winnie wanted to drive on, I reckon. She hates drunks, her father…'

'OK,' said Bell. 'Now, as you passed the car, did you see anyone else in it. In the back, maybe?'

Johnson shook his head. 'Well they could have been lying down, I suppose, but I didn't see anybody, no.'

'And can you be sure about the time?'

'Oh, aye. When we got moving again Winnie checked her watch 'cos she was worried about the time, you know. Twelve forty-three, she said.'

'Could you show us exactly where all this happened, Mr Johnson?' said Skaife.

'I could try,' said Walter. 'Looks a bit different in daylight, doesn't it?'

'We'll go in our car,' said Skaife, 'and we can bring you back here. Can Mrs Johnson come too?'

'No problem,' said Walter getting up. He went to the door, 'Winnie, get your coat, we're going out.'

It was only a few minutes' drive on the main road from the Johnsons' house to the driveway that led towards Axelby Hall. As they approached, Bell slowed down. 'On a bit,' said Winnie. 'Past the gate, and further on.' They drove further on, about fifty yards on the other side of the gate. 'About here it was,' she said. 'Did you say about them throwing something over the hedge?'

Bell braked suddenly, then pulled the car to the side of the road. 'Which one threw something over the hedge?' he asked.

'The one in the long coat,' said Winnie. 'The other one was trying to get it, but he could hardly stand up straight. Well, when we'd gone past, I looked in the side mirror and I saw the person in the coat move their arm, you know, like throwing something, and this little thing sailed over the hedge, that way.' She pointed towards the hedge on the other side, away from the grounds of the Hall.

Bell said. 'The thing that was thrown. Could it have been a phone, one of those new little ones?'

'Might have been,' said Winnie. 'But we'd gone past and it was dark. Could have been anything.'

Skaife said, 'Would you walk back along the road with us, to see if we can pinpoint the place where all this happened?'

'All right,' said Winnie, 'if it's important.'

'It could save us a lot of time,' said Bell.

The four of them walked back a few yards. Mrs Johnson stopped and looked around. She walked a little closer to the gate and stopped again. 'About here I reckon,' she said. She looked at

Skaife. 'The man in the jacket, that was Jimmy Bramall wasn't it?'

Skaife hesitated. 'Yes, it probably was.'

'That poor woman,' said Winnie. 'She worshipped that boy.'

'Spoiled brat, if you ask me,' said Walter.

Winnie hit him on the shoulder. 'Walter, manners! He's dead, poor thing.'

Skaife looked at Bell. 'Anything else, Sergeant?'

Bell shook his head. I think we've got what we need, sir.'

'Right,' said Skaife. 'Could you take both the statements, Sergeant, when we get back to the house? Then we'll get another search party in there.' He pointed at the hedge where the item had been thrown. 'Who owns the land beyond the hedge, do you know?'

'Braithwaite keeps his cows in there,' Walter said. 'Could be a messy business.'

Statements taken, and more tea drunk, Bell drove them back to Workington. 'That was useful,' said the DCI. 'A precise time, a precise location, a pretty good ID and the chance to recover that missing phone. Good morning's work so far.' He turned to Bell. 'And you said you'd done some checking yourself over the weekend, Sergeant. What did you find out? Anything useful?'

Bell was pleased to have the DCI's undivided attention as they drove, and the chance to make a good impression. 'Yes, sir. We knew that young Bramall spent most weekends away, and his girlfriend's workmate said they went to Carlisle, clubbing. Out late, Saturday night and sometimes Sunday too. So, we reckoned they had to stay somewhere in the city, seeing as Bramall had enough money to do that.'

'Yes, yes, I know about that,' said Skaife. 'Did you go to the Royal Hotel yourself?'

'I did sir,' said Bell. 'Saturday afternoon, before the match finished and the place filled up with hooligans. The woman behind the bar knew Bramall and the girlfriend. Heavy drinkers and good tippers. She said they were in there last Sunday, the night Bramall was killed, with someone else, a woman, American, she thought.'

'Could that be the woman who was with Bramall, on the road?'

'Almost certainly, unless there are two American women hanging around. The bar girl said the American was drinking coke all night, but the other two were pretty legless.'

'So the American could have been driving Bramall back home. What about the girlfriend?'

'Could have dropped her off already in Whitehaven. She had to get back sometime before Monday when the landlady found her.' He hesitated. 'Or she could have been in the car, out of sight.'

'Well,' said Skaife. 'It's beginning to come together. Well done, Sergeant. You seem to be moving this case on nicely.'

'Local knowledge, sir,' said Bell. 'You can't beat it.'

'Absolutely,' said Skaife. 'The Super will be pleased. Edward Bramall has friends in high places.'

'Well, his son seems to have been a problem,' said Bell. 'Unsuitable friends, drinking, drugs too, from all we hear.'

'But still the apple of his mother's eye,' said Skaife. 'Let's get this phone found, if that's what it was chucked over the hedge. With any luck by the end of the day we might have this part of the case sorted, even if we're still missing a suspect.'

'I reckon the American woman's involved,' said Bell. 'If Bramall was as drunk as it sounds, he could have fallen down and she could have driven straight at him, then dragged him off the road so the body might not be found for hours. Plenty of time to get away.' He paused, thinking. 'Still haven't found the car, but it'll turn up somewhere.'

'What about the girlfriend?' Skaife asked. 'Is that PM report back yet?'

'Not yet,' said Bell. 'People tell me Dr Patel is good, but slow.' He looked at Skaife. 'You know these women, sir. No sense of urgency.'

Skaife didn't respond.

They were pulling into the car park at Nook Street when the radio crackled. Skaife picked it up. 'DCI Skaife here. Yes Geoff?' He smiled at Bell. 'Can you get Dr Patel to call me on the phone at Nook Street, in ten minutes? Thanks.'

'What were you saying, Sergeant?'

'That it's about time we got the full PM report on Sandra Evans, sir.'

'And your wish is granted. Do you want to come through while I take this call? We can have some decent coffee instead of Mrs Johnson's ghastly tea.'

Bell made a point of stopping at his new office on the way, just to make sure that everyone knew he was installed in the DI's office, and about to take coffee with the DCI. To his disappointment, no one was around except Bob and DC Sergeant, and he didn't need to impress those two. 'Bob,' Dinger said. 'We might be recovering Bramall's mobile phone, and it could be damaged, or full of cow shit. Who's the best person to deal with that?'

Bob hesitated. Mention of cow shit didn't augur well.

'I'll check with Chorley, sir,' he said. 'I can do some of the stuff, but their people are better.'

'Tell them with any luck we'll have it by the end of the day. Where is everybody?'

Bob shrugged. 'Canteen?' he suggested. 'It's Sergeant Andrews' birthday, I think there's cake.'

Bell shook his head. 'If Findale gets back before I've finished with Skaife, tell him to hang on. I need a word.'

'Sir,' said Bob. He wondered what those two would have to say to each other.

When Bell reached the tidy tranquillity of Skaife's office the DCI was already on the phone and gestured for him to take a seat.

'When can we expect the full report on paper, Dr Patel?' Skaife was asking. 'Good, so just give me the headlines, can you…Yes, we know Evans was pregnant, twelve weeks you reckon.' Bell got out his notebook and started doing some calculations.

Skaife continued his conversation. 'Yes, we know when she finally died, but do you have any idea when the overdose actually happened… Ah, right…What? A real mixture… Good lord… She was found at four in the afternoon… That long?… Right, right. Fax that report to us here, will you, quick as you can. Thanks, bye.'

'Vodka', said Skaife, 'mixed with heroin and cocaine. The combination killed her. The heroin would have been injected a few hours before she was found.'

Bell said, 'The landlady said Sandra had her sleeve rolled up when she was found. Could have injected herself I suppose. The drug works on the bedside table had traces of heroin.'

'However it got into her system,' said Skaife, 'her death was preventable, if she'd been treated in time. By the time she got to A&E the damage was done.'

'What about this pregnancy? We know that Bramall wasn't the father. If she was twelve weeks gone, that takes us back to the middle of September, about the time Sandra was on her way back from the States.'

Bell leafed back through the notes he'd made from his reading of the case papers over the weekend. 'Can I go through this with you, sir, before I say anything at the briefing?'

Skaife glanced at his watch. 'I've got half an hour, no more, Sergeant.'

Bell looked around for a whiteboard or even some paper to map things out, but there was nothing in the room except an empty desk and a redundant computer.

'OK,' he said, 'Sandra's into leftie causes, according to her sister, had been for years. She went off to New York in the spring – not sure exactly when – and came back in mid-September according to the sister, ranting on about saving the planet. Bramall was there over the summer, we can get exact dates from the family. He met some people he was impressed with apparently, and he too came back going on about saving the planet.'

'Right,' said Skaife. Bell wondered how much the DCI really knew about this case he was supposed to be in charge of. 'Sandra got pregnant mid-September if the doctor's dates are right. We know it's not Bramall's but he might have thought it was. He and Sandra are having a fine time, then this woman turns up looking for Sandra. We have them all drinking together in Carlisle less than twenty four hours before she was found comatose by the landlady. Now we have Bramall and a tall person, could have been female, having a row in Axelby in the middle of the night, right where Bramall's body was found.'

Skaife's face lit up. 'So, you think the American woman is Bramall's killer. Could she have done for Sandra as well?'

'It all fits,' said Bell. 'The question is, why?'

'Maybe Bramall was upset about Sandra's baby and threatened to dump her or tell his family about the Earth Liberation stuff, so they had to shut him up to protect themselves,' said Skaife. 'But why kill him first and then Sandra, if that's what she did?'

Bell shook his head. 'Bramall's phone might help, if we can find it.'

Skaife picked up a briefcase. 'Carry on, Sergeant,' he said. 'I'll be back for the briefing at five-thirty. Good work, so far.'

'Thank you, sir,' said Bell. The plan was working so far. If Skaife did the decent thing and retired, then Sam would go to DCI, and the DI's job should be Bell's. Mission accomplished.

Back in the office Rob Findale was obviously annoyed. 'Your lad says you want to see me,' he said. 'Since when do you get to boss me around, Sergeant?'

'Since I was put in charge of this case, Sergeant,' said Bell, 'alongside our esteemed DCI of course.'

'So, what is it?' said Findale.

Bell explained about Mrs Johnson and something being lobbed over the hedge. 'We only searched the roadside,' he said, 'not the field on the other side of the hedge. So we need to do that pronto.' He checked his watch. 'About three hours of daylight left. Can you get a team of anybody you can find, cadets, uniforms, anybody, and get out there?' He went to the sketched map on the whiteboard and drew in some details. 'Here's where the car was stopped. Unless the killer dragged the body a long way down the road, and why would she, Bramall must have staggered about ten yards or so towards his gate before he fell down. Before he could get up, the killer had time to drive the car straight at him.'

Rob looked at Bell and his self-satisfied smile. He had a strong urge to punch the bossy little man in the face, but now was not the time. Instead, he peered at the sketch map. 'So, if something was thrown from the point where the car had stopped, it would be further away from the gate, somewhere behind that hedge,' he said, tapping the spot. 'You're sure it's a phone?'

'The woman just said it was something small. What else could it be?'

'Drugs?'

'Worth looking for, whatever it was.'

'OK,' said Rob. 'If we can't find it before dark, it'll have to wait till the morning.'

'Before you go,' said Bell. 'Weren't you checking some address in London, off one of those lefty leaflets?'

'Dead end,' said Rob. 'The address is an empty shop, email address doesn't exist and the phone number just rings out. Either it was all a front, or else the organisers have disappeared.'

'Good riddance', said Bell. 'Report back by five-thirty, right? And take the touchy Scottish lassie with you.'

Findale controlled his temper with some difficulty, picked up his coat and left.

Chapter 15

Sam was at the Sellafield Visitors Centre ahead of his ten o'clock rendezvous with Conall Smith. The place was officially closed on Mondays but they had arranged to meet the head of security there without having to worry about visitors being around. From the carpark the Centre looked incongruous, more like a shopping mall or a planetarium than part of a nuclear plant. Maybe that was the idea, Sam thought. There'd been a big refurbishment not many years before, so they must have designed it quite deliberately to look safe and accessible against the backdrop of industrial towers and cranes. He'd never actually been to the place as a visitor. It tended to attract families, or school trips, with activities designed for kids. Security must be a bit of a nightmare, but someone must have weighed those problems against the necessity to keep the public on side and decided it was worth it.

As he waited, he wondered what was happening at Nook Street, and whether there would be fallout from Bell's clumsy sneering at Marion Sharp on Friday. Skaife would deal with Bell only if someone leaned on him hard, and Sam couldn't see how a lowly DC like Sharp would have the means or the courage to do so unless the Police Federation supported her, and he wasn't even sure about that. On the other hand, if Bell could control himself and felt he had something to prove by being put in charge of the case, Sam wondered how long it would be before Dinger identified the person that Special Branch wanted them to leave alone.

Smith pulled up next to him in the empty carpark. He looked as young and cheerful as ever. If he was bothered by the choice between short-term policing and long-term security, it certainly didn't show. He was telling Sam about the joys of his trip to Crummock Water the previous day when the front door of the Centre opened, and a man emerged and walked over to them. He was built like a rugby player, and probably was one.

'Alan Robinson,' he said. 'Head of Security.'

Sam and Smith introduced themselves and flashed their ID cards, and Robinson ushered them into the Centre.

It was just like any other modern science museum, with displays designed to interest children. As they looked around, the conversation was about access points, security checks, weak spots, and previous experiences with protests.

'Were you around in '95?' Robinson asked Sam.

'I certainly was,' Sam said. 'Busy times, eh?'

Robinson shook his head. 'It's always been a problem. The government says it wants public engagement, the people who work here are enthusiastic about their work, and I have a permanent headache about some lunatic going crazy, setting fire to himself or something equally bonkers.'

'You get your share of crazies, do you?' Smith asked.

'There's one bloke who wanders about outside wearing nothing but a leather thong, and we have hippy types dancing and singing 'Kum Ba Yah', all sorts. It's been going on for years, so what's bringing you lot here, why now?'

Sam kept quiet while Smith explained the anxiety around the Millennium, with as few specific details as possible.

'You're sure something's going to happen?' said Robinson.

'No, that's the problem. We think there may be some publicity stunts planned at an iconic place, to grab some headlines. Nothing too dire or life-threatening but it could be an embarrassing nuisance.'

'Iconic?' said Robinson. 'The girls who work here will love that,' he hesitated, 'but you don't want me to be heavy-handed about this, do you? If the local press gets a sniff they could make a story out of it even if nothing happens.'

'Right,' said Smith. 'Unless we hear anything more specific, all we can advise is that we need you to be aware and extra careful around New Year's Eve. You'll be open, will you?'

'Oh yes, school holidays are always busy.'

Smith said, 'Is there anyone else we need to talk to today? How about the Sellafield police force?'

Robinson led the way through various levels of security checks to the offices of the UKAEA Constabulary. The security of the actual nuclear plant was obviously tight, and the Sellafield police were licensed to carry firearms. Smith and Sam looked at the detailed map of the site. 'What about the railway line that runs on the seaward side?' Smith asked, tracing the line with his finger. 'The Constabulary here control all round the site and up to fifteen miles beyond it,' Robinson said. 'There are secure boundaries between the railway line and the plant, and there are armed officers on the trains that bring in nuclear materials.'

'And out to sea?'

Robinson nodded. 'We've had trouble out there before. You'll know all about that,' he said to Sam. 'Again, it's been a protest rather than a serious attempt to attack the place. I can't see us taking any extra precautions unless you tell us there's a need. Don't want to draw media attention and spook the locals or give anyone ideas.'

'OK,' said Smith. 'We all know it's the Visitors' Centre that's the most vulnerable, but in terms of the intelligence we have, such as it is, I don't think there'd be much mileage in blowing up somewhere that looks like a shopping centre. The outline of the main plant is the iconic part, and that's pretty well protected, as it has to be.'

'So, what do we do about the Visitors' Centre?' Robinson asked.

'I'll check with my superiors,' said Smith. 'If they want you to close the place for New Year's Eve and the following day, that's what you'll have to do I'm afraid. The trouble might happen at night, but whoever's planning it might want to be around during the day. Short notice I know, but it may not come to that. In the meantime, you need to keep your eyes and ears open locally for any rumours or unusual activity, anything out of the ordinary. DI Tognarelli is your local contact, closer than my operational base in Penrith.'

'And where do we find you?' Robinson asked Sam.

Sam scribbled down his new mobile number. 'Any time,' he said, 'day or night. I'm not at Nook Street at present, while I'm working on this.'

'Sounds like a cushy number,' said Robinson. 'Let's hope I don't need to contact you.'

'He's right, it is a cushy number,' said Sam. They were walking back to the carpark. The wind off the sea blew fine rain at their backs. Smith opened the door of his car. 'Get in quick before the rain gets worse,' he said to Sam.

'Look,' said Smith, before he started the engine. 'Do you think this whole Millennium threat business is a bit of a wild goose chase?'

'It's crossed my mind, yes.'

'And mine too. But someone in London, or possibly in Washington DC, has convinced themselves that something is being planned, and the orders have come down the wires.'

'Washington?'

'The FBI. They have their fair share of conspiracy theorists, and MI5 have some too. They think the ELF threat is real and that nuclear facilities could be the target. The Millennium thing is the more fanciful notion, but it has a certain appeal.'

Sam was puzzled. 'This idea came from the FBI?'

'Partly, yes.'

'And the people you say you're after are American?'

'Some of them, yes.'

'So why are we looking for them here?'

'Because the FBI found that one of the New York group, Sandra Evans, came from here. Sandra comes back to Cumbria, and an American person turns up to see her. The FBI think they may be up to something and they contact our people to tell them so.'

Sam shook his head. 'Any hard evidence for any of this?'

'I've not seen it myself. But if my bosses tell me to go to Cumbria, find a good local copper and check out the security risks, that's what I do.'

'You sound doubtful.'

'Frankly, I am. And it hasn't taken you long to wonder if this is all a bit far-fetched.' He paused. 'What do you want to do?'

Sam thought about his options. 'Look,' he said, 'I was frustrated at work, I'm worried about my wife's health, and it's only two weeks out of my life. But, and it's a big but, I think the person you're after may also be a suspect in one killing here, maybe two, if Sandra Evans didn't take her own life. I want them caught and waiting for them to show their hand may mean waiting too long.' He thought for a moment. 'Do you have any images of the New York ELF people? That might help to pin down who this American woman is.'

'I can check and fax them to you,' said Smith. 'But the question remains, what do you want to do?'

'I need to talk to DCI Skaife. If I think they're close to finding whoever killed Bramall and Evans, they can do it without me. If not, if they're messing up the investigation, I may have to go back. Two murders trump a political gesture.'

'How long will it take to make that decision?'

'A day or two.'

'OK. Give it till the end of the week. By then we'll have checked the other sites in this area that might be under threat, and if they look OK I can close this whole operation down.'

Sam shook his head, trying to work out the confusion in his mind. 'Look,' he said finally. 'If they really can't close this case without me, you don't really need me to hold your hand, do you? Our friends Mr Truelove and Ms Gordon will think I've bottled out, but that's just too bad.'

'It wouldn't look good,' said Smith.

Sam shrugged. 'I'm not saying I will back out, but I'm a policeman at heart, a detective. I'm not sure I can stand back and watch the case flounder.'

'Your choice,' said Smith. 'Don't expect anyone to admire you for your integrity, if that's what you're worried about.'

There was a pause. The car was feeling stuffy and Sam was uncomfortable. 'Can I ask you a personal question?' said Smith. 'You and Marianne Gordon have met before, right?'

The question was unexpected. 'Yes,' said Sam.

'How well do you know her, really?'

Sam felt his face getting hot. He was stuck in the car and couldn't avoid saying something.

'Why do you ask?'

Smith smiled. 'Just a feeling, seeing you together the other day.' He tapped the side of his nose. 'I'll call you tomorrow, when you've checked what's going on.'

As Smith drove back towards Parton, Sam sat in the car for a few minutes saying nothing, gathering his thoughts. Obviously, he would have to avoid Marianne Gordon if at all possible. He'd never been good at lying and the last thing he needed now was gossip about his private life. He just had to be alert to possible occasions when Marianne might appear and keep well away.

'Can't get used to this,' said Judith. 'You being home in the middle of the day. It makes me feel guilty.'

Sam laughed. 'Me too. I'm even worrying about taking Bill out, in case someone sees me.'

'Well one of us at least has some proper work to do,' she said. 'Ted's finally asked me for an article about the Millennium bug stories that are floating around. I can do the research on the computer. It'll take me a while to gather stuff together, but it's good practice. When are you going to start using yours?'

Sam looked at the slab of metal that squatted on the sideboard alongside the fax machine and the charger for his new phone. 'Looking at it makes me feel old,' he said.

'Guilt and ageing,' Judith said. 'That's what this new assignment seems to be offering so far. Are you sure it's a good idea?'

Sam finished his cup of coffee and looked at her. 'Actually, I'm having second thoughts already. I hate the thought of the Bramall investigation being fouled up.'

'Is it being fouled up? You're not indispensable you know.'

'OK, I know that. Maybe I'd like to be.'

'You can't just stroll into Nook Street as if you're still in charge.'

'I know that too. Skaife made it pretty clear how he feels about me, and I don't want a row with him. If I want to change my mind and go back to work I honestly don't know what he would say.'

'Well if you can't go to Nook Street, don't bring him in here,' said Judith. 'He's a neat freak, and this house would give him apoplexy.'

'Never fear. I'll keep him well away.'

❖ ❖ ❖

DCI Skaife's house in Lamplugh looked like a show home that no one actually lived in. Sam had spoken to Skaife on the phone, apologised for any embarrassment he might have caused by being too frank about Bell at the Penrith meeting and asked to meet him away from the station. Skaife had obviously calmed down and suggested that they meet at his house, which had been a surprise. Maybe he too was trying to make amends for his previous behaviour and the outburst in the car a few days earlier. Now that they were here, Sam was careful to take off his shoes inside the front door and line them up straight before he followed Skaife into the shiny kitchen. He was on his best behaviour. 'Nice place,' he said. 'Have you lived here long?'

It was just a polite question to break the ice and Sam was surprised by Skaife's response. 'You remember my wife Carol?' Skaife said. We bought this house just before Carol was diagnosed. It was the kind of house she'd always wanted, and we were finally able to afford it. At least she had a few years here before…' his voice tailed away.

Sam had never heard his boss talk about his dead wife and looked at him carefully out of the corner of his eye. He had a feeling Skaife was going to start crying and had no idea what to do if that happened. Fortunately, the moment passed. Skaife bustled around making coffee, before opening a cupboard, taking out a bottle and pouring a hefty tot of whisky into a glass for himself. 'I'd never have done this when Carol was around,' he said. 'But now she's not.' He took a sip and looked across at Sam. 'Never take life for granted,' he said. 'Work is just a job, it's family that matters. Take it from me, Sam. I wish I'd realised that earlier.'

Sam didn't respond. He was thinking about Judith. Skaife broke the silence. 'So, what do you want to see me about? I thought you'd agreed to step back for a few weeks.'

'That was the plan, sir,' said Sam, 'but I've been having some doubts about whether the assignment I agreed to is actually worth doing.'

Skaife raised his eyebrows. 'Is that your decision? If the Home Office and MI5 and your senior officers think it's worth doing, then it's your duty, surely?'

Sam said, 'I thought I was given a choice.'

'Well it had to be put to you like that, I suppose, but realistically you could hardly refuse. And now you're saying you've changed your mind?'

Sam could hear the man's irritation in his voice. Maybe this meeting wasn't a good idea, but Sam decided to keep going. 'I'm beginning to gather what this Millennium threat really amounts to in our area,' he said, 'and it looks pretty far-fetched.'

'Far-fetched to you, maybe, but that's not your decision either, is it?'

'But it's a delicate balance, sir,' said Sam. 'I'm worried about compromising the chance to close a murder enquiry while I'm chasing shadows all around the county.'

Skaife put down the whisky. 'Am I hearing you correctly, Inspector?' he said. 'Are you saying that without your presence our current investigation is doomed to failure?'

Sam back pedalled. 'No, no, sir, of course not. Maybe I just want to be part of it, part of the action.'

'Well, you should have said so when you had the chance. What does it look like if you come back now? It looks as if we can't cope without you, and that's simply not the case. DS Bell and I can handle this, Inspector, with help from the team, and without you. We're making good progress and I have to say Bell has really got things moving.'

This was a surprise, but Sam tried not to show it. 'That's excellent news, sir,' he said. 'Has there been a breakthrough since last week?'

Skaife told Sam about the Johnsons, how they'd witnessed the altercation involving Bramall early on Monday morning. 'And,' said Skaife, 'at this very moment there's a search team out expecting to find Bramall's phone.'

'But we combed the roadside, sir,' Sam protested.

Skaife's face was getting pinker and his voice louder. 'As I told you, Tognarelli, things have progressed, and now we know where to look.' He poured himself another drink. 'And another thing,' he said. 'DS Bell may have his detractors, but it was his persistence, in his own time, that has given us more information about the mystery woman who could be involved in both these deaths. The barmaid at the Royal Hotel in Carlisle is another witness we seem to have uncovered without your help.'

'The mystery woman, you mean the one the FBI are looking for? The one we're supposed to be leaving at large?'

'MI5 are more involved than the FBI, as far as I know. And you said yourself, Inspector, that the whole eco-terrorist business looks pretty flimsy. In the meantime, we may have the chance to pick the suspect up ourselves, under our own steam. The security people will have to be kept in the loop, but my boss is the Chief Superintendent and police work has to be done.'

You old bugger, thought Sam. You do want the credit for yourself, no matter what the bigger picture might be. Out loud he said, 'I'm beginning to understand, sir.'

'Good,' said Skaife. 'Some people might think I'm past it, Inspector, but DS Bell and I make a bloody good team, and we can bring this case home without you.' He drained his glass and put it down with more than necessary emphasis.

Sam got to his feet. 'Right, sir, that seems to be very clear. So, I assume you'll be getting good descriptions of this American person, from the barmaid and from Sandra Evans' friend who saw them in the street.'

'Of course,' said Skaife.

'And you won't be needing the images I've already requested from the FBI?'

'Of course we'll want those too.'

Sam smiled as sincerely as he could. 'You're obviously doing splendidly without me, sir. I'll leave you to it.'

'Good,' said Skaife. 'I'm getting tired of these games. The world doesn't revolve around you, Tognarelli. Now if that's all you have to say, I have things to do.' He led the way to the front door and opened it, and Sam walked past him without a word.

That was a mistake, Sam thought. Another one. Never underestimate the deviousness of a senior officer, even if he's near to retirement. If there are points to be scored, Skaife will be right at the front of the line with DS Bell close behind. Now Sam had to decide what to tell Smith. Nothing, he decided. It might all come to nought, and if Skaife did actually close in on the woman he was looking for, he would have to check with Chief Superintendent Williams before picking her up. It was a tangled mess and Sam suspected that some of it was his fault.

'What did you expect?' said Judith, after Sam told her about his meeting with Skaife. 'They got lucky, and they want to take the credit. And I bet Dinger got a free pint out of his trip to the hotel in Carlisle. Who tracked all that down, by the way?'

'Bob Carruthers. He sits there in his corner like a spider, doing his policework without getting off his arse.'

'That's the future, right there,' said Judith. 'Dinger's no fool. He knows how useful Bob is and he keeps him sweet.'

The fax machine on the sideboard started to screech and they both looked at it. 'Did you put paper in it?' Judith asked.

'Christ,' said Sam. 'I forgot.'

Judith laughed. 'So much for the white heat of the technological revolution.'

Five minutes later, with the fax machine now able to do its job, half a dozen grainy pictures chugged slowly out of the machine. Smith must have checked his files for the New York ELF people. Sam peered at the faces. All male. Useless. These pictures wouldn't help, and he hid them away in a folder.

Judith had opened a fresh bottle of red wine and poured two large glasses. 'Here's to Skaife and Bell,' said Judith, 'Workington's answer to Morse and Lewis. It's a great story for Tommy.' She took a generous mouthful. 'Do we know when he's arriving?'

Sam had almost forgotten about Tommy's visit. He'd have to warn Smith that there would be someone in the house for a while who didn't know anything about Sam's new assignment.

Taking Bill out for his walk was a good time to try out the new phone and contact Conall Smith. To Sam's surprise the mobile phone signal on Parton beach was strong. Chris was right about the signal from the Isle of Man. Smith didn't answer. What if it had been an emergency, Sam thought as he left a message. A few minutes later, the phone shrilled in his pocket. 'Who's this visitor you're telling me about?' Conall asked.

'Just my nephew, not seen him for years.'

'Right. Well, remember the OSA, Sam. You're working on a new assignment for a few weeks, OK? That's all he needs to know. Have you spoken to Skaife? How's it going without you?'

Sam hesitated before he said, 'Oh, they seem to be muddling along.'

'So, you'll stick with me for the time being? Good, because we're going to Barrow on Thursday.'

'Whoopee,' said Sam.

Chapter 16

At the start of the working day on Wednesday Nook Street CID room was far busier than the house in Parton where Sam was enjoying a lie-in. Conall Smith had faxed through information to him about the technicalities of nuclear waste and its route to Sellafield for reprocessing, which Sam was to read before their trip to Barrow, but that was only an hour or two's work.

At Nook Street Maureen Pritchard took up her usual position during briefings at the back of the CID room where she could take in the performance from the team leaders while watching the reactions of her peers. Marion Sharp was in her usual place. She'd obviously decided against pursuing a complaint about DS Bell's racial slurs, which Maureen was disappointed about but not surprised. Life was hard enough for a young female DC without inviting further hostile attention. DC Sharp might well decide that West Cumbria was not the place to make her career. And Rob Findale, Maureen wondered, how long will he stick around, the butt of Bell's sarcasm and gamesmanship? He must have seen enough of that in just a few days to encourage him to move on.

The surprising thing about the current set-up was the unexpected enthusiasm of DCI Skaife. He still seemed to regard the main CID room as somehow beneath him, but here he was, standing alongside Bell as if to the manor born. Information was accumulating on the big whiteboard and the mobile phone had been recovered from a field, found by a search party led by DS Findale. The phone was wet and muddy when it was found, but it had been sent to Chorley for analysis and might possibly reveal even more about the connection between the mystery woman, Bramall and Evans.

'Which brings us to the whereabouts of the Toyota car which damaged a headlight in the collision with Bramall,' said Skaife. 'DC Carruthers, any progress?' Bob rose from his corner, smiling, and beside him DC Sergeant was almost bouncing with excitement. 'Just a few minutes ago, sir,' said Bob. 'Someone reported a van missing from a long-stay carpark near the station in Carlisle, and in the corner of the same carpark they found a Toyota car, 1998 plates, with a damaged headlight. I'm just about to check the reg. with the car hire firm where Evans rented her car last Saturday.'

Good work, Bob, Maureen thought. The lad might be another Bell in the making, but he knew his way round that computer, and it was paying off. The pieces of the picture were beginning to fall into place. DC Sergeant was still bouncing on his seat and put up his hand. 'Sir, what about the van that was stolen from the carpark? We could check the CCTV at the carpark, and at the station too.'

Bell chimed in, 'And we need the barmaid at the Royal to do a photofit.'

Skaife raised his hand. 'OK, calm down everyone. Carruthers, check with the car rental people about the Toyota, and sort out the CCTV we need access to. And try and find out how long the Toyota has been in the carpark. DS Bell will arrange for forensic examination of the Toyota and get a photofit of the mystery woman from the barmaid. DC Pritchard, you've got Drug Squad experience. See if you can track down a local drugs supplier that Bramall and Evans used. Findale and Sharp, you have to find the van that was reported stolen from the carpark, and I want someone to hurry Chorley up with Bramall's phone, so Sergeant Findale that's for you too. DS Bell and I will be going to Axelby to see the Bramalls this afternoon. I promised them progress, and that's what's happening. Good work everyone. Five-thirty this evening for an update.'

Well, well, Maureen said to herself through the buzz of activity that greeted the end of the briefing. There's life in the old dog yet. Dinger might have to wait a bit longer for Skaife to leave, Sam to step up and the DI role to be ripe for plucking.

❖ ❖ ❖

Sam's Wednesday was far less productive. It didn't take him long to read through the information Smith had sent, and Judith seemed to have perked up now that she had a job to do for the newspaper. Bill the dog enjoyed a longer walk than normal. Sam took him north along the beach and then up across muddy fields until the westerly wind brought heavy showers rattling in from the sea and they sheltered among some tall trees for a while before making their way back to the house.

Judith was on the phone to her office while Sam finished rubbing Bill dry and went to put the kettle on. She seemed to be more cheerful. 'OK, quick cuppa and then we're off to that hire place to get me a wheelchair,' she said. 'That way I can get out of the house for a while and you get to show off what a good carer you are, taking time off work to look after the crippled wife.' She smiled. 'I'll do my best to look careworn.'

By the time they arrived home again the day had cleared, and Sam managed to push Judith in the new wheelchair a little way along the path down to the beach. They sat side by side for a while watching the ebbing tide. 'I feel bad about Tommy, in a way,' she said. 'When he was a child and you lived with him and Elspeth, you were like a proper family. And then you and I moved on and Andy came along and everything changed. Did you ever meet Andy?'

'Just once, I think,' Sam said, 'at their engagement party, just after I got back to Barrow.'

'Why wasn't I there?'

'Not sure. It was in Preston, maybe you couldn't get away.'

'What was Andy like?'

'I didn't like him,' said Sam. 'He came across as a real Prince Charming, but there were a few things Elspeth told me that didn't sound right, him telling her off about what she was wearing and for being too lenient with Tommy. She seemed to think that showed how much he cared for them both, but I wasn't convinced.'

'Did you say anything to her?'

'No. I thought it would cause trouble.'

'You should have done,' said Judith. 'That could be why she never wrote back to us, maybe Andy stopped her.' She shook her head. 'I wonder if Tommy will tell us what happened?'

Sam said, 'Maybe, but we can't push him, not when he's only just arrived. If he wants to tell us, he will.'

'A few beers should do the trick,' said Judith.

Sam was suddenly annoyed. 'No, Judith. Don't get the poor bloke drunk.' He hesitated. 'And don't get drunk yourself either.'

'There you go again,' she said, turning towards him, angry. 'On and on about me having a drink. It's nothing to do with you, right, so lay off.'

For a moment she struggled to get up, to walk back to the house under her own steam, but it was hopeless. 'Come on,' she said. 'Make yourself useful. Take me home.'

Fortunately, things had calmed down by the time Sam went out to pick up Tommy at the station. The wind had dropped, and the sky was clear and sprinkled with planets and early stars as Sam waited on the platform at Workington. He had to remind himself that the man he was meeting wasn't the eleven-year old he'd seen at Elspeth and Andy's party in 1974. He'd be about thirty-six now, perhaps unrecogniseable. And would Tommy recognise him?

And then the train pulled in, doors banged and there he was, taller but much the same. The years have been kind, Sam thought. Tom's long body was lean and the face as lively as ever. It was when he spoke to greet Sam that the years between their meetings made a difference. 'G'day, Sam,' he said. He dropped the bag he was carrying and put both arms round Sam, hugging him close. 'So good to see you, mate. It's been too long,' he said, and the New Zealand accent was clear. They shook hands, laughing. 'You look well, Tommy,' said Sam, standing back to look his nephew up and down.

'Tom, please! Tommy makes me feel about ten!'

'Sorry,' said Sam. 'Tom it is. Come on, Judith will be waiting.'

'I thought she might be here,' said Tom. 'Is she OK?'

'She's fine, but she had an accident about two weeks ago and broke her leg. It's such a hassle getting in and out of the car that she stayed home. We've rented a wheelchair so she can get around without the crutches.'

When they arrived at the house Judith had hopped to the front door, opened it and was standing just inside, too excited to bother about the cold. Sam carried Tom's bag and Tom bent to hold Judith, lifting her up as she shrieked with delight. 'Look at you,' she said when he put her gently down again. 'Sweeping me off my feet.'

Sam made a big pot of tea as Judith sat at the table next to Tom. 'It's been a long day,' he said. 'So good to be here at last.'

'Don't get too comfy,' said Judith. 'We're planning to celebrate your visit by going out for a meal. I wangled a table for us at the Chinese by telling them we'd do a piece about how welcoming they are to disabled people.'

Sam laughed. 'Judith! Honestly, what a scam!'

'But it's true,' she protested. 'Ted will run the piece, I asked him. In fact, he's asked me to test out all sorts of places to see how wheelchair friendly they are. That's another job, but I might need your help. Perfect while you're off work.'

Tom looked at Sam. 'You're off work? Is everything OK?'

'Oh, it's fine,' said Sam. 'I had some leave owing and took it, just while Judith's so incapacitated. Come on, if we've got a table booked, we might as well go straight there. It's not much by city standards Tom, but we like it.'

'And we've not been out together for months,' said Judith, struggling to her feet. 'You should visit more often Tom, take us out of ourselves.'

Judith's wheelchair was folded up in the boot and they drove down to the harbour at Whitehaven. The sea was calm, protected from the breeze by the old harbour walls that stretched out in two great arms, encircling the boats and yachts that bobbed on the black water, cables tinkling against masts. While Sam and Judith struggled with the wheelchair Tom stood looking around.

'This is fantastic,' he said. 'I thought Whitehaven was full of coal and phosphates. What happened?'

Sam looked up and followed Tom's gaze. 'All the mining stopped. No coal to export. Marchon's on its last legs. So the harbour has been cleaned up and become a small boats harbour again, some fishing too.'

Tom gestured with his arm, taking in the sweep of the harbour. 'If this was in New Zealand there'd be restaurants and bars right along the front here, people strolling around. Where is everybody?'

Judith settled herself in the wheelchair. 'It's like we've lost the old industries and the new ones haven't really started yet,' she said. 'Whitehaven's quite a small town, and not enough visitors to keep places going. Tourism's picking up in the Lake District, but people don't often come as far west as this.'

'Old reputations die hard,' said Sam. 'West Cumbria was always an industrial place, dangerous work, poor housing, plenty of pubs but not many decent restaurants. Whitehaven will have to reinvent itself. That takes a while.'

'In the meantime,' Judith said, 'we do have at least one good place to eat out, so let's move, I'm starving.'

Judith wanted a bottle of prosecco to celebrate but Tom said he would stick to jasmine tea. Sam was relieved, wondering what Judith would say if there was too much alcohol flowing. They tried not to ask Tom intrusive questions, but he seemed to sense what they wanted to know.

'I have to explain a few things,' he said as they waited for the first course of the order to arrive. 'I'm afraid Andy wasn't the open-hearted bloke you might have thought he was.'

Sam kept quiet about his doubts on that score. Tom went on, 'He insisted that we all make a clean break, a "fresh start" he called it, and he meant it. Nothing of our old life here could be mentioned. Any letters that came from the UK were hidden away by him before we even knew anything had arrived. When I found a stack of them when I was about sixteen, Andy was really angry, saying I'd "betrayed" him by wanting to read them. Then he burned them, can you believe that? I tried to tell Mum what he'd done, but by that time things were so bad that she didn't want to listen.'

Sam was shocked. He'd written to Elspeth a number of times in the early years but had never had a reply.

'We didn't know where you were,' said Tom. 'For a while Mum fretted about not hearing from you, but Andy just wore her down, saying that we had a new life and didn't need the old family any more.'

'That's awful,' said Judith. 'Why did she go along with it?'

Tom shook his head. 'I never really understood. I was only twelve or so when we went to New Zealand, didn't understand how things like that work. As I got older, I began to suss it out, but Mum wouldn't listen to me. It was as if she had to believe that Andy was always right and that she'd made the right choice. And of course, there were the other two to think of.' He took another sip of his tea.

'What other two?' Sam asked.

'The other two kids. They came along when we were living in Tauranga. Richard was born in 1976, Ngaio two years later. Mum was busy with them, and then went back to teaching when they were both in school.'

Judith and Sam looked at each other. 'You mean Sam has another nephew and a niece and no one told us?' Judith said.

Tom frowned. 'It's awful, I know. But that's the way it was. And then, after all that, the bastard upped and left her. Ran off with someone from work about eight years ago. Ngaio was just fourteen.'

'Bloody hell,' said Sam. 'What a shitty thing to do.'

They stopped talking while the food was presented with some ceremony and various explanations. The restaurant clearly wanted to impress the person who would be writing about them in the local paper, although Judith was thinking less about the food and more about their guest's life story.

'Where is Elspeth now?' Judith asked.

'She and the kids moved down to Petone, near Wellington. I think Mum just wanted to start again and it's a completely different life down there. Great place to live actually and much cheaper housing than Wellington itself. I was well away by then. I moved out when I was eighteen to go to uni in Dunedin and after that I went to the States for a while and then to London.'

'What do you do?' Sam asked. He was curious about work that seemed to take Tom all over the place.

'Computer stuff,' said Tom. 'Got in at the beginning of it all and it gets busier every year.'

Judith smiled. 'Don't get too technical with Sam,' she said. 'His eyes will glaze over.'

They shared out the various dishes that had arrived. 'I've always wanted to go to New Zealand,' said Sam. 'There's a pride about the place, and they take a stand on things, don't just blindly follow the USA like everyone else does.'

Tom nodded. 'We feel as if we're on our own,' he said, 'making our own way. The anti-nuclear thing is all part of that. And when the Rainbow Warrior was blown up in 1985, that just made us stronger.'

Judith said, 'I remember that. It was a Greenpeace boat, wasn't it?'

'Blown up in Auckland Harbour by the French secret service, and a guy on board was killed,' said Tom. 'When the two blokes who did it were convicted the French government insisted that they should be in a French jail, and as soon as they were shipped back, they were released.' He laughed. 'Most Kiwis won't drive a French car, even now. The whole business had a big impact on me.'

Sam said, 'You know we have a nuclear plant just a few miles from here, don't you?'

'Of course,' Tom said. 'But it's just processing other people's waste now isn't it? Messy business.'

'Didn't you go there the other day?' Judith said.

'Just a routine visit,' said Sam quickly. He wanted to kick Judith under the table but daren't risk hitting her bad leg. 'Well,' he said, changing the subject as quickly as he could. 'I can't eat any more right now, don't know about you two. Could we box the leftovers and take them home?'

Half an hour later, they were back at the house in Parton. They finished off the food, Judith tucked into the wine, and Sam showed Tom the spare room where he would stay overnight. Sam was earnestly hoping that Tom would be too tired to stay up much longer, as Judith had opened the bottle of wine as soon as they got home and seemed determined to share what she knew about Sam's 'special assignment'.

Upstairs, Sam said to Tom, 'I'm so sorry to hear what you've all been through. I could have tried harder to keep in touch, but I had no idea Andy was so determined to keep us away.'

Tom sat on the bed and ran a hand through his hair. 'It was all about control,' he said. 'I realised that as I got older. He made Mum more and more dependent on him, and then left her for someone much younger. I suppose he started all over again with the new woman. I hope she manages to stand up to him.'

'Now that Elspeth's on her own, I'll write to her again,' Sam said. 'I'll be retiring in a few years, I expect. Judith and I could go out there and see her, make up for lost time.'

Tom said, 'And now that we're back together, can I ask you a favour?'

'Anything,' said Sam.

'You know I'm on my own, no family of my own.'

'I guessed that, as you said nothing about it.'

'My housemates in London all go off to their families at Christmas, but it's just too far to go home this year, and the airfares go sky high. Could I come and stay with you and Judith for a few days?'

Sam was delighted. 'That's a wonderful idea,' he said. 'Judith's brother and his family live in St Bees. We spend time with them over Christmas every year and they'd be thrilled to welcome you as well.'

Tom gave Sam a hug. 'Thanks, mate,' he said.

Tom was obviously tired, and Sam left him to it. 'He's gone to bed,' he said to Judith. 'Damn,' she said. Sam put a finger to his lips, and she lowered her voice. 'I was looking forward to finding out a bit more. He's not told us much about himself at all. Did he say anything to you?'

'He said he's on his own, but I'd guessed that already, hadn't you? No mention of anyone in his life.'

'Not now, maybe, but I can't believe an attractive bloke like that hasn't had a few flings at least.'

'Oh, and he invited himself for Christmas. That's OK isn't it?'

Judith clapped her hands. 'That's great! Wait till I tell Helen.'

Chapter 17

'What time is Tom's train?' Judith asked as Sam got out of bed the following morning.

'Just before nine, plenty of time.'

'What else did he tell you last night, as well as inviting himself to stay?'

'Keep your voice down,' he whispered.

'He's gone downstairs already,' she said. 'I heard him. So, what else did he tell you?'

'I told you he's on his own, that's why he wants to stay at Christmas. It's too expensive to go back home.'

'He's not short of money, is he?'

'I don't know, we didn't talk about money. Anyway, I thought you'd be pleased about him coming to stay.'

'I am,' said Judith. 'Just curious. He's too much of a catch to be on his own. There must be a story there, waiting to come out.'

'Well, it's not coming out yet, so control yourself. Are you getting up to say goodbye?'

Judith hobbled slowly down the stairs wearing the special dressing gown she kept for holidays. Tom leaned down and gave her a hug. 'Thanks for the hospitality,' he said. 'Did Sam tell you I invited myself for Christmas?'

'He did and you're very welcome,' she said. 'I'm really glad you took the trouble to track us down.'

'Me too,' he said.

'Time we were off,' said Sam, tapping his watch.

Half an hour later, he was back at the house. He retrieved the file from the box upstairs where he kept all the details of his assignment and checked through it, reminding himself of the details of the day's visit to Barrow.

'Where are you off to today?' Judith asked.

'Barrow. Don't ask me where we're going. In fact, the less I tell you, the better. For a nasty moment last night, I thought you were going to start telling Tom about my assignment. What you don't know, you can't give away.'

Judith laughed. 'You make it sound as if it's really important. But OK, my lips are sealed. Am I allowed to ask when you might be back?'

'Mid-afternoon, I guess. I'll do the shopping on the way home, and I'll cook dinner too. How's that?'

'Excellent, 007,' she said. 'Give me a kiss.'

Conall Smith was waiting when Sam pulled into the layby where they'd planned to rendezvous. Sam climbed into the rental car beside him.

'Any news from the investigation?' Smith asked.

'Not since Monday night,' said Sam.

'And how did the visit from your nephew go?'

'Fine, thanks. We hadn't seen him for years, all sorts of family problems. He seems to be doing well, something in computers he said. Travels all over.'

'You didn't tell him what we're doing, did you?'

'Of course not,' said Sam.

Smith pulled away, and the blue van that had been parked just behind them pulled away too.

It was a long time since Sam had driven to Barrow. Living where they did Whitehaven was the local town and Barrow seemed a long way, on a road which was notoriously difficult, winding at one point through a farmyard where heavy traffic regularly got stuck or scraped the old barn walls.

After a while, watching from the passenger seat, Sam began to recognise views that reminded him of past times. The slopes of Black Combe loomed to their left and then came the sharp left turn up the Whicham valley and across the River Duddon on the old bridge.

Sam said, 'You know this is the only bridge across the river unless you detour inland for several miles. Everyone travelling by road between Sellafield and the docks at Barrow has to cross the river here. The other road route is so steep and winding that it can't take heavy traffic.

'Nothing surprises me now about this area,' said Smith. 'It's like the land that time forgot.'

'What are we looking for in Barrow, anyway?' Sam asked.

'We have to check out the docks where they bring in the nuclear waste. One of the ships is in, and we're due there around eleven. Then there's the business of getting the stuff onto the train. All those links are potentially problematic, at least that's what I'm told. I'm relying on you to get us to the right place. You used to be stationed here, didn't you?'

'Yes, but thirty years ago. Things have changed, but the docks haven't moved. You can see the nuclear ships from quite a distance. They're white and blue and the colours stand out.'

The view from the main road into the town from the north looked like any other declining northern town with big stores on its outskirts. The high ground between the road and the sea channel to their right could have been natural, but Sam knew it was actually a mountain of slag from the old iron and steel days, grassed over and now a favourite place for dog walking.

Sam directed, and Smith drove on, round a couple of roundabouts.

'What's that big place?' Conall asked, looking at the red sandstone tower that rose over the buildings.

'Town Hall,' said Sam. 'Impressive isn't it. This was a busy important place for a hundred years and more, until iron and steel and shipbuilding all moved overseas and left it behind. Now it's a shadow of itself. If we're going to the docks, we need a road on the right. Here.'

Smith steered the car right at a big junction into an area that looked like something out of an old Soviet film. Red brick blocks of flats stood in severe rows, interspersed with low terraced houses. 'The blocks of flats are tenements,' said Sam, 'flats built round courtyards, like the ones in Glasgow.'

'Do people still live here?'

'Oh, aye,' said Sam. 'They're probably some of the worst housing conditions, worst rates of poverty and illness and premature death. They should have torn them down years ago. I think they keep them as some kind of monument to industry.'

Ahead of them they could see the outline of a ship, gleaming white and blue against the drear grey and terracotta of the streets and the dark sky. 'Looks out of place, doesn't it?' Sam said. 'Did you tell the dock people when to expect us?'

Conall glanced at his watch. 'Right on time,' he said.

There was a gate ahead of them standing half open, and Conall spoke to the man who waved them down, showed him the papers he had, and they were waved on. There were high walls and razor wire on either side. 'Is that it for security?' Conall said. 'This place looks wide open.'

'Nothing of much importance moves by road,' said Sam. 'Everything round the docks moved on rails, then and now. Used to bring workers in by rail, too, when the place was humming.'

'Humming' said Conall. 'Not much of that going on that I can see.'

'Just a fragment of what there was,' Sam agreed. 'But see what you make of the ships and the movement of the waste canisters. Ask them to show you the video of the train crash too.'

'What train crash?'

'The one they set up to test the safety of the canisters they use to carry radioactive material. It was done a few years ago now.'

They were obviously expected and there was an air of complacency as they were shown round the ship that was moored at the dock. Two of every key piece of equipment in case of breakdown, safety systems second to none, the list of features went on and on. Sam could see that Smith was impressed.

'Any worries about the Y2K stuff?' he asked.

The Captain smiled and shook his head. 'We were checking all our computers for those issues months ago. No problem.'

'And security?' asked Smith.

'No worries on that score either,' said the Captain, who was a northerner by the sound of his voice. 'We've been running these ships in and out of this port for many years now and we've got it pretty tight. Transfer of the canisters from ship to train or vice-versa is as fast as possible, and away they go. When we're at sea we're monitored constantly.' He smiled. 'Good ship, safe as houses, we know what we're doing. Best job I ever had.'

'What about security round the docks?' Smith asked.

'Best ask the authorities about that, not me. They use sniffer dogs, I know that, probably trained to detect anything that shouldn't be here. They come on board with them too, it cheers the crew up no end to see them.'

Sam said, 'Can you show us the train crash video?'

The Captain smiled. 'Everyone wants to see that,' he said. 'I think one of my security team should be able to show it you. They show it to people at Sellafield, in that big Visitor Centre place. In fact, the more people realise how safe these canisters are, the better. Makes the people who live here feel safer and warns off anyone who thinks they might be handy things to steal.'

Sam enjoyed the tour, but he still felt the whole exercise was an elaborate waste of time. Some civil servant at the Home Office was ticking things off a list so they could cover their backs if anything untoward actually happened. The security team seemed pleased with the attention they were getting, and they provided a convivial lunch for the two visitors.

On the road back north in the early afternoon Smith glanced frequently into his rear-view mirror. 'Something behind us?' Sam asked.

'There was a blue van I kept seeing as we drove down,' said Smith. 'Nothing particularly sinister about that, seeing that there's only one road into Barrow, but I was wondering whether it would still be around on the way back. I asked the blokes on the security gate at the docks to have a look at the CCTV they have there, just in case. They can let me know when they've had a look. Probably nothing.'

'Is it behind us now?'

'No sign. You get paranoid in this job, even if there's no indication that anything's amiss.'

'Who might be following us?' Sam asked.

'Let's get a cup of tea somewhere and have a think,' said Smith.

There was a food van in a layby just outside Broughton. Steam from their paper mugs fogged the windows of the car. Smith said, 'We need to think about the connections between the case your colleagues are dealing with and what we're up to.' He opened a window a fraction to clear the air. 'The two people who have died in your case both have connections to Sellafield through their work, both have recently been to New York and came back apparently more radical about the environment and suchlike than they were before. Right so far?'

Sam nodded. 'We, on the other hand,' Smith went on, 'are acting on a rumour – that's all it is really – that someone is planning a stunt on New Year's Eve to highlight an issue that's dear to them.'

'A stunt?' Sam said. 'Is that all we're worried about?'

'Who knows? One man's stunt is another man's symbolic gesture. What matters to us is that HMG, who employ both of us, want nothing to happen that might embarrass them. So here we are, checking security procedures that seem to me to be perfectly adequate for purpose. The only thing that's bothered me all day has been that blue van.' He thought for a moment. 'Do you think we've found any serious weak links so far?'

Sam shrugged. 'Not my field. Things look OK to me, but I'm not thinking like a terrorist, or like a Special Branch man either, come to that.'

'Maybe it's the years in Northern Ireland that make me think everywhere else is OK,' said Smith. 'Or else I'm getting soft. Just to be on the safe side, ask your Workington team if they know anything about a blue van, will you? Your DC Pritchard should be able to tell you.'

'OK,' said Sam. 'I was going to ring her tonight anyway.' He finished his coffee and crumpled the empty paper cup in his hand. 'Are you in touch with the other teams round the country who are checking likely places out?'

'Someone will be,' said Smith. 'The lovely Ms Gordon probably.' He turned towards Sam and winked. 'Do you want to talk to her about it?'

Sam frowned. 'No. Do you?'

'Don't want to waste her time as well as ours,' Smith said. 'Actually, I have a call booked with Truelove later this afternoon, to report on everything so far and see what else they want us to do. You're local. Can you think of places round here that might be targets, beyond the places we've already checked?'

Sam shook his head. 'But let me think about it. How long will you be staying in Cockermouth?'

'That depends on Truelove and Gordon. They might decide to send me elsewhere.'

'So, what about me?'

'Let's see. You've been given official leave. Judith still needs your help. Unless your Chief Super insists on your return, I'd stay put. You can keep tabs on what the other investigation is showing up and let me know if anything sounds relevant. There's only a week to Christmas, then the few days run up to New Year's Eve. Things might be clearer by then.'

Smith dropped Sam back at the layby where his car was parked. 'I'll call you later, after I've spoken to Truelove,' Smith said, and he was gone.

Sam looked around. Almost the shortest day of the year and already the sun that had appeared as they drove north was sliding towards the horizon. It felt like a long evening stretching ahead. There was no doubt that Sam was missing the routines of his job and the way it occupied his mind. He would ring Maureen later and ask how life in the real world was developing.

At about the same time in the late afternoon that Sam was arriving home, Bell was doing something that he could and probably should have done earlier in the day, had he not been dealing with the forensic examination of the Toyota found in the carpark. That report might come in before the end of the day, but he didn't wait at Nook Street to find out. Instead he'd headed up to

Carlisle. With any luck, if he could find the delightful barmaid from the Royal, bring her down to the station to do the photofit and then take her home, he might be able to persuade her to make an evening of it.

He parked the car near the station and walked across to the hotel. Pavel from Krakow was not at the reception desk and a woman he'd not seen before looked up and smiled with her mouth but not her eyes. 'Good evening, sir,' she said.

Dinger pulled out his ID and opened it, and the woman took it and examined it closely. 'DC Bell,' she said, 'what can we do for you?'

'One of your barmaids, Mary Brady. I'd like to speak to her please, official business.'

The smile faded. 'I'm afraid Mary isn't here at present,' she said.

Dinger checked his watch. 'Will she be here later this evening, Mrs...?'

'Mrs Tomkinson,' said the woman. She hesitated. 'Would you mind waiting a moment please?'

She turned and went through a door behind her. The partition between reception and the back office was frosted glass and Dinger could see two people facing each other, but he couldn't hear what they were saying.

The door opened again and it was Pavel who emerged. 'Sergeant Bell,' he said, 'you're looking for Mary Brady?'

'Is there a problem?' Bell asked.

'Yes, the problem is that Mary doesn't work here any more. She gave in her notice this afternoon. It was very sudden.'

'Did she give a reason?'

'No, but Mrs Tomkinson tells me that someone came in at about two this afternoon, went straight through to the bar and a few moments later she and Miss Brady came out together. Miss Brady took off her name badge, put it on the desk, said she was leaving, and then walked out with the person.' He smiled. 'Mrs Tomkinson tells me they were both laughing.'

'Can you or Mrs Tomkinson describe this person?' said Dinger.

Mrs Tomkinson was obviously expecting to be summoned. 'A woman,' she said, 'tall, short cropped hair. She was wearing a long black coat, very striking.'

'So, you would know her again?'

'Oh yes, sir,' she said. 'It's one of the things you learn in this job, to remember a face.'

Dinger acted fast. A few phone calls later, he and Eileen Tomkinson were sitting with a photofit technician in Carlisle police station. It wasn't the way DS Bell had planned to spend his evening, but Mrs Tomkinson had demonstrated her excellent memory for faces and the image of the mystery woman was staring out from the page. It was indeed a striking face. High cheek bones, slightly slanting eyes, a strong chin.

'Can you recall anything else about this woman?' Dinger asked.

'Only that as she and Miss Brady walked out, they were talking. I think the woman had an American accent.'

'Is the DCI still around?' Bell asked when he rang Nook Street from the CID room at Carlisle.

'At six?' said the duty sergeant.

'Well, who's still there?'

'The new lad, Sergeant, I think he's still huddled over the computer, and Maureen is just leaving. Do you want me to call her?'

'Sarge,' said Maureen when she came to the phone. 'Are you sure you want to talk to a, what was it, 'fucking feminist'? There's a proper DC, with all the right equipment, on the other side of the office.'

'Don't be sarky, Pritchard,' said Dinger. 'Look, I'm faxing over the photofit of our mystery woman. It's a belter. Put a copy on Skaife's desk, and pin one up on the whiteboard, will you? I want it there first thing.'

'Why can't you do it?'

'I've a missing witness to track down, last seen walking out of the Royal Hotel with, guess who?'

'Not the mystery woman?'

'The very same. It's a long shot, but we need to try the witness's home address.'

'Where is it? And what do you mean by "we"?'

'Wigton. And I mean you, actually. No point in two of us trailing out there, and you're better at that kind of stuff.'

By seven, Sam had finished his supper and picked up the phone to call Maureen at home.

'She's not here, Sam,' said Paddy. 'She rang about an hour ago, said she was going to be late. Something about Wigton. Do you want her to ring you when she gets in?'

'Yes,' said Sam. 'What's at Wigton?'

'No idea,' said Paddy. 'How's your Judith? I hear she broke a leg?'

'Fine, thanks,' said Sam. 'Bye Paddy.'

Sam hung up. Something was going on, and he wanted to be part of it.

Chapter 18

Ten o'clock. Judith was dozing in her chair, her injured leg resting on a stool. Sam looked at his watch and wondered whether Maureen had forgotten to ring him, or how long it would be before she did. Getting Judith to bed would take a while, and he couldn't wait much longer. If she slept too long in the chair, she'd probably wake up grumpy and uncomfortable and would struggle to get back to sleep when she finally got to bed. He thought again about suggesting that he might move into the spare bedroom for a while until she was sleeping better, but he knew that she would think he had finally given up on sex. It was something else they had to talk about, in the conversation that never seemed to happen.

He was just about to wake Judith when the telephone did it for him. He picked it up as quickly as he could, and Judith turned slightly before dropping back to sleep. Sam took the phone into the front room and closed the door.

'Are you there, Sam?' Maureen said.

'Yes, trying not to wake Judith.'

'Is she OK?'

'Yes, basically, but she's fed up with the leg problem. So, come on, has something happened? I was expecting you to call ages ago.'

'Where to start?' Maureen said. 'Look, are you busy tomorrow morning, early? It would take too long tonight to explain, and if you can get away I could catch you up properly over breakfast somewhere, before I go into work.'

'Is that OK with you, you've had a long day obviously.'

'I'd rather do that than keep both of us away from our beds now.'

'OK,' he said. 'Let's do it properly at that café near the harbour in Maryport.'

'That's twice as far for you than for me,' said Maureen. 'Are you sure boss?'

'Absolutely,' said Sam, 'and it's my shout. They open at eight, I'll see you there.'

The Harbourside café was exactly that, perched on South Quay overlooking the small harbour in Maryport. The town was smaller than Whitehaven but it had a history stretching back further, exemplified in the rows of sandstone Roman memorial plaques in the museum on the site of the Roman fort on the cliffs. As Sam approached the café they were just opening up.

'You must be hungry,' said the woman in an apron. 'Two of you? Anywhere you like, I'll be with you in a minute.'

They took a table by the window. Maureen was pleased to see him and said so. 'I'm not going to ask about what you're up to,' she said, 'but I hope it's not for long. Very tense at work, needless to say.'

'Dinger seems to thrive on it,' said Sam. 'Always did.'

'Well, he creates most of it himself,' Maureen said. 'Mind you, give him his due, he's working hard on this one. That's where I was last night.'

'Where?'

'Wigton. Dinger went looking for the barmaid at the Royal in Carlisle, to get her to do a photofit. When he got there about five last night she'd gone, a couple of hours earlier. Packed in the job and walked out, happy as Larry according to the boss. Remind you of anyone?'

'Sandy Evans?'

'Exactly. And the description of the woman she was with matched with the woman Anne-Marie saw with Sandra in Carlisle.'

'Hang on a minute,' said Sam. 'I've been out of this loop for a few days.'

Sam had time to catch up while they waited for their breakfasts, full English for Maureen, porridge and toast for Sam, and Maureen took him back through the various stages of the investigation. 'So,' Sam said, 'now we think that young Bramall and Evans met this person in New York, and it was she who called at Evans' flat in Whitehaven and was seen with her in Carlisle, right?' Maureen nodded. 'And now this same woman has lured the barmaid away as well. Sounds like a female Pied Piper.'

'And don't forget about the people who saw a tall person that could have been female with Bramall near where he was run over.'

'What about the Toyota?' Sam asked. 'If this woman was driving, there should be some traces.'

'Nothing yet. Forensics reckoned the car had been cleaned up by someone who knew what they were doing, but they're still looking. The DCI wasn't happy, told Forensics to try harder. I think he's bothered about Bramall senior complaining.'

Sam poured himself another cup of tea from the huge pot that sat on the table between them. 'So, that brings us up to last night. What were you doing in Wigton?'

'Dinger got the barmaid's home address.'

'Barmaid's name?'

'Mary Brady. It was a couple of hours since she'd left work, so he reckoned that was the first place to check. Dinger asked me to go out there.'

'That was noble of you,' said Sam, 'considering the spat you had the other day.'

'I don't trust the bloke,' she said. 'He takes risks and wants to take the credit for everything. I reckon he's after your job.'

'That thought crossed my mind too. Skaife finally quits, I bump up to his job and Dinger goes for mine. He's halfway there now that Skaife made him Acting DI, and he must be betting on Findale moving on.'

'Rob won't stay long,' said Maureen. 'Too quiet for him here. And Dinger winds him up all the time.'

'Did you find the barmaid?' Sam asked.

'No, or I would have more to tell you. No sign of her at home. Her mum said when she got home from work just before six Mary's room was a mess. Clothes, personal stuff, a big holdall all missing. No note.'

'What about Mary's mum, what did she think?'

'Not a lot. She said Mary used the place more like a lodging house than a home. Came and went at all hours. I think Mum would be glad to see the back of her.'

'Any idea where Mary might have gone, or about this woman?'

'All she said was that Mary had seemed quite distracted the past few weeks, nothing more than that. I don't think there was much mother-daughter sharing going on.'

'We need to go back to her and have a proper look at the girl's room. If she left in a hurry, there might be something worth finding.' He finished the last of his porridge and pushed the bowl away. 'So, what did you do next?'

'Checked with the neighbours. No CCTV out there.'

'Any joy?'

'Only one of the neighbours had seen anything. A van parked outside the Brady's about half five. He thought it must be a delivery and didn't take much notice. It wasn't there more than a few minutes.'

Sam was buttering a piece of toast and stopped. 'A van? Any details?'

'Hard to see the colour in those funny streetlights. First the chap said black and then he changed his mind. Blue, he said. Dark blue. There was a blue van stolen from the carpark where the Toyota was dumped.'

Sam sat back. 'Did the neighbour see anyone? The driver?'

'No, but I'm pretty sure it'll be the same woman who was with Brady at the hotel.

'Tall, short hair, American accent?'

'Yep.'

Sam asked, 'Have you got a phone number for Brady's home in Wigton?'

Maureen took out her notebook and scribbled a number on a paper napkin. Sam put it in his pocket. 'Anything else?' he asked. He left his toast uneaten and called to the woman for the bill.

'I think that's it so far,' Maureen said, watching Sam's reaction. 'More forensics on the Toyota still to come, and now a full-on search for the barmaid. We've got a photofit of the tall woman from the woman at the hotel. Dinger faxed it through last night. It's a good one. Skaife should have it by now.'

'Right,' said Sam, reaching into his pocket for the money to pay for their food. 'Got to go. Thanks for the information. Can you keep this to yourself for a while, an hour or two?'

'OK,' said Maureen. 'You'll call me, right?'

'When I can,' said Sam. 'Bye.'

Mercifully there was a good mobile phone signal. Back in the car, Sam called Conall Smith.

'You know that blue van you saw behind us yesterday? Any news on it?'

'Still waiting to hear from the blokes at the security gate at the docks. Why?'

'Where are you?' Sam asked.

'At my digs in Cockermouth, just finishing breakfast.'

'Stay there,' Sam said. 'I'll be with you in twenty minutes or so. See if you can talk to the security gate guys before then.'

'What have you got?' Smith asked.

'Not sure yet. But we need to talk.'

Smith was out at the front of the guest house smoking a cigarette when Sam arrived.

'Housekeeping's in my room already,' said Conall. 'OK if we talk out here?'

'In the car,' said Sam.

'OK, what's up?' said Smith as the two men sat side by side. The acrid smell of the cigarette lingered and Sam rolled down the window. 'Any word about the blue van?'

Smith checked his watch. 'I'm calling back in ten minutes. They were still checking the CCTV.'

'It may be a coincidence, but I don't think so,' said Sam. 'The car that ran down young James Bramall was a Toyota. It turned up in a carpark in Carlisle and a blue van was stolen at the same time. Nook Street will have the number for it, but I haven't checked yet. What if that same blue van was the one you saw behind us yesterday?'

Smith said nothing for a moment, then turned towards Sam. He looked puzzled. 'You think the person involved with your murders is now following us as well? What about those pics I sent you?'

'All male. No use. But now we have a photofit of this woman.'
'Where?'
'DCI Skaife has it and we need a copy.'

'I'll make that call to the security blokes at the docks,' said Smith. He did. Smith said into the phone, 'It approached the gate and then just turned round?…Did you get the reg?…OK, give us what you could see.'

He fumbled for his notebook with his free hand and scribbled down letters and numbers. 'OK, thanks,' he said. 'If you see that van again, contact me right away. OK, bye.'

Smith waved the notebook and smiled. 'Partial plate but should be enough given what else we have.' He punched numbers on the phone and waited. 'DCI Skaife, please… Do you know where he is?… OK, could you get a message to him and tell him that DS Smith will meet him there in…' he looked at Sam.

'Where?' Sam asked.

'Axelby,'

'Great,' said Sam. 'Two birds with one stone. Ten minutes.'

'Ten minutes,' said Smith into the phone.

'OK,' said Smith. 'If Skaife's one of these birds, who's the other one?'

'Bramall senior, at Axelby Hall,' said Sam. 'I told you a while ago that both our fatalities had links with Sellafield. Maybe Bramall senior could tell us if James was involved in anything that the ELF might be interested in.'

'What's Skaife doing there, do we know?'

'Keeping his old pal in the loop, I should think. Those two know each other from way back.'

'He might think we're treading on his toes,' said Smith. 'But it may be time for a reminder about his instructions about this case.'

❖ ❖ ❖

'Good morning, Sergeant,' said Edward Bramall as Mrs Harvey the housekeeper ushered Sam and Smith into the sitting room at Axelby Hall. 'Shall I bring coffee?' said Mrs Harvey. 'Yes, for four, thank you, Audrey,' said Bramall, gesturing to the new arrivals to sit down. DCI Skaife did not look pleased to see them.

'DCI Skaife has kindly dropped in to provide an update on the investigation into my son's death,' said Bramall. 'DS Tognarelli I know of course, but you are…' he said looking at Smith. Conall Smith stood up, 'Conall Smith, I'm from the Met, helping with your son's case,' he said, extending his hand. Sam was impressed with how easily Smith managed the lie.

'The Met, goodness,' said Bramall, shaking Smith's hand. 'You didn't tell me they were involved, Arthur.'

Skaife looked uncomfortable. 'The Chief Superintendent briefed us last week on the big picture,' he said, 'and Mr Smith is working up here for the time being.'

Bramall looked at Smith again. 'And what has this "big picture" as you call it got to do with the death of my son? I agreed to meet the DCI here for a specific purpose, and if you don't need me, I should get to work.' He checked his watch. 'I'm already very late.'

Sam leaned forward. 'With your permission, sir, some explanation is in order, if I may provide it.'

Skaife looked at Smith who nodded.

'Very well,' said Bramall. 'I hope it doesn't take too long.'

Sam said, 'It's possible, sir that your son James's death is connected to a wider investigation. There are some details involved that are covered by the Official Secrets Act.'

'And so is most of my work, Sergeant,' said Bramall.

'Of course,' said Sam, 'so you will appreciate that this meeting is included in that.'

'Get to the point, man,' said Bramall.

Sam wished he'd had longer to work out how to approach the interview. He thought Smith should be leading, but Smith was clearly leaving it to him. Sam said, 'Sir, can you explain to us the main projects Bramall Engineering are involved in at Sellafield?'

Bramall frowned. 'I fail to see what that has to do with my son.'

Sam tried again. 'The investigation that DS Smith and I are pursuing involves a possible threat to security at Sellafield. One of the people that your son was involved with, the person who may have been driving the car that killed James, may be part of that security threat.'

Bramall looked at Skaife. 'Arthur?'

Before Skaife could respond there was a tap on the door. Bramall roared 'Come,' and Mrs Harvey pushed a trolley into the room bearing all the makings of fresh coffee for four. Bramall waved Mrs Harvey away and poured the coffee himself before turning his attention back to Sam.

'Let me get this straight, Sergeant. You're suggesting that my son was killed because he was part of some plot or other? Ridiculous. James would have nothing to do with anything like that. He wasn't,' he hesitated, 'he wasn't in a position to be of use to anyone. He occupied quite a lowly position in our firm, and would have done for a while at least. In time, perhaps…' He stopped.

'Forgive me, sir,' said Sam. 'His name, his connection with you, might have been interpreted differently by others. They might have assumed that he had more access to confidential information than was the case.' He paused. 'We have heard from some of James's friends that he tended to exaggerate sometimes, to make himself sound more important, perhaps to impress people.'

Sam was expecting a denial from Bramall, but the old man hung his head before he responded. 'As I recall telling you myself, Sergeant, my son was very immature. My wife indulged him, I'm afraid. James always wanted to make himself sound important. I hoped he would grow out of it, but…' He looked at Sam, 'You're implying that James boasted about his place in the firm and attracted someone who was hatching some kind of plot? With all due respect, that sounds pretty far-fetched.'

Sam glanced at Smith, who raised his eyebrows, and Sam took this as a hint he should carry on. 'I asked you what the main Bramall Engineering project is at Sellafield. Could you tell us that?'

Bramall sat back. 'If you must know, we're involved in the decommissioning of the old no. 1 reactor stack.'

'The one that was involved in the 1957 fire?'

'Yes. It was badly irradiated at that time. The plan to decommission and remove it has been under consideration for some time. It's too contaminated to be demolished in any conventional way.'

Sam turned to Smith. 'The reactor stack is part of the Sellafield skyline,' he said. 'It has a very distinctive shape, with the filters on the outside, like a cap on the top. It can be seen for miles around.' Smith nodded. He understood what Sam was saying, that the stack might be attractive to anyone wanting to make a symbolic gesture about the perils of nuclear power.

'Was James involved in this project?' Sam asked Bramall.

'No, he wasn't.'

'But knowing James's habit for self-promotion,' Sam continued, 'it's possible that he might have bragged about being involved?'

Bramall shook his head. 'It's possible.'

Skaife said, 'I've been updating Mr Bramall about some of the developments, and how we're gathering fresh evidence.'

There was an awkward silence. Edward Bramall threw up his hands. 'For God's sake, what's going on? Why aren't you out looking for whoever ran my son down like a dog in the street instead of sitting here drinking my coffee?'

Skaife got to his feet. 'I think we've intruded on the Bramalls quite long enough,' he said. He turned to Edward Bramall. 'My apologies, Edward. Please thank Mrs Harvey for the coffee.'

'She made it, I paid for it,' said Edward Bramall. He was on his feet now, walking towards the door which he opened wide. 'I trust that when you people have done your jobs properly,' he said, 'you'll be able to make more sense. I'm only glad James's mother wasn't here to listen to such idle speculation before the poor boy is even buried.'

They filed out, Skaife hanging behind to apologise again to Bramall. Sam and Smith waited for him by the car, their backs to the house. Sam knew that Skaife would be angry, and he was.

'Well?' the DCI said, looking first at Smith and then at Sam.

'Perhaps we need to talk somewhere else,' Smith said. 'Mr Bramall clearly wants to see the back of us.'

'There's a layby on the main road, right at the end of the drive,' said Sam. 'We can talk there.'

Still without a word, DCI Skaife got into his car and drove away up the drive, with Sam and Smith following behind.

Chapter 19

Skaife got out of his car in the layby and marched towards them. 'This better be good, Sergeant,' he said to Sam. 'I'm in no mood for the conspiracy babble you dished out back there. What the hell's going on?'

'We needed to ask Mr Bramall if James could have been involved in any high-security projects at work. Someone wanted to befriend him, and then killed him, and we need to know why,' said Sam. 'And of course, we wouldn't want to interview Mr Bramall without involving you.'

'Don't try and butter me up, Sergeant,' said Skaife. 'And don't waste my time with pointless meetings with a busy man who's lost his son and is wondering what we're doing about it. I've told you before that Acting DI Bell and I are managing very nicely, thank you.'

'And that's another thing,' Skaife said, his anger showing in his face. 'Clearly someone is telling you about our investigation. I'm guessing that it's DC Pritchard, is that right? You've no right to go behind my back to one of my officers.'

'That's my fault, sir,' said Sam. 'I asked DC Pritchard for information. I pulled rank, it's my doing, not hers.'

'What information?' Skaife said.

This time Smith responded. 'We understand there's a photofit of a woman who was seen with Bramall at a hotel in Carlisle. We need to see it. And the registration number of a blue van that was stolen in Carlisle. Could we have that too?'

Before Skaife could object, Smith said, 'We can't explain why these are both important, I'm afraid. Can you fax them to DI Tognareli, at home, please?' He wrote the number on a page of his notebook, tore out the page and gave it to Skaife, who peered at the unfamiliar number.

'You're saying this is vital for your work?'

Smith nodded. 'Yes, it is. I know my bosses will want us to have it.'

Skaife frowned, but Sam could see that he understood. He said nothing more, got into his car and drove away.

Sam and Smith looked at each other.

'Oh dear,' said Sam. 'It seemed like a good idea to meet the DCI here with Bramall, but now I seem to have pissed them both off. I'm not very good at navigating these things.'

'I can see that,' said Smith. 'Let's hope Skaife comes through with that photofit. Can we go to your house to pick it up? Will that be OK with your wife?'

Fortunately, Judith was already up and dressed and the house looked reasonably tidy when Sam and Smith arrived. Bill was so excited to see Sam home that he had to be put outside to calm down. Conall Smith introduced himself. 'The man from the Met,' said Judith, smiling. 'Good to put a face to the name.'

'We're expecting a fax,' said Sam. 'I'll take Conall into the other room, out of your way. Can you give me a shout when it arrives?'

'Do you want coffee?' she asked.

Sam shook his head. 'We've just had some, thanks.'

Sam was trying to explain to Smith about the tensions within Workington CID when Judith knocked on the door and handed over some papers without a word, closing the door again behind her. Sam spread the papers on the small table.

'Looks like I was right about the van,' said Smith. 'The partial from the CCTV at the docks matches the van that was stolen. We have the details of the original owner but that's not much help.' He looked at the photofit. 'This looks as if it might be a good likeness,' he said, 'Distinctive.'

'The woman who supplied it works at the hotel in Carlisle,' said Sam. 'She's obviously good with faces. Does it ring any bells?'

Smith shook his head. 'Not with me but might need to check with the FBI. We need more details, not just a face and a vague description.' He thought for a moment. 'Can we get any more information from Skaife about the barmaid?'

Sam smiled. 'I think I may be "persona non grata". Maybe leave that for a while.'

'What do we do about the van?'

'Wait, that's all we can do. It's a stolen vehicle. Skaife will want it found for his own investigation.'

Smith leaned back in the armchair. 'I'm curious about the effect that the tall woman seems to have on the people she meets. Evans was obviously very taken with her, and now this barmaid has followed her off somewhere.'

'You think there's some kind of sisterhood going on?' Sam asked, smiling.

'Don't you? Two women gladly give up their jobs at the drop of a hat when this charismatic person turns up. The barmaid, what's her name?'

'Mary Brady?' said Sam.

'Mary must have known the tall woman before that chance encounter in the hotel. Surely Dinger asked her about that?'

'She'd have lied, wouldn't she?' said Sam, 'and then got out quick before anyone twigged that she was involved.'

'But involved in what?' Smith said. 'We still have no idea.'

'It must be the Earth Liberation Front,' said Sam. 'Their followers don't necessarily know each other, but they could recognise each other somehow and the bonds would be pretty strong. It's hard to imagine putting absolute trust in someone after just a few code words, but it could happen.'

'And so the sisterhood grows,' said Smith. 'Who's next, I wonder? Judith, maybe?'

Sam laughed. 'Judith has a questioning and sceptical nature, thank God,' he said. 'I promised I'd take her out today if the weather was OK, and Bill needs a walk. Just down the path to the beach. Want to come?'

The wind had swung round to the south and the air was less cold than it had been earlier in the week. Even in the middle of the day the sun was low in the sky, but it was still bright with the light reflected off the incoming tide.

'Were you brought up by the sea?' Judith asked Conall as he helped Sam with the wheelchair.

'Ballycastle? Wonderful beach,' he said, 'but I don't get back there often. London has its pleasures but a sight like this isn't one of them.'

'How long will you stay up here?' she asked. Sam hoped she wouldn't be too nosy.

'Not sure,' said Conall. 'I need to talk to my bosses. I'm hoping to get to Ireland for a few days at Christmas and then come back before New Year.'

'We'll be here,' she said. 'With a visitor this year, that'll be fun. He's coming back for New Year too, isn't he Sam?'

'We'll see,' said Sam. 'Can we leave you here for a few minutes Judith, while Conall and I stretch our legs a bit and Bill gets a bit more exercise? Are you warm enough?'

She snuggled into the big coat and scarf. 'Snug as a bug in a rug, but don't be long.'

Out of earshot, Sam said, 'Should we put the Sellafield reactor stack on our list of potential targets?'

'We could, but it's protected as well as the rest of the site. Those guys are armed, with dogs, several layers of security. I can't see that being breached without some pretty heavy armoury and that's not what these "Elves" are about, as far as I can see.'

'So what do we have?'

Smith shrugged. 'Not a lot. We have the possibility that James Bramall's boasting about his role at Sellafield might have made him interesting to the ELF people, and that his big mouth also got him killed. That doesn't explain anything about Sandra Evans, or what the tall woman is up to.'

'We need a name for her,' said Sam. 'Can't keep calling her the tall woman.'

'Leave that with me,' said Smith. 'Now we have a good likeness we could make progress with identification. I'll get on to that this afternoon. Who's going to be looking for the barmaid?'

'Skaife will decide about that. Maureen might not be involved directly, but she'll be able to keep us updated. I'll have to be careful what I ask her to do now that Skaife's on to her.'

They walked back to Judith. 'Just in time,' she said. 'Too cold out here for sitting still.'

❖ ❖ ❖

The smell of bacon that lingered in Mrs Brady's kitchen in Wigton made Maureen Pritchard hungry. 'Sorry I was a bit late,' she said. 'I had to go all the way into work just to turn round and come back here. I live in Aspatria, could have been here in ten minutes.'

Mrs Brady stood, hands on hips, resenting the intrusion. 'Look,' she said, 'I should be at work. I called in sick this morning to meet you here 'cos I didn't want them knowing my business. It may be a charity shop, but they're not particularly charitable, pretending to care about you when it's an excuse for being nosy.'

'Just a few questions,' said Maureen.

'Well, if you want to know where our Mary's gone, I can't help you. We moved here together a few years ago because we all wanted to get away from Dublin, but we haven't had much of a conversation about anything recently, since she came back.'

'Came back from where?'

'Down south, Brighton, for the summer. Bar work and clubs, and getting well away from here. She's always had itchy feet.'

'When did she get back?'

'October, near the end. Just turned up, no warning, you know what they're like. Have you got kids?'

'Aye,' said Maureen, 'just the one, he's in London. He couldn't wait to get away too.'

'Come home often, does he?'

'No, not often. He needs to be where the work is.'

'And when she does get home,' Mrs Brady went on, 'it's like she just lodges here. Comes and goes as she pleases, cooks for herself, all that veggie stuff, sits in her room. Like we're not good enough for her any more. It drives her dad crazy, but if he tries to say anything she just shouts at him. Even worse since she went to Brighton. Feels like she despises us now.' She poured water into the kettle and set it on the stove. 'To be honest with you, I'd not be sorry if she's gone off down south again.'

'Can I have a look at her room, Mrs Brady?'

'Help yourself, love. At the back upstairs, on the right. It's even more of a tip than usual. If you find any teaspoons up there, can you bring them down?'

Maureen pushed open the door of the small bedroom and stood looking around. The wardrobe was open and empty hangers hung there, with more on the bed. Half a dozen in all, so not many clothes taken. Drawers were open, one of them almost empty, underwear probably. She stepped across the littered floor to the bedside table, pulling on her plastic gloves. Nothing much there, no drug works or pills. She opened the drawer. A box of tissues, a small mirror, some eye drops. Whatever exciting things happened in Mary Brady's life, it looked as if they happened elsewhere.

In the wardrobe was a shoulder strap that probably belonged to a holdall, but the bag itself was missing. Most of the clothes still hanging on the rail were black. A lonely pair of high heels, hardly worn. Maureen looked around the room again. No photos. In fact, the room had no personal traces of the person who had inhabited it. Skaife would probably insist on forensics taking a look but Maureen doubted they would find anything interesting. She left the room untouched and went downstairs.

'Did Mary ever bring friends home?' she asked, watching Mrs Brady pull washing out of the machine.

'Not since she was at primary school in Dublin, before we moved here. She was fourteen then, went to high school here.'

'What did she do after she left school?'

'College in Carlisle for a year or so, but then she dropped out, started doing bar work as soon as she was old enough, in Carlisle again. The train's handy, you know, she could get around. Started stopping out late, not coming home at all sometimes.'

'Any trouble with drugs?'

Mrs Brady sniffed. 'If there was, we never saw anything. She smoked, you could smell that a mile off. Filthy habit.'

'What about politics?'

'Politics? You mean elections and such?'

'Well, you know, issues, women's rights, saving the planet, that kind of stuff.'

Mrs Brady rolled her eyes. 'You wouldn't believe the lecturing me and her dad had to put up with, especially the past few months. On and on, in the end her dad just told her straight, "Shut up or get out." That's why I'm not surprised she's gone. It's been brewing for a while.'

Maureen said, 'The people at the hotel said that a woman was with Mary when she packed in her job and walked out. A tall woman, short dark hair, quite mannish by the sound of it. Any idea who that might be?'

'No one I know,' said Mrs Brady, 'but Mary did mention some woman she'd met, another of these tree hugger types. Ursula this, Ursula that.'

'Ursula who?'

'No idea, and I didn't ask. Who's called 'Ursula' these days? Sounds so old-fashioned.'

'And this was just after Mary got back from Brighton?'

'Aye. Do you think this tall woman might be her?'

Maureen shook her head. 'Can't discuss that, sorry. Are you worried about Mary, Mrs Brady? Do you think she might have come to harm?'

'To be honest, I think she's been itching to leave for a while. She's been away before, for months at a time. If she needs help, she'd probably ask us, but she can look after herself.'

She shrugged. 'What can you do? You raise them, and they leave.'

Maureen nodded.

'I have to report to my boss, Mrs Brady. It's just possible that he'll want some people to search Mary's room properly.'

'Do what you want,' she said. 'It can't get any messier than it is now.'

Back in the car, Maureen radioed in, and spoke to DCI Skaife. 'There's nothing at Brady's home to indicate that she's been coerced into leaving. No drugs in evidence, no signs of violence, beyond the room being a tip. Mother says there were arguments, I think she's glad Mary's gone.'

Skaife said, 'Any mention of radical views?'

'Yes, ranting about the planet and all that, but that's not uncommon with young people these days, is it? It was worse after she got back from Brighton in October.'

'Brighton? What was she doing there?'

'Bar work, hanging around.'

'Do we need forensics?'

'Might be worth checking for prints or traces that could belong to that woman Mary was with.'

Skaife said, 'Have you checked with your drug contacts about where Bramall and Evans might have got their supplies?'

'I'll do that now. Has the missing blue van turned up yet?'

'No,' said Skaife. 'Every lead seems to be going cold. That photofit of the tall woman was a breakthrough, but no one seems to know who she is. We're putting out feelers overseas, following the American accent, but that takes time. Briefing at five-thirty, OK?'

Maureen wondered how much Skaife knew about whatever Sam was doing. If he knew that she was in touch with Sam, he was keeping very quiet about it. What on earth are they all up to, she wondered. And where is Mary Brady?

❖ ❖ ❖

In a small rented holiday cottage overlooking the Solway, a fire was crackling in the open hearth and the smell of frying bacon hung in the air.

Mary Brady looked at the bacon sandwich on the plate in front of her. 'Don't tell anyone about this,' she said. 'I'm veggie most of the time but never could resist bacon.' She bit into the sandwich and closed her eyes. 'Some ketchup would have been good.'

The woman standing at the sink turned and laughed. 'I thought it was just Americans who cover everything in ketchup.'

'Not everything,' said Mary, her mouth full. 'Just bacon sandwiches.'

'The bacon's different here too,' said the woman. 'I'm used to it being very thin, not meaty like that stuff you bought.'

Mary took another bite of her sandwich. 'This is real bacon like we used to have at my gran's. It has to be chewy, not just crumble away to nothing. If you were staying longer, you'd get used to it.' She looked across at the woman. 'How long are you staying?'

The woman shrugged. 'As long as it takes.'

'To do what?'

'To do what I came to do. I may have to go back to Brighton after that, but I'll need to be careful. I'm not sure what Special Branch have on me, or the FBI, but someone will be checking.'

'That wig makes a difference,' Mary said. 'Take it off. Let me see if I'd recognise you.'

The woman took off the blonde wig and ran long fingers through her own short black hair. 'It itches,' she said. 'I'll leave it off for a while.'

Mary licked her fingers. 'They won't find us here, will they?'

'They'll still be looking for a blue van, and that won't be easy to find,' said the woman. 'We got here after dark, and the Landrover we picked up is in the shed, out of sight. That was lucky, wasn't it, to be able to swap cars so easily.'

Mary pouted. 'It wasn't luck. I told you where to find that Landrover, and where to dump the van. You see, I'm useful, not just a hanger-on.'

The woman put her arms round Mary. 'Of course, you're not just a hanger-on. Everyone in the movement is useful, we all have a part to play. And now we have transport for a few days at least.' She stood back. 'What about me? Do I look different enough?'

'The wig helps, that's for sure,' said Mary, 'but can you do something about the way you walk?'

'You mean, walk like this?' She demonstrated, walking round the small kitchen like Quasimodo and Mary couldn't help but laugh.

'What about your mum?' said the woman.

'She hasn't got a clue. I never tell her anything.'

'Not even when you got back from Brighton?'

'No, as far as she was concerned, I went down there looking for work and came back at the end of the summer. So long as I gave her some money for rent, she never asked.' She hesitated. 'Was it you who suggested that Jim and Sandra should stay at the Royal?'

'Yep,' the woman said. 'It seemed obvious when you got the job there. Then I could meet up with all three of you.'

'Jim really was an idiot,' said Mary. 'Such a loudmouth. When there were other people around in the bar, I was always afraid he would start spouting something, draw attention to us. Sandra was constantly having to quieten him down.' She was silent for a moment. 'What happened to them, you never said?'

'Don't ask,' she said. 'It was a mess, but unavoidable. What did that pig policeman say?'

'Just that they were dead.'

'That's all you need to know.'

The woman scratched her head again and pulled the wig back on. 'I'm going out for a bit, just down to the shore. Are you coming? Wear your coat with the hood up. You never know who's around.'

They walked along the muddy shoreline, the far side of the Solway just a smudge across the grey water. 'When will your friend get here?' Mary asked.

'Sometime over the weekend, probably. Just a quick visit to see how things are going, before I go to Glasgow.'

'Do you trust him?'

'As much as I trust anyone. We go back a long way, and he's useful to us right now.' She took Mary's arm and they stood together watching birds that scurried across the sand and pebbles, camouflaged by dappled feathers.

Back at the cottage, darkness folded round them. They lit candles and stoked up the fire with wood off the beach that fizzed and spat. Mary fell asleep lying on the settee, her legs bent like a baby in the womb. The woman watched her closely, wondering, thinking about Sandra and her unborn child. Such a disappointment that had been, so unnecessary, so complicated. Sandra knew that Jim Bramall was a liability and would have to be silenced. So why the tears, the remorse? Had she overdosed on purpose? Probably not, just careless. When she'd got into the flat by the back door and found Sandy deeply asleep it hadn't taken much heroin to make sure that she would never wake up. Just one less complication to worry about, Ursula said to herself, and so easy. People were expendable after all. The journal could have been a problem, but she'd found it in the end.

Mary was sound asleep. The woman went upstairs to the bedroom where Mary's bag sat on the floor, contents scattered around. She went through everything, checking all the pockets.

No phone, no camera, no notebook or diary. The girl left no footprint. She'd give her a couple of days. If all was well, she might survive. If not, no one would hear a scream or a shot. Or it could be quiet, like Sandra. So easy.

Chapter 20

The five-thirty briefing at Nook Street added still more details to the whiteboard. Since the blue van had been spotted outside the Brady house there'd been no more sightings.

'They could have dumped that one and stolen another,' said Findale.

'Carruthers,' said Skaife, 'check all cars reported stolen in north Cumbria over the past twenty-four hours, and put out an alert for sightings of the blue van. If it's found, get forensics in. This woman may be good at covering her tracks but we have to hope she gets careless.'

Maureen reported on the conversation with Mrs Brady, and Bell added "Ursula?" to the board, alongside the photofit. 'We can't assume that's her real name,' he said. 'Check with your FBI contact, Findale, see if it rings any bells.'

'I had a message from him,' said Rob Findale. 'He said that one of his bosses had taken it on and he couldn't tell me anything.'

Bell snorted. 'So much for the Met and its worldwide links.'

Skaife frowned. 'Leave the FBI connection with me,' he said. 'And I'll check with the Met, or the Brighton police. They might have something.'

'If Mary Brady and this woman have gone back to Brighton,' said Marion Sharp, 'they could have gone on the train.'

'Check with the stations, DC Sharp,' said Skaife. 'Two women, one distinctively tall, travelling together. It's a long shot. Having their own transport makes more sense.'

The briefing broke up in an air of irritation. Other work that had been put on hold now demanded attention as the major enquiry faltered. Skaife went back to his office fuming that the case he'd put himself in charge of was going nowhere.

Bell knocked on his door. 'Sir,' he said, 'I'm not sure how much further we can go with this one if nothing else turns up.'

Skaife was irritated. 'Do you think I don't know that, Sergeant? Is that all you've got to offer?'

'You do know that Pritchard is telling DS Tognarelli everything that's going on?'

'Yes, I know that too. I can hardly prevent her from talking to him.'

'I could tell her to lay off, sir. She's been around a long time, sometimes forgets she's only a DC.'

Skaife looked at the short podgy man in front of him. 'DS Bell,' said the DCI. 'When I want your help with managing my team of officers, I'll let you know. In the meantime, do your job, and get this enquiry moving. That means thinking about your own activity, Sergeant, not everyone else's. Understood?'

'Yes, sir,' said Bell, and he turned and walked out without waiting to be dismissed.

'Miserable git,' Bell muttered as he went back to the CID room. The two computer-mad DCs were perched side-by-side in front of the screen. 'Right lads,' he said. 'The DCI wants answers on the whereabouts of this blue van. Presumably it was in Carlisle when that stupid barmaid left with Lanky Ursula, and then they went to Wigton, to the barmaid's house. Check all the

CCTV you can find on the route they would have taken, petrol stations, the lot.'

Carruthers looked at his watch.

'Yes, now Bob,' said Dinger. 'Don't whine on about the time. I don't care how long it takes, just do it.'

❖ ❖ ❖

At the Solway cottage, the expected visitor arrived just as the day began to dawn on Saturday morning, parking his car behind the building where it couldn't be seen from the road. He let himself in. Mary was still in bed upstairs. The tall woman crept down quietly when she heard the door. 'Fernando,' she said. 'Come here.'

The two hugged for a long time before the woman pulled away. 'Our friend Mary's upstairs,' she said. 'We'll try not to wake her. Are you hungry? Can you wait a while for breakfast?'

'Just tea for now,' he said. 'I'll need to sleep later. I left about two, easy drive with the roads emptier.'

He went to the bottom of the stairs and listened. 'Do you want to check on her? We need to talk. How much does she know?'

The woman smiled. 'Nothing. She was so pleased to get out of that job and away from her mother that she's not really asked me anything. The policeman who came checking at the hotel told her that Jim and Sandy were both dead, but that's all she knows. I told her we have things to do and can't afford people getting in the way.'

'Is she frightened?'

The woman shook her head. 'I don't think so. She trusts me. And she calls me Ursula, by the way, so you should too.'

'What have you told her about me?'

'Nothing, except you're an old friend called Fernando.'

He reached for her. 'An old friend or a lover?' He kissed her, holding her very tight, his hand pressing her hips into him.

'We have to be careful,' she said, pulling back.

'I've missed you.'

'Well, you might have to wait, just a few more days. Once it's done, we can disappear again, anywhere we like.'

'What if it goes wrong?'

She smiled. 'It won't.'

They heard the stairs creak and Mary stood in the doorway. She was rubbing her eyes, wearing a long shirt, her legs bare.

'Is this him?' she asked.

'Mary,' said the woman, 'this is Fernando. I told you about him, he's one of us and an old friend.'

'I'm Mary Brady,' said the girl. 'Is that your real name?'

Fernando raised his eyebrows. Ursula laughed. 'Tea?' she said.

'It's nearly Christmas,' said Mary later that morning. Fernando was asleep upstairs and Ursula was reading. 'What am I going to do when you go away? I don't want to stay here on my own.'

Ursula looked up. 'You knew that I would be going away,' she said. 'I told you what this life would be like. There will be times of confusion and anxiety, and loneliness.'

Mary looked away, out of the window towards the flat plain of the Solway estuary and the Scottish shore beyond. 'I know that, but you get to do things and I don't. I thought I might come to Glasgow with you.'

Ursula shook her head. 'Impossible. I have people to see and things to do that you can't be part of. I have to go alone. Not even Fernando can come with me.'

'So, do I have to stay here?'

'They'll be looking for you, won't they? That nasty policeman has probably been back to the hotel to ask you more questions and they'll know you left with me. What did he ask you, by the way?'

Mary smiled. 'He asked me if I'd ever seen you there before. Well, he was so rude that I just said 'No' and didn't explain that I knew you in Brighton.'

'Good. Look, Mary, I'm used to avoiding being seen but you're new to all this. If you try to get away from here now, they'll find you, and put pressure on you to tell them about me, about all of us. It'll only be until the beginning of January. After that it won't matter.'

Mary was adamant. 'If they find me, I won't say anything, you know I won't.'

Ursula got up and stood next to the young woman, a hand on her shoulder. 'I can't be sure of that. This isn't personal, it's political. Our lives are political. We believe in things beyond ourselves, things that drive us on. We can't let anything get in the way.'

'I know that,' Mary insisted. 'How long is that man staying? It's awkward having him here.'

Ursula bent to look into the young face. 'We all do what we need to do. We don't have to explain things to each other. I need to be sure I can trust you.'

Mary twisted away from her. 'Of course you can trust me. I'm not a kid.' She stood at the window, looking out. 'Can I at least go out for a walk?' Her voice was childish, petulant.

'I'd prefer you to wait until it's dark, after four o'clock.'

'I can't wait that long,' said Mary. 'No one will see me, I'm going out now, just for a while. I'll put my hood up. You can't stop me.'

Ursula turned away, disappointed, and went back to her book. Mary said nothing more, put on her coat, pulled up the hood and went out into the grey of the morning.

When Fernando came down, the room was quiet. Ursula was still sitting by the fire reading.

'Where's the girl?' he asked.

'Out for a walk. I asked her to wait until it's dark, but she insisted.'

He frowned. 'That's not good. What do you think?'

Ursula closed her book and put it down. 'I don't understand these young people. They know what we stand for, they know how we live, but they don't understand the sacrifice. Is it about being young, or where they've come from? Even Sandra let me down.'

'What happened with Sandra?' he asked. 'Tell me, while she's out.'

Ursula sat quiet for a while, choosing her words. Then she said, 'She'd seemed so promising. She read, asked good questions, volunteered for all the worst jobs. A man called James Bramall arrived, after you'd left. He told us he worked at Sellafield. When we realised what Bramall might do for us, Sandra didn't hesitate, even though he was a bore and a braggart and it was Mark she really wanted to be with.'

'Mark?'

'The man Sandy hooked up with in New York. One of us. They had a thing going.' She shook her head, remembering. 'That idiot Bramall told us his dad owned a company based at Sellafield. He made out he had an important job there but he was worse than useless. He couldn't actually help us with anything at Sellafield and he couldn't keep his mouth shut.' She hesitated. 'It was ridiculously easy to get rid of him.'

Fernando looked hard at her. 'What do you mean?'

Ursula hesitated. 'He had an accident. I had to cover it up.'

'An accident?'

'I told you,' said Ursula.

'And what about Sandra?'

'She'd got herself pregnant. After James left New York she and Mark were fucking all the time. I thought she'd be careful, but obviously not. When I got over here, she announced she was pregnant, as if I'd be pleased. I begged her to get rid of it, but she wouldn't. She kept saying she wanted out, to start a new life. I think it was James' accident that freaked her out.'

Fernando asked, 'Was Sandra there when it happened?'

'In the back seat. She was crouching down, no one would have seen her. I got out to drag the boy off the road, and when I got back in the car she was snivelling like a teenager. Then she told me she'd been keeping a journal about everything that had happened, as if that gave her some kind of leverage. She wouldn't show it to me. It took me a long time to find it, afterwards.' She pointed to the fire. 'It's gone now.'

Ursula turned around to face Fernando who was standing with his back to the fire that smouldered in the grate. 'She gave me no choice,' she said. 'After Bramall's accident she'd been drinking in the car and then she started with the heroin. I could have stopped her, but I didn't.'

He stared at her. 'She died?'

Ursula nodded.

'The baby too?'

'Collateral damage,' she said.

Suddenly the door opened. Fernando stood in front of Ursula, his arms outstretched to protect her. 'Sorry,' Mary said. 'Am I interrupting something?'

Ursula pushed him away and shook her head. 'It's nothing,' she said. 'You weren't out for long.'

'It started raining, so I came back.'

'Anyone around out there?' Fernando asked.

Mary shook her head. 'I just wish I had something to do,' she said.

'There's an old pallet in the shed, at the back behind the Landrover,' said Ursula. 'And there's an axe there too. Someone must have used it for storing wood. Why don't you and Fernando chop some wood while I make a meal for us?'

Mary looked at Fernando, who nodded. 'OK, Mary,' he said. 'Let's make ourselves useful.'

For a while they worked in silence, Mary gathering the wood that lay around the old shed, Fernando breaking down the pallet to create more. Fernando put down the axe and straightened up. 'It's a big step you've taken,' he said. 'Are you sure it's what you want?'

She looked at him in the dim light from the half open door. 'It's better than what I had before,' she said. 'Brighton felt like another world, full of ideas and things that matter. I can't wait to get back there.'

'And what about Ursula?'

'She's changed my life,' said the young woman. 'Without her I'd never have done any of this. She's incredible, don't you think?'

'Is it her that's important to you, or what she stands for, what we all stand for?'

'Her,' said Mary, without hesitation. Fernando's heart sank. 'Without her, it would feel empty.'

'You love her?'

'Yes. It must be love. I've never felt this about anyone before.'

'What if she told you to do something that might hurt someone else?'

Mary hesitated. 'But she wouldn't do that, would she? She's about saving people, not hurting them.'

Fernando stared at the girl for a moment, as if making up his mind about something. Then he pushed the shed door so that it was almost closed, and darkness lay between them. He lowered his voice. 'Mary, listen to me. When Ursula leaves here, don't stay. Don't wait for her to come back. Things might get difficult, and you could get hurt. As soon as you have the chance, get to the nearest station and take a train. Do your best not to be seen or followed, but go, do you hear me?'

Mary was puzzled. 'But Ursula told me to stay here.'

'I know she did, but I'm telling you to get right away, to be safe.'

'I can't go home. I hate it there.'

'OK, go anywhere, London, Brighton. Do you need money?'

'I've got some, not much.'

He reached into his back pocket for his wallet. 'Look,' he said. 'A hundred, it's all I can spare, but it will get you started, OK?'

'I don't understand. Ursula said to wait.'

'And I'm telling you to go, as soon as you get the chance. Don't tell Ursula. Just go.'

He thrust the money into her hands. 'And don't say anything about this. It's between us, a secret.'

Mary looked at him, felt the notes in her hand and put them carefully into an inside pocket.

When they went back into the house carrying the wood Ursula turned from the range. 'Great, thanks,' she said. 'Everything OK?'

'Fine,' said Fernando. 'It's cold out there.'

❖ ❖ ❖

Conall Smith was just out of the shower when his phone rang. It was Marianne Gordon.

'DCI Skaife's been on to Truelove,' she said. 'He's not happy. He thinks Tognarelli is interfering in his case, and he's not getting what he needs from the FBI about his main suspect.'

'Has he talked to the Chief Superintendent?' Smith asked.

'I don't think so, not yet. What's your take on it?'

'Tognarelli's frustrated,' Smith said. 'He thinks this Millennium threat stuff is a waste of our time and wants to help the Bramall-Evans case along, but Skaife has pushed him out. Is the FBI blocking us? What's going on?'

'I think they're embarrassed,' said Marianne. 'Whoever this woman is, it's caught them on the hop, looking foolish. They're stalling while they try and find out. Last I heard they were getting on to the Canadians about her.'

'Canadian? That's a thought. Most people here couldn't tell the difference in the accents. Don't the US and the Canadians share everything anyway?'

'Obviously not,' she said, 'or they wouldn't be keeping us waiting. Where's Skaife's case up to?'

'Another key witness has gone missing, lured away by the same tall woman they've heard about before, and they seem to have vanished.'

'You told me about the blue van. Has it turned up?'

'Not yet, as far as I know. Sam should be up to speed on that if his loyal DC is still in touch with him. Skaife knows about that too. It's a bit of a mess.'

'Look,' said Marianne. 'I'm due a few days' leave over Christmas, but I could come up before that, just to see for myself. Sam may be right about the potential threat being a myth, but we can't afford to forget about it entirely, and he needs to be on board. Do you two have anything planned for Monday?'

'No, that's half the problem We don't have enough to do.'

'Where's a good place for us to meet?' she asked.

'Not County HQ, that's for sure,' said Smith, 'and you don't want to have to drive. How about Oxenholme Station? All the London trains stop there. It's quiet, not many people around.' He hesitated. 'What's the point if there's nothing new to tell us?'

'There may be by then. And see Sam if you can over the weekend. Make him feel we're aware of his concerns. Find some questions we need to sort out. I'll check the trains.'

'It's about three hours to Oxenholme from Euston for you,' said Smith, 'and about an hour and half for us from here. It'll be about lunchtime, let me know.'

He rang off, finished dressing and picked up the phone again.

'Sam? Conall. How's things?'

'I'm on the beach with Bill,' said Sam. 'I hope you've got some news. Everything seems to have ground to a halt.'

'Meeting on Monday,' said Smith. 'Marianne is coming up and we'll meet her at Oxenholme station.'

Sam felt his stomach turn. 'What about? Has something happened?'

'No, not yet, but she's pushing to get more out of the Americans. We need more on this tall woman that keeps appearing. Skaife's on about her too. He has orders not to pick her up, but I'm sure he would if he could. We might have to rein him in. Have you heard any more from your DC?'

'She rang last night,' said Sam. 'Where are you?'

'At the digs.'

'Do you want to come here for lunch?' Sam said. 'Judith's not feeling great, it would take her mind off things.'

'Are you sure?'

'Just another of her dizzy spells last night. She says she's fine.'

'OK, why don't I go to that nice café near here and bring lunch with me?'

'Great, thanks.'

Conall Smith arrived at noon with a bag full of food, far more than they would need.

'Heavens,' said Judith. 'Where's the rest of the rugby team to help us eat all this?'

'It's practice for Christmas,' Smith said. 'I hope you're feeling better by then.'

She smiled. 'I'm sure I will, it's nothing really, just a headache. Being at home all day, I have too much time to think about things. I'm better when I'm working.'

'What about that piece you're doing about the 'Millennium Bug'?' Sam asked. 'What have you found?'

'Well,' said Judith, pleased to think her work was worth talking about, 'The first surprise was how long ago people started worrying about it. 1993, the first stuff appeared about what might happen. After that, it depends how much of a big deal you want to make of it. The bigger story now is about how it's been overhyped, I reckon.'

'Newspapers,' said Sam. 'They wind everyone up and then tell us not to get wound up. They win both ways.'

'It's not all gossip and conspiracy theories,' said Judith. 'Journalists have done some good work over the years, haven't we, Sam? Remember what we did in 1984?'

'True,' he said. 'I thought I might drag Conall out for a walk this afternoon with Bill, love, if that's OK with you?'

'OK, if you promise to get back in time to help me down to look at the sea. If it stays as clear as this, we might get a sunset.'

Conall and Sam set off on the path north out of the village after their lunch. 'So why does Marianne want to meet? Couldn't we just talk on the phone?' Sam asked.

'I think she fancies a train ride, getting out of the office before she goes on leave next week. They all have to be around right through New Year, just in case, so she'll be stuck there then.' He looked at Sam. 'Is it a problem for you?'

Sam shook his head. 'No, of course not. Did you tell her that we seem to be drawing a blank?'

'I did, but that doesn't prove anything really. We still don't know what kind of 'action' to expect. Could be anything.'

Sam said, 'I'm fairly sure there's a link between the Bramall death, Sellafield and these Earth Liberation people. There's a thread about saving the planet that connects the ELF with Bramall and Evans, and the barmaid from the Royal in Carlisle too, by the sound of it.'

'What have you heard?'

'That the barmaid spent time in Brighton, came back raving about the environment and full of some woman she called 'Ursula', who they think is the woman who lured her away from work just after Bell's visit.'

'Ursula? Sounds like a code name. Is that all we have?'

'Yes. It's something else for the FBI to dig around for.'

They were climbing up steeply and Smith stopped to catch his breath. 'No hills where I live,' he said. 'Running on the flat isn't the same.'

'Hard to walk here without hills,' said Sam. 'The dog keeps me fit.'

'This connection with the ELF puzzles me,' said Smith as they reached the brow of the hill and the path flattened out. 'Most of the environmental groups are ostentatiously non-violent. They make a lot of noise and can be a nuisance, but they don't set out to harm people. Maybe the political and the personal just got mixed up.'

'Could be,' said Sam. 'It's a fine line. And what's to stop someone with psychopathic tendencies joining a group and then not playing by its rules? What would the group be able to do?'

'Tricky,' said Smith. 'It's hard to keep someone quiet or under control if they're determined to go their own way.'

'Which brings us back to the tall woman, Ursula.' Sam stopped and looked back at the sea where a patch of white cloud was reflected in the water. 'She was definitely involved in the death of James Bramall, and probably in Sandra Evans's too, although it would be hard to prove that her death wasn't accidental. There were no usable prints on the syringe found in her room, or on the vodka bottle.'

'If Sandra had witnessed what happened to James, she could have been upset.'

'And deliberately overdosed? But what about the baby, assuming she knew she was pregnant.'

'Twelve weeks, you said,' said Smith, remembering. 'She'd know by then.'

'Hard to imagine a pregnant woman wanting to kill herself,' said Sam. He paused, thinking. 'Judith and I wanted a child so badly, but in the end, we gave up. Having a child would have changed our lives.'

'For the better?'

'I think we need a responsibility beyond the two of us,' said Sam, pulling Bill towards him. 'We're too bound up with each other, especially now when neither of us is really working.'

Smith smiled. 'I told Marianne you were keen to get back to proper work,' he said.

'Talking of that,' said Sam. 'I forgot to tell you. Pritchard's been in touch. The blue van was spotted at a petrol station just west of Carlisle. Our blokes checked the CCTV. There was a blonde woman driving, and someone in the passenger seat whose face was hidden by the visor, presumably the barmaid.'

'When was that?'

'About an hour after they left the hotel. They were probably heading for Wigton to pick up the barmaid's things. A neighbour saw the van there, but nothing since then.'

Smith stopped again, finding it hard to keep up with Sam. 'The driver was blonde?' he asked.

'A wig, it must be. That short dark hair is easily changed. A few wigs, glasses, it's easy to change her appearance. The only thing she can't change is her height.'

'So,' said Smith, 'that lead's gone cold as well. Are they checking on any other stolen cars, if they've switched cars again?'

'Yes, but nothing as of this morning when Maureen rang.'

'Let's see what turns up by the time we meet Marianne on Monday,' said Smith. 'She may have news from across the pond by then.'

'What pond?'

'The big one, the Atlantic. The FBI are checking with the Canadians.'

'The Mounties?'

'No, the Canadian Security Intelligence Service. Maybe they know who 'Ursula' is.'

'Well, I hope someone does,' said Sam. 'The words 'needle' and 'haystack' are on my mind.'

Chapter 21

The little café on the down-line platform at Oxenholme station was quiet. It was long and narrow, and the woman working in the kitchen was twenty yards away from the group of three who sat huddled over their coffees, their heads so close together that Sam could smell Marianne's perfume. It was the same one she'd been wearing on that night they'd spent together. That was fifteen years before. Sam remembered every detail and wished he had forgotten.

'Any news?' Smith asked.

'Plenty,' said Marianne, 'and what's happening here?'

'Sam got a call this morning about the blue van that was following us when we went to Barrow docks. It was found last night in deep cover near the Solway coast, a place called Finglandrigg Woods. And there was a Landrover reported missing on Saturday from quite close by. The owner leaves it at his place for when he comes up at the weekends. He turned up on Saturday morning and it was missing.'

"Forensics?"

'They're on it now,' said Sam. 'We're pretty sure it was the tall woman. We're calling her "Ursula", it's probably a code name but it's what the barmaid, Mary Brady, called her.'

'Talking of names,' said Conall. 'Do you have one for us?'

Marianne smiled and sat back, both hands on the plastic table. 'I do,' she said, 'and it's the same name, which is reassuring. Nothing much else that helps us very much.' She pulled a file from her briefcase and laid it on the table. 'First, this is the image we have.' She laid a grainy photo in front of them. It was of a long face, with a strong square jaw and eyes slanted slightly, staring defiantly into the camera. The dark hair was brushed back, off the forehead. Sam picked it up. 'That's the same image we have, near enough. She's very striking,' he said. 'And tall, five foot eleven the police record says,' Marianne added. 'No wonder she's often mistaken for a man.'

'What do we know about her?' Smith asked.

Marianne pulled another sheet of paper from the file. 'This is all from CSIC, the Canadians. The FBI finally admitted they needed help. I'll read you the important bits.' She skimmed down the page. 'OK, real name Tania Oleshenko, Ukrainian heritage, born in Winnipeg, Manitoba, 1958. Code name "Ursula". She looked up, 'Could be after Ursula le Guin, feminist author, iconoclast, she has a big following in North America. Our Ursula has political affiliations to various left-wing causes, mainly the Earth Liberation Front. Arrested during the Love Canal environment protests in Buffalo – she must have been about twenty then, and then at the big anti-nuclear protests in New York in 1982. Nothing recently, but she must be pretty skilled at staying under the radar.' She scanned down the page. 'Must have other aliases too but no mention of those here.'

'Just a run-of-the-mill leftie, by the sound of it,' said Smith.

'Yes, but when you dig a bit deeper, she has quite a mean streak. The arrest in New York was for a violent assault on a police officer, and she served time for that. The prison authorities added to her file apparently, saying they considered her dangerous, but nothing concrete. Looks as if she went back to Canada for a while.'

Sam said, 'Bramall and Sandra Evans both talked about meeting someone like this in New York, and Mary Brady's mother said Mary talked about "Ursula". It must be the same woman.'

'And now she's here,' said Smith, 'stealing cars, running people down, just one step ahead of us.'

Sam put his head back. 'I knew it. I'd be better off trying to find this homicidal woman than messing around with a wild goose chase about security threats and the Millennium.'

Smith put a hand on his arm. 'Keep your voice down.'

Marianne put the papers back in the file. 'Obviously, we need to find her, but she's no amateur. Well-organised, savvy about police procedures, bold.'

'And all in a good cause, as she sees it,' said Smith. 'You two won't know about this, but it reminds me of Michael Collins, one of the IRA leaders in 1920. He hunted all over the country and constantly avoided capture by using local safe houses and disguises. He was driven by passion, resourceful. They got him in the end though.'

'So,' said Sam. 'Looking for our modern-day Michael Collins, what do we do next?' He tapped Marianne's file with his finger. 'Workington CID has other work to do. It can't spend all its resources chasing zealots. DCI Skaife will do as he's told in the end, he always does despite all the bravado, so what's he going to be told?'

'That's down to the Chief Super,' said Marianne, 'and my bosses in London. My guess would be they keep all the alerts in place, but it sounds as if there's nothing much to go on right now, until the woman betrays herself in some way.' She turned to Conall Smith. 'Michael Collins relied on safe houses and local support to protect him, right? So, does "Ursula" have local protection, anyone we can think of?'

'That would be Earth Liberation people, I suppose,' said Conall. 'Do you want me to check with Special Branch about that? Anyone local who might be helping?'

'It's something to do,' said Marianne. 'Otherwise, we're just waiting for something to turn up. What do you think, Sam?'

Sam shook his head. 'Christmas next weekend, New Year's Eve the following Friday. We're looking for an old Landrover in north Cumbria, not exactly a rarity. We'll have the reg number but that could be changed, if our Ursula is as resourceful as it seems. I'm worried about the barmaid, just a girl apparently, not a hardened terrorist. If Bramall and Evans were expendable, maybe she's in danger too.'

'If she realises that, she might try to get away,' said Marianne. 'It's a potential weak link. I'll get the word to the Chief Super, and thence to the DCI.' She looked at Sam. 'What about you?' she said. 'I know you'd like to get back to proper police work.'

Sam leaned back in his chair, watching as a southbound train slid into the station on the other side of the tracks. 'I've thought about it,' he said. 'But I'll stay where I am for the time being. Judith still needs me, and Christmas will be here in a day or two. It could be the most time we've spent together in quite a while.' He ran a hand through his hair, wishing that Marianne wasn't quite so close.

'OK,' said Marianne. 'Conall, what about you?'

'I'm taking a few days off over Christmas too,' he said. 'I have a flight booked to Belfast on Wednesday, back on the 27th. Sam and I will be on duty through the New Year, obviously.'

'Me too,' said Marianne. 'All of us will be on high alert in London, waiting for the banks to crash and planes to drop out of the sky.' She smiled, 'Or not, as the case may be.'

'Will you pass all this intel. about "Ursula" on to my bosses?' Sam asked.

'Will do. Not sure what they'll be able to do with it, but we have to make sure they don't do anything prematurely.'

Many miles away on this cold Monday morning, a young woman with a hundred pounds in her back pocket was wondering about how she could get to a station without being seen, to spend Christmas with people who knew how to have fun.

❖ ❖ ❖

Judith Pharaoh and her sister-in-law Helen were making plans. Helen's husband Vince would be at work at Sellafield until Thursday lunchtime, but Helen's school term had finished and she could focus on Christmas.

'What's he like?' Helen asked.

'Tommy? Actually he doesn't want to be called Tommy, it's Tom, Tom Phelps.'

'Why not Tognarelli?' Helen asked.

'He kept his stepfather's name when he left, which surprised me, considering how badly they got on. But who'd want to carry the 'Tognarelli' handle around if they didn't have to? Sam has to spell it out for people every day, and you get all those tired jokes about ice cream.'

' "Pharaoh" is nearly as bad,' said Helen. 'We get all sorts of spellings even though it's a local name. Anyway, come on, what's he like?'

Judith was lying on the settee with the phone in her hand, Bill snoring quietly beside her. 'Honestly, Helen, he's gorgeous. How old?' She worked it out. 'He's well into his thirties, not married apparently. Can't believe there's not a long line of women pining for him.'

'Could he be gay?' said Helen.

'OK, a long line of men pining for him. But I don't think he's gay, none of the signs.'

Helen laughed. 'They're not all as camp as a row of tents,' she said. 'But it doesn't matter, does it? You're not thinking of abandoning Sam and running off with the nephew, are you?'

'Dream on,' said Judith. 'Me with my pot leg and middle-aged spread and dizzy spells.'

'What dizzy spells?'

'Oh, nothing much. It could be my blood pressure, but the pills the doc gave me made me feel dozy.'

Helen sounded concerned. 'Have you seen the doc lately? You could have an ear infection or something that affects your balance. Don't want any more falls.'

'No, I haven't seen the doctor, just the nurse checking on my leg. It's doing fine, by the way. Sam's been taking me out in a wheelchair.'

'Not great for chasing a younger man around, then,' Helen said.

They talked for a while about the logistics of Christmas, who's bringing what, timings, presents.

'How's Mum?' said Judith. 'I haven't seen her for a while.' She hesitated. 'It's that care home, Helen, I can't bear going there. The smell, that old lady who shouts about her handbag all the time, it makes me want to retch, or scream, or both.'

'Dad goes almost every day,' said Helen. 'He doesn't say much, but I don't think he enjoys it. It says the walk down the hill and back again does him good. I don't think he'd go so often if one of us had to take him.'

'When's your visitor arriving?' Helen asked.

'Wednesday, I think. He was a bit vague. I think it depends on the work he has to finish. I'm not even sure where he's coming from. We'll come to you Christmas Day, and you come here Boxing Day, as usual?'

'It works OK for us, if that's fine with you. Tom will want a few hours' peace between work and our two grandkids climbing all over him. What does he do, by the way?'

'Something to do with computers. It's a bit vague. Takes him all over the place, whatever it is. You'll like him Helen. Sam and I are thinking of going out to New Zealand to see Elspeth now she's on her own again, but it might have to wait till Sam retires in a year or two.'

'So soon?'

'He'll have done his thirty years in 2001, so that could be the time to stop.'

Sam was thinking about retirement as he drove back from Cockermouth having dropped off Conall Smith. He realised now that just stopping work wasn't going to feel right, he would have to have something to do, a project of some kind, to occupy his mind. Maybe a trip to New Zealand would soak up his energy for a while. He and Judith had never travelled far for their holidays over the years and this would be a major undertaking. Such a long trip wasn't worth it for less than a month, he thought.

But that's well ahead, he said to himself as he approached the junction where the A596 would take him to Workington and the A595 would take him home. Later he tried to remember what made him decide to head for Nook Street. Curiosity was the only reason he could think of, and a lingering regret about being away from the action. He needed time to clear Marianne out of his head and Judith wasn't expecting him home yet, so why not?

He parked at the shopping centre rather than risk taking one of the precious parking spots at the police station which lay tucked away down a narrow side street. Ridiculous place for a police station, but the move out of town to the new place was still years away. Bits had been added to the old building, but it still looked like a Victorian school, which it probably was.

Duty Sergeant Geoff Simpson looked up as Sam walked in and smiled broadly. 'Look who's here,' he said. 'The wanderer returns. How are you Sam?'

'Bored,' said Sam, 'but that's for your ears only. Officially I'm on personal leave looking after my wife for a couple of weeks. Who's in?'

'The DCI's at a meeting in Carlisle, Findale and Sharp are out with a robbery in Allonby, Bell dashed off somewhere, never tells me anything. Pritchard disappeared an hour ago, something about that Wigton girl who's missing. Bob and the new lad are in their corner, as ever.' He stood, hands on hips. 'I'm getting old Sam,' he said. 'Too much on the computer these days. It's the people stuff that matters.'

'That's right,' said Sam. He felt suddenly self-conscious about being there and wondered whether Skaife would resent his presence in the building. 'Geoff, if Skaife checks in or gets back here, can you forget to tell him that you've seen me?'

The radio on the desk crackled. 'Sarge,' said a familiar voice. 'We've picked up a young woman, the one from the hotel in Carlisle, Mary Brady. Bringing her in now. Can you let the DCI know?'

Sam put his hand out and Geoff passed the radio over. 'Maureen?' said Sam. 'It's Sam. Are you bringing her in now?'

'Should be there in half an hour, boss. Do you want to see her?'

'What's she done?'

'Nothing. Helping with enquiries. But she's got a fair amount of money on her that came from somewhere. Do you want to talk to her?'

'It would be useful. I'll stick around. See you later.'

Mary Brady was not happy. 'You can't keep me here,' she said. 'I know my rights, I've done nothing wrong.' She stared at Sam. 'Who are you?'

'DI Tognarelli,' said Sam.

'Where's that other one, the fat bloke who tried to pick me up?'

Maureen whispered to Sam. 'She says Bell asked her what time she finished work, first time he talked to her.'

'DS Bell is busy,' he said. 'DC Pritchard and I have every right to interview you about a case. It's called "helping the police with their enquiries".'

'I want a solicitor,' said Mary.

'Why do you want a solicitor, Mary,' Maureen asked, 'if you've done nothing wrong?'

'I know about people like you,' Mary said, twisting in the chair. 'You'll put words in my mouth, make me tell you things.'

'What things?' Sam asked.

She shrugged. 'You know, personal things, secrets.'

'Would you like a drink? Coffee, maybe?' Maureen asked. 'I can get you some.'

'And leave me alone with him?' Mary said, jerking her elbow at Sam. 'That's another trick. I'll have a coffee, but only if you both go and fetch it.'

She sat back in the chair in the monochrome interview room and folded her arms.

'Fine,' said Sam. He and Maureen both stood up and left the room.

Through the one-way window they watched as Mary inspected her fingernails.

'Where was she?' Sam said.

'Hitching a lift near Abbey Town, about two o'clock. The farmer who picked her up said he'd heard about a girl missing from Wigton. He called us after he dropped her off and I found her sitting by the side of the road. Terrible place to hitch. She said she was waiting for the bus to Wigton.'

'Was Bell with you?' Sam asked.

'No, good job too, she'd have legged it. Keeps on referring to him as 'the fat one'.'

'Where is Bell now?'

'Call came in about the Landrover, the one we were looking for. He went off to Kirkbampton to check it out. We're tight on people since Skaife reined in the investigation. He said we had to clear some of the backlog until something else broke on this case.'

'And it just did,' said Sam.

'You reckon the girl's going to be helpful?' Maureen asked.

'Could be, if she doesn't clam up,' Sam said.

'Do we need the mother in? No love lost there from what I gathered when I talked to her.'

'Mary's over eighteen. Keep Mum out of it. We'll get her that drink and see what she gives us. Not exactly a criminal mastermind, is she?' Sam looked at the young woman again, who seemed unaware that they would be watching her from the other side of the glass. 'I think we have to approach her as someone who can help us, not as someone with something to hide. If you lead, I'll listen. And I've got some information to add, when the time's right.'

'Here you are, Mary,' said Maureen. 'It's canteen coffee, not brilliant I'm afraid. I brought you sugar in case you want it.' She pushed the coffee over the table and Mary looked at it for a while before adding the sugar, stirring and taking a sip.

'I'm glad we found you,' said Maureen. 'Your mum was upset when I spoke to her.'

'When?' said Mary, looking up.

'Just after you went missing. She got home and found you'd taken some things and gone.'

'She doesn't care,' said Mary. 'She'd just be worried about the rent.'

Maureen smiled. 'I thought you might have gone back to Brighton. Your mum says you liked it down there.'

'I did. It was cool. I want to go back for Christmas, not stay up here.'

'But you didn't go straight away after you left the hotel. Why was that?'

Mary hesitated, sipping some more of the coffee. She shrugged.

'Was it because the person you were with had other plans?' Maureen asked.

'What person?'

'We checked, Mary. You jacked in your job at the hotel and just walked out, didn't you? The woman on reception said you were with someone else and you were both laughing.'

Mary smiled. 'It was funny, seeing the look on the old cow's face.'

'So, who were you with?'

Mary shrugged again. 'Just a friend,' she said.

Sam leaned forward. 'It was Ursula, wasn't it?'

The girl looked at him. 'Who told you about Ursula?'

Maureen said, 'Your mum told me you talked about Ursula when you got back from Brighton. You like her, don't you?'

Mary looked at Sam again. 'So, who told him about Ursula?'

'He's my boss,' said Maureen. 'He knows all about it.'

'Nothing to know,' said Mary. 'So, I've got nothing to tell you.'

Sam said, 'Would you like me to tell you some things about Ursula?'

Mary looked but said nothing.

'She comes from Canada, did you know that? Winnipeg, Manitoba. And Ursula's not her real name. Her real name is Tania Oleshenko.'

Mary looked surprised, then she laughed. 'You're having me on.'

'No, really,' said Sam. 'Her dad came from the Ukraine. That's near Russia. And do you know how old she is?'

'Bit older than me,' said Mary.

'How old are you?'

'Nineteen.'

'Well, Tania is forty-one, old enough to be your mother.'

'So?'

'So, isn't it a bit odd that she should be so interested in you, with such a big age gap?'

Mary frowned. 'We were friends. I met her in Brighton. She said I could do something for her. Nothing wrong with that, is there?'

'What did she want you to do?'

'Work in that poxy hotel, keep an eye on things.'

'What things?'

'Some people she knew.' She looked from one face to the other, then turned away.

'Mary,' said Maureen. 'Do you know what happened to those people? They're both dead.'

Mary bit her lip. 'I don't want to say any more.'

'One of those people was murdered,' said Sam. 'This is a murder enquiry, Mary, and if you have information about any of this, we need to know. Do you understand?'

Mary's eyes began to fill with tears. 'I'm not saying any more. You can't make me. I want a solicitor.'

Sam and Maureen looked at each other. 'OK,' said Sam. 'Do you have someone you can call?'

The girl shook her head.

'Well, we'll find someone for you,' said Sam. 'It'll take a little while. Are you hungry?'

Mary looked up. 'Can I have a bacon butty?'

Chapter 22

Sam and Maureen went to the canteen while they waited for the duty solicitor to turn up.

'Was that right, about Ursula's real name?' Maureen asked.

'Straight from Canadian security services,' said Sam. 'They also said that Ursula is known for being pretty ruthless, nothing's off limits.'

'Is that where the money came from that Mary had on her?'

'That doesn't feel right.' said Sam. 'Why would Ursula basically kidnap the girl and then give her money to leave?'

'What else do you want to know from her?'

'Where Ursula is now, what she's got planned, if anything. If the duty solicitor's got any sense, they'll let Mary talk. Her worst offence so far is poor judgment.'

Maureen said, 'She reminds me of a teenager, stroppy but no clue what's going on.'

'She is a teenager,' said Sam. 'In over her head. I just don't want her to clam up. The longer Ursula is out there, the more worried I get. She's up to something.'

Maureen leaned back in her chair. 'This all fits with that job you're doing with Special Branch, doesn't it, the one I'm not allowed to talk about?'

Sam said, 'I just hope Skaife remembers that meeting we had with the bigwigs and doesn't start grandstanding, telling me not to darken his door again.'

'Really?' She shook her head. 'Ego and turf protection in full flower.'

An hour later a young woman blew into Nook Street, a bulging rucksack slung over one shoulder and another bag from which sundry personal items clattered onto the duty sergeant's desk.

'Connie Eversholt,' she said. 'Duty solicitor, here to see…' she hesitated.

'Mary Brady?' Geoff suggested.

'That's the one,' she said.

'I'll call DI Tognarelli,' said Geoff, picking up the phone.

Sam pushed open the door and ushered Connie through.

'Mary Brady,' he said, 'aged nineteen. Missing from home in Wigton for two days and picked up this afternoon, hitching near Abbey Town.'

'Any charges?'

'No, not so far, but she's insisted on talking to a solicitor.'

'As is her right,' said Connie.

'Exactly,' said Sam. 'So far we don't think she's committed any offence, but we do think she has information pertinent to a murder enquiry.'

'OK,' said Connie. 'Let's see what we can do.' She hesitated. 'Anything to do with that Bramall boy?'

'I couldn't possibly comment,' said Sam.

Half an hour later, Connie called Sam and Maureen back into the interview room. Mary's eyes were red. 'My client and I have had a useful meeting, Inspector. She has some things she'd like to tell you, and I'll be here to advise her. She's quite insistent that the interview should not be tape-recorded. I said I was sure this was just a conversation, as she's done nothing unlawful.'

Sam agreed and the recorder remained off. If Mary had anything to offer that might constitute an offence, or if he believed she was lying to them, then more formal proceedings would follow. Connie nodded and put a hand on Mary's arm. 'Go ahead. The Inspector will ask his questions, and I'll tell you if you don't need to answer him. It's OK. He might have to interview you later with the tape running, but let's hope not.'

Mary looked at Sam nervously.

'First of all, Mary,' he said, 'can you tell us where you've been the past two days, since you left your house in Wigton?'

'In a cottage, not sure where exactly, but we went through Finglandrigg to get there. It was a bit further on, by the shore.'

'Finglandrigg, that's where the Landrover was stolen.'

Mary looked at Connie, who nodded and said, 'You didn't steal it, Mary. You're not responsible. Remember what we talked about.'

Mary nodded. 'It was just a small place. I think it was a holiday cottage.'

'So Ursula would have rented it?'

Mary shrugged. 'She had a key. We didn't break in. It was a pretty rough place, but it was clean.'

Sam opened the file in front of him and pretended to read something, shielding the blank paper from Mary's eyes. 'Now Mary,' he said. 'When we found you, you said you were waiting for a bus.'

'To Wigton,' she said.

'Going home?'

She shook her head. 'No chance. I was going for the train, back to Brighton.'

'Long way,' said Sam. 'It would cost a bit to get down there.'

Mary looked away.

'How much money do you have on you?' he asked.

'Enough,' she said.

'How much, show me.'

Mary looked at Connie, who nodded. Mary reached into her pocket and pulled out a wad of notes. She spread them out on the table. 'It's a hundred,' she said.

'And where did it come from?' Sam asked. 'Did Ursula give it to you?'

Mary shook her head. 'No, she said I should stay there and wait for her to come back.'

'So where did it come from? That's a lot for you to have saved.'

Mary hesitated. 'Someone gave it to me,' she said, after a long pause.

Sam was surprised. He hadn't considered anyone else being involved. 'Who was that, Mary?' he asked, keeping his voice even. He wanted the girl to stay calm.

'A man, he was a friend of Ursula's. They were, you know…' She raised her eyebrows. 'They were all over each other.'

Sam's perception of Ursula began to shift. He'd been sure that Ursula was attracted to women. Maybe she was. But here was a man in the picture too.

'Was this man at the cottage when you got there?'

'No, Ursula said he was coming, and then he did. He had a car.'

'What can you tell us about him? His name?'

Mary pursed her lips. 'Ursula called him "Fernando", but that can't have been his real name, can it, unless he was foreign or something?'

'Do you think he was?'

She shrugged. 'He spoke English, but he had a funny accent. Maybe from down south.'

'London?'

'No, not like people I know from London.' She shrugged again. 'I dunno. There was an Ozzie bloke in Brighton, who spoke like that. Different from us.'

Sam leaned back in his chair. 'This is really interesting Mary. You're being very helpful. This was the man who gave you the money?'

She nodded.

'OK, let's talk a bit more about that. What happened exactly?'

Mary settled into her chair. Connie Eversholt could see that she was more relaxed and admired the policeman's skill in putting the girl at her ease.

'Well,' said Mary. 'Me and Fernando went to the shed to chop some firewood. I was bored and I wanted something to do. He started talking to me, like he didn't want Ursula to know.'

'What did he say?'

'He said I wasn't safe, and I should get away. Then he gave me the money. He said to wait until Ursula went off, and then go.'

Suddenly Sam remembered something that Marianne had said at the meeting at HQ in Penrith. Could this man have been working undercover for MI5 or the Special Branch? Why else would he have wanted to get an innocent person out of the way? 'What did the man look like?' he asked.

'Older than me, maybe a bit younger than you.' The girl shrugged again. 'Old, you know, but fit looking.' She squinted at Sam. 'Eyes like yours actually, I could see why Ursula fancied him.' She giggled. 'Quite fancied him myself.'

Maureen touched Sam's arm before she interrupted. 'We've got people who draw pictures of faces from someone's description.'

'I know that,' said Mary. 'Seen it on the telly. They call them photo something.'

'Photofit, that's right. Do you think you could do that for us? It would take a little while, but it would be really useful.'

'How long?' said Mary. 'I want to get a train to Brighton.'

'Tell you what,' Maureen said. 'I have to go to Carlisle later, to see my Dad. I could drive you up there to do the photofit, get something to eat, and then take you to the train. Much quicker than getting the train from here. How about that?'

Mary looked at Connie Eversholt, who nodded. 'Sounds like a good offer to me, Mary.'

The girl smiled and pushed back her chair. Sam held up his hand. 'Just a couple more things I'd like to know, if you can help,' he said. 'Do you know where Ursula was going when she left the cottage?'

'Glasgow,' Mary said. She was answering more quickly now, after Maureen's offer of help.

'Did she take the Landrover?'

'No, the train.'

'OK, and one last thing. You said Fernando told you to get away for your own safety. Why do you think he said that?'

Mary's expression altered. She frowned and looked at her hands. Sam looked at Connie Eversholt, who shook her head. Sam waited. Mary leaned over and whispered something to Connie that Sam couldn't hear. Connie said, 'Could you give us a minute, Inspector? Mary has something she wants to ask me before we go on.'

Sam and Maureen got up. 'That's fine,' said Sam. 'We'll be outside.'

Outside, Maureen said. 'What are you going to tell Skaife about all this? It's his case officially.'

'But he's not here, is he? And Mary could give us an image of this bloke, "Fernando." Can you arrange for that, Maureen? The more information we have the better, while she still remembers all the details.'

'Will do,' said Maureen. 'Do you want to see it, when it's done?'

'Please,' said Sam.

Connie Eversholt beckoned them back in.

'Inspector, Mary will tell you what she knows, but it's very clear that she's not guilty of any crime.'

Sam smiled. 'We need to be the judge of that. I hope your client remembers that we may have to caution her if she's not being honest?' Mary nodded.

'So, Mary,' said Sam, 'I was asking why this man Fernando thought you weren't safe.'

Mary sniffed. Connie put a hand on her shoulder and the girl went on, speaking quietly. 'I think it was because of what happened to Jimmy and Sandra.'

'You mean, James Bramall and Sandra Evans?'

Mary nodded. 'The fat policeman told me they were both dead. I asked Ursula about it. She said it was "unavoidable". That's what she said, "unavoidable", and she said it was a mess.'

Sam nodded. 'So when Fernando said you weren't safe, was it because he thinks that Ursula might have harmed those two others?'

Mary shrugged. 'I told him Ursula wouldn't kill anyone. But he offered me the money, so I took it. I want to go to Brighton, get away from here.'

'Do you think Ursula killed Jimmy and Sandra?'

Mary's eyes filled with tears. She looked down.

'I think that's enough, Inspector,' Connie said. 'I can't see that you have any further reason to detain my client. I trust that DC Pritchard's offer of help still stands?'

'What if Mary is in danger?' said Maureen. 'We have a duty to protect her.'

'Just do as you said,' Connie said, her hand on Mary's arm, 'Stay with her until she's safely on the train south, and your duty of care has been met. That's what she wants.'

Suddenly the door of the interview room opened. Mary saw who it was and stood up, the chair crashing to the floor behind her. Sam turned to see Bell standing in the doorway.

'Get him away from me,' Mary shouted. 'I won't talk to him.'

Sam pushed Bell out of the room and into the corridor.

'What the hell are you doing here?' Bell said. Spittle landed on Sam's face and he blinked.

'Calm down, for God's sake,' Sam said. 'And remember who you're talking to. I'm still your senior officer.' He pushed Bell away. 'I came in to see the DCI, but he's at a meeting apparently. DC Pritchard brought in the barmaid from the Royal, so we decided to talk to her, unofficially.'

'So why's Eversholt here, poking her nose in?'

'Mary wouldn't talk to us without support. She's been very helpful, and now Maureen's taking her up to Carlisle to get a photofit done of another key witness.'

'Who?' Bell demanded.

'I'll discuss that with the DCI, not you, Sergeant.'

'Inspector,' Bell insisted.

'Acting Inspector,' Sam corrected him. 'You're still my junior officer on this case, just remember that.'

Maureen joined them outside. 'Keep your voices down, you two,' she said.

Bell flexed his shoulders. 'This girl's going nowhere until the DCI comes back, right?' he said. 'It's his case, and his call. And you,' he said pointing a chubby finger at Maureen. 'It's time you sorted out who you're working for. You're still just a plain old DC, Pritchard, however many years you've put in.'

'That's enough,' Sam said. 'DC Pritchard has my authority to take our witness to Carlisle to do a photofit, which will happen more quickly in Carlisle than here. I will explain it to DCI Skaife. If he wishes to detain Mary Brady further, that can be done in Carlisle nick before she's released. Eversholt insists her client isn't guilty of anything except foolishness, and I think she's right. So, back off Sergeant, right now.'

Connie opened the interview room door. 'We had an agreement, Inspector. My client is upset and wants to leave. If you need to check with the DCI, do it and do it soon.'

Sam hesitated. He had to get Mary Brady away from Bell or the girl would tell them nothing more. 'Go,' he said to Maureen. 'Get the photofit done in Carlisle, give her some food, take your time over getting a proper statement and don't get her to the train until you hear from me or Skaife, OK?'

'Right,' said Maureen.

Sam turned to Bell who was still standing there, hands on hips like a boxer before the bell.

'You'd better go before Mary comes out or she'll scream the place down. If you see the DCI, keep your mouth shut. I'll talk him through it all.'

Bell hesitated, and then stomped off down the corridor.

Connie led Mary out of the interview room, and they stopped for a moment. 'Has he gone?' Mary said.

Sam nodded. 'DC Pritchard will take you to Carlisle, as we promised,' he said. 'You've been very helpful, Mary, thanks.

Hopefully we won't need to see you again.' He watched as they walked away.

'What's going on?' said Connie. 'Trouble in the ranks?'

'Nothing we can't handle,' said Sam. The last thing he wanted was gossip about CID officers in Workington shouting at each other.

When things quietened down Sam had time to think. He needed to see Skaife, and he also needed a plausible reason for being in the station at all. Back at the reception desk, Geoff called him over. 'DCI's just come in,' he said, 'and Dinger looks like he's going to explode. What's going on?'

'Later, Geoff,' said Sam, 'I'm off to see Skaife myself.'

When Sam reached Skaife's office, Bell was already there.

'What are you playing at, Tognarelli? I leave the station on important business and all hell breaks loose,' said Skaife. 'DS Bell here tells me you've been interviewing a witness without reference to him, or to me, when you're supposed to be off this case altogether.'

Sam decided to be conciliatory. 'Yes, sir. I apologise for that. I came into the station to check with you about another matter and DC Pritchard had just brought in Mary Brady, the barmaid who'd been seen with our suspect.'

'The barmaid I interviewed in Carlisle,' Bell interrupted. 'The one who served Bramall and Evans at the hotel just before they died.'

Sam ignored him. 'For some reason, Mary Brady refused to speak to DS Bell again and you weren't available, so DC Pritchard and I interviewed her.'

'And why was Eversholt here?'

'Brady wanted a solicitor present before she would talk.'

'She watches too much TV,' said Bell.

Skaife held up his hand. 'Right, right. Carry on, Inspector. Explain, from the top.'

Sam went on. 'Mary Brady was picked up this afternoon near Drumburgh trying to catch a bus into Carlisle,' he said. 'She'd voluntarily gone to a cottage out there with the tall woman, the one we need to find, who she calls 'Ursula'. She told us Ursula was going to Glasgow. She also mentioned a man who arrived at the cottage, who also knew Ursula. It's clear to me that Mary knows nothing about what happened to Bramall and Evans, beyond the fact that they're both dead, which she learned from DS Bell. I believe there are no grounds at present to hold her. If we need her to make a case later, we can pick her up again.'

'Was she cautioned?'

'No, and she was very reluctant to have her statement recorded.'

'So, it could be a pack of lies?' said Skaife.

'Exactly,' said Bell.

Skaife sat, thinking. 'Is that all she told you?' he asked. 'And who's this man she talked about?'

'We know nothing much about him, beyond what Mary told us, which will be in her statement. A good-looking man in his middle years. And we're getting a photofit done.' Sam paused. He could see that Skaife was struggling to absorb all the information. 'I apologise for interfering in the case, sir,' he went on, 'but you and DS Bell were both unavailable. I had actually come into the station to speak to you about the other matter I'm currently involved with.'

'What about it?' Skaife said.

'I need to talk to you privately about that, sir,' said Sam.

Skaife looked at Bell. 'Ah,' he said. 'DS Bell, can you alert all units that our tall suspect may be heading for Glasgow. Unless she's taken another vehicle, she'll be taking the train.'

'There's a bus into the city from Kirkbampton,' said Bell. 'Shall I check it out? And what about the girl, sir?'

'Check the bus, and the trains. Leave the girl to me,' said Skaife.

Sam could feel Bell's irritation as he left the room.

'Well, Inspector?' said Skaife.

'I was thinking about something Ms Gordon said at the meeting in Penrith, and came in to discuss it with you.'

Skaife nodded.

'It was about the possibility of there being a police informant within the ELF group. I thought you might enquire if any similar operation was in place here, with some of the left-wing groups operating locally, anarchists and such like.'

Skaife looked puzzled. 'What if there is?' he said.

Sam was struggling to say something sensible. He was making it up as he went along. 'Well, sir,' he said, 'we might be able to check with local informants if they'd heard anything about plans for a political 'happening' of some kind around New Year's Eve. That might be of help to Mr Smith in his investigations here.'

Skaife still looked puzzled, but he nodded. 'You want me to make some enquiries?'

'Yes, please, sir.' Sam had another thought. 'As I said, sir, the witness we've just interviewed told us about a man who appeared, warned Mary off and gave her money to get away. That's why we were able to pick her up. It seemed an odd thing to do, but if he were actually one of us, working undercover, it would make more sense.'

'Ah, I see,' said Skaife. He was leaning back in his chair, his hands together close to his face as if in prayer.

Sam went on, more confidently now. 'I thought it was important to get a proper image of this new potential witness, that's why I asked DC Pritchard to take her up to Carlisle, to speed up the photofit process.'

'Right,' said Skaife, and Sam steamed ahead. 'Miss Eversholt claims that from the evidence we have there is nothing we could charge Miss Brady with. She's had a lucky escape, and she's been very cooperative. With your permission, I feel we should let her go once she's signed a full statement and done the photofit.'

Skaife thought for a moment. Sam guessed he was trying to find a way to reassert his authority. 'I'll make the enquiries you asked for, Inspector, about any undercover operatives in this area. But there was clearly no need for you to come into the station to ask me about that. It could easily have been done by phone.' He was right. Sam said nothing. 'So, I want to reiterate,' Skaife went on, looking up at Sam who was still standing in front of the desk, hands clasped behind his back. 'Your orders are very clear, Inspector. You are off this case. There should be no reason for you to be around here, interfering in any way. Am I making myself clear?'

'Yes sir,' Sam said.

'As for Mary Brady,' Skaife went on. 'I shall speak to DC Pritchard myself to check that everything has been done before Brady can be allowed to leave. That decision is mine, and mine alone. Clear?'

'Yes, sir.'

'You can go,' said Skaife, dismissing Sam with a wave of his hand.

Outside, Sam leaned against the wall. He'd manoeuvred his way through this awkwardness, but a question had begun to itch at the back of his mind, and it continued to bother him as he drove home.

❖ ❖ ❖

Two hundred miles away, in a dingy bedroom of a hotel near Queen Street Station in Glasgow, Ursula turned towards the man lying beside her and put a hand on his stomach. 'You shouldn't have come here,' she said. 'Are you sure you weren't followed?'

'Certain. I left the car in Edinburgh and came across by train. No one knows me anyway. It's you they're looking for.'

'Which is why you shouldn't have come.'

'I couldn't stay away any longer,' he said.

'You knew I'd be out of reach for a while. It's easier travelling alone. And I've got things to do. I had to get out of Cumbria for a while. MI5 are trying to frame me, you know that don't you? They're just using Bramall as an excuse.'

The man turned to face her. 'You must have realised that Jimmy Bramall was just small fry. He was too much of an idiot to have any serious responsibility, even if his dad owned the firm. You could tell that just by listening to him.' He propped himself up on one elbow. 'What really happened to him?'

'I told you,' she said. 'An accident. He was very drunk. I started the car and he ran out in front of it raving about something, waving his arms. I tried to stop in time, but he just stood there.'

She rolled away from him. 'Anyway, don't go on about it. He was a nuisance, and now he's gone. That's all you need to know. And now you have to go too. Sean's expecting me at nine, he wouldn't want anyone else hanging around.'

'We shouldn't be mixed up with men like him.'

She sat up, exasperated. 'We've tried being nice about some very important political issues, it doesn't work. People like Sean and his mates know that, and it's something I've learned too.'

The man sat up too, pulling the sheet up round his shoulders. It smelled as grubby as it looked. 'Ten years ago, when you and I got together, it was different. You've changed.'

'Don't be childish. We've all changed. The world's changed. It's no good bleating about what used to be.' She looked at him. 'Are you in this, or not?'

He sat still for a while, listening to the traffic outside. 'I'm in for this job, yes,' he said. 'After that, I'm not sure.' Ursula didn't respond but shook her head, as if she was rebuking a child. The man's voice rose. 'The girl who died was pregnant! Doesn't that bother you?' he asked. 'And don't just give me that "Collateral damage" line. I've heard enough of that.'

Again, she didn't respond, and his outrage faltered. He remembered how much he loved her, what they'd been through together. After a while he said, 'I'll help you with this last job but no one else gets hurt, right?'

'We've talked enough about this,' she said. 'Time you were going.'

Chapter 23

When Sam got home, Judith was making lists, as she always did when there was a lot to do.

'You'll have to do the shopping, so I'm making the food list very precise, OK?' Judith said. 'And we need to check with Tom about when he's going to get here, so I know how many to plan for. Do you have a phone number for him?'

'I put it somewhere,' Sam said.

She looked up, 'Oh, sorry, I forgot. Conall Smith called a little while ago. I said you'd call him back. I'm making supper in a minute, so don't go poking around for food.'

'Yes, ma'am,' said Sam. 'I'll take the phone in the other room.'

'Sam,' said Conall. 'What have you been up to? I had a call from Skaife.'

Sam groaned. He should have known that Skaife's irritation would spill over, and he wondered who else the DCI had been talking to.

'Ah, yes,' said Sam. 'Bit of a mess this afternoon, sorry. What did Skaife say?'

'That you'd gone into Nook Street to talk to him about undercover police operations and then interviewed a witness without checking with him, which he wasn't best pleased about I can tell you.'

'To be honest, I was just being nosy about what was going on and went into Nook Street on a whim. I had to make up that stuff about the undercover operation to give Skaife a reason for me being there.'

'You may have made it up, but it's a question worth asking,' said Smith. 'Didn't Marianne Gordon mention something about MI5 having undercover people in the ELF? That's where a tip about a possible Millennium attack came from in the first place.'

'Exactly,' said Sam. 'Listen to this. While I was at Nook Street, Pritchard brought in Mary Brady, the barmaid from the Royal Hotel in Carlisle. Mary mentioned a man who turned up to the place where she and Ursula were hiding out. Called himself "Fernando" but that sounds like a code name to me. He was very friendly with Ursula apparently, but he gave Mary Brady £100 and told her to get out, for her own safety. That's how we found her. I've been trying to work out who this bloke is and why he might do that, and if he was working undercover for you lot that would make sense.'

'First I've heard of it, if he is one of ours,' said Conall. 'Do you want me to ask?'

'You're more likely to find out than I am,' said Sam. 'If there is someone on the inside, I think we deserve to know, don't you?'

'OK,' said Conall. 'I'll ask, but don't hold your breath. These deep undercover placements are usually kept very dark indeed. So, anything else I need to know?'

'I apologised to Skaife as humbly as I could muster,' said Sam.

'To be fair,' said Conall, 'he did tell me that. He thinks I'm your boss, and it's my job to rein you in. You're not going to make a habit of interfering in his case, are you?'

'No,' said Sam, and they ended the call.

'OK,' said Judith. 'Supper in half an hour. Don't forget to call Tom.'

Sam searched for the number Tom had given him and called it, but there was no response, and no way to leave a message.

It was Judith who took the call from Tom later that evening. They had a long conversation, mainly about food and the family they would be spending time with over Christmas, Judith's brother Vince, Helen and their growing family. 'And my dad, John,' Judith said to Tom. 'My stepdad actually, but he's always been a real father to me. My mum's in care, and John lives with Vince and Helen now. It seems to work really well… What? Oh no, don't bother with presents, it would be too much. Let's just keep it simple. Having you here is present enough.' She laughed. Sam could tell she was enjoying herself, talking to the handsome man who had reappeared in their lives.

'He'll be here Thursday evening,' she said to Sam after she rang off. 'Coming across from Newcastle, so he could be delayed.'

'Train?' Sam asked.

'No, he's rented a car apparently. He has people to see over there and a car is easier. I told him not to bother with presents, so I'll tell Helen. Don't want them buying loads of things for him, could be embarrassing.'

'Right,' said Sam. 'Do we have any more idea yet about his job?'

'Just something in computing is all he ever says,' said Judith. 'Probably some inexplicable title. It doesn't really matter, does it? I'm just so happy he found us again.'

The following day passed in a blur of activity. Judith had a hospital appointment and at last was fitted with a cast that she could walk on with a stick, rather than the hateful crutches. To celebrate, they did the food shopping before it got too manically busy. Judith waited in the car while Sam took the detailed list and did his best to gather what Judith had requested. In the afternoon Judith insisted that they go to see her brother's family in

St Bees, with the presents to go under the tree and a contribution to the drinks cupboard. Vince was still at work, and Judith and Helen talked yet again about food and timings while the grandchildren amused themselves writing their names on Judith's fresh cast.

On the way home, Judith said. 'I'm really looking forward to having Tom with us, aren't you? After all these years of feeling that there was a hole in your family, and now we're slowing getting back together. When we get the chance to go out to New Zealand and see Elspeth, the family will be complete again. Or maybe Elspeth will come here? We can ask Tom about that.'

After they got back, there was a phone call from Maureen.

'How did you get on yesterday?' Sam asked.

'Fine. Once we'd got away from nasty Dinger, she calmed down again. I took a proper detailed statement from her, no problem. I had to get some food for her before she did the photofit, and she was very cooperative apparently. I've got the image you wanted. What's the best way to get it to you?'

'Let's try the fax,' said Sam. 'That'll save you a journey. If it doesn't come through well enough you might have to post a copy. And give a copy to Skaife.'

'Oh yes,' said Maureen, 'what happened when you went to see him?'

'I grovelled,' said Sam, 'and I think that did the trick. And he'll be pleased to have something else to put on the big whiteboard.'

'Bell tracked down the bus driver who took Ursula into Carlisle, by the way,' Maureen added. 'Apparently the driver thought the tall passenger with slicked down hair and a rucksack was a man.'

'What about the voice?' said Sam.

'The driver said the man pointed at his throat and whispered that he'd lost his voice.'

'Shit, it's too easy. Where did she go?'

'Centre of Carlisle. Could have gone anywhere from there. Probably the station. Bell's got Carruthers and his little friend checking all the CCTV.'

Sam said, 'Thanks for calling, Maureen, but you'd better leave me out of the loop for a while. Bell will score as many points as he can about you being in touch with me, and I promised Skaife I'd back off.'

'OK, boss,' said Maureen. 'If you need anything, just give me a call.'

It was windy now and cold, with showers rattling in off the sea, but Sam insisted on taking Bill for a walk, just to get out of the house. He had some thinking to do, trying to connect the formless bits of information that were floating round his brain. The evening brought the usual tedious Christmas TV offering of old films, but it passed the time as they waited for Tom to arrive. By ten, Judith was ready for bed, but she dozed in the chair, determined to greet their guest on his arrival. It was almost eleven when they heard a car door slam and a knock on the door.

Tom was full of apologies, an accident on the A69, traffic backed up. He looked very tired. Sam carried his bag and a small computer case in from the car and Judith fussed with offers of drinks and food, most of which were politely declined. By midnight they were all in bed, but Sam couldn't get to sleep. It was after one in the morning when he got up and went downstairs. He'd been expecting the fax from Maureen but there was nothing, a fact explained when he noticed that the machine was switched off. He switched it back on, but it would be hours before Maureen would try again. He opened up the computer and typed in the word "Fernando". A number of links showed up, too many to deal with in the middle of the night as the words began to swim before his tired eyes. He closed the lid of the laptop and went back to bed.

When he woke it was still dark, but the clock by the bed said it was almost seven. Sam heard a noise downstairs. It must be Tom, he thought, and he got up, pulled on his dressing gown and went down to the kitchen. Tom was standing at the sink, looking out at the darkness through the rain-spattered window. He turned when he heard Sam but didn't smile. He looked just as tired as the night before.

'You OK?' Sam asked. 'You look tired.'

Tom nodded. 'I am. I need a break, and that drive last night seemed endless.'

Sam filled the kettle and switched it on. 'Were you working in Newcastle?' he asked. 'I'm not clear what you do. Some of these new jobs are a mystery. Make mine feel really old-fashioned.'

'Being a policeman?' Tom said, smiling. 'The basic idea is pretty old, but the methods change, don't they?'

'True,' said Sam. 'The younger people coming in understand all that better than I do.' He picked up two mugs. 'Tea?'

'Please,' said Tom, sitting down at the table. 'It feels good to be in a real house after so many hotel rooms.'

'You travel around a lot.'

'Clients all over,' Tom said. 'Everyone wants the latest computer equipment but most of the time they have no idea what to buy, or how to use it. Sensible people look for help before they spend a lot of money on new kit. Some of them come to me.'

'You have your own business?'

'I have a partner, an American guy, who's based in New York. We have plans to expand, but both of us like the flexibility we have now. It would be different if we just managed the business and other people got to do the hands-on stuff.'

'Sugar, milk?' Sam asked.

'Just milk, thanks.'

Tom sipped his tea appreciatively. 'Gumboot tea, we call it at home. No fancy names, no ghastly herbal infusions, just good strong tea, brewed in any holder within reach.' He looked at Sam. 'Nothing pretentious about New Zealand. It's a great place. One of these days I'll go back for good.'

'Anyone special waiting for you back there?'

'A woman, you mean?' Tom shook his head. 'No. I've been away a long time. Maybe when I get back…'

Sam smiled, 'Judging by the flutter you've been causing with my wife and her sister-in-law, you shouldn't have too much trouble finding someone if you want to. Judith says a straight man who's solvent, healthy and independent is as rare as hen's teeth.'

Tom didn't respond and Sam backed away from the personal. 'I'll make some porridge,' he said. 'Want some?'

Half an hour later, the porridge had been made and consumed and they were on their second pot of tea when Judith came slowly down the stairs. Sam noticed she was wearing her best dressing gown again. It was long and deep red and showed off the gold of her hair.

'Morning, Tom,' she said. 'Sleep OK?'

'Fine, thanks,' he said.

Sam said, 'Tom and I have had our porridge. I'll take Bill out when it gets light. Want to come, Tom, just down to the beach?'

Sam was showered and dressed and sitting alone in the kitchen when the fax machine began to rattle. Judith had gone back to bed, and Tom was upstairs getting dressed. Sam stood by the fax, waiting while the paper chugged into sight, blank side up. When it was finished, he picked up the paper and turned it over.

He stared at the image in his hand, then pulled out a chair and sat down, taking a deep breath to steady himself. Slowly, he folded up the paper and put it in his pocket.

Half an hour later, the two men were walking down towards the beach as Bill pulled ahead of them, straining on his lead. Sam was trying to frame a conversation in his head. When Bill was finally released and raced away, they stopped side by side.

'Tom,' said Sam. 'I have a question for you.'

Tom looked at him. A shaft of early morning sun illuminated his face. 'OK,' he said.

Sam said, 'Do you know someone called Ursula?'

For a moment Tom stared, his eyes wide. He blinked and looked away. 'What do you mean?'

'We picked up a young woman called Mary Brady and interviewed her,' said Sam. 'She told us about a woman called Ursula and mentioned a man called Fernando too, someone who looked and sounded like you.'

Tom gazed out to sea, saying nothing. Then he turned. 'Who interviewed this Mary Brady?'

'Me, with Maureen Pritchard and a solicitor that Mary wanted, a woman called Connie Eversholt.'

'Where, when?'

'Yesterday, in Workington.'

'Is it on tape?'

'No.'

Silence. Sam pulled the paper from his pocket, unfolded it and handed it to Tom.

'Where did this come from?' Tom asked.

'From Mary Brady,' Sam said. 'It looks very like you, Tom. So like you, it took my breath away.'

'When did you get it?'

'This morning. Maureen might have tried to send it yesterday, but the machine was switched off.'

'Has Judith seen it?'

'No, just you and me and Maureen, but she's never met you.'

Tom turned away and walked towards the sea. Sam waited and then followed him. When he caught up, Sam pulled on Tom's arm and turned him round. 'Tell me, do you know Ursula? Is it you that Mary Brady described?'

Tom looked away and said nothing for a while, then, 'Can I trust you, Sam?'

Sam hesitated. 'I'm a policeman, Tom. You're my nephew, but I couldn't just stand by and watch you break the law or threaten someone. You understand that, don't you?'

Tom nodded. Sam went on, 'If you want to tell me what's going on, that's your choice, but I can't promise you that it'll go no further.'

Tom said. 'You're sure Judith knows nothing?'

'I can promise you that, and she'll hear nothing from me.'

'Can you give me twenty-four hours?'

Sam shook his head. 'To do what? Run away? This is your chance to put things right, and the longer you leave it the harder it will get.' He gestured at the empty beach that lay around them. 'There's no one here, this is just between you and me.' He pointed towards the bank at the top of the beach. 'Come on, we can sit there. Bill will come back to us when he's finished playing in the sea.'

Sam began to walk towards the bank and Tom followed. It would be too cold to sit for long. Tom dropped his head. 'I'll tell you some of it,' he said. 'I may have to think about the rest. There's a lot at stake.'

Sam waited.

Tom said, 'I took the code name Fernando in memory of a man who was killed on the "Rainbow Warrior", the Greenpeace boat, in 1985. I told you, didn't I, that it changed my life? I was already in Greenpeace, but it pulled me further into the movement. "Radicalised", that's what they call it. After that I left New Zealand, like many Kiwis do. I had the chance to set up my own business and I took it. I met Tania, that's Ursula's real name, in New York ten years ago.' He looked up at Sam. 'Have you met her? She's incredible. Passionate, beautiful. People fall for her, I did myself.'

'But she kills people,' said Sam.

Tom looked away. 'I don't believe that.'

Sam said, 'MI5 have told us that someone's planning some kind of propaganda event on New Year's Eve. They think someone like Ursula might be involved. Do you know about that?'

Tom shook his head. 'That's news to me,' he said. 'MI5 have been after her for years, and the CIA, and everyone else who hates radicals like us. I wouldn't believe a word they say.'

A shriek of wind and rain tore across the beach and hit them. Bill was at Sam's feet, sensing danger. Sam stood up. 'We can't stay here.' He put his hand on Tom's shoulder. 'We have to talk again, but don't say a word about this in the house. I've told no one, and I won't, not until we work out what to do. Promise me, leave Judith out of it.'

Tom nodded. They struggled back to the warmth of the kitchen and shut the back door against the storm.

'Look at you two,' said Judith, laughing. 'Two drowned rats and a dog. Hot showers and a change of clothes needed and available. We don't need to go anywhere today, just please ourselves. I've got things to do, but you guys can relax.' She smiled. 'It's so good to have you here, Tom. Your first Christmas with us since 1971. Too long.' She stood on tiptoe and kissed his cold cheek. 'Now you can tell us all about what's happened in between, can't he, Sam.'

Sam tried to smile. 'Give the poor bloke a chance,' he said. 'Maybe he doesn't want to tell us everything there is. We all have things we'd like to forget about.'

She nodded cheerfully. 'I bottled things up when I was younger,' she said. 'But it doesn't help.'

'You first in the shower, Tom,' said Sam, pushing him towards the stairs. 'I'll persuade Judith not to hassle you.'

Tom left without a word.

❖ ❖ ❖

Tension hung in the house, but when Tom offered to help Judith make mince pies, the atmosphere lifted. Judith was in awe of Tom's pastry-making skills and Sam watched as the two of them worked side by side, chatting about baking and Christmas in New Zealand where the full Christmas dinner was prepared as the summer sun shone and the cook sweltered.

When the phone rang late in the afternoon Sam rushed to pick it up. Judith and Tom were both resting, while the results of their efforts filled the house with the smells of Christmas. Sam had been trying to read, but he couldn't settle. Doubts and possibilities jangled in his brain.

'Sam?' It was Maureen. 'Just called to wish you and yours a happy Christmas,' she said, but Sam knew she'd never done that before in all the years he had known her. 'Everything OK down there?' she added.

'Fine,' he said. 'My nephew and my wife have been baking all day.'

'Yes, you told me he was coming, Tommy isn't it?'

Sam laughed, to give himself time to think. He would have to be careful what he said. He hadn't yet decided what to tell Conall

Smith about Tom, and there was certainly no need to mention anything about it to Maureen. 'It's not "Tommy" any longer,' he said. 'We have to call him Tom these days. He's grown into a fine man. "Gorgeous" is Judith's summary.'

'Gorgeous and baking!' said Maureen. 'Wow. Is he married?'

'Not as far as we know,' said Sam. He hesitated. 'About yesterday,' he began. 'I feel bad about involving you. Skaife can be a sly bugger sometimes, and Dinger will keep on about it no doubt.

'Don't worry about me Sam,' she said. 'I can handle those two.'

'Thanks, Maureen. Love to Paddy and Jack by the way. Is Jack home?'

'On his way,' said Maureen. 'First time since last Christmas, and only for three days, but a joy all the same.' She paused. 'When are you back at work, officially?'

'First Monday after the New Year, I'll be there. Dinger better clear out of my office by then.'

'I'll remind him,' she said. 'Acting Inspector Bell has been a pain in the arse, but that's nothing new. Have fun, Sam. Love to Judith.'

It was Maureen's trust in him that cemented Sam's decision. He went quietly up the stairs and pushed open the door of the spare bedroom. Tom was lying on the bed in the dark, but he was awake and turned to look at Sam standing in the doorway. Sam put a finger to his lips and beckoned Tom to follow him downstairs. Tom sat at the kitchen table as Sam closed the door and put his back against it.

'Listen,' Sam said. 'I'll be as clear as I can, and you have a decision to make.'

Tom said nothing.

'You say you don't believe Ursula killed those people. The evidence we have is very strong, but she's escaped us time and again. We need to bring her in, to prove the case once and for all.'

Tom stared. 'You want me to help you get her?'

'I could turn you over to my Special Branch colleagues on the basis of what you've told me so far. They would turn your life upside down. Or you could help us bring Ursula in.'

'How?'

'I told you that MI5 think someone's planning some kind of attack to mark the Millennium. I'm working with them at the moment, checking security on all the possible weak spots.' He waited, watching for a sign or recognition in Tom's face. There was nothing. Sam went on, 'I even thought you might be a Special Branch mole, working undercover.'

'Me?' said Tom. 'I hate that kind of stuff, and the people who do it.'

'You told me you don't know anything about it,' Sam said. He hesitated, but Tom didn't respond. 'If you do know anything, Tom,' Sam went on, 'you need to tell me now. If something happens, I won't be able to protect you.'

There was a long silence. Sam heard the floorboards creak upstairs. Judith was awake. Suddenly Sam felt so angry with Tom, wanted to shake him, wake him out of the trance he seemed to be in. 'Tom,' he hissed. 'For fuck's sake, make a decision. If Ursula's planning something, we need to know.'

'What if she is?' Tom said, 'you want me to betray her?'

'Yes. She's a murderer, Tom. She ran a man over, made sure he was dead and dumped his body in a ditch. There was a woman who died too, and an unborn baby.'

Tom hung his head. 'She said that the man died in an accident, and that Sandra overdosed.'

'And you believed her?'

Tom said quietly, 'Yes, of course I believe her. I love her.' He sat back in the chair and looked at Sam. 'What do you want me to do?'

'You have her number, call her. She's been lucky so far, but that can't last. Offer to help her get right away.'

'And if she believes me, and shows herself?'

'Then we pick her up before any harm's done, you've proved your innocence and we can leave you alone.'

They both looked up as Judith pushed open the kitchen door. 'You two look very serious,' she said. 'You OK, Tom?'

Tom stood up. 'Fine. I just remembered something I left in the car.' He went out of the back door. 'What's going on?' Judith said to Sam.

'Nothing,' he said. 'Tom's a bit preoccupied with some work problem, that's all.'

Chapter 24

The normal Christmas festivities didn't lighten Sam's mood. There was no outward sign of tension, but Sam knew that Tom's choice could change both their lives. As they were washing up after a mammoth Christmas dinner Helen said to Sam, 'Judith said Tom was gorgeous, but didn't say what a lovely bloke he is. The kids adore him. How long is he staying?'

'Just a couple of days,' said Sam. 'I'm not sure about his plans after that.'

'It's amazing, him just turning up like that, isn't it?' She laughed. 'You could make a film about it, but then he might be an imposter. What do we really know about him?'

'Judith and I both knew him as a child, thirty years ago.'

'And nothing since?'

'No,' said Sam.

'There you are then,' said Helen. 'It's a mystery. A case for DI Tognarelli, super sleuth.'

Sam smiled. 'Christmas Day isn't the best time for doing background checks.'

The family festivities continued on Boxing Day at Vince and Helen's house in St Bees, with even more people and noise and food. Tom did and said everything that a good guest should, and everyone was delighted with him. Everyone except Sam, who watched his nephew carefully, looking for signs of deceit and finding none.

It was late when they got back to Parton. Judith was feeling under the weather and went straight to bed. Sam and Tom were sitting opposite each other at the big kitchen table, enjoying a last whisky before they went to bed.

'Have you made up your mind?' Sam asked.

'I don't feel I have a choice,' said Tom. 'You know about Ursula and me and the ELF, and MI5 are out to get us anyway. I don't want to give them more ammunition against her. What do they have on her already?'

'They think she killed two people to protect her identity.'

'That's rubbish,' said Tom. He poured himself another whisky.

Sam was watching him carefully. 'Helen asked me today if I'm sure you are who you say you are,' he said. 'I think she was kidding.'

'What did you say?'

'That Christmas Day wasn't a great time for doing background checks.'

Tom sipped his drink. 'I want to help Ursula,' he said.

Sam shook his head. 'I can't let you help her get away. The evidence against her is too strong, even if you don't believe it.' He hesitated. 'The only person I can help is you. I have a Special Branch man working with me. If I can convince him that you have nothing to do with this alleged plot, you could walk away, back to your life. That's what I want. You're my sister's eldest, I know what you mean to her, and to us.'

'Have you told the Special Branch man about me?'

'No, not yet. The fact that you have a secret name and know Ursula doesn't amount to much. But if there was something going on, I would have to tell him.'

Tom looked into his glass. 'If there was something planned for New Year's Eve, and I told you about it, what then?'

Sam leaned forward. 'Tom, you have to tell me. Can't you see? If Ursula is involved, she's facing a whole new list of charges. Even if she wasn't convicted for killing those two people, they would still have enough to put her away for a long time. It's over. All I have to do is make a phone call.'

Tom stood up suddenly, his chair scraping on the flagged floor of the kitchen. Sam winced at the noise, praying that Judith wouldn't wake up. He watched as Tom paced up and down, the whisky glass in his hand. Tom stopped by the back window, looking out into the dark.

'Look,' he said, turning back to face Sam. 'I'm going away for a few days and I'll see what I can find out. But you have to keep your word and not say anything to your Special Branch man, not yet. Will you promise me that?'

Sam thought about it, and then nodded. 'If you talk to Ursula, tell her that MI5 have got wind of a possible threat around New Year's Eve. If she tells you anything specific, tell me, but don't call me here. I'll give you my mobile number. I'm giving you a few days' grace, for Elspeth's sake.'

'What if I can't find her, or she won't tell me anything?'

Sam knew he had no choice. 'If I hear nothing from you before December 31st, I'll have to report to my superiors that my nephew has a secret life as 'Fernando'. What happens after that is out of my hands. You have three days.'

Tom turned back to the window. 'Mum always said there was a dark side to you,' he said. 'She said it was because your parents died young.'

Sam shook his head. 'They were her parents too. She made some bad choices.'

'About me, you mean?' Tom said, facing Sam again.

He looks sad, Sam thought. 'No, Tom. Having you was a good choice. Don't prove me wrong on that.' He got up. 'What time are you leaving in the morning?'

Tom drained his glass and put it down on the table. 'You can't wait to get rid of me, can you?'

'To be honest, Tom,' Sam said, 'it's tearing me up having you around and not being sure I can trust you. But don't go without saying goodbye to Judith. She's very fond of you.'

It was nearly mid-morning the following day when Tom said his goodbyes. He hugged Judith. 'Thanks for being so kind,' he said. 'It was the best Christmas I could have had away from home.'

'You'll be back, right?' said Judith, 'in a few days.'

'See you soon,' said Tom. He shook Sam's hand. 'I'll be in touch,' he said.

They watched as he drove away, before the sharp rain drove them indoors.

'Did Helen tell you what she said to me about Tom?' he asked.

'You mean that she fancies the pants off him?' said Judith.

He laughed. 'She asked me how we can be sure that Tom is really the Tommy you and I remember from thirty years ago. She says he might be an imposter.'

Judith looked puzzled. 'How could he be? How could he know so much about us?'

He laughed again. 'It's a mystery,' he said.

The next day or two felt very flat. The rain was almost ceaseless, and the days were short and gloomy. Judith still wasn't feeling well. Sam managed to help her into the car one afternoon when a weak sun appeared for a while, and they drove to the beach at St Bees, watching through the car windscreen as the high tide reached the top of the beach.

'I feel as if I'm getting old,' Judith said.

'It's just the frustration of your leg,' he said. 'You'll be fine when you can walk about again. And you need to talk to the doctor about these headaches. They don't seem to be getting any better.'

'They're not,' she said. 'I should be able to see him next week. Dizzy spells too. Helen says I might have an inner ear problem.'

'Helen's full of ideas,' said Sam.

That evening Sam's phone rang and he rushed to answer it, thinking it might be Tom. But it was Conall Smith. 'Still no word from Glasgow,' he said. 'It's a worry though. We know there are links between the ELF and a remnant of the Provisional IRA, and that could be connected to Glasgow.'

'Strange bedfellows, aren't they?' Sam asked.

'What they share is a hostility towards the state, for whatever reason. Zealots seem to attract each other.'

'If that is what's taken Ursula to Glasgow, what might she do next?'

'Any kind of mayhem,' he said. 'We haven't heard anything specific.'

'Are your bosses still thinking there might be something on New Year's Eve?'

'No change on that score,' Smith said. 'I'll be on duty that night, and you need to be available. No alcohol, clear head, phone charged up, ready for anything.'

'Where will you be?' said Sam.

'Penrith, probably, unless my bosses say otherwise. It's not exactly central, is it, but close to the M6.'

'That's not much use for anything that happens in the west,' said Sam. 'You'd be better off at Workington nick.'

'I'll check that out and let you know,' said Smith. 'Let's hope we get through without having to go anywhere.'

Sam rang off. There was still no word from Tom, but Sam hadn't given up hope that he would do the right thing.

The phone call came late on December 30th, just before Sam knew he would have to tell Conall Smith everything he knew, and that Tom's future would be at risk. Sam took the phone out into the street, leaning against the wall of the house to escape the wind.

'I can't talk on the phone,' Tom said. 'You'll have to trust me. I'll be with you tomorrow morning, and we'll talk then.'

'I said before December 31st,' Sam said. 'That was the deal.'

'I called you, didn't I?' Tom argued. 'You'll have to wait till the morning. Don't do anything before then.'

'Do you have information for me?'

'Yes, but not now.' He rang off.

'Who was that?' said Judith when he went back into the house. 'It was Tom,' Sam said. 'The line was bad and the signal's better outside. He says he'll be here before lunch. He said to say "Hi" to you.'

'Great,' Judith said, smiling. 'I might have got rid of this headache by then.'

Sam and Judith both slept late on New Year's Eve. For a while after he woke, Sam lay still, thinking. For weeks December 31st 1999, the Millennium Eve, had loomed in his mind, large but formless, promising something significant but he didn't know what. All that traipsing up and down the coast with Conall Smith had produced only frustration and a growing scepticism about the idea of 'an event' of some kind marking the occasion. The public were only worried that the video recorder or the cash machine might not work, not about some apocalyptic wake-up call. Sam was still hoping that Tom would come good, help them find Ursula and let the law take its course.

Judith's first question when she woke was, 'What will Tom want to do tonight?'

'I don't know,' Sam said. 'He doesn't drink much, and he's not a hokey-cokey kind of bloke, is he? Are they doing fireworks down at the harbour this year?'

'Probably, but earlier so the kids can see them. About nine, I think. If we watch those, what then? Home and cocoa and an early night?'

'Nothing wrong with that,' said Sam. 'I'll have to stay up though, and not drink anything in case I'm called out.'

'Ah, the hush-hush project,' said Judith. 'You've not mentioned that for a while. What about your Special Branch buddy, is he back from Ballycastle yet?'

'Came back on the 27th,' Sam said. 'He called me the other night. Nothing to tell me.' He pushed back the duvet.

'I'm staying here for a while,' Judith said. 'Can you get me some water?'

'More painkillers?' said Sam. 'I'm sure they're not good for you.'

Sam was downstairs and Judith still in bed when his phone rang. 'Can you talk?' he said.

'Judith's upstairs,' said Sam.

'It took me a while to track our friend down,' said Tom. 'She took some persuading.' A pause. Sam strained to hear his voice. 'She says she has something planned.'

'What?'

'She wouldn't say.'

'Did she say where?'

'She mentioned a Visitors' Centre. Does that make sense?'

Sam was surprised. 'It's an easy target,' he said. 'Maybe that's what she's been looking for.'

'So, you know where she means?'

'Oh, yes,' said Sam.'

'That's all I can tell you for now.'

'You've done the right thing Tom. That's a great relief. I'll do what's needed at this end.'

Tom said, 'I'm leaving soon, see you around lunchtime.' Sam had more questions, but Tom had rung off. He picked up the phone again and called Conall Smith.

'Conall,' he said. 'I've got some things to tell you.'

By one o'clock, Tom was knocking on the door and Judith was clearly pleased to see him again. 'Just in time for lunch,' she said. 'Have you had a good time, wherever you've been?'

Tom looked well and more rested than before. Sam was curious to know where he'd been, and who with, but Judith was excited, and Tom was quick to respond. 'Busy,' he said. 'I thought more people would take time off between Christmas and New Year, but I was wrong.'

'Well now you can relax for a day or two,' said Judith, taking his arm. 'I'm not sure what we'll find to do tonight, but Sam says we can't go far. There's some flap at work apparently.'

'Tom doesn't want to hear about it,' Sam said, hoping Judith wouldn't say any more.

'I wouldn't know what to tell him, anyway,' she said. 'Bit of a dark one sometimes, my husband, though I say it myself.'

They lingered over lunch and it was only when Sam took Bill out and Tom offered to go with them that the two men got the chance to talk. The winter sun was bright but there was no warmth in it, and they were muffled up against the cold. Sam wanted Tom to talk, but they were well down the beach before he pulled the scarf away from his face and turned to face Sam. 'You've passed on the information I gave you?' he said.

Sam nodded. 'All done. Now we just wait and see. I told my contact as little as I could. If you want to, you could talk to him yourself.'

Tom shook his head. 'It's not as simple as that. You trust these security people, but I don't. They could kill her.'

'That's not going to happen, Tom, I promise you.'

'What if she defends herself?'

Sam realised what Tom meant. 'You mean, she'll be armed?'

'She's carried a gun for years. She's always said she'd rather die than rot in a jail somewhere. She knows they're out to get her.'

Sam stopped to think. This complicated everything.

Tom went on. 'So, I've decided I have to be there too, to be her witness, to keep her safe. It's not what she wants, but I can't let her do this alone.'

Sam was horrified. 'It's too late to save her now, Tom. The trap is set. If that's how you feel, you shouldn't have told me anything.'

Tom's eyes were watering in the wind. 'I have to stop her harming anyone, or herself. I can only do that if I'm there with her.'

Sam came to a decision. 'If you go, I go too,' he said.

Tom shook his head. 'Why don't they pick her up now?' he asked.

'Not my decision,' said Sam. 'I told my bosses what you told me, and they want to catch her in the act, to make the case against her stronger. After that it'll be a fight between MI5 and the Cumbria police about who has first crack at her.'

'What about me?' Tom asked.

'We have nothing serious to charge you with, so far. You helped Mary Brady get away, and you're helping us now. All that will help. If I'm with you tonight, I can make sure nothing happens to spoil that.'

Tom turned away and said nothing more as the two men walked back to the house.

Judith looked up from her chair. 'You've been a while,' she said. 'Everything OK?'

Sam forced a smile. 'Fine,' he said. 'Tom's asked if we might catch some fireworks tonight. I think there's some at the harbour.'

'What about leaving Bill, he hates fireworks?' Judith asked, as Sam knew she would.

'Could you stay with him?' Sam asked. 'You might struggle with that leg if there are lots of people around, and we won't be out for long.'

'OK, I'll stay here,' said Judith smiling. 'Just for you, Tom. We want you to have a good New Year's Eve.'

Tom smiled and gave her a hug. Sam looked away.

The evening passed in a blur. Tom chatted to Judith as if he had nothing on his mind but a few fireworks. When they ate supper, the food tasted like sawdust in Sam's mouth. He pushed his plate away. 'Too much food the past few days,' he said. 'My stomach's upset.'

'I wondered what you were looking so dismal about,' said Judith. 'I hope the fireworks cheer you up a bit.' She checked her watch. 'Nearly nine,' she said. 'You'd better be off. They won't last long once they start.'

Sam hugged his wife.

'Steady on,' she said, laughing. 'You're only going out for an hour. Put your big jacket on,' she said, handing it to him. 'It could be cold standing around. And take your little phone with you, in case you need to call me.'

'Will do,' Sam said. He took the jacket from her and put it on, feeling the weight of his phone in the pocket.

'My car or yours?' Sam asked.

'Yours,' said Tom. He was carrying a rucksack and put it at his feet when they got into the car.

'What's in there?' Sam asked.

'Just another jacket,' Tom said. 'I'm still not used to how cold it gets here.'

As they drove away Sam said, 'OK, we're heading south towards the Visitors' Centre. My people will already be there, out of sight. They'll let Ursula get well inside their cordon before they close in.'

They turned south on the main road. As they approached the road towards the Visitors' Centre, Tom said, 'Not down there, drive straight on.'

'But Ursula told you…'

'I lied,' said Tom, 'I had to. You'll come to no harm, but you have to come with me.'

'Where?'

'I can't tell you. Keep driving south.'

Sam felt sick. 'You set me up,' he said. He wanted to stop the car, leave Tom behind and go home. He saw a sign for a layby and began to slow down.

'Don't stop,' said Tom. 'Drive on.'

'Why should I do what you say?'

Tom pulled the rucksack onto his lap and patted it. 'Because I have a gun in here, and if I have to, I'll use it.'

Sam stared. 'I don't believe you.'

Tom reached into the bag. When he pulled out his hand it was clasping a small pistol. 'Believe me now, Sam? Drive.'

For a few minutes they drove in silence. The roads were busy with people on their way to celebrate the New Year. Sam felt numb but forced himself to think. Tom was looking straight ahead. Sam took his right hand off the steering wheel and let it drop towards his side. In the pocket of his jacket he could feel the hard outline of the phone. Desperately, he tried to remember the procedure Chris had made him practice, finding the speed dial button first and then the one that would record what was said. He couldn't drive for long with only one hand on the wheel, and he couldn't work out which button was which.

Headlights swerved towards them and Sam needed his right hand to steer the car to the left, hitting the hard shoulder and lurching back to the right as he struggled to keep control.

'Slow down,' said Tom. 'There's plenty of time.'

'Time for what?' Sam asked, but Tom didn't answer.

There was a wide junction on the left and Sam steered the car into it and stopped. Tom looked at him, furious.

'What are you going to do, Tom?' said Sam, surprised at the sound of his own voice. 'Are you going to shoot me, here in the car? They'd find you so easily. Is it worth it?'

'You don't understand,' Tom said.

'Damn right,' said Sam. 'I understand you want to save the Earth, but does it help to kill innocent people? What will that do for your precious cause?'

'Collateral damage,' said Tom. 'I warned you.'

'No. Ursula warned us, all of us, wiping out James and Sandra as if they were insects. I thought you could see the folly of it all.'

Tom shook his head. 'I was wrong. I needed time to find the right thing to do.'

'And this is it?' said Sam.

'We need you,' Tom said. 'If things go wrong, you're our ticket out of here.'

Sam shook his head. 'This time you don't understand. I'm a middle-ranking copper in a place that no one's ever heard of. You think you can bargain using me? No chance.'

'That's enough,' said Tom.

Sam hesitated. He needed to wait, bide his time, play along and take any chance he had either to escape or use the phone to call for help. He tried to breathe deeply, to stop the hammering in his chest. Then he put the car into gear and pulled out into the main road, two hands on the wheel.

He knew the main road heading south well and recognised the long pull up and over Muncaster hill, round a sharp right-hand bend and then steeply down to another sharp bend where the road turned towards the bridge over the Esk. All the while he was thinking. What could Tom and Ursula be planning? Sellafield was impregnable and lay behind them now. The docks at Barrow would be shut up tight, too tight for two zealots on their own to penetrate. Between the two there was nothing but the long stretch of railway, along which the train carrying canisters of nuclear waste trundled several times a week, thundering over the viaduct over the Esk estuary, south of Ravenglass.

Suddenly, Sam knew where they were going.

Chapter 25

They were climbing the hill, passing the sign for Waberthwaite. Sam knew that soon they would be turning right, down a lane, twisting towards the viaduct that took the railway across the wide estuary of the River Esk, supported on solid sandstone pillars.

Sam knew this place. At the southern end of the viaduct the road ran under the rail tracks, close to the water's edge. At high tide the road leading to the viaduct would be flooded as sea water surged into the estuary, up the muddy creeks, unstoppable. With a westerly wind the tide would be deep, flooding the road for an hour each side of its highest reach. Sam tried to remember the pattern of the tide over the past few days, but even before the final stretch along the side of the river he knew that there would be flooding. A stream by the side of the road had backed up and water swirled round the car as he drove through. Tom didn't seem to notice.

As they turned the final corner towards the viaduct Tom peered ahead into the darkness and swore. The moon had risen into a clear sky, although the wind was fierce. Where the road should have been ahead of them, light gleamed off water.

'High tide,' said Sam, stopping the car. 'We'll not get through.'

'How deep? How long?' Tom asked.

'It depends,' said Sam. 'If it's ebbing already it'll go down fast, within half an hour or so. If it's still rising, it'll be longer. We could wade through it here, but not under the bridge further on.'

Tom looked at his watch. 'It's not ten o'clock. We have time.'

'To do what?' Sam asked. He felt for the hard shape in his jacket pocket.

Tom opened the car door. 'We'll have to wade through,' he said. 'Get out of the car,' Sam hesitated. 'I said, get out!' Tom yelled, 'And shut up. We're done talking.'

Sam got out and stood watching the water stretching out on both sides of them.

'Walk,' said Tom. 'She's waiting. The water's not moving much, we can wade as far as that place ahead that's still clear of the water.'

The water was cold, so cold that after a few moments it began to hurt. Sam held his jacket away from the water that reached to his knees, then higher. He could hear Tom ahead of him, grunting with the exertion of pushing through the flood against the wind. Where the road rose slightly on a low bridge over one of the creeks, they both stopped, pulling for breath. Sam began to shiver. The light ahead of them was closer now, and higher, shining from the edge of the viaduct. His fingers were almost numb with cold and fright, but he aligned the small shape in his pocket, trying to picture the position of the buttons he needed. Tom was ahead of him and he stopped for a moment, closed his eyes and turned the phone on, feeling the buzz in his hand. Tom turned round, a torch in his hand, shining it into Sam's face. 'Come on,' he said. 'She's waiting.'

Tom looked away and Sam put his hand back into his pocket. One more press, on the speed dial this time. Done. Now he had to speak clearly and hope that someone would be listening.

'Where is Ursula?' he said, as loudly as he could. 'On the viaduct?'

Ahead of them, in the middle distance, a light appeared, moving from side to side.

'She's there,' Tom said. 'She's waiting for us.'

Sam said. 'Tom, please. It's not too late. We can turn back, forget whatever you think you need to do. It's pointless.' Tom stared ahead. 'You're not a violent man,' Sam said. 'This is not the way. Two people have died already, and for what?'

'It's too late to go back,' Tom said.

'No,' said Sam. 'I'll vouch for you. So far, you've done nothing except plan some stupid prank to draw attention to yourselves. This is Ursula's fight, not yours.'

'Is the water still rising?' Tom asked, peering at the flood ahead of them.

'I think so,' said Sam. He knew that if they could wade another few yards there was a road leading away to the left towards a house that stood by the side of the railway tracks. If they could reach that, they could scramble on to higher ground, away from the deepest water right under the viaduct.

Suddenly something snaked into the sky to the left and an instant later exploded into a shower of gold that scattered in the wind. Then another, and another, red and then green.

'Rockets,' said Sam. 'Someone's letting off rockets.'

'Move,' said Tom. 'We can't wait here.'

They started to walk on, but now the water seemed less deep and Sam noticed the current round their legs flowing down towards the main body of the river. 'It's going out,' he said. 'But it's deeper under the bridge. We'll go up to the left where the road bends. I know where. Just follow me.'

Tom looked up and Sam followed his gaze. They could see a figure silhouetted above the parapet of the bridge. 'She's here,' said Tom. They waded the last few yards and then along the drive that led to the house where every window was lit, and they could hear the sound of voices. Sam felt sick. If they were discovered, what would Tom do? What would Ursula do?

Over a final fence, dead brambles tugged at their sodden clothes. They were standing by the railway, moonlight glinting off the tracks that ran straight on either side. 'Get down,' hissed a voice from the other side of the track.

Sam sank to his knees, trying to control the shivering that had seized him.

'Down here,' the voice hissed again, and they stumbled down off the tracks into a clearing, out of sight of the house and the people having fun in the garden.

'Fucking kids,' said the voice with the unmistakeable North American twang. 'And the fucking tide. Why didn't you warn me?'

'I didn't know,' Tom said. 'We had to wade through it.'

'And you brought good old Uncle Sam,' she said. 'Excellent.' She looked at Sam. 'You do as you're told, OK? If you pray, get praying.' To Tom she said, 'It'll take three of us to carry the stuff. We've got time. I want to wait till those people go back inside. Can't afford to be spotted, not now.'

'How much do we have to carry?' Tom said.

'Fifty pounds,' she said. 'It's all I could get, but it's enough to blow a fucking great hole in the middle of the viaduct and light up the sky. Great headlines. It'll take them weeks to repair. We'll carry the stuff out there, set the timer, then you and I can head south. I've parked out of sight and no one comes along here anyway. We can be in London before dawn.'

'You're going to blow up the viaduct?' Sam asked.

'Shut up,' said Ursula.

They waited. Doors banged and the noise from the house diminished until all they could hear was the whining of the wind and the rush of the ebbing tide under the bridge. Ursula stood up and gestured for Sam to do the same. She was holding a gun in her hand and waved in the direction of the far corner of the clearing where something was covered by a plastic sheet. She pulled off the sheet, picked up a large bag and handed it to Sam.

'Is it safe to pick up?' he asked. 'Will it go off?'

She laughed. 'Not yet. Put as many of the packets as you can into the bag. You'll have to carry it.'

'Where to?' he asked, 'Onto the viaduct?'

Ursula pointed. 'Right to the middle,' she said. 'You never guessed, did you, you and that Special Branch moron? Why would we risk armed guards and dogs when we could blow up this place by climbing over a fence?' She laughed. 'So easy.'

Sam started to load the packets into the bag. 'What about detonators?' he asked.

'None of your business,' said Ursula. 'Get on with it.' She spoke to Tom, 'All here,' she said, pointing to the bag on her shoulder. 'Timer, the works. Sean took me through it all. He wanted to come but I said we didn't need him. This is just you and me, Tom. This is where we make history.'

Ursula went up onto the tracks and looked around. She gestured for the other two to follow and they did so, crouching low to reduce the chance of being seen, although the place was deserted. Stooping, they carried their burdens towards the middle of the viaduct while the ebbing tide beneath them rushed towards the sea. The moon had disappeared behind a racing cloud and they had to step carefully along the tracks. Sam felt the weight of the bag he had slung over his back and knew he had to stay strong. And he had to speak, trusting that the phone line was still open and someone would be listening. 'How much further,

Tom?' he asked. If anyone was listening, would they understand that three people were there, about to plant enough explosive to blow the viaduct into the river?

Ursula had stopped. She looked in one direction, then the other. She put down her bag and leaned over the railings at the edge of the viaduct, looking to the left and right, checking. 'We need to put it between the pillars.' She walked on a few more yards and leaned over again. 'Here,' she said. 'Drop the stuff right in the middle between the tracks.' She checked her watch, pressing a switch on the side so that the face glowed in the dark. 'Almost eleven,' she said. 'The timer is set for an hour. You and I will be well away by then, Tom.'

Tom put down the bag he was carrying. 'What about him?' he said, pointing at Sam.

'Dear old Uncle Sam,' she said. 'Worried about him, are you?'

They were both standing, and Sam crouched between them, looking up. Suddenly Ursula said, 'You checked him, didn't you?'

'Checked him how?' asked Tom. 'He doesn't have a gun.'

'A phone, stupid. Did you check he doesn't have a phone?'

Sam held his breath. 'Stand up,' Ursula barked at Sam. She took the gun out of her pocket and held it steady, aimed at Sam's head. 'Check his pockets, Tom, all of them.'

Sam stood up. Tom felt Sam's trouser pockets first, then patted the jacket. He felt the phone, reached in and held it up. Ursula held out her hand, took the phone and threw it as far as she could into the water below.

'Careless,' she said to Tom. 'Now, make a better job of this.' She took a length of rope from the bag at her feet and handed it to Tom. 'You're going to tie up Uncle Sam right here. We get to wreck the viaduct and take out the old pig at the same time.'

'No,' Tom said, after a long pause. 'I promised we wouldn't harm him.'

She stared. 'You promised? You had no right to promise him anything.' She hesitated. 'Just tie him up for now, so he can't get in our way. We have to get this done.'

Without a word, Tom tied Sam's hands behind his back and put another length of rope round Sam's ankles, holding them tight.

'Tom,' Sam said, 'Tom!' but there was no response and Tom turned away to train the light on where Ursula was preparing the detonators and the timer. Sam wondered whether the phone had worked. If it had, how long would it take for help to arrive? Tom and Ursula were both armed. He might be able to tackle one of them but not both.

Ursula sat back on her haunches. 'OK,' she said. 'Now, tie the old man to the railings, right here,' she said as she stood up, pointing to a spot just a few feet away from the explosive at Tom's feet. Tom stood quite still. 'We could leave him further away. Why kill him too?'

'You getting soft, Fernando?' she said. 'I've told you before. Collateral damage.'

Tom didn't move. 'Did you kill the other two deliberately?'

'Jimmy and Sandra? Yes,' she said. 'Of course I did.'

There was a sudden movement. Sam saw the gun in Tom's hand and crouched down, expecting death.

'Oh, you want to shoot him yourself, right here?' Ursula asked Tom. 'OK, we could just tip his body into the water.' She stepped to one side.

Tom said, 'You killed those people? You told me they were accidents, both of them.'

She laughed. 'And you believed me? Time you grew up, Fernando. Shooting your Uncle Sam will help. Just get on with it.'

Tom stared at Ursula. Then he raised the gun and pointed it at her. 'I can't go on with this,' he said, his voice tense and strained. 'Collateral damage? For God's sake. We're not killers. What happened to you?'

Before she could speak, they heard the sound. Sirens, wailing in the distance.

Ursula's eyes were wide. 'What have you done?' she said.

Along the south side of the river was a procession of blue flashing lights.

Ursula turned towards the other end of the viaduct, away from the road and the flashing lights. She shouted above the noise.

'Run Tom, now. Leave the old man. The car's waiting. We can reach it before they get here.'

Tom didn't move. 'Untie Sam,' he said. 'Then you can go.'

She stood, not moving. 'We worked so hard for this,' she said.

'You killed for it,' said Tom. 'Untie him. It's over.'

Ursula began to run but tripped and fell over the rails. She got to her feet and stood with her back against the railing and Tom could see the gun in her hand. Figures appeared at the far end of the viaduct. There was shouting and the unmistakeable sound of a barking dog. Ursula looked back at Tom, wide-eyed and desperate. The dog was racing along the tracks towards them. Ursula raised her hand and pointed the gun at the dog. Before she could fire, Tom shot her. The bullet ripped into her chest, the force of it tipping her backwards over the top railing and down into the water below.

Suddenly there was shouting. The dog stopped running and one of the approaching figures ran towards the spot where Ursula had fallen. It was Marion Sharp. As she ran, she pulled off her jacket and then kicked off her boots before she climbed over the parapet and disappeared. Sam wriggled to the edge of the viaduct and looked down but could see nothing. A helicopter clattered overhead, its searchlight piercing the blackness. Sam felt himself being lifted up and carried. 'You're safe now, sir,' said a voice. 'Bomb squad's here.'

'Tom,' said Sam. 'Where's Tom?'

There was no answer. The movement stopped. Sam was lying on the floor and someone was taking the ropes from round his arms and ankles. He lay back, powerless.

'Sam,' said Conall Smith's voice. 'Are you OK?'

'Where's Tom?' Sam said again.

'We've got him,' said Conall.

Later, Sam remembered very little about the next hour. They told him he was in shock, shaking and mumbling as they drove up to Workington in convoy. They gave him tea and he looked up to see Smith and Bell standing close by. Bell said nothing, watching with his arms folded across his chest. Conall Smith sat down next to him. 'Tom Phelps is in custody, Sam,' he said. 'We don't know what to charge him with, but there's no rush. He's not going anywhere.'

'What about Ursula?' said Sam. 'Did Sharp get her?'

Smith shook his head. 'It was a brave effort. She managed to reach Ursula, but she was already dead. The current was too strong to get her out. Sharp's OK, but she had to let Ursula's body go.'

Bell snorted. 'She's an idiot,' he said, and he walked away.

Sam held Conall's arm. 'Tom didn't know what she was planning, Conall,' he said. 'When he realised that she wanted me dead and that she'd killed Bramall and Evans, he turned on her. He saved my life.'

'Only after he'd put you in harm's way,' said Conall. 'He may be family, Sam, but he's used you like a pawn in a chess game. He has a lot to answer for. Anyway, we'll take statements from both of you when the dust's settled,' said Conall. 'It's been a busy night.'

'The phone,' said Sam. 'Did it work?'

'Like a dream,' said Conall. 'We were standing around at the Visitors' Centre when all of a sudden my phone rang and there you were. Didn't take long to work out what was going on. We knew there was a bomb involved and the Bomb Squad were on alert already. Pretty straightforward after that, although there wasn't long to go before they made it safe.' He looked up. 'I'll have to see Skaife before he goes. Maureen's here, I'll leave you with her.'

'What a night,' Maureen said, smiling at him. 'One way to welcome the new year, I suppose.'

'What time is it?' Sam asked.

Maureen checked her watch. 'Nearly one,' she said.

Sam tugged at her arm. 'Maureen, what about Judith? Tom and I left the house hours ago, just for a short while. She'll have no idea what's happened.'

'Do you want me to call her?'

'I'll do it,' he said. 'Can you bring me a phone?'

He dialled the familiar number and waited, expecting Judith to pick up almost immediately, demanding to know what had happened to keep them away so long. The phone rang and rang, but there was no response. He wondered where she was, then dialled another familiar number. This time someone picked up almost immediately. It was Vince.

'It's Sam,' he said. 'Happy New Year, Vince. Is Judith with you?'

'Judith?' said Vince. 'No, she's not here. Where are you?'

'Too complicated,' said Sam. 'I'm at work.' He hesitated. 'Vince, could you and Helen go to my house and see where she is? Maybe she locked herself out or something. I left around nine, that's nearly four hours ago. I'm stuck here for a while. Can you call me here at Nook Street when you find her?'

Sam had just finished giving his statement to DCI Skaife in his office when the phone on his desk jangled. Sam picked it up. It was Helen. Her voice sounded odd. 'Sam,' she said, 'we're at the hospital in Whitehaven. Can someone bring you up here?'

'Why?' said Sam. Then he went cold. 'Is it Judith?' he said. 'What's happened?'

'We'll meet you outside,' said Helen. 'Come now, Sam, please.'

Sam put down the phone. Maureen was standing at the door of his office. 'What's wrong?' she said.

'I need to get to the hospital,' he said. 'Now.'

Helen was waiting at the main entrance when they arrived. Maureen helped Sam out of the car. He was feeling dizzy. Helen took his arm and Maureen followed them into the warmth of the building, across the busy entrance hall and down a corridor. 'Where are we going?' Sam asked. 'Where's Judith?'

Helen opened a door and guided Sam into a small empty room with comfortable seating.

'Sit down,' she said, and sat down beside him. Maureen waited outside.

Helen took Sam's hand. 'We found Judith at the house, Sam,' she said. 'She was in the bathroom, on the floor. She wasn't breathing. We called the ambulance straight away, but there was nothing they could do.'

Sam stared at her.

'She's dead, Sam. I'm so sorry, sweetheart. They brought her here, but they couldn't revive her. The doctor said it was a stroke. Very quick. She wouldn't have suffered.'

Sam couldn't speak. He sat, disbelieving, waiting for the nightmare to be over.

Chapter 26

'Sam? Are you awake?'

Sam turned his head towards the sound. Helen's face was very close. 'Helen? Where am I?'

'You're with us,' she said. 'We brought you back last night.'

A dream swirled in his head. 'Judith, where's Judith?'

Helen stroked his forehead. 'I've brought you some tea. Can you sit up, drink it while it's hot?'

She helped him up. He closed his eyes, trying to clear the nightmare from his head.

'Judith's dead,' he said.

Helen stroked his face, looked into his eyes. 'The doctor at the hospital said she'd had a stroke. It would have been very sudden. No pain.'

'The headaches,' he said. 'She was going to the doctor on Thursday.' He hesitated. 'Will there be a post-mortem?'

Helen nodded. 'They'll want to know for sure.'

Sam hung his head. 'I can't believe it.'

'None of us can,' said Helen.

'What do I have to do?'

'Nothing,' she said. 'Rest, recover. Maureen is coming later. Drink the tea and go back to sleep if you can.'

'Tom? Is he OK?'

She nodded. 'The police have him.'

Sam shook his head. 'She was going to kill me, like the others. He stopped her.'

Helen held the tea out to him. 'Here,' she said. 'You need this. Drink.'

When Maureen tapped on the door and came into the small spare bedroom at Vince and Helen's house Sam was sitting up, propped on pillows, staring out of the window at the tall trees outside thrashing in the wind.

'I'm so, so sorry Sam,' she said. 'How are you feeling?' she said, pulling up a chair to sit beside him.

'I don't know. Numb. When I woke up, I thought I'd dreamed that Judith had died, but it's true. She's gone Maureen, I'll never see her again.'

She stretched out and took his hand. 'It's a terrible shock,' she said. 'We all feel it.'

'Does everybody know?'

She nodded. 'They all send their condolences. The Special Branch man, Conall Smith, said he'll come and see you later. I said I'd ask you if that was OK.'

Sam nodded. 'I want to see him. I can't just lie here thinking.'

'Is there anything you want me to do?'

'Can you let Judith's editor know, at the paper?'

'Anyone else?'

'No, the rest of the family are all here. They'll have to decide what to tell Maggie, Judith's mother. And poor John,' he said. 'He loves Judith so much.'

Suddenly, tears came. He turned his head away and covered his eyes with his hand. Maureen took his other hand and held it tightly, waiting for the storm to pass.

'I'm sorry,' he said.

'It's OK,' she said, stroking his hand. 'You need to grieve.'

When Conall Smith arrived later in the morning, Sam was up and dressed and sitting in a chair downstairs. Helen brought them coffee and then left them alone.

'What a dreadful thing to happen,' said Conall. 'Did you know she was ill?'

Sam shook his head. 'She'd been complaining about headaches, and there was that fall down the stairs. She said she'd felt dizzy before she fell.' Sam put a hand to his mouth. 'I thought she'd drunk too much. I told her off. Oh God.'

'You can't blame yourself,' Conall said. 'It happens sometimes. Things go wrong.'

'But if I'd been there…'

'Yes, but it could have happened any time. You could have been at work, on a normal day.'

Sam nodded. 'I know, but I keep thinking about it.'

Conall said, 'Do you want me to tell you what's happened since last night?'

'Yes. I can't bear to think about Judith all the time. Did you find Ursula?'

Conall shook his head. 'The tide will have carried her out. The Coastguard is looking, they know how the tides work. We've got a team out on the viaduct now, looking for anything that might show us exactly what happened.'

Sam leaned forward. 'I don't think Tom was sure she'd killed the other two, until she told him, at the viaduct. She sneered at him about it, no remorse. What are you going to do with him?'

'Not my call,' said Smith. 'We'll talk to the CPS about charges. There are all sorts of things to consider.'

'Like what?' said Sam.

'How much we want to make public, for a start,' said Smith. 'Truelove and his pals will have views on that. I'm staying out of it.'

'He saved my life,' said Sam. 'He might have saved Mary Brady's life too, by helping her to get away. Ursula could have killed her.' He remembered something. 'Ursula mentioned someone called Sean, in Glasgow, who supplied the explosive and the kit. No surname.'

Smith nodded. 'We'll probably know who that is. I'll deal with it.' He sipped his coffee. 'Don't think too much about all that. It's out of our hands. Look after yourself, Sam. Honour your wife.'

'The undertaker's coming later on,' Sam said. 'Helen and Vince are wonderful friends. They'll help me deal with everything.'

'Is there anyone else you want to see?' said Smith.

Sam shook his head.

❖ ❖ ❖

Judith's funeral at Distington Crematorium was packed. The shock of her sudden death reverberated round the communities where she'd lived and worked during her life. Sam tried to think of it as a time to celebrate her life, but his sadness was deep and raw. John Pharaoh's grief was hard to witness, as if he was mourning his demented wife as well as his beloved daughter.

Sam wanted to speak at the funeral and had written down what he wanted to say, but in the end he couldn't face it and left it to Vince. Later he regretted his cowardice, but at the time it was all too much, too soon. The service passed in a blur. Outside the crematorium the wind was icy in their faces and people hurried to their cars, heading for the warmth of the Seacote Hotel in St Bees for the funeral tea.

'This is where Judith and I got together, nearly thirty years ago,' Sam said to Helen when they reached the hotel. 'It was at Frank's funeral. Judith and I had fallen out about something, but she wanted a bacon butty instead of the funeral tea, so we escaped to Hartley's Café over there by the sea, on our own.' He smiled. 'Typical.'

'I didn't know you then,' Helen said. 'Maybe we could organise a proper wake for Judith, a bit later on. Bacon butties all round.'

'That would be good,' he said. 'It's too early yet. I feel as if my life has suddenly collapsed.'

'Give it time,' she said. 'Can you get some leave from work?'

'I'm going to ask,' said Sam. 'I'm not fit for work yet, I know that.'

Work intruded on Sam a few minutes later when DCI Skaife appeared at his side. 'My sympathies, Sam,' said Skaife, looking even older than Sam remembered. 'I know what you're going through. The pain will ease, but not for a long time.'

Sam remembered that Skaife too had lost his wife only a few months before.

'Work, that's what you need,' said Skaife. 'It takes your mind off things.'

'Not quite ready yet, sir,' Sam said. 'I'm going to ask for a few weeks' leave, to properly clear my head.'

'That shouldn't be a problem. Drop me a note, I'll take it up the line.'

Sam was suddenly curious. 'You and Bell put some energy into finding Ursula, didn't you,' he said, 'after Truelove asked you to hold back?'

Skaife shrugged. 'I knew that Williams really wanted us to find her, no matter what he told Truelove. No love lost there, I can tell you. Those two have crossed swords before.' He looked around, wanting to be seen to be chatting confidentially with the hero of the hour. 'Oh, by the way,' he said. 'Sergeant Findale has told me he'll be moving on. I can't say I was surprised.'

'What about Sharp?' Sam asked.

'Nothing yet,' said Skaife, 'but I can't see her and Bell working together, and Bell's not going anywhere.'

'That's a pity,' said Sam.

Skaife shrugged again. 'I know, but what can you do?'

Mercifully, Maureen intervened, guiding Sam away to meet some ex-colleagues who'd come from Barrow.

'The man's just marking time,' Sam whispered to her.

'I know,' she said, mimicking the DCI's plaintive voice. 'But what can you do?'

❖ ❖ ❖

Tom's flat in London was on a quiet tree-lined street. Sam had the street map in his hand, trying to read the tiny print and shielding the paper from the rain that slanted down from a dark grey sky. Tom was on bail while the CPS decided the full list of charges he would be facing. Sam wondered whether he'd been told about Ursula's body being found by the coastguard further up the coast.

At the top of the steps up from the street Sam put down his bag and pressed the bell by the front door marked 'Phelps'. A tinny voice said, 'Who is it?'

'It's Sam,' he said. 'Can you let me in? It's wet out here.'

The buzzer grated and the green front door clicked open. 'Come up,' said the voice. 'Second landing.'

Sam climbed the stairs slowly and saw Tom standing on the landing above him, silhouetted against the light from the open door to his flat. Tom turned without a word and left the door open for Sam to follow. In the large sitting room Tom stood facing him, the long windows refracting the orange street lights through rain-spattered glass. There was music playing somewhere and the smell of garlic.

'I knew you'd come,' Tom said. 'Do you want a drink? I've just opened a bottle of red.'

'Just tea, please,' said Sam. 'Red wine reminds me of Judith.'

Tom looked distraught. 'I was so sorry to hear what happened,' he said. 'They said I could go to the funeral, but I didn't want to intrude.'

'To be honest, I wouldn't have wanted you there,' Sam said, taking off his wet coat. 'You deceived us, Tom. Judith would have been devastated if she'd known.'

Tom didn't respond. He took Sam's coat and hung it on a hook behind the door. Then he sat down, but Sam stayed standing, looking down at him. 'Judith died while you and that woman kept me away from her. I should have been with her, not with you.'

Tom hung his head. 'We couldn't have known what would happen.'

Sam pushed on, 'Did you know Ursula planned to kill me too?'

'No, believe me,' Tom said, raising his eyes to Sam's face. 'I wondered about the other two, but she never admitted it, not until that night.'

'That's what I told the Special Branch bloke, hoping it was true. I really wanted to believe you'd been cheated by her as much as we all were, but you could have been a murderer, just like her.'

'I wasn't,' he said, 'I'm not.'

'So why, Tom, why?' Sam said, more loudly now. 'Tell me.'

'I need that drink,' said Tom, getting up. 'I'll make your tea. Are you in a hurry?'

Sam shook his head. He sat down and leaned back, closing his eyes, listening to Tom moving around in the small kitchen. He'd been sleeping badly, dreaming of black rushing water and the thud of the helicopter. It was a few days after Judith's funeral, just long enough to make a decision and book a plane ticket to New Zealand. He'd given his statements and they didn't need him until the trial which would be months away. A few weeks' leave would help him put the pain and guilt behind him, hopefully, or at least ease them a little. And Sam needed some answers too, answers that only Tom could provide.

'You're asking me why?' Tom said when he came back with a tray and put it on the small table between them. 'It goes back a long way.'

'Go on,' said Sam.

Tom leaned back, trying to find the words. 'I told you about the impact the Rainbow Warrior business had on me,' he said, 'but even before that I was unhappy. I had to get away from Andy, but that meant leaving Mum as well.' A pause. 'I suppose I was looking for another family. The Greenpeace people were that. We cared for each other.' He looked up, and Sam could see that his eyes were wet. 'When I met Ursula in New York everything made sense to me.' He looked up. 'She was still Tania then, Sam, passionate about everything, not obsessed and callous like the Ursula you saw. I told you when we talked about her before, people were drawn to her, just like I was.'

'Needy people,' Sam said. 'Tyrants feed on needy people.'

'No,' Tom shot back. 'That's not fair. She wasn't a tyrant, not then.'

'But she became one,' said Sam.

'She hardened,' Tom said. 'In the end she despised people who fell for her.'

'She used them. Did she ask you to spy on me?'

Tom shook his head. 'That wasn't my idea, Sam, believe me. I told someone in our group that you'd been in the police when I was a child, but I had no idea whether you were still there.

Someone did the research to track you down, and then they put the pressure on me.'

'To do what?'

'To make contact with you, find out what the local police were up to. Ursula had this idea about Sellafield, to attack it at the Millennium for publicity. She got the idea from Jimmy Bramall. I had no idea what she was planning, or what she would do to make it work.' He looked at Sam in the orange light of the streetlamps. 'Do you believe me?'

Sam got up and walked to the window. Rain was still sluicing down the glass and the bare trees in the street outside were spangled with drops. 'I want to,' he said. 'What do you want me to tell Elspeth?'

'Mum? Are you going to see her?'

'I'm going to Heathrow when I leave here,' said Sam. 'I need her address and phone number. Have you been in touch with her yourself since all this happened?'

Tom shook his head. 'She'll be ashamed of me.'

'I'll tell her that you saved my life,' said Sam, 'and what you did for Mary Brady. That'll come out at the trial too, eventually. It should help you.' He sat down again. 'I've got a few hours yet. If you write to your mother, I can take it with me, if that would help. Easier than trying to talk on the phone.'

'I don't know what to say to her,' Tom said.

'Just tell her what you've told me. She deserves to hear it from you.'

For a while the room was silent as Tom sat at the big table and wrote a letter to his mother. Sam sat waiting, his mind quiet for the first time in days. He closed his eyes, and all he could see was Judith. In his wallet he kept a tiny photo of her, taken around the time they were married. She looked so happy on a beach somewhere, her hair blowing in the wind. He took out the photo and touched her face with his fingers.

If you've enjoyed this book, here are Ruth Sutton's other titles.

A Good Liar
Forgiven
Fallout
Cruel Tide
Fatal Reckoning
Burning Secrets
Out of the Deep
Corruption